Cinderella
SCREWED ME OVER

Also by Cindi Madsen

The Accidentally in Love Series
Falling for Her Fiancé
Act Like You Love Me

For Teen Readers
All the Broken Pieces

Cinderella

SCREWED ME OVER

CINDI MADSEN

Entangled Publishing, LLC
2614 South Timberline Road
Suite 109
Fort Collins, CO 80525
Visit our website at www.entangledpublishing.com.

Edited by Stacy Abrams
Cover design by Libby Murphy

Ebook ISBN 978-1-62266-030-8
Print ISBN 978-1-62266-031-5

Manufactured in the United States of America

First Edition October 2013

To my daughters, Kylie and Sydney. I hope you learn that you don't need a prince charming to make all your dreams come true, but that you find one anyway.

CHAPTER ONE

Cinderella screwed me over. And really, she doesn't deserve all the blame. Jasmine, Ariel, Belle, Sleeping Beauty—whatever her real name was, she had, like, three of them—they all added to it. This idea of happily ever after. Of finding Prince Charming.

If you rewatch *Cinderella* now, you'll realize there are some similarities between Prince Charming and the guys you've dated. Cute, charismatic, and kind of lazy. After all, what did the prince in *Cinderella* really do? He danced with Cinderella, thought she was pretty, and picked up her shoe.

Then, did he go after her? Nope. He sent the duke. You'd think if he were as in love as he claimed, he would've gone himself. Instead he was, like, *Well, as long as her foot's that small, she'll probably be about right for me.* That's what's sold to us. Forced down our throats as one of the greatest romances of all time.

The brainwashing starts at about two or three years old, when you first hear fairy tales about princesses, castles, ball gowns, and everybody living happily ever after. It's no wonder that by sixteen, you're shocked when your boyfriend cares more about looking cool or copping a feel than sweeping you off your feet. So you tell yourself it'll get better when you're older.

Then you get older.

You remain optimistic, because you watch romantic comedies now—they've become your new, more realistic fairy tales. You see lovey-dovey couples everywhere you go, proving that romance is still out there. Around the early- to midtwenties, some of your friends start getting married. You keep waiting for it to happen to you.

I waited. And waited. But the more dating experience I got, the more I realized that guys aren't princes and love fades, replaced with either mediocre feelings or full-on contempt. I looked back at my relationships and noticed my dating life had been more like *Con Air* than *Cinderella*—you know, bumpy and full of bad guys.

Still, I tried to stay positive. Kept hoping the right guy was out there. I dated every man in the city—well, not literally, but after a while they all started to blur together. Dating became this sadistic ritual that always ended the same way—disappointment. With each bad date, each failed relationship, I grew more and more cynical.

It was on my twenty-sixth birthday that it finally hit me: Love is bullshit. There was no happily ever after.

I swore off men and threw myself into work. I started spending lots of money on shoes. A pair of great heels was much more satisfying than a man. They lasted longer, and better yet, they didn't leave me for someone prettier.

Sure, there were some lonely nights when I wished I had someone to talk to. So I'd stroll past the pet shop and wonder exactly how much that kitty in the window was. On more than one occasion I'd been tempted to buy myself a furry companion. But I wasn't quite ready to be the crazy cat lady. I was saving that for my forties.

At twenty-eight, I had a relapse. I fell in love; I was sure it was meant to be. But then it ended and I was left brokenhearted.

Again. You'd think, after all the disastrous relationships I'd been through, I'd know better. That I wouldn't be crushed in the end. But as all history teachers say, those who don't learn from history are doomed to repeat it. So right then and there I recommitted to my previous decision that two people couldn't really work it out. I also watched a few of the friends who'd gotten married in their early twenties get divorced, which only reaffirmed my decision.

That's why, at thirty years old, I'm a year sober from love, fairy tales, and happy endings. And it's not so bad.

Really.

• • •

If I had a theme song—and I totally should—it would be one of those power ballads about being an independent woman and not needing a guy. That's the mood I was rocking tonight. Today was a big milestone for me.

A cool, air-conditioned breeze washed over me as I stepped into the restaurant. My best friend, Stephanie, was already there, and, of course, she was on the phone. She probably hadn't even checked in yet. Lucky for her, I love her as much as her phone-dependent fiancé does.

I walked up to the hostess. She was obviously new, because I didn't recognize her, and I ate here more than I did at my own place. "Darby Quinn, party of two."

She ran a finger down her list, made a checkmark with her pen, then smiled at me. "Give us just a minute, Ms. Quinn, and I'll have someone show you to your table."

I glanced back at Stephanie, who looked like she was talking into thin air. "I understand," Stephanie was saying. "But she's *your* mom. You'll have to talk to her about it." Underneath her pale curtain of hair, she had her Bluetooth earpiece on. Her gaze caught mine and she held up a finger.

One minute, my butt.

Stephanie and I were often mistaken for sisters. We had the same blond hair—mine was naturally straight, whereas she was a slave to her flat iron—same hazel eyes, and after fifteen years of hanging out together, we'd developed similar mannerisms. Though she was far more detail-oriented than I was. Perfectionist was an understatement, but it worked out well for her. Who wants to hire a sloppy accountant?

"Hi, Darby," Mindy, my usual hostess, said as she walked up to the front. She grabbed two menus. "How are you doing today?"

"I'm well, thanks." I raised my voice and looked at Steph. "If I could just get my friend off the phone, since she's supposed to be hanging out with me, I'd be even better."

Stephanie stuck out her tongue. "Okay, honey, I've gotta go. I'll see you at home." Pause. "I don't know, a few hours." Pause. "Love you, too." She pushed the button on her earpiece, disconnecting the call, then smiled at me. "I'm all yours."

Steph and I followed Mindy through Blue. The place was a mix of espresso-colored wood, white, and dark blue. Miniature lamps lit the tables, casting a soft bluish glow. Blue was my favorite restaurant in Denver. My favorite restaurant anywhere, actually.

The fact that it was five minutes from my building and about ten from Metamorphosis Interior Designs, where I worked as an interior designer, made it even better.

As soon as Stephanie and I were settled into a table in the corner, she picked up her menu. "So what are we celebrating again?"

I took the white cloth napkin off the table and placed it on my lap. "It's been a year since I've had my heart broken. No more relapses."

"Oh, that's right." Stephanie shook her head. "You're celebrating your jaded stance on men."

"I prefer the term *realistic*, thank you very much. I'm just a girl who realizes love is not only overrated but downright impractical."

"For the past year, anyway."

"Right," I said. "Before that I was miserable."

"You weren't miserable the entire time. You had happy moments, too."

"That's my point. I'm not saying I won't find a guy to have a few happy months with here and there, but I realize now that's enough for me. No future. No big wedding. No forever. Just low-risk here and now."

Stephanie frowned. "I can't believe my maid of honor doesn't believe in love. Please don't tell my mom."

"Well, you and Anthony are an exception."

"I thought you said there are no exceptions."

I smiled. "I did. But not to my best friend who's getting married in two months. That would just be cruel." Honestly, I hoped she and Anthony were an exception. If anyone deserved happiness, Steph did.

"What about that saying?" Steph tapped a finger to her lips. "'No man is an island.'"

"No man is an island because he'd never survive. Men are like overgrown babies. Women, on the other hand—well, without men, I think we'd be relatively problem-free. I could totally be an island."

But the thought of being *all* alone, without anyone else, was pretty depressing. "I suppose I'd need my family and friends. I'm more like a peninsula."

Steph sighed. "At least you admit you need me. I still think, though, that if you just found the right guy—"

"We're not puzzle pieces, Steph. There's no 'you complete me' guy out there, and the beauty of this day and age is I don't need one."

"So why are you dressed like that"—she waved a hand at me—"if you don't have anyone to impress?"

My red dress hugged in all the right places and showed off my legs. "One, because I run my butt off so I can pull it off. And two, what am I supposed to do? Look like a slob because I don't think relationships last forever? I'm not itching to run off and become a nun or something."

Steph laughed. "Yeah, you'd be a great nun."

Chad walked up to the table and shot me a big, toothy grin. "Darby. Hey."

I returned his smile. "If it isn't my favorite waiter. How are you today?"

"Good. We're getting kind of slammed right now, so it's crazy. But good." He lifted his pad of paper. "What can I get for you ladies?"

I didn't even bother with the menu anymore. I rattled off my order, then waited as Stephanie placed hers.

Steph watched Chad walk away. "What about him? He's super cute and you two seem to have a vibe."

"We don't have a vibe. We have a I-come-here-all-the-time-so-we-say-hi thing. Besides, he's way too young, not to mention I have a strict policy against dating people I run into all the time. No guy's worth losing my favorite place to eat."

Steph rolled her eyes. "You're completely hopeless."

"No, you're the hopeless romantic. They call it that for a reason, you know."

Steph's phone rang and she hovered her finger over her earpiece. "Anthony's probably calling to tell me what his mom said about the flowers. I'll just be one minute."

"I knew you'd never make it." I dug through my purse until I found the envelope I was looking for and took it out. "I'll be right back," I whispered.

Making my way toward the back of the restaurant, I took in all the different kinds of people out on a Saturday night. One couple sat, smiling at each other but not saying anything, neither one eating much of his or her food.

On a date. Probably first or second.

The next table over, a woman in her late thirties to early forties had her arms folded across her chest, a scowl on her face. The guy across from her leaned in, looking frustrated and confused, saying, "I'm sorry, okay."

Married and not speaking—well, she's not speaking.

The kitchen would be a madhouse tonight, so I didn't bother heading in that direction. Brent, the head chef and owner, had done me a huge favor last week, making a special plate for one of my clients. The list of items she couldn't have had been lengthy, but he'd managed to pull off a delicious meal anyway. I'd written him a thank-you note because that's the kind of girl I am.

The office in the back corner had a plastic in-box attached to the door. Brent had mentioned I could place notes or special requests in there if he was ever too busy to come out of the kitchen. I dropped my note inside, then headed back the way I'd come.

A large group of people walked toward me, taking up most of the walkway, and I flattened myself against the wall to let them through. After they passed, I stepped forward, my thoughts on getting back to my table, when the heel of my stiletto caught. To keep from falling, I had to leave the shoe behind.

"Whoa," I muttered as I recovered from my almost-fall.

I turned around in search of my shoe and saw a guy bend over to retrieve it.

"I think you lost this," he said, tugging it loose from the crack in the floor.

"Yeah, it kind of stuck in there and... Let's just say it wasn't my smoothest move."

He stood up, a big smile on his face. His very handsome face. His bright blue eyes, killer smile, and short, dark hair made it hard to look away. So I didn't bother trying.

"Well..." He held my black stiletto out to me. "Here you go."

Oh, that's right. I'm standing in the middle of a crowded restaurant, one foot four inches higher than the other.

"Thanks," I said as I took the shoe. Balancing on my other foot, I bent my leg back and attempted to slide the shoe on. Stepping into this pair wasn't an option. They took a little extra work—a finger on the back—to wedge in the heel.

He reached out and put a hand on my hip to steady me. It sent my heart racing, which just goes to show you how long it had been since my last physical contact with a guy.

The shoe finally slipped into place and I put my foot down. When he didn't move his hand, I glanced at it, then back up at him.

"I didn't want you to fall," he said, one corner of his mouth lifting.

A deep stirring I hadn't felt in a long time burned through my core. "I wouldn't fall."

"You see how I might worry, since you did trip just a minute ago."

Between the grin he was flashing me and the heat radiating from his hand, my pulse was having trouble staying steady. I smiled back, pulling out the flirty grin that was rusty from lack of use. "I suppose I do have that against me. Although I choose to blame the faulty flooring and not my coordination."

He took his hand off my hip and held it out to me. "I'm Jake."

I placed my hand in his—firm shake. Bonus points. "Darby."

"Interesting name."

"Interesting is one word for it. For a long time, I thought my parents chose it to torture me. People used to tell me that because of my name, they thought I was a boy."

Jake's gaze ran down my dress, then lifted back to my face. "I doubt anyone makes that mistake now."

My throat went dry, and with him staring at me like that, I got a little light-headed, too. "Yeah, well, the dress and the heels, they kind of put it all in perspective."

"So did you need something?" Jake asked. "I saw you near the office. Complaints? Compliments? Just so you know, we prefer compliments. And I'll remind you that I did help you out with your shoe problem. Although with the flooring issue, that's probably going to be a wash."

It took me a moment to shift gears. Was he saying…? I looked him over again. All the waiters wore white shirts and black slacks. Jake had on a red button-down shirt with a black tie and nice black pants. In fact, we matched.

"You work here?" I asked.

"I do a little of this, a little of that." Jake scooted to the side as Mindy led an older couple down the walkway, bringing him even closer to me. I caught a whiff of his musky, masculine-smelling cologne. "Actually, I manage and own the place. Well, my buddy and I do."

That pulled me out of my he-looks-and-smells-amazing daze. *Sure you do, you big fat liar.* "Funny, I've never seen you here before."

"Oh, do you come here often?"

I narrowed my eyes at him.

"It's not a line," he said. "Unless it worked, then I'll go with it."

"You know, I've got to get back to my friend. Thanks for the help with the shoe and everything." I turned to walk away.

"Wait."

I glanced back at him.

He leveled those dangerous blue eyes on me. "Could I take you to dinner sometime?"

I motioned around. "Like, here? In this lovely restaurant you own?"

"Wherever you want," Jake said. "It doesn't have to be here."

"I'm going to have to pass. Now if you'll excuse me, I've really got to get back." Before he could say anything else, I turned and walked away from the best-looking guy that had ever hit on me.

It's such a shame he's a liar. Otherwise, I might've been tempted. And I haven't been tempted in a long *time.*

Our food was at our table by the time I got back. Steph was even off the phone. "Where did you disappear to?" she asked.

I slid into my seat. "I was walking back from dropping a note off to Brent and my shoe got caught. This guy got it out for me."

Steph grinned. "Did he slip it on for you, too?"

"No. I did that." I picked up my fork, ready to devour my dinner. "Stop looking at me like that."

"It's just funny that the girl who is so anti-fairy tale had her shoe rescued by a guy. It's very *Cinderella*."

"The guy was definitely cute and charming. But he claimed he owned this place, making him a liar."

"Maybe he wasn't lying."

"Steph, I've never seen him before and I eat here *all* the time. And I happen to know Brent, who *actually* owns the place. So, yeah, the very handsome guy's a liar. And ever since Allen, I have a strict no-liars policy."

"Liars are the worst," Steph said.

I lifted my glass, ready to recommit myself to what I'd come here to celebrate. "To male sobriety."

• • •

Being burned time and time again takes an emotional toll on a girl. I'd know. After my last failed relationship, I called Steph, like I always did, and she came over for calorie splurging, guy bashing, and binge drinking. Over pizza, Steph and I rehashed our worst relationships.

The next afternoon, I got the idea to lay out all my relationships, so I'd avoid making the same mistakes. Since fairy tales were partially responsible for my messy love life, I'd drawn parallels to my failed relationships.

The first of my case studies demonstrates why I never date liars—even charming ones.

Aladdin Case Study: Allen/Aladdin

My Age: 22

You know in *Aladdin* how he's all charming and you're rooting for him, even though he's been lying to Jasmine the whole time? He comes in, says he's a prince, and you think, okay, he had his reasons. He even tells her to "trust him." Well, people do have their reasons for lying. It doesn't make it okay, though.

Allen and I met at a cocktail bar. I was there with my coworkers, celebrating the end of a project. At the time, I'd had a few heartbreaks but was still optimistic about love. After all, this was the stage in my life when guys were supposed to be different—more mature.

Allen smiled at me from across the room. He was older, which made him more interesting to me. Feeling bold—thanks to the strong cocktails—I walked over and introduced myself. He and I chatted for hours. It was like everyone else in the room had disappeared.

"Twenty-two, huh?" he said after I'd told him my age. He studied me for a minute, then reached out and squeezed my shoulder. "I wish I would've met you back when I was twenty-two."

"Instead, you met me now. I don't really think age makes much of a difference." I dug into my purse and found a card for Metamorphosis Interior Designs, where I was doing my apprenticeship, and scribbled my number on the back. I wasn't usually so forward, but I hadn't met a guy I'd liked in a while. "Give me a call sometime."

Three weeks went by before he called. After talking on the phone for an hour, he asked me out.

Enter the magic carpet. Or in Allen's case, a red Dodge Viper. Showy, yes. Fast, yes. Impressive, very. It didn't fly, but it came pretty damn close.

Allen opened the passenger door for me and I slid inside, taking in the smell of the leather seats as I studied the gauges. My stepbrothers had taught me enough about cars to be impressed.

"So," I said as he got into the driver's seat, "let me guess. You boost cars for a living."

Allen grinned, the dimples in his cheeks deepening. "I'm an Oral and Maxillofacial Surgeon."

"Sounds fancy."

"It pays the bills." Allen started the car and zoomed away from my apartment. "I was thinking we'd head up to Boulder. It gives me a chance to drive on the freeway, and there're some nice places to eat there."

"I'm game." The fact he wanted to spend extra time with me seemed promising.

The night only got better from there.

Allen was thirty. He was different from all the other guys I'd dated in college. In fact, the whole relationship was quite the ride. Sometimes he couldn't seem to get enough of me; sometimes he'd ignore me for a few weeks. After three months of trying to figure him out, I finally lost it.

"Look," I said over dinner, my irritation now at a boiling point. "I know that no girl thinks of herself as clingy, but I'm really not. If you need some space, whatever. But I'm tired of the hot and cold. I never know when you're going to be sweet or when you'll decide that I don't exist."

Allen set down his fork and placed his hand on my knee. "I'm sorry. It's just that...I'm a little embarrassed about my current situation. I'm staying with some friends, trying to get my life together. That's why I always suggest your place." He sighed. "I know I probably should've brought it up sooner, but I went through a really messy divorce last year. No matter what I did, it was never good enough for my wife. The money, my job. *I* was never good enough."

He shook his head, pressing his lips together, and his voice came out strained. "I like you, and I feel myself getting really attached, and then I worry I'm never going to be good enough. So I throw myself into work." He squeezed my knee and flashed me a smile. "Then I start thinking about you and call again. We have a great time, and the cycle repeats. I wish I could just forget about my past and stay in the perfect moments with you."

I was happy he felt close enough to open up to me. "I think you're good enough. I think you're amazing, actually. Instead of ignoring me, just tell me what's going on." I looked up, into his eyes. "Cool?"

His posture relaxed and he nodded. "Okay. It might take me some time to readjust, though. Please just be patient with me."

I walked away from that dinner feeling confident. His confession explained a lot. After that, he'd send a text saying he was thinking of me but was hanging with the guys. Or he had training. Sometimes an emergency surgery came up.

It always started with, *Wish I had more time*, or *Wish I could be with you right now, but...*

I know what you're thinking. You're thinking, *Wow, she's a moron.* But I was young and naive, and I tended to believe people back then. I didn't match the sob story with the fact that we always headed to a different town. At the time, I wasn't even bothered by not knowing where he lived. I thought it was endearing how much he wanted to impress me.

One day, I decided to surprise him. To let him know how much I cared by showing up at his office. Because he often called me on his break, I knew he took lunch at twelve thirty. Most of the time I had client lunches, so I was especially excited to sneak in an extra hour with Allen.

His dental practice was in one of those older brick buildings with lots of medical offices inside. I took the elevator to the third floor and pulled open the door that had a Dr. Allen Booth plaque on it. The waiting room was empty except for chairs and magazines.

I walked up to the receptionist window. "Hi, could you tell Allen that Darby is here?"

The woman looked up from her computer. "Do you have an appointment?"

"No, I—"

"I'm sorry, ma'am. We're about to close for lunch." She slid out a business card. "Give us a call to schedule something."

"Actually," I said, "I'm here to see if Allen wants to go to lunch."

"Dr. Booth has lunch scheduled with his wife."

"You mean his ex-wife?"

The woman frowned. "No, ma'am. I mean Mrs. Booth."

My heart dropped. Surely she didn't mean—

"Is that Alicia?" I recognized Allen's voice. "Tell her I'll be right out."

"Actually, it's Darby," I yelled back, rage taking over as I realized what this meant. "And I think you'd better get out here now."

A few seconds later, Allen walked into the waiting room. "What are you doing here?" he whispered. "I really wish you would've called first."

I didn't bother whispering back. "I thought I'd surprise you and take you to lunch. You know, since you've been so busy lately. But I was just informed that you're having lunch with your wife. I was sure she meant ex-wife, but she made it sound like there was no ex in front of it."

"Look, it's complicated. We were about to get a divorce, but then..." He lowered his voice to a whisper. "She's pregnant. What am I supposed to do? Leave her anyway?"

I shoved him. "How about not keep calling me." I stepped forward and shoved him again. "How about not telling me that you love me?"

"I *do* love you. Look, what I told you about her is true. She's demanding. She makes me feel like I'm not good enough. Then I met you and you just lit up the room. You made me feel special." He reached out for me. "Is it so wrong I tried to hold onto that?"

Instead of yelling all the insults I wanted to, I clenched my teeth, feeling like screaming and crying and not knowing which one to grab onto. I'd sworn that if this ever happened again—if a guy ever did me wrong again—I wouldn't freeze up; I'd let the guy have a piece of my mind. But the giant lump in my throat made it impossible to say anything.

The door swung open and a raven-haired woman with a round, protruding belly walked in.

Allen's eyes widened as he looked over at her, then back at me. "Please don't say anything," he whispered. "She's already having a high-stress pregnancy, and they're worried about her losing the baby." He raised his voice, turning to his wife. "Honey, hi. Just give me a minute."

He tried to tug me toward the back, but I was done being jerked around. I didn't know if what he said about his wife's pregnancy was true. She deserved to know her husband was a cheating dirtbag, but was I willing to risk her health? No. Besides, she'd probably just blame me anyway.

"He's all yours," I said as I bolted past her, out of the office.

For two days I called in sick to work. It wasn't even a lie; I felt ill every time I thought of how I'd been with another woman's husband.

Allen called off and on for a few weeks, leaving me sorry excuses and apologies in my voice mail I couldn't believe. He told me how much he wished things were different. He said he still loved me.

See, in the end of *Aladdin* it was all okay because Aladdin came clean, admitted his feelings...and let's face it, Jasmine was rich enough to take care of him, so it didn't really matter. I think she should've held out for longer—maybe even ruled the kingdom without him—so girls out there wouldn't think a little apology and flying off into the sunset repaired all. I mean, how did she know he wouldn't lie again? He probably did.

But they never bother showing what happens after.

In real life, coming clean doesn't always make a difference. Because some dirty laundry is too ruined to get clean again.

Time Wasted: Five months

Lessons Learned:

Don't date someone obsessed with his car.

Insist on seeing his place.

Don't buy sob stories.

Dentists are evil.

A person who lies about one thing won't hesitate to lie about something big.

Never EVER date a liar!

Chapter Two

Nadine, my partner at work, insisted we go to lunch at Blue to get away from the office—our boss was on some kind of warpath today, and it was best to steer clear when she was looking for someone to blame. After what happened Saturday evening, I'd been planning on staying away for a while. Even though Jake didn't own the place, he might actually work there, and I didn't want to have an awkward run-in with him. Especially since I couldn't stop thinking about his handsome face, his smile, and the way my heart jumped into my throat when he put his hand on my hip.

"Hey, Darby. Nadine," Mindy said when we walked in. "Just you two today? Or do you have clients joining you?"

"Just us," Nadine said.

Mindy ushered us to a table and left so we could look over the menu.

Nadine lifted her menu and studied it, even though we both knew she'd end up getting the grilled chicken salad. I lifted mine, too, simply for something to look at, when deep male voices caught my attention, and I glanced in their direction. Jake and Chad stood near the back, discussing something. I threw my menu up, not wanting Jake to see me.

Okay, so he does work here. He wasn't wearing the normal waiter attire, either. *Hmm, guess I'll see what I can find out from Mindy.*

"So, what do you think about Mrs. Crabtree's remodel?" Nadine asked. "Are we going to go with the Pepto-pink color, or are we going to try to talk her out of it?"

I peeked around my menu—*no sign of Jake*—then lowered it. "I suggested a lighter pink that wouldn't make me think of an upset stomach, but she insists she wants that particular pink."

"It's going to be the most god-awful bathroom."

"I talked her out of painting all the walls—told her accent walls are all the rage these days. She seemed to buy it, so that'll help tone it down. Then, next time we meet, I'm going to tell her that stripes are in. If we're really lucky, we'll end up with one pink-and-white-striped wall that we can work accent decorations into. It might be kind of cute, actually."

"Hello, are you ladies…?" Jake trailed off when his gaze lit on me. "Darby. Hi."

I was impressed he remembered my name. Most people could only remember it was unusual. Even without his hand on my hip, my body reacted to him, my pulse quickening and my stomach churning with a mixture of nerves and attraction. "Hi, Jake."

He rubbed his fingers across his jaw—such a simple motion, but it drew my attention to his handsome features. He was the exact type of guy I used to lose my mind over. "I didn't expect… Well, you did imply you came here a lot," he said.

"And *I* wasn't lying." Yes, I needed to remember the lying part and ignore how hot the guy was. I gestured to Nadine. "This is Nadine. Nadine, Jake. Nadine and I work together. And we do end up eating here and bringing clients in a lot."

"Hi," Nadine said with a giant grin, adding in a healthy dose of eye batting. "So, what do you do?"

I crossed my arms and looked up at him. "Yeah, and before you answer, maybe I should mention that I know most everyone who works here. Including the guy who actually owns this place."

Jake's brow furrowed. "You mean me?"

"I mean Brent."

"Right. Brent and I own the place." Jake's confused expression turned into one of amusement. "But you don't believe me."

I looked down at my menu, not wanting to have to call him a liar to his face. Sarah, one of the waitresses, walked up to our table, notepad and pen in her hand.

"Sarah," Jake said. "Could you tell these ladies why I'm here?"

"By their table?" Sarah asked. She was a little on the ditzy side.

"At the restaurant. Why am I at the restaurant now, when I haven't been for the past several months."

"Jake was opening up another restaurant in Las Vegas, so he's been there for a while, and just got back." Sarah glanced at him. "Is that what you mean?"

"It's exactly what I mean."

Heat crept up my neck and into my cheeks. He wasn't lying— he actually owned the place. My foot was inserted so far in my mouth, I couldn't form words. I just stared up at him like an idiot.

He tapped the edge of the table. "Enjoy your meal. I'm sure Sarah will take good care of you. And feel free to let me know if there's anything else you need."

Nadine watched him walk away, then turned her attention back to me. "Holy hell, he's hot. How do you know him?"

"I don't," I said. *And after insulting him like that, I'm never going to.*

• • •

As if my day hadn't been bad enough already, I had a date tonight. Unless you're in an actual relationship with someone, a Monday night date is basically a throwaway. It's like, hey, if you suck, at least I didn't waste a good day of the week on you; if you're actually normal, we can always make a plan for the weekend.

Believe it or not, I've been accused of being pessimistic. Pardon the hell out of me for being what I'd call realistic, because my optimism had slowly been drained one horrible relationship at a time.

"Oh, they weren't all bad," Mom had said when she'd called to set me up on the blind date and I informed her why I didn't want to go. While I've accepted the idea of never having a serious, full-blown relationship again, some people—especially my mom—don't want me to give up on finding "the one" yet.

Apparently her friend had a son who'd recently moved to the city and "needed to be shown around." Yeah, there's Internet now. Most people in this country have a GPS device of some kind. They don't need to be "shown around." And if they're too stupid to read a map or do a little exploring on their own, why would I want to be trapped anywhere with them?

But I digress.

No, my boyfriends weren't all bad. Until they suddenly were. There's that moment when you look at your significant other and think, *Did I ever like you? I'm sure I did. But why?* And right then, you know it's not going to last. It's sad, but true, and the final result is the same: the end of the relationship and heartbreak.

So while I had my doubts about this date, I knew it'd make Mom happy. If I could at least have a decent conversation with the guy, I'd consider it a win. After all, I'd sworn off relationships, not going out altogether, and if I didn't start meeting new people, I'd have no one to hang out with when Stephanie was a busy wife with other obligations.

My date, whose name was Nick, buzzed in to tell me he was here. I loved that feature about my building. It made random drop-bys from guys I never wanted to see again a thing of the past. The building also had a pool, large hot tub, and a fitness room. If you were willing to drop a few more zeros than I was (or had), the top half of the building had floor-to-ceiling glass views of downtown.

Glass views or not, buying my one-bedroom condo four years ago was one of my proudest accomplishments. Since I'd worked on the building with Metamorphosis, I'd gotten a deal. I loved the hardwood floors, black granite countertops, cherry cabinets, and stainless-steel appliances. I'd done the living room in red and aquamarine and it'd turned out pretty good if I did say so myself.

I grabbed my purse off the granite countertop, locked up, and took the elevator down to the lobby, where Nick was waiting for me.

"Darby?" a guy said as I stepped off the elevator. He was in his midthirties, had a little extra love in the gut area, but not enough to be called fat, and was wearing a sweater vest. A bit on the preppy side for my tastes, but better looking than I'd imagined when Mom suggested I go out with her friend's son.

"That's me," I said. "You must be Nick."

He extended his hand. "Yep. Nice to meet you."

I took it and we shook—weak and a little clammy. *He's definitely no Jake.*

I quickly tried to shut that thought down. Not only was it an unfair comparison, but I shouldn't be thinking about him right now. Not that flutter of attraction, or his nice jawline and firm handshake.

A sinking sensation went through my gut. I'd already blown any chance of even being friends with the guy. *I can't believe I called him a liar.* I always insisted guys were the jerks, but I'd win, hands down, when it came to the guy who actually did own Blue.

I realized I was still holding Nick's hand, even though we weren't shaking anymore, and quickly dropped it.

A short walk later, we reached his car. "So, it's a little embarrassing to be set up by your mom," Nick said as he fired up the engine. "But it is nice to meet someone. So far, I just work and go home."

"That's about all I do," I said. "My best friend is getting married, so she's busy with all this wedding stuff and I'm left to hang out with myself."

He glanced at me, that nervous OMG-she-just-said-marriage look on his face. Guys freak out about that. Like if your friend is getting married you must be desperate to do it, too.

"I've been kind of thrown into helping her plan, even though it's not my thing," I said, trying to smooth it over. "I'm not big on marriage in general."

Now he looked even more disturbed, the creases in his forehead deepening.

Just stop talking, Darby. So much for thinking we could have a decent conversation. Maybe I really was destined to spend most of my nights alone.

The next few minutes were filled with nothing but the jazz music coming from his stereo.

Finally, we got to the restaurant. At least inside, the buzz of conversation and people eating made the silence between us less awkward. As we sat down and started talking, one thing was clear: we didn't have a whole lot to talk about. Even though our moms weren't here, it was like they were on the date with us.

"I heard your mom makes the best cherry pie," Nick said a few minutes after we got our food.

I had to finish my bite of pasta before responding. "It is really good." Then I felt like I should reciprocate. "And your mom is famous for her peach jam."

A nod from him. More eating. Another comment about what he'd heard about my mom.

Toward the end of dinner, the conversation steered to his job. He *loved* talking about his job managing a store that sold golfing gear. To hear him tell it, he was the most important thing that had happened to the store. He prattled on about shipments, sales, and a slew of other things I couldn't care less about, but tried to pay attention to anyway.

"I have to admit," I said when he finished a lengthy discussion on the types of drivers, "I've been golfing and it's about the most boring thing I've ever done. Old men drive around in golf carts pretending they're sporty and getting grouchy if there's any noise. It's like the nursing-home Olympics."

Nick's mouth dropped open. "It takes great athletic ability to know how to aim and drive the ball that far."

"I get more exercise shopping at the mall," I joked. "I don't come home and tell everyone that I won at shopping." *Although those red shoes I got on sale the other day felt like a win.*

Nick frowned. "I think you'd change your mind if you got into it."

Obviously, he didn't think my jokes were funny—it wasn't the first time I'd said the wrong thing, and I doubted it'd be the last. At least I knew to not add any more to the golfing conversation. I needed someone I could at least joke with, though, or there was no point in putting effort into going out. *Sorry, Mom, but looks like it's not gonna be a love match.*

Nick tossed his napkin onto his plate and pulled one of those flossers out of his pocket—the plastic, Y-shaped thing you thread floss through. I watched in horror as he proceeded to take care of business.

So I ask you, what's worse? A little something between the teeth or flossing at the table? I'm casting my vote for the table. If you must use the floss that's been in your pocket gathering lint, take it to the bathroom and go to town. Because digging meat out of your teeth is just something I don't want to see.

"Shall we go, then?" he asked a teeth cleaning later.

I couldn't get out of there fast enough.

The ride home was filled with talk of golf and instrumental

music. Being around this guy made me feel tired and boring and blah. When we pulled up to my building, I fought the urge to run for it. "Thanks for dinner."

"So…" He leaned toward me.

No way he expects a kiss.

On the bright side, at least I know his teeth have been flossed recently.

"I've got a huge presentation first thing tomorrow morning, so good night." I grabbed the door handle and exited the car. I purposely didn't use the "see you later" line, because I was hoping there wouldn't be a later. I'd had more than enough.

Chapter Three

I'd lied to Nick last night. I didn't have a presentation this morning. Actually, I was working from home because I had to meet Stephanie later to get my bridesmaid dress altered. Since it'd always been on the tighter side, I decided to go run off last night's dinner.

I gathered my hair into a messy bun, grabbed a bottle of water, turned on my iPod, and headed downstairs to work out.

The exercise room was pretty empty, so I didn't have to wait around for a treadmill. As I ran, I went over my projects in my head. I mentally rearranged the furniture in Mrs. Crabtree's living room, mixed color schemes, and played with the few items she'd purchased at a gallery in California.

Three miles later, I wiped my face with a towel and took a big swig from my water bottle. I stepped off the treadmill, thinking about all I had to do that day. And came face-to-face with Jake.

"I thought that was you," he said.

I tugged the earphones out of my ears and blinked, hardly able to believe my eyes. He was wearing long mesh shorts and a T-shirt that stretched tight across his well-defined chest.

Last night after my date, when I'd had trouble falling asleep, I'd thought of all the things I should say to him the next time we ran into each other. But they'd abandoned me somewhere around the time I'd checked out his pecs.

"W-what are you doing here?" *Smooth, Darby. Real smooth.*

"Same thing as you," he said. "Going for a run."

I really wished I wasn't so sweaty. My face was probably all red, too. "But… You don't live here? In this building?"

One corner of Jake's mouth twisted up. "It would be kind of strange for me to go running here if I didn't live here."

Heat filled my cheeks and I took another swig from my water bottle. Time for the apology. Then maybe I could stop feeling so guilty and get this guy off my mind. "Look, I'm sorry about the misunderstanding at the restaurant. I just thought you were one of those guys who tells everyone he owns the restaurant or runs the company or whatever to seem impressive. I thought that since I knew everyone, you were lying to try to impress me."

There. I'd apologized. Now I could move past this guy and get back to my normal life.

"I *was* trying to impress you, but not with my job." He tucked his thumbs into the pockets of his shorts and shrugged. "I guess I need to work on my skills, because obviously my natural rugged charm wasn't enough." He flashed me a smile to punctuate his statement and I tried—and failed—not to let it melt me the tiniest bit.

"Oh, you were plenty charming. Just not enough to make up for being a liar. Which for all I know, you're not, so again, sorry."

"Do you always assume the worst in people?"

I crossed my arms. "Yes. That way I'm never disappointed. It saves a lot of time and trouble."

His eyebrows shot up and his smile faded. It only lasted a moment; then the smile returned. "I guess there's only one thing to do about that. Let's go to dinner, and I'll prove to you I'm not a liar."

Is he seriously asking me out right now, while I'm all sweaty and makeup-free? My gaze accidentally drifted to his toned chest and arms. My pulse quickened and the temperature in the room climbed even higher. I'd be lying if I said I wasn't tempted.

I swallowed, forcing from my mind thoughts of how good he'd look shirtless, and reminding myself of the rules that had kept me heartbreak-free for a year. Guys like Nick, they were safe. The guy standing in front of me was the total opposite. "Sorry, but you've got two strikes against you already. You work at my favorite restaurant, and you live in my building. That's just asking for trouble."

Jake took a step closer. "Or maybe it'll be convenient."

"A girl does like to be called convenient." My voice shook a little, thanks to his proximity. He was tall, too—in my sneakers, I barely came to his shoulder, which meant he'd still have a few inches on me in my highest heels. Forcing as much indifference into my expression as I could manage, I glanced at my watch. "I've got to go get some work done."

Jake reached out and put his hand on my hip, just like he'd done the other night. My skin heated under his touch and my breath caught in my throat. Part of me was screaming, *Just go for it,* and the other part was yelling, *Mayday, mayday, we're going down!*

"Just so you know," he said, leaning close enough his chest bumped my arm, "I'm an expert on baseball, and two strikes isn't enough to get out. You need three."

I stared up into those startling blue eyes of his, and worked at keeping my voice steady. "I'm sure the third will come up soon."

The wattage on his smile kicked up a couple extra notches. "I'll see you around, Darby."

• • •

"I think you should go out with him," Stephanie said after I'd relayed the story. The woman tailoring my dress tugged on the pale pink fabric and I almost fell over.

"He lives in my building, Steph. I can't go out with him."

"So? I say you go for it anyway."

I shook my head. "Not gonna happen. You remember what happened to Evan and me. That was awkward forever. I swore that I'd never date someone who lived in my same building ever again."

Stephanie pointed at my hem. "I think an inch higher," she said and then looked back up at me. "All I'm saying is you seem to be getting all worked up over this guy. You admitted you think he's smokin' hot, and he asked you out again, even though you shot him down once *and* called him a liar. You've got to admire his determination."

"It'd be admirable if he didn't live in my building and work at my favorite restaurant." I groaned when I realized I'd have to avoid Blue. "Where am I going to eat now?"

Stephanie's cell rang and she held up a finger.

As she talked on the phone, I thought about Jake again. The way he'd smiled at me, how he'd implied he still had another strike left, the way he said he'd see me around. Okay, he'd gotten to me. But all I had to do to snap back to reality was remember what happened with Evan. Back then I'd lived in an apartment complex. After things went sour with him, I had to find a new place to live.

Nope. Stick to the rules. That's history I don't want to repeat.

Little Mermaid Case Study: Evan/Prince Eric
My Age: 24

Stephanie and I had lived in a tiny, run-down apartment the entire time we were going through college, so after a few years in the work force, we decided it was time to get a place that didn't smell like cat pee and curry. Drew and Devin, my twin stepbrothers, were helping Steph and me haul all of our furniture and boxes into our new place.

After unloading the truck, Drew, Devin, and Stephanie went on a food run. I had the doors and window to our apartment open, airing it out. I turned on my iPod and started moving boxes around. I guess I got a little carried away with the singing. I was belting out the lyrics along with my music when I looked up and saw a guy standing outside my door. He had an athletic build, blond hair, and a big grin.

Before I could figure out whether to wave or run and hide, Drew, Devin, and Stephanie showed up with the food, and he walked on past our open door.

A week later, I ran into him at the mailboxes.

"Hey, you're the singing chick," he said. "Nice voice, by the way."

I stood there staring, unable to say a word.

"I'm Evan. I'm just a few doors down, so if you ever need anything…" His eyebrows drew together and he gave this adorable half-shrug thing. "Well, I probably won't have it—our apartment's pretty bare, actually. But try the next door over because that lady's really nice."

I smiled, still working on forming words. Finally, I got a few out. "Thanks for the tip. I'm Darby, by the way."

He gave me The Nod. "I'm sure I'll see you around."

After that, we bumped into each other on a regular basis: at the pool, the laundry room, while taking the stairs instead of the elevator. We'd have short conversations about our days; laugh about Gertrude, the old lady who walked her cat on a leash; or complain about the neighbor who cooked something that smelled awful and permeated our half of the building. Of all the people who lived in my complex—except Steph, of course, who was logging so many hours at her job I hardly saw her—I knew Evan the best. Things were easy between us. We clicked.

One night, after an especially stressful day at work, I went down to soak in the hot tub. The jets shut off, and I sat there with my eyes closed, trying to gather the energy to get out and restart them. Before I'd psyched myself up to brave the cold air, the bubbles started again. I opened my eyes to see who I'd be sharing the hot tub with.

Evan stepped into the bubbling water. "Hey, Darby. How's it going?"

"Oh, you know, stressful day, so I'm unwinding."

"I had the same idea after unloading trucks all day." Evan smiled at me. "Not many people come out in this weather."

I glanced up at the sky and took a deep breath of the fresh air that contained the promise of rain. "I like being in the hot tub when it's like this."

When I looked back down, Evan was right next to me. "I keep almost asking you out, then chickening out," he said.

I swallowed, staring at the way the steam rose off his body and swirled through the air around us. "You shouldn't. Chicken out, I mean."

He put his arms around me and we spent the rest of the night kissing in the hot tub. I know, every sleazy reality show contains a hot-tub make-out—or ten. Believe me, the next morning I was wondering if that was all it would ever be. Then I started stressing about how I was going to act when I saw him again.

Pulling into our apartment complex after work the next day, I noticed his truck in the parking lot. I debated between the elevator and stairs for a few minutes, wondering which one might bring me face-to-face with Evan, and then trying to figure out if I wanted to be face-to-face with him. In the end, I took the stairs. I scurried past his door and locked myself in my apartment.

I clicked on the television and flipped through the menu. Twenty minutes of channel surfing later, a knock sounded on my door. I peered through my peephole and saw Evan on the other side, holding a pizza box.

I ran a hand through my hair before pulling open the door.

"Hey, I was thinking we could eat some pizza and hang out," Evan said.

My heart skipped a couple beats. It wasn't a one-night thing! I didn't belong on an episode of *The Bachelor*, the discarded girl who didn't get a rose—or a greasy slice of pepperoni, as it were. I stepped aside and motioned for him to come in. We ate pizza, then kissed some more.

From then on, we hung out more often than not. We cooked dinner together, went to movies, and made frequent visits to the hot tub. Before long, the entire apartment complex knew we were together. It was pretty convenient, being able to get home from his place in under a minute.

And then—you know how in *The Little Mermaid* the shell on Ursula's (disguised as Vanessa's) chest hypnotized Prince Eric? Other girls' chests hypnotized Evan. I saw him ogling them all the time. I didn't love it, but you know, I still took a moment to admire a cute guy when I encountered one. Much more subtly, but still. And it wasn't like he forgot to check me out, either—he always told me I looked hot.

A couple months in, Evan started pulling away, spending less time with me and saying he needed to get up early. Fine. I was busy, too.

When I ran into him in the hallway one day, he told me he needed a break from us. He said we'd gone so fast, living next door and all, and he wasn't ready for that big of a commitment.

The confusing part about the whole I-need-a-break speech was that it made it sound like we might resume the relationship, even though deep down, I knew things were over. Still, when a week later I ran into him and he had his arm around another girl, I felt a little blindsided. According to his roommate, Evan's new girlfriend was a singer in a local band, and he was completely mesmerized by her.

Three months later—while I was collecting the giant stack of bills from my mailbox—he told me he was getting married.

I lost my voice again. I tried to nod like I was fine. I'd been running into *her* more and more, though. When I left for work, she was there in the hall, kissing him good-bye. She was in the laundry room when I tried to do my laundry. She always gave me dirty looks, too, simply because I was his ex. She was the one who'd lured him away; I don't know why *I* got the dirty looks.

The night after he confessed he was engaged, I went downstairs to soak in the hot tub. And there Evan and his new fiancée were, making out like we used to.

As far as I know, no sea creatures interrupted their wedding.

Of all the princes, Prince Eric used to be one of my favorites. When you think about it, though, he fell in love with a voice— with an idea. And I can't hold much against Ariel, because she was young and naive and easily amused by things like forks. At least Disney tried to make the ending happy. In the original story, she turned into sea foam. But see, if I'd watched the original growing up, maybe I wouldn't have had such high hopes. Maybe I wouldn't have expected a guy to accept all my quirks, love me for me, and ride out the storm together, no matter what life tried to throw at us.

Time Wasted: Three months with him; four months trying to avoid him and his new girlfriend/eventual fiancée.

Lessons Learned:

Guys who ogle shamelessly must not be all that satisfied with what's in front of them.

Hot tub hookups are always, always a bad idea.

Never date anyone who you'll be forced to run into on a regular basis if it goes wrong.

CHAPTER FOUR

I groaned as I approached Blue. It was the last place I wanted to be, but I'd been unable to convince Mrs. Crabtree to meet for lunch somewhere else—I should've never brought her here for the lamb the first time, because now she was hooked.

I already had a headache from my marathon work meeting with my boss, Patricia, that morning, where Nadine and I had gotten accused of not turning in our reports, even though my e-mail said it sent. I didn't need any more drama in my life. After yesterday morning's run-in with Jake, I'd resolved to avoid him at all costs, and walking into his restaurant was pretty much the opposite of that.

Why did my stupid shoe have to get stuck? If I hadn't lost it, none of this would've happened. And why did Mrs. Crabtree have to be so set on the place?

I'd tried to get Nadine to come, too, so I had an extra buffer, but she'd begged off, stating she was swamped between printing off our reports so she could hand a physical copy to Patricia and finishing up one of her smaller jobs.

I took a deep breath and made my way inside.

The entire meal I was on edge, barely nibbling at my food and glancing around every few seconds. Mrs. Crabtree and I finalized plans, and then she gave me updates on her grandchildren.

By some miracle, we'd made it through our meeting without seeing Jake. All we had to do now was slip out and I'd be home free.

"I love the idea about the stripes," Mrs. Crabtree said as we walked toward the front of the restaurant.

"And that chandelier you picked for the living room is going to look amazing." I draped my gray peacoat over my arm. It had been a bit breezy today, and I thought it might rain. Colorado was like that. One day you'd think summer had hit, and the next you could see your breath.

Jake rounded the corner, headed my way. I stepped behind Mrs. Crabtree, but even with her puffy, white hair, she was too short to provide good cover. Jake glanced up and our eyes met. I was caught. So I waved, accidentally inviting him over.

"Can't stay away, I see," Jake said.

I let out a nervous laugh that made me inwardly cringe. Crap. Why did he mess me up so badly? He was just a guy. A very good-looking guy who'd asked me out. Twice.

I swiped my hair behind my ear. "Hi, Jake. This is Mrs. Crabtree. Mrs. Crabtree, this is Jake. He's one of the owners of Blue." *At least I got that detail right now.*

Jake extended his hand to Mrs. Crabtree, flashing that damn charming smile of his. "Nice to meet you."

Mrs. Crabtree grabbed his hand and shook it enthusiastically. "Oh, I just love this place. You're doing a great job with it."

"Thank you so much. As the owner" —Jake shot me an extra-large and extra-smug grin— "that's so nice to hear."

I died a little inside, but his teasing also sent a spark of desire through me. As I'd been recently reminded, a guy who didn't take things too seriously was hard to find, and a good sense of humor was such a turn-on.

Would it really be so bad to go out with him just once?

But I didn't do very well with just once, not with guys like Jake. I got sucked in, started thinking this would be the guy who would be different, and ended up missing another piece of my heart.

My defense mechanism clicked in, the same danger warning from yesterday going off in my mind, only stronger. This was a guy who could hurt me. Would if I let him.

He turned back to Mrs. Crabtree. "So, how'd you get Darby to have lunch with you?"

"I'm an interior designer and Mrs. Crabtree's one of my favorite clients," I said, kissing up and brushing off in one smooth move.

Jake kept his eyes glued to mine. "You're saying I need to become a client in order to have dinner with you?"

"I don't date clients, either." Another lesson I'd learned the hard way. "And technically, I did help design your place. I assisted on the building we live in." I tried to tug my coat on, to show him Mrs. Crabtree and I were on our way out. I slid one arm in and reached back to get the other.

Jake turned to Mrs. Crabtree and gave a dramatic sigh. "You see, I keep trying to get Darby to go out with me, and she keeps refusing. Can you believe that?"

Mrs. Crabtree looked from him to me. "I cannot."

"I come here all the time, and we live in the same building. It would be awkward." My sleeve was still not cooperating.

Jake grabbed my coat, guiding my arm into the hole I couldn't seem to find. He leaned down, his breath hitting my neck as he whispered, "More awkward than the obvious chemistry between us?"

Goose bumps traveled across my skin, and I prayed my coat covered them up so he couldn't see the way he was affecting me. I stepped away, putting some space between us. "Good-bye, Jake. I'm sure I'll be seeing you around."

He winked—actually, full-on winked at me! "Count on it."

• • •

A couple of blocks from my building, there was a bookstore I frequently killed time in, and I needed something to distract me after a long day at work and the encounter with Jake that I could not. Stop. Thinking about.

I used to read romance novels, but nowadays I went for action-packed and a high body count. I read the back cover of a bright yellow book, decided it wasn't something I wanted to read, and slipped it back into its place.

When I looked up, I thought I saw Jake. *No way! He's seriously everywhere.*

Trying to get another glimpse, I moved through the aisles. Leaving before he saw me would probably be the smarter option, but I was curious. The types of books he looked at might give me some insight into the guy. Plus, he was nice to look at.

The guy paused in front of a section, and I craned my neck to try to get a better view. He glanced up, toward the top of the shelves, and I was sure it was him. Before he could see me, I ducked behind a stack of books. When I peeked around the shelf, he was coming my way.

Looking for an escape, I hurried down the aisle. Darting out in either direction wasn't an option—he'd spot me for sure. It looked like he was going to anyway. As he stepped into unobstructed view, I whipped around and snatched a book off the shelf in front of me.

"Darby? What are you doing here?"

"Oh, I'm just checking out books." I glanced at the one I was holding. Somehow, of all the places I could duck into, I'd wound up in the erotica section. In my hands was a book about bondage. *Somebody kill me now.*

Jake cocked an eyebrow. "Looks interesting."

My face heated and I shifted my weight to the other foot. "I-it's for a friend. Not me. I mean, it's not what you think. My friend's getting married. Wow, I'm making me really uncomfortable."

A smile spread across his face. "It's okay to admit you were stalking me."

Quirky sex books or stalking? The fact that I'm actually weighing these two options proves how desperate I've become.

"I've gotta go." I slammed the book back down on the shelf and hurried away.

Well, that'll either spark his interest even more, or he'll never speak to me again.

Right now, I still wasn't sure which option I truly wanted.

• • •

Kinky stuff seemed to be the theme of the evening. A politician who'd been caught cheating on his wife was on all the news channels. This particular guy preferred prostitutes. I picked up my TV remote to change the station but found it impossible to look away. Here was this guy holding a giant press conference, and his wife was right there next to him, looking shell-shocked, but still standing by his side.

"I apologize for my actions," the politician said. "I regret that people's faith in me has been shaken. I especially regret hurting my family…"

"Oh, admit it," I said to him, even though he couldn't hear me. "You just regret getting caught. Otherwise you'd be with a prostitute right now."

It was disgusting to see him apologize to his wife in a press conference. You know what his wife didn't want him to do—besides prostitutes, of course? Hold a press conference to apologize. If he were really sorry, he'd apologize to her in a nice private setting where she could slap him across the face and tell him what an ass he was.

Of course he was groveling like an idiot, claiming he regretted his actions. What else was he going to do? Get up there and say, in front of the entire nation, "Hookers are awesome. I especially love how you can pay them to do kinky stuff that my wife won't do." I think I'd actually admire that; at least I'd know he wasn't full of crap. Because like I said, he's not really sorry. He's only sorry he got caught. It's just how guys are.

With my resolve against Jake wavering, this was the wake-up call I needed. The more I reminded myself why I wasn't dating Jake, the better.

CHAPTER FIVE

Now, I realize I've compared myself to Cinderella. I may not have two evil stepsisters, but I do have two evil stepbrothers. Actually, Drew and Devin aren't really evil, and I love them to death. *Now.*

But having to spend the end of my childhood in the tiny town of Longmont, when they were making fun of me and lining the horse pens with my clothes, I was sure they were evil. When Mom and I moved in with three guys, it had taken some time to adjust. Eventually, though, they became part of my family. Drew and I had gotten even closer the past few years.

He'd called me this afternoon to say he was driving down to hang out, which usually meant he wanted to go trolling for women. Which meant he and Michelle must've broken up.

Drew showed up a few minutes after six and announced he was starving. I grabbed all my take-out menus from the kitchen drawer, flopped onto the couch, and handed them to him.

He started flipping through the stack. "I'm surprised you don't want to go to Blue."

"I'm sick of eating there," I said. "Now, tell me what happened with Michelle."

"You know I'm not a girl, right? I don't need to talk it out." He glanced at me. "Besides, this is a good thing for you, remember? You need me to stay single forever, because you're obviously not having any luck."

My mouth dropped open. I smacked him across the chest with the back of my hand. "Thanks for rubbing it in, but we're not close enough to our fifties to decide that yet."

Drew and I had both had a string of failed relationships. One night, we'd made a pact. If we hit our fifties and were still single, we'd get a big place together. We'd be kind of like Marilla and Matthew Cuthbert in *Anne of Green Gables*. Except we wouldn't adopt an orphan; we'd hire someone to do the chores instead.

Drew rubbed the place where I'd smacked him. "Jeez."

"Like it really hurt. Spill it."

"I told Dad and Janet that Michelle and I broke up because she wanted to get more serious than I did, which I'm sure she probably did. Really, she was just irritating me more and more by the day. I started wondering if her voice had always sounded so nasally—"

"She does kind of have an annoying voice," I said.

"And she'd call, like, every hour and ask what I was doing. I wanted to shout, 'I'm working. Some of us work.'"

I leaned back on the couch. "You always attract clingy girls."

Drew shrugged. "I guess I should start trying relationships with women I don't think are my type."

I swiped a hand through the air. "I tried that before. I hunted out guys I'd never usually go for, but all I got were several short relationships with noncompatible people."

"I'm not looking for anything serious right now, anyway."

I shook my head at him. "Typical guy."

He huffed and shoved my knee. "Like you're any better. You don't even believe in long-term relationships."

"I don't believe in short-term flings, either." I knew this conversation would only get us arguing about women and men, so I grabbed the menu for the Yellow Dragon out of his hands and pointed at the chicken lo mein. "This is what I'm getting. What do you want?"

Drew pointed out the orange chicken and the Szechuan beef. "I'll eat the leftovers tomorrow morning."

"Ew. You can't eat Chinese leftovers for *breakfast*."

"Fine. I'll eat them for lunch. What time do you have to go in tomorrow?"

"I can slide in a little late."

"Okay, then!" Drew tossed the rest of the menus onto my glass coffee table. "Chinese food, then we go find us some insignificant others for the night."

"You know, you really are a bad influence." I grinned at him. "You should come over more often."

· · ·

The Wagon Wheel, a rustic bar with a jukebox full of country music, seemed like a good place to take Drew. I didn't think the girls there would mind that he was a full-on cowboy, even though he didn't so much look the part in his T-shirt and loose-fitting jeans. Plus, it was a nice break from the norm for me. Stephanie's fiancé, Anthony, always insisted on going to the nightclub hot spots. Which meant my options were hanging out alone at home or being a third wheel. Neither was all that great.

"Now that's more like it," Drew said, eyeing a couple of girls who sat down at the opposite end of the bar.

"Which one?" I asked.

"The redhead with the—" Drew froze, cupped hands out in front of his chest. He dropped them. "Who looks like she's really smart."

I'd gone off before about him looking at girls like they were pieces of meat. At least he'd tried to edit this time. Drew was very charismatic, and I'd seen what he did with his charm. He got a girl all wrapped up in him, then got bored and moved on. So far tonight, he'd flirted with three women but decided none of them was worth a drink or more than a few minutes of his time.

Drew slapped the bar with his palms. "I'm going in."

He walked over, sat down next to the redhead, and introduced himself. Immediately, she was laughing, leaning in as he told another joke or story. She was already hooked. So it looked like he'd settled on her—at least for tonight. Or the next five minutes. You never knew with him.

A guy with enough hair gel for ten people walked up to me. "Yo, hot stuff, how you doin' tonight?" His Jersey Shore accent was so thick I lost a few IQ points just listening to it.

"I'm okay."

He puffed out his chest. "You need Romeo to buy you a drink?"

"Is your name actually Romeo, or do you just think you're a Romeo?"

He put his hand on the bar and leaned closer to me. "Both."

I held up my glass—cranberry juice and Sprite, because I'd had a feeling I'd be driving home. "I'm good, thanks."

The guy didn't even look old enough to be buying drinks, which just made me feel old. And only the tiniest bit flattered.

"I get you. You playin' it cool. Let me guess, you're one of those uptight gals. All wound up. Let Romeo unwind you."

"Okay, you can move on now. Thanks for playing." I glanced over at Drew, who had his arm around the redhead.

Romeo looked back at his friends, seeming unsure whether he'd been rejected or not.

I waited for him to get the hint.

When he didn't, I leveled my eyes on him. "Look, if you're worried about saving face, you can tell your friends I have a boyfriend or that I'm meeting you later or whatever you want. But I'm not interested."

He lowered his head and walked off.

Some people might think that was mean. What *would* be mean was if I let him waste his whole night on me. Drew had taught me that. He said hint once, then be brutal if they didn't get it. Some of my girlfriends had guys hanging around not just for a night, but weeks—months even—because they didn't want to be mean.

Romeo's head perked up when another girl walked into the bar. He walked past his friends' table and over to talk to her. See, he'd recovered just fine. In fact, I did him a favor because he might actually have a chance with that girl.

The girl smiled. Romeo put his arm around her and led her to the bar.

Looks like Romeo found his Juliet.

Now there's a story for you. I used to think there was something so lovely, so powerful about *Romeo and Juliet*. To be so much in love that you were willing to die for it. Now that I'm older and wiser, I can't help thinking the lovers jumped the gun—or dagger, in Juliet's case. The two of them barely knew each other. If they'd just played the relationship out a bit, they'd probably find that they didn't even like each other all that much.

"Hey, is this seat taken?" a guy asked.

I looked at him, contemplating my answer. He was cute, and maybe he—

"Because my friend needs a place to sit and there's not enough stools at our table."

That put my ego back where it belonged. Karma must've been getting me back for dissing Romeo. "Go ahead."

As he dragged the stool away, I turned my attention back to my empty glass.

I should've brought my headphones so I could at least listen to my audiobook.

Thinking about my book reminded me of my embarrassing encounter with Jake yesterday. I'd been standing there holding that stupid book on bondage, and he'd just flashed his perfect smile at me, melting my resistance to him even as embarrassment burned through me. I heard his voice in my head. *It's okay to admit that you were stalking me.*

For a brief second, I was tempted to break my rules, to see what going out with him would be like. Then I remembered the last time I'd had my heart broken and came to my senses. The rules had gotten me this far.

•••

I climbed out of Drew's truck and pocketed his keys. Since he'd gotten a little tipsy, I'd driven his giant Dodge Ram back to my place. "So, did you find a lust connection with the redhead?"

"Lust, yes," Drew said as we headed across the parking garage toward the elevator. "She was funny, too, so I'll be giving her a call. What about the guy you were talking to at the end of the night?"

"He was nice, and I needed someone to chat with, since you left me stranded." I gave him a mock dirty look. "But after talking to him for a while, I knew we'd never go anywhere. I gave him a fake number. If he calls, he'll be able to order the best pizza in the city, so at least there's a possible consolation prize."

"Cold."

I pushed the up button on the elevator and the doors opened. "Hey, you're the one who said you have to stab the knife in deep enough for them to get the point." Drew and I stepped into the elevator and I pushed the five button. "And I quote, 'Otherwise they waste months taking you out, spending all their money on you, when they have no chance. That's far crueler than rejecting them. So you don't scrape or barely poke, you jab hard enough to pierce the heart.'"

"I forgot about telling you that. I should probably take my own advice." He held up his phone. "Five missed calls from Michelle. Apparently, I didn't go deep enough for her to get the point."

"Yeah, rookie mistake."

The elevator stopped on the first floor. When the doors opened, I automatically scooted toward Drew to allow space for whomever or however many were coming in.

Of course it was Jake. Because he was *everywhere.*

Our eyes met and the air around me thickened. No, I definitely couldn't deny the obvious chemistry between us, as he'd put it. Now to decide what to do about it. I lifted my hand to wave, the word *hi* on my tongue, when Drew said, "I can't believe you're calling me a rookie. I taught you how to do it. Then again, you're the one who's taken it to the next level. Like when you slapped that guy in front of everyone at the wedding and told him you never wanted to see him again. Now *that's* driving the point home."

Jake's eyebrows shot up as he settled into the corner.

The elevator suddenly felt way too small. And way too hot. "Yeah, but that guy deserved it. He said disgusting things to the whole wedding party, hit on the bride, all the bridesmaids, and then came back to me. He was a special circumstance."

"Don't be ashamed," Drew said. "That was good stuff. I tell everyone that story. It's what keeps my friends from hitting on you."

I thought about explaining to Jake that I wasn't really a mean, horrible person, but I knew it would come out wrong. And why did I care anyway? I didn't want to date Jake.

Of course, I didn't want him to think I was an awful person, either.

And okay, maybe I did kinda sorta want to date him. Hell, I was more confused with every encounter, and if we were going to keep seeing each other every time I turned around…

"Chinese food never fills me up," Drew said. "I say we eat the leftovers now, then I'll make a real breakfast tomorrow morning."

The elevator landed on five and the doors slid open. I thought about waving or saying good-bye to Jake. But in the end, I just decided to walk out with the small bit of dignity I had left.

CHAPTER SIX

The sound of pots and pans clanging together woke me up. I squinted at the clock and pulled my covers over my head. Drew had gotten chatty last night and we ended up laughing and talking while we ate leftover Chinese food. It'd been fun, but I'd had a hard time falling asleep. Even after a solid six hours, I still felt exhausted.

Whistling accompanied the clanging pans, and I cursed myself for not closing my bedroom door. Groaning, I threw off the covers, got out of bed, and padded down the hall.

Drew was already up and cooking eggs. He put down the spatula and headed over to the fridge, where he took out the carton of orange juice and set it on the island. "You don't have any bacon or sausage."

"I don't usually have time for real breakfast. Mostly I just grab cereal and toast." I took two glasses out of my cupboard and filled them with orange juice. "I thought you'd sleep in."

"I did. I'm used to waking up at six, and I made it all the way to seven. Besides, I feel bad leaving Dad and Devin doing all the work."

I covered my yawn with my hand. "How is Devin anyway? I know last time I was there, things between him and Anne were tense."

"Ava's still in that crying-all-the-time baby stage. It'll get better once she's older. At least it did after Levi got older."

"I just think it's sad. They used to be so in love. Ever since they had the kids, all they do is fight."

"It's not like they're going to get divorced." Drew scooped out the steaming scrambled eggs onto the two plates.

"Yeah, but it proves my point. Love—the I'm-crazy-about-you kind—never lasts. You still care for and love the person. But you don't stay *in* love."

Drew shoveled a forkful of food into his mouth. "I remember when all you ever talked about was finding a guy and getting married. You'd hog the TV, watching those sappy chick flicks—"

"Then I grew up and learned why they always end the movie after the guy and girl get together. That's when everything falls apart."

• • •

While I waited for the elevator, I listened to the voice mail message Steph had left for me. "Just thought I'd remind you to be nice to Karl. He's Anthony's best man, so you'll be seeing him again. No pressure," she teased, and I couldn't help but smile despite my reservations.

I'd already had a failed blind date on Monday, and two in one week made me feel desperate, even though it was everyone else who was desperate to set me up with someone. But I'd quickly learned you don't argue with the bride when it comes to anything even semi-wedding related, and as she'd pointed out, I had to meet Karl eventually. She also said this guy was different, and if anyone had a chance of setting me up with someone I could have a casual dating relationship with, it was Stephanie.

The elevator doors opened, and I walked in, my gaze on my keypad as I sent Steph a text. IF THIS ADVERSELY AFFECTS YOUR WEDDING, YOU AND ANTHONY WILL HAVE NO ONE TO BLAME BUT YOURSELVES. I WANT A STATEMENT DETAILING SUCH IN MY OFFICE BY NOON.

I hit send, knowing she'd get that I was joking, then glanced up to make sure the elevator was going down to the garage.

I wasn't the only person in the elevator. Jake—of course—was in the corner. He smelled like a combination of fresh, soapy scent and that amazing-smelling musky cologne. It filled up the elevator, and I wanted to take a big whiff and hold it in all day.

"Hey," I said. "Off to work?"

He nodded. Nothing else.

Is he snubbing me? Maybe it's because of last night.

I twisted a strand of hair around my finger. "I should've said hi last night, but it was kind of crazy."

"You had company. I get it," he said, his voice lacking its usual carefree quality.

I realized he'd probably gotten the wrong idea about who Drew was, and suddenly, I was desperate to explain. Because first of all, ew, and second of all, I didn't want him thinking I brought guys home all the time. "That was my brother. He was in town for the night, and we actually spent most of it trying to land him a new girl. I won't know for a few weeks how successful it was." The memory of Drew saying in front of Jake how mean I was came rushing back to me. I put my hand on his arm. "You know, Drew was exaggerating. I'm a nice person. Most of the time."

Jake raised an eyebrow, the hint of a smile on his lips. "So, you didn't really slap a guy in the middle of someone's wedding?"

I bit my lip. "Technically, it was at the reception, and I know it sounds bad out of context, but I swear he deserved it."

Jake looked down at me and I noticed again how blue his eyes were. My gaze moved to his lips.

Mayday, mayday, mayday.

I dropped my hand from his arm and swallowed.

"And what did I do to deserve the brush-off?" he asked.

The elevator doors opened and I let out a sigh of relief. Saved by the *bing*! I moved for the doors, but Jake beat me to them. Only he put a hand out to hold them open and turned to face me, eyebrows raised. So much for escaping the question.

I could feel every beat of my heart, and the walls of the elevator seemed to be closing in on me. "It's nothing against you personally. You seem nice—you're very charming, actually, which I'm sure you know. But you live in my building, and I've got certain rules about that kind of thing. Before I stuck to the rules, my life was much messier." I ducked under his arm—damn he smelled good—and started for my car.

Jake stayed by my side, our footsteps echoing through the garage. "I live in the wrong place and just like that, I've got no chance with you?"

I kept my eyes on my car, afraid that if I looked at him, I might give in. And yes, last night I'd considered trying one little date. But he noticed too much, and he pushed against boundaries I wasn't ready to let go of. It was time I pushed back. "Why have you chosen to pursue me? I'm not playing hard to get. It's not some game you've got to win." I pointed my remote at my silver Dodge Durango and pushed the unlock button.

Jake stepped ahead of me and opened the car door for me. "I'm sure plenty of guys hit on you. Obviously you're beautiful. But there's something different about you that makes me not want to give up."

"You don't even know me," I said.

"And whose fault is that?"

"Cinderella's."

Two creases formed between Jake's eyebrows. "Cinderella's?"

"Yeah, Cinderella screwed me over." Without any more explanation, I got into my car, pulled the door closed, and fired up the engine.

. . .

My seventh birthday was one that stuck out among the rest of my birthdays. Mom and Dad had been fighting a lot, but on that day they'd come together and thrown me a princess party at the local McDonald's. I wore my Cinderella dress; the other girls were decked out in various other princess costumes. (Mine was the most authentic—Mom had gone all out.)

Another party was going on at the same time. A group of boys dressed as superheroes sat across the room. Their fighting and yelling drifted over, interrupting our party. The girls and I frowned, shook our heads, and wrinkled our noses at them. *Ugh. Boys.*

Mom took a picture of all my friends and me in our dresses, which remained remarkably clean. In the photo, you can see the boys in the background. They have ketchup on their clothes, and for some reason, Batman has a sword—basically, it's an unorganized mess.

I could've saved a lot of stress over the years if I'd just realized then that boys didn't want to be princes from fairy tales. They wanted to act cool, talk cool, and get into fights.

I made the mistake of thinking they'd grow out of it someday.

Cinderella Case Study: Charlie/Prince Charming
My Age: 23

I met Charlie at a dance club. It wasn't exactly a ball, but my dress was sparkly, my shoes covered in rhinestones—so practically glass slippers. I'd been to enough dance clubs to know that you didn't meet guys at dance clubs—not good guys, anyway. Stephanie had just broken up with Jimmy Delfino, this jerk she'd dated for way too long. To celebrate, she'd wanted to go dancing.

Charlie, a cute guy with light brown skin and huge brown eyes, asked me to dance shortly after we'd arrived. We danced another song after that. Then another and another, until we'd spent more of the night together than apart. As the club was closing down, he told me he'd love to see me again.

Stephanie gave me that look. The one that said, *We have rules about dance-club guys.*

I sighed. "You know, I don't think that's a good idea."

Charlie leaned in and kissed my cheek. "Well, it was nice meeting you. I hope that someday we'll cross paths again." He gave me a sad smile, hung his head, and then slowly turned away from me.

"Wait," I said. "I'd rather not leave it up to fate. Sometimes fate needs a little help."

A huge grin spread across his face. He whipped out his cell and programmed my number into it. "I'll call you tomorrow."

"Tomorrow? You're not going to play it cool for a few days? Isn't that what guys like you do?"

Charlie reached out and squeezed my hand. "I'm the kind of guy who doesn't wait around when I run into a girl like you. I'm not stupid."

I had to hand it to him, he had the sweet-talk thing down. I'd heard plenty of lines before, but there was something about the way he delivered that one that made me think he might just be different.

The next day, I told myself over and over that if he didn't call, it wouldn't be a big deal. But when an unfamiliar number lit up my display, I shrieked and jumped around for a few seconds before answering it.

"Hello," I said in my best, I'm-casual-sexy-cool voice.

"Darby?"

His voice sent my blood rushing through my body. It was him! He called! "Yeah?"

He exhaled. "Oh, thank goodness. My boys bet me you didn't give me your real number. I'm glad they're wrong."

I smiled. "You had a certain something that made me break my rule about giving my number out to guys at a club." But then reality hit. My last serious relationship had been Allen, and that made me gun-shy to dig in. "Hey, Charlie, you're not married are you?"

"Hell no! And why would I hit on you if I was married?"

I shrugged even though he couldn't see me. "I just like to check." I cringed, thinking I'd blown it—that he'd hang up and never talk to me again.

But then he said, "So how do you feel about my coming and picking you up tomorrow night? I don't want to have to wait longer than that."

I was officially swept off my feet.

For the first month, Charlie and I had nothing but fun. We hit dance clubs and went to party after party together. One of his friends was always having a get-together, and they were usually big, extravagant things—money was obviously not an object. It was a blur of fun, loud, good times.

By then my apprenticeship at Metamorphosis was almost up, and I was working like crazy to make sure I got a coveted designer position. I spent a few weeks mixing and matching color swatches for an upcoming pitch while downing muffins and energy drinks.

Since Charlie was what Steph and I referred to as a "trust-fund baby," he didn't have a job. I think he occasionally went to the one college class he was taking, and though he didn't have much purpose in life besides having a good time, he was very good at it.

One night when I was putting the finishing touches on my pitch, he took my laptop away and held it out of reach. "If you don't get busy living, you're going to look back at your life and find it empty."

When I reached for it, he kissed me, keeping my computer out of reach. "Come on, baby," he said. "Let's go out. You deserve a break." He kissed my neck, then moved his lips to my jawline. "Wherever you want to go. Whatever you want to do."

So we went out and hit the party scene, the way we had before my life had gotten so busy. And I liked that he made me take time for myself so I didn't get too burned out.

Then I got my full-time job at Metamorphosis, life slowed down a bit, and Charlie and I started spending a little quiet time together. We didn't do that well with quiet time. Remember how in *Cinderella* Prince Charming has, like, three or four lines? My relationship with Charlie would've been better had we stuck to four lines.

A few big fights later, I knew we weren't going to work. But because I had so much fun when we went out, I hesitated to end it.

I was sitting in his apartment with him and his friends when things took a turn for the worse. They were watching sports, like they did every minute they could.

"Can you believe those chicks at the club last night?" Joe, one of Charlie's roommates, said.

"There should be a weight limit on girls dancing in the cages," Charlie said.

"And at Hooters."

Charlie tossed a handful of chips in his mouth. "Unless their boobs are what tips them over the scale," he said through the crunching.

I sat there for a moment, not believing what I'd just heard. "Seriously?"

Eyes still locked on the screen, Charlie kissed my cheek. "Don't worry, baby. You're not even close to that weight."

I injected my words with sarcasm. "Yes, that's what I'm worried about. Not that my boyfriend is a chauvinistic pig."

"When did you get so serious about everything?" he asked.

I shoved the magazine I'd been looking at into my purse and sighed. "Good-bye, Charlie. You and I aren't going to work out."

Charlie's gaze actually left the screen this time. "Come on, baby. It will work if you just loosen up."

"Well, this is who I am."

"No, you used to be cool."

"No, you don't really know me." I'd never been very good at the break-up part, but I didn't wan to end on a completely horrible note. "So, good luck with everything and all that. It was fun while it lasted."

"I don't need this!" he shouted. "Just go!" He then proceeded to act like he was dumping me, even though I'd already ended the relationship.

So I packed up my practically glass slippers and hit the road.

Cinderella was the first fairy tale I remember—the one I was most obsessed with because of the gowns and magic and pretty shoes. Yes, her home life was less than ideal—and considering the talking mice and birds, she probably needed serious therapy. But she gave me the most unrealistic expectations of all. Falling in love at first sight, becoming a princess with everything she'd ever need at her disposal, and a relationship that ended happily ever after, with never an argument or bad day in sight.

And worst of all, she made me think all I needed in life was a man to come and whisk me away.

Time Wasted: Four months, but honestly, two of those were pretty fun.

Lessons Learned:

You have to actually talk to the person to get to know him.

You need to know how to work as well as play. It's about balance, not having some guy come in and show you how to have fun. Or tell you what an uptight workaholic you are.

Make sure he at least has aspirations or ambitions of some

kind.

Never date a guy who thinks you're more an object than a human being capable of using a brain.

No sports fanatics.

NEVER give your number out at a dance club.

CHAPTER SEVEN

I punched the elevator button repeatedly, like that would make it come to pick me up faster. If I wasn't wearing five-inch heels, I might've even considered running down the stairs. I hated being late, the stress when you had to rush to get somewhere. Which was why I was never late. Really, I wasn't even *that* late. I'd probably get to the restaurant about ten minutes after my date did, but still, it drove me crazy. I didn't even have Karl's number to let him know.

The elevator finally arrived.

On the way down, I sent a text to Stephanie, stating I was running a few minutes behind for my date, hoping she'd pass on the information to Karl.

I stepped out of the elevator and hurried across the parking garage toward my car. When I went to put my phone in my purse, I dropped my keys. I bent to pick them up and the contents of my unzipped purse poured onto the ground.

"Argh!" Squatting down to get the items was no small feat, considering the binding black ruched skirt I was wearing. *The things I do for fashion.*

I was gathering the last of it when a tube of lip gloss was thrust in front of my face. I looked up and saw Jake. I took the lip gloss from him, tossed it in my purse, and stood.

"You look nice," he said. "Hot date?"

My skirt had inched up, exposing much more of my legs than I meant to. I tugged it back down. "I don't know about hot, but I've got a date. It's something my friend set up."

"Let me guess." Jake counted the list off on his fingers. "He doesn't live in the building, doesn't work at your favorite restaurant… What are your other requirements?"

I was sure he was mocking me, but I went ahead and rattled off more of the list, just so he'd see it wasn't something I took lightly. "No oral surgeons—I'll just generalize and say dentists of any kind. No lawyers. No liars. No dance-club guys, workaholics, or slackers."

He arched an eyebrow. "That's it?"

It almost sounded like a challenge. I met his gaze and raised an eyebrow of my own. "Pretty much. Until I find something else to add, which I'm sure I will." I double-checked I'd zipped my purse, then slid it over my shoulder. "Now, if you'll excuse me, I'm running late. I'm sure I'll see you around. You do seem to be everywhere."

He flashed his signature drool-worthy grin. "Well, you didn't say 'no stalkers' in your list, so I'm thinking of going with that."

I shook my head, though I couldn't help but smile. My heart was also doing a fluttering thing it shouldn't be doing. "Good night, Jake."

"Good night, Darby."

• • •

Conversations on blind dates are a crapshoot. You start off with general, boring getting-to-know-you questions. Then you make a few stabs in the dark, testing the waters, trying to figure out the other person's likes and dislikes before finding anything you can really talk about. Since Anthony and Stephanie had set us up, they were the common thread for Karl and me, making our mutual friends the safe topic.

"How long have you known Anthony?" I asked after our food arrived. I'll give it to Steph—Karl was good-looking. Blond, with lean muscles, and the guy knew how to dress, too. Perhaps a night out with this guy would end up being just what I needed. Maybe Karl would even be my first venture into low-risk semi-dating. With mutual friends, it might even be convenient.

Of course my mind chose that moment to go to when Jake had said something similar about living in the same building, and I made a joke about being called convenient.

Karl took a sip of water. "We met in college. Lived right next to each other, then we moved in together."

"Sounds like a great love story."

Karl stared across the table at me. His blond eyebrows puckered when he drew them together, and he gazed at me blankly with his pale blue eyes.

"You know, because a lot of relationships start like…" His expression didn't soften, so I abandoned my pathetic attempt at a joke. Maybe no one got my humor, and I should just stop trying to use it. "And you two were roommates for a while?"

"Right. For three years."

"Steph and I have been best friends for a long time. Before she moved to Longmont, I didn't really have girl friends. She and I instantly hit it off and started spending all our free time together. Until Anthony. If he wasn't such a good guy, I'd never let him marry her."

Karl swallowed his bite of chicken. "From what I've observed, she and Anthony have excellent communication. That's one of the best signs of a good relationship."

"I don't believe that," I said, shaking my head. "You see, the key to a relationship isn't communication…"

I got the confused, eyebrow-puckered look again. "It isn't?"

"Nope. It's knowing that men and women will never be able to communicate effectively with each other. I've decided that communication is just what therapists preach, because they know that no one can do it. That way, they can keep getting paid."

Karl set down his fork. "So if I told you I was a marriage counselor…?"

I laughed. "Funny."

Karl remained stone-faced, not a hint of humor showing on his features.

A lump settled in my stomach. "You're not kidding, are you?"

"No. But apparently I only preach communication so I can keep getting paid."

Check please.

• • •

I'd insisted on paying for our dinner. After all, I *had* slammed the guy's profession. He'd resisted at first, but I finally won out. Then I told him I'd see him at the wedding, while wishing I'd never have to see him again. I should've known going out with a groomsman before the wedding was a bad idea.

Since I hadn't gotten my mail in a few days, I popped into the lobby. I tucked the few envelopes under my arm and attempted to call Steph. When I got her voice mail, I said, "I pretty much wrecked that date, so I hope you don't start second-guessing your decision to make me your maid of honor. I think I better give up on blind dates before someone else gets hurt. Call me later if you get a chance."

I made my way across the lobby and pushed the elevator button.

The doors slid open and Jake stepped out. He wore a crisp, white button-down shirt, the top buttons undone, the sleeves pushed up. "Hey. I thought you had a date." He narrowed his eyes.

"Or was that just to get rid of me?"

I ran a hand through my hair and sighed. "I did have one. It didn't go so well."

He jerked a thumb toward the door. "I'm headed out to a gallery a few streets over. I'd love some company."

"Thanks, but I think I'll just go upstairs."

"And watch a movie with your cat?" He grinned, obviously thinking he was hilarious.

I smacked him with my mail. Dang guy and his sexy sense of humor. "I don't have a cat, thank you very much." *Yet.*

Jake laughed, then reached out and put his hand on my hip. My heart jumped into my throat—it made it so hard to think clearly when he did that. "Come out with me, then. You're all dressed up, and it's Friday. Don't you want to try to redeem the night?"

My resolve wavered. I'd spent longer getting all dolled up than I'd spent on my date.

Jake dropped his hand. "It'll just be two neighbors getting to know each other."

I had a hot, funny guy asking me to go on a casual night out with him, even though I'd shot him down again and again. Finally, I decided to just try it out—I was only human, after all. "Okay. Guess I'll stick this"—I waved my mail through the air—"back in the box." Jake waited for me, then we headed outside.

I loved this time of year, when summer was finally here to stay, the city lights glowed against the dark skyline, and people were out and about, enjoying the perfect nighttime weather. Winter was a different story.

"It's over on Bannock," Jake said, tilting his head to indicate direction. Side by side, we headed down the sidewalk.

"What are you doing going to an art gallery by yourself anyway?" I asked. "Big art enthusiast?"

"I'm not going by myself. I'm going with you."

I raised an eyebrow at him.

He looked at me for a couple beats, lopsided smile on his lips, then said, "My friend Tina's got an exhibit, and I told her I'd come see it."

"Did it ever occur to you that this friend of yours invited you, most likely, because she's interested in you? You showing up with me is probably going to ruin her whole night."

"She's dating one of my friends, so trust me, bringing you isn't going to ruin her night. If anything, she'll probably be thrilled that I brought someone. She's always trying to set me up." Jake stepped around a lamppost, bringing him closer to me. "Speaking of setups, what happened on yours tonight? I could use an entertaining story."

"How do you know it's going to be entertaining? What if he took one look at me and ran away? You think I want to rehash that"—I clutched my chest and got all dramatic—"pain and suffering?"

His eyes lit up as a grin spread across his face. "You found out he was a dentist or a lawyer, didn't you?"

"Worse. A marriage counselor."

"What's so bad about that?"

"Everything." I shook my head, thinking of how quickly the date had gone downhill once his job came under discussion— Stephanie had purposely withheld that information, I was sure of it. "I offended him, and it was awkward. And it's even worse because of all this other stuff. In order to explain it, I'd have to start from the beginning."

"Start from the beginning, then," Jake said.

I took a deep breath while figuring out how much to say. I started with the fact that Stephanie was getting married in a couple months, then who Karl was, and how I'd managed to offend him. "Needless to say, things were awkward after that."

Jake nodded, amusement flickering across his features. "Yep, that'd definitely do it."

"See, this is why I avoid dates with guys I'll have to see again. He'll probably be shooting me death glares all through the wedding."

"It's right here," Jake said, putting his hand on the small of my back and guiding me toward the entrance to one of the many downtown art galleries. He pulled the door open, and I stepped inside. The floor was pale wood; the walls, ceiling, and pedestals were all lacquered white. The neutral colors made the colorful art in the room stand out.

"This reminds me of college," I said. "I went to the Rocky Mountain College of Art and Design. There were always cool displays everywhere."

As Jake and I rounded the corner into a large open room, my heels echoed, each step sounding loud in the quiet space. We stopped in front of a large painting done in red, thick paint in some places and barely a hint in others. There were two tiny blue squares, one just left of center and one in the right corner.

Jake crossed his arms and studied it. "Ah, yes, a lovely impressionist piece, reminiscent of…that one painter." He tapped a finger to his chin. "Let's see, what was his name?"

I looked at him, waiting for him to come up with it. Then his lips curved up and he asked, "How'd I do? Get any of it right?"

I shrugged. "No idea. I had one Art History class late at night, and the guy dimmed the lights and showed slides as he lectured in a monotone voice. It was almost impossible not to fall asleep. Plus, I always sucked at dates, so I studied enough to pass the class and immediately forgot everything."

"I was waiting for you to tell me one of your rules about dating included finding a guy who knew art," he said, his smile widening.

I nudged him with my elbow. "Very funny."

He put his hand on my back again, leading me toward the next painting. I was so caught up in the warmth of his touch and my quickening pulse that the next painting took me off guard.

"Whoa," I said as I looked at the gruesome image. There was a face with sagging gray skin, one missing eyeball, and blood covering its teeth and chin. "It's a zombie."

He gave me this smile that made me feel like I'd been caught, even though I wasn't sure what I'd done. "I notice you stated a fact instead of your opinion."

Okay, so I had been caught. "Well, the detail is impressive, but if I had that in my house, it'd give me nightmares." It hit me then that we were here to see his friend's work. "Please don't tell me this is your friend's piece, because I'll feel horrible."

He leaned closer to read the card by it. "Nope, not hers. And it says 'self-portrait.'" He glanced back at me. "I always knew zombies existed."

I laughed. "Irrefutable proof, right there."

Jake laughed, too, and of course I had to notice that on top of everything else, he had a sexy laugh. He tipped his head toward the other room and I followed him. Inside was a giant, metal sculpture of a skeleton riding a bicycle.

"That's actually really cool," I said. "Interesting and unique."

"Should we have them wrap it up and take it to your place?"

"Um. Yeah, it's more of a look-at-once kind of cool. See, when you decorate a place the size of mine, you have to exercise proportion control."

The murmur of voices floated from a room in the back. I peeked past the divider and saw a couple people milling around the area. "I'm guessing your friend is in there."

"I bet you're right."

The back room had a sea of colorful, twisted glass sculptures. Sculptures I could easily place in my clients' homes. I turned to study one that looked like blue-and-silver flames.

"Jake, you came!"

I turned to see a petite girl with choppy black-and-red hair— like the brightest, most unnatural shade of red—hug Jake.

"What do you think?" she asked.

Not wanting to intrude, I moved to study the rest of the sculptures. There was a yellow-and-purple one with thin, squiggly pieces exploding from it. Then I saw the little pink sculpture up on a pedestal. It had a green stem and a giant pink bud flopped over the front. Mrs. Crabtree would love it.

Jake and Tina walked up to me. Anyway, I assumed it was Tina. For some reason, the girl was looking at me like I was some kind of adorable woodland creature.

"This is Darby," Jake said. "Darby, this is my friend Tina."

"Your stuff is amazing," I said.

"Darby's thing is honesty, so you can be sure she wouldn't say that unless she meant it."

I pointed at the flower. "And I need this. Mrs. Crabtree's got a pink bathroom and it has this shelf that needs decorations. That piece will fit perfectly there and luckily the shelf's high enough her granddaughter won't be able to reach it, so it won't get broken." I smiled at Tina. "Sorry, you don't know her, so you probably don't care."

Tina returned my smile. "I just like hearing that my stuff will be in a bathroom."

I laughed. "This bathroom is the size of most people's bedrooms, so I swear, it's going to be very well done." I glanced around the room. "Actually, I'd love to get your card. I'm an interior designer and I'm always on the lookout for good accent pieces. And these are all extraordinary."

Tina nudged Jake. "I like her."

Jake's eyes locked onto mine and I forgot how to breathe for a second. "Me, too."

• • •

"I better take that," Jake said as we walked out of the gallery.

I had Mrs. Crabtree's sculpture in a bag hanging from my arm.

Tina had wrapped it in padding and stuffed it into a box. "It's not like it's heavy."

"No offense, but I haven't known you very long, and I've already seen you lose your shoe and dump everything out of your purse."

"I swear I'm not normally clumsy."

Jake flashed me a skeptical look and held out his hand. I hesitated for a moment, then went ahead and gave him the bag. "We fixed the floor in the restaurant, by the way. There was a crack that needed to be filled in. I think that's why your heel caught."

"Then it's a good thing you took care of it." I bumped my shoulder into his, no longer able to keep myself from flirting with him a little bit. "Especially if someone as clumsy as me is going to be in there again." And who was I kidding? I couldn't avoid Blue much longer.

After being around Jake and Tina, I'd seen another side of him. He was still his charming self, but there was something more. The way he talked to Tina, the way he listened as she went into excruciating detail about how she made each sculpture. I'd also been in the elevator with him enough times to know that his floor was at the top, where the expensive, great-view condos were. "So, you're a good-looking, successful guy…"

"Thanks," Jake said.

"Not a compliment. I'm wondering why you're still single. And I'm sure you're thinking the same about me. The truth is, I don't really believe that I'll ever have a successful relationship."

He pressed his lips together. "Isn't that a little cynical?"

"No. It's a lot cynical. Doesn't mean it's not true."

Jake slowed his pace and studied me for a moment. "I guess I just haven't found the right person yet. It doesn't mean I don't believe she's out there."

"You don't have to pretend you believe in"—I threw up my hands and made air quotes—"'the one' and falling madly in love to impress me. I wasted too much time believing in all that, so now I'm realistic. The odds of you and me working aren't great."

"But what if we do work out? What if we end up being perfect for each other?"

I shook my head. "See, that's the problem. Everyone's been taught this unrealistic idea that there's someone out there who's perfect for us. A soul mate who completes us. But I've found that's just not the way things work."

Jake grabbed my arm, pulling me to a stop. "I'm going to make a guess as to why you feel that way. If I guess right, I get a date."

I twisted to face him. "You think you know enough about me to guess how I got so cynical?"

He met my gaze, a challenging glint in his eye. "One date."

"If you guess right." I knew he couldn't. It had taken a lot of bad relationships to get me to this point. The analysis of all of my exes as I turned them into case studies probably hadn't helped with the cynicism, but it had made me smarter. They say the truth will set you free.

He looked me up and down, like I might be hiding all my secrets in the way I was standing. "Child of divorce. Watched your parents never find love, so now you don't believe people can be happy together."

I crossed my arms. "Wrong. My parents *are* divorced, but both of them found love. They're both happily married to other people now."

"I was still right."

"Half-right," I corrected.

Jake grinned. "So I get half a date. We'll go somewhere and get an appetizer. Or we'll go to a movie and walk out in the middle of it."

I stared at him for a moment, not sure whether to smile or laugh or shake my head and sigh. "I can't figure you out. Why are you so determined? We've had a few good conversations, and I'm sure you've noticed I'm attracted to you, what with the fact that I get all flustered whenever you're around—but really, you don't know that much about me." I stuck my hand on my hip. "And don't even try to tell me it's in my eyes, that you just have a feeling about us, or something like that."

He took a step, bringing us so close our bodies were almost touching. "I guess it's how when you talk about your clients, I can tell you care about them. You're more honest than most people I know. You're witty and make really funny jokes about art. And I think it's cute how you put your fist on your hip when you're about to tell me all your rules."

I dropped my fist. "And how is it you think you know all this?"

"Because whenever you're around, I pay attention." His eyes bored into mine with such intensity my throat went dry. "You might not believe in seeing someone and knowing something's different about them, but I do. And there's something different about you." Jake ran his fingers down my arm, leaving a trail of goose bumps. Then he grabbed my hand and continued down the sidewalk. "So? Where do you want our half date to be?"

Chapter Eight

$\mathcal{Y}$ou know what I was not doing as I scrubbed my bathroom floor Saturday morning? Singing. The only thing coming from my mouth as I scoured that brown crap between the tiles was a stream of profanities. Not exactly princess behavior, but as I've mentioned, I'm no princess, and the guys I've dated are far from princes—evidently I have trouble identifying the good guys and end up picking ones who'll hurt me.

Sometimes I wonder if my dating life would've gone differently had my first boyfriend not ended up being a huge jerk. That boy taught me a big life lesson about trust. Apparently not enough to keep from making several mistakes, but he taught me that not everyone is as great as they seem.

Snow White Case Study: Sherman/The Prince
My Age: 17
In order to get the full effect of why and how things happened with Sherman, I need to go back to when I was thirteen and my

entire life was uprooted.

Mom and Dad had been divorced for three years when Mom met Dwight. After four months of dating, he proposed. Six months later, they got married, and I suddenly gained a stepdad and twin stepbrothers. Mom and I moved from Aurora to Dwight's ranch in Longmont. Even though it was only an hour drive away, it felt like moving countries.

The entire summer before my freshman year, Drew and Devin tortured me. They called me a baby for still watching Disney movies, pointed out when I got zits, and used my clothes and bedding to line the horse pens for reasons I still don't understand. And everything I did was "like a girl." I threw like a girl, talked like a girl, cried like a girl, dressed like a girl. They spat it out like the biggest insult, and I took it as one. I don't know why. Because after all, I was *a girl*.

Mom assured me life would get better—that I'd meet lots of new friends when school started.

Then school started.

Everyone hated me. I was going through this phase where I was all knees and elbows, with string-bean legs up to my neck. The other students made fun of my clothes even though they were wearing trends from three years ago. At the time, finding pants to fit my long legs was impossible, meaning I got asked when the flood was coming on a regular basis.

Two months into the school year, I couldn't take it anymore. I missed my old life and my old friends. I parked myself at a table in the back of the school cafeteria, looked at the food on my plate, and started crying. I hoped no one would notice.

No such luck.

Drew and Devin sat down next to me, apparently sensing weakness and preparing to attack. I was just waiting for them to tell me what I was doing like a girl now.

Ross, the leader of the popular boys, walked by, stuck his

thumb up and said, "Nice high-waters, dummy."

Instead of Darby, some jokester had decided to start calling me dummy. It caught like wildfire.

Devin stood up, double-fisted Ross's shirt, and slammed him against the wall. "Apologize to Darby."

"Uh…s-s-sorry, Darby," Ross said.

Drew stood on the other side of him and jabbed a finger into his chest. "You tell everyone you know that making fun of Darby means getting your ass kicked by Devin and me. And never, *ever* call her dummy again."

Drew smacked the back of Ross's head with his open palm. "Got it, dummy?"

"I got it," Ross said.

Devin released him, he hurried off, and then my stepbrothers came and sat back down by me.

I stared at Devin and Drew in shock. "But…why did you do that?"

"Do you want him to call you that?" Devin asked.

I shook my head. "No."

"We're family now," Drew said. "And families stick together."

At the end of lunch, Devin ran a hand over my head, mussing my hair. "Later, you girl."

After that, Devin, Drew, and their five friends sat by me in the lunchroom; Ross and his gang never picked on me again. There was still a group of snotty girls that made life hell, but I couldn't exactly ask my brothers to beat them up for me.

Most days after school, I hung out with the guys. They were far from dwarfs—in fact most of them towered over me—but they were my group. My seven giants. Thinking of going home and being able to ride my horse or hang with the guys, I knew I could make it through the day of school.

Nothing much changed over the next few years. I was never what you'd call popular, and when I went out, it was with my seven giants.

The first day of my junior year, I was feeling pretty good about life. I'd finally stopped growing, filled out a little bit, and Mom had taken me to a store in Denver and bought pants that fit me perfectly. The poofy, big-bang hairdos weren't in anymore, so my straight, blond hair wasn't as out of place.

Tabitha Newton walked up to me as I was loading school supplies into my locker. Since she'd made no secret of her hatred for me, I was surprised when she didn't immediately insult me.

"Hi, Darby," she said.

I stared for a few seconds before responding. "Hi."

Tabitha ran a hand through her hair. She'd gotten "The Rachel" cut over the summer and had chunky blond highlights running through it. "You should try out for cheerleading."

Because the cheerleaders made no secret of the fact that they didn't like me, trying out had never crossed my mind. But it did have a certain allure. "Sure. Maybe."

"Let's see how you'd do on a pyramid." Tabitha shoved me.

Someone had set up behind me on her hands and knees—I believe they call it a tabletop—and I toppled backward over her body.

Tabitha's face floated above me. "Looks like you failed." She and her friend giggled and walked off.

That's what you get for trusting the biggest witch in school, I thought as I lay there, not wanting to deal with life.

A hand extended toward me. It was no True Love's Kiss, but it got me on my feet again. He had shaggy, brown hair, and tan, I-spend-lots-of-time-outdoors skin.

"Thanks." I didn't recognize him, and I would remember a face like that. "Are you new?"

"Just moved in. I'm Sherman." He shook his head. "Don't ask about the name. It was my granddad's and now I'm lucky enough to have it."

"My name's Darby, so I completely understand."

"Actually, I think Darby's a cute name." He tapped my nose. "It fits."

This was the kind of guy I'd been dreaming about.

Two days later, when Sherman and I were sitting outside after lunch, he kissed me. I'd been anticipating my first kiss for a long time, and it didn't disappoint. After that, the kissing increased at steady intervals. So did his roving hands. He wanted to take things fast; I wanted to take it slow. I didn't want to lose him, so I kept asking him to be patient.

Around our three-month anniversary, Sherman and I had plans to go to a party out by Burch Lake. Unfortunately, the school had called to talk to Mom earlier that day. The secretary had asked why I was always late for class. (Sherman and I often snuck outside for a few uninterrupted minutes of kissing, but I wasn't about to tell her that.)

I sat, sulking in the kitchen, thinking about how unfair life was when Drew, Devin, and the rest of the guys came in.

"You need a ride to the party?" Devin asked.

I stared at the back of Mom's head. "My mom thinks I've been spending too much time with Sherman."

"We can take her with us, Janet," Drew said. "We'll make sure she and Sherman stay in sight at all times. In fact, I've been meaning to talk to that kid anyway."

Mom sighed. "Fine. Don't you let her get into trouble, or there'll be heck to pay."

Mom didn't believe in swearing, and even using "heck" was pretty colorful for her.

"Understood," Devin said.

My entourage and I squished into Devin's quad-cab Dodge and headed to the party. The second we got there, I scanned the place for Sherman. Every night away from him was like torture.

Then, I spotted him.

Making out with Tabitha Newton.

I didn't know what to do; I'd never been in a relationship before. The two of them were sitting on Sherman's open tailgate, feeling each other up, even though people were nearby. Tabitha pulled her mouth off Sherman's to catch a breath. When she looked up, her eyes met mine. She flashed an evil grin before going in for round two.

You'd think I'd charge over there and yell or slap him or do something. Anything. Instead, I stood there frozen, watching my boyfriend—I'd thought he was my boyfriend, anyway—make out with the witch. My eyes burned as tears formed; a sharp pain shot through my chest.

"Did you find Sherman yet?" Gil, the nicest of my brothers' friends, asked. He must've seen what I was staring at then, because he said, "Oh. Darby, I'm sorry."

When Sherman and Tabitha broke apart again, Ross tapped Sherman on the shoulder and pointed at me. Sherman slowly stood and walked over.

"How could you?" I asked as a few tears escaped and ran down my cheeks.

"We never said we were exclusive," Sherman said. "Did you think we were?"

"Of course I did." I leaned in and whispered, "You were trying to get me to have sex with you. I wouldn't do that with someone I thought was going to shove his tongue down Tabitha's throat."

Sherman shrugged. "What can I say? You snooze you lose."

Gil grabbed my hand. "This guy's a loser. You don't need him." He pulled me away from Sherman and the crowd that had gathered to watch the drama.

I just caught the sight of Devin approaching Sherman. He yelled something at him and shoved him, hard enough my boyfriend—er, ex-boyfriend—went down on his butt.

Then the guys and I were back in the truck headed home, me fighting tears and losing. The stupid thing was, even after all of that,

I couldn't stop wondering if Sherman would call and apologize so we could go back to the happy couple we used to be.

Time Wasted: Three months

Lessons Learned:

Tabitha Newton truly was the biggest witch in school.

Some guys are only about one thing.

Charming boys are dangerous.

Assuming does, in fact, make an ass out of *U* and *Me*. But mostly just him.

. . .

I answered the door and invited Jake inside. "I've got to throw on some jewelry, so have a seat, or look around or whatever." I gripped his arm just below the elbow and said in my most serious voice, "No matter what you do, though, don't look in the hall closet. That's where I keep all my skeletons."

I walked back to my bedroom, wondering how long it'd take him to open the closet. Last night when Jake and I had discussed when and where we were going to go on our half date, we'd found out that we both were planning on attending the same charity function. Nadine and I had worked on Mr. and Mrs. Hammond's houses — that's right, plural. Virginia Hammond had a soft spot for me and insisted I come to all her social events. She'd actually called the office yesterday afternoon to double-check I'd be attending the Hammond's Children's Hospital fund-raiser.

I stuck in my chandelier earrings and slipped into my purple stilettos. When I came out of the bedroom, Jake wasn't looking in the closet; he was looking at the plant I had on the window ledge.

Jake poked one of the brown, crispy blades. "I like that you keep this plant, even though it's dead."

"It's not dead. Malnourished maybe, but look at that leaf." I pointed to the green one in the middle.

"Okay, so in the middle of all the brown, dried-up leaves,

there's a single struggling one."

"As long as he's still trying, I'll keep watering him. When I occasionally remember to." I turned my attention from the plant to Jake. A lot of guys wore suits a size or two too big, but his was tailored to his body, the black simple yet striking, and for a moment I forgot that I needed to make a point before we left. "By the way, my boss is going to be there tonight, so we need to keep things low-key."

"Hmm. That's going to mess with my plans to steal the microphone and sing karaoke for you. I was going to do a big dedication and everything." One of Jake's dark eyebrows cocked up. "How do you feel about Journey?"

My earrings rattled together as I shook my head. "Don't make me regret this."

"Meatloaf it is."

What escaped my lips could only be described as a giggle. We hadn't even started our almost-date and I was already *giggling*.

Pull it together, I told myself, but I wasn't going to freak out, either. I had this situation totally under control.

I opened the hall closet, picked my keys off the hook inside, and threw them in my purse.

Jake put his hand on my back and looked past me into the closet. "Those skeletons don't look too bad. Nothing I can't handle."

I closed the door. "I keep the really scary ones in a different closet."

Jake offered me his arm. "Ready?"

All day I'd thought about this. There had to be a happy medium. I didn't want to stay away from him anymore, and we had a good time together. *I can do this. All I gotta do is relax and enjoy the night. No pressure, no strings attached.*

I didn't sit and type up all my case studies just to get burned again for the same stupid thing. I'd broken the rules before, and I always paid for it in the end.

I ignored his arm and pulled open my door. "Ready."

• • •

I'd circled the room a couple times, talked shop with Patricia—due to all the champagne she'd had, she was friendlier than usual, though she managed to insinuate I was slacking on the Seventh Street job she'd told me *she* wanted to take point on—and said hi to a few clients. Virginia was always recommending me to people, so I'd also done some networking. Jake seemed to know everyone, too, and I'd lost him somewhere along the way.

The orchestra played in the corner of the room, there was a large area in the middle for dancing, and couples swirled around the floor. Tables draped in white tablecloths dotted the edges of the room. Sweet peas filled the vases in the centers, scenting the air. During dinner they'd had the keynote speaker, people had pledged lots of money to the hospital, and now everyone was up enjoying their evening. It was about as close to a ball as I'd ever been to.

Virginia came up and put a hand on my shoulder. She had on a black-and-white dress and was wearing her signature string of pearls. "Darby, honey, you simply must meet this man. He's handsome, successful, and perfect for you in every way."

I looked around the room, trying to find Jake. The place was packed, making it hard to find him in the crowd. "Thank you, but actually I—"

"I won't take no for an answer." Virginia gave my arm a gentle tug. "You at least have to allow me to introduce him. If after a few minutes you're not completely intrigued, I'll let you make an excuse to take your leave of us."

I'd learned that when it came to Virginia, it was easier to go along than to argue, so I allowed myself to be led away to what was sure to be an awkward encounter with a boring, self-centered, but oh-so-handsome-and-successful man. They were Virginia's specialty.

A woman with a familiar face I couldn't put a name to waved as I walked by. I waved back, trying to recall how I knew her.

"Here he is!" Virginia said. I peeled my eyes away from the mystery lady to meet the guy she was sure I'd be intrigued by. "Darby Quinn, I'd like you to meet Jake Knight. This charming young man has been a lifesaver." Virginia gestured to me. "Darby is a very successful interior designer. She transformed my places into the most beautiful works of art. And look at her! I'm sure you'll agree she is lovely."

"I definitely agree." Jake stepped next to me and slid his arm around my waist. "In fact, I thought she was so lovely, I asked her to accompany me here tonight. She tried to resist, but as you pointed out, I'm just so charming."

Virginia put both hands over her heart as she stared at us. "I simply knew you two would hit it off. I'm so glad to see that you're together."

I shook my head. "Oh, we're not—"

"Thank you," Jake said, dropping his arm from my waist and taking my hand. "Now, if you don't mind, I think I'll steal her away for a dance."

He led me to the dance floor, we assumed the formal position, and then we were twirling around the floor with the rest of the couples.

"Your last name is Knight?" I asked.

"Is something wrong with that?"

"No." *Just that I'm anti-fairy tales and you're a Knight. It's not ironic at all.* "Your dancing skills are rather impressive."

Jake spun me out and brought me back in. "I've had to attend functions like this for a long time. My parents were on the board of everything. Still are, actually."

I wanted to ask more about his family. From the sounds of it, he'd probably always had a trust fund, which most girls would've swooned over. But since I'd learned the value of hard work, I found most guys born with silver spoons were lazy. Jake managed a restaurant, though, which I assumed wasn't easy.

Jake slid his arm tighter around me, pulling me close enough I was pressed against his firm body. My heart rate screamed into the danger zone, and with how close we were, I was sure he could feel it thumping against his chest. And speaking of chests, I wanted to relax fully into the dance and lean my head against his. I wanted to close my eyes and melt into the perfect moment before it ended.

He tilted his head, the hint of a smile playing on his lips. "Hmm. I kind of expected you to try to take the lead."

"Do I seem like the type of girl who can't follow simple dance moves?" I was relieved my voice didn't come out as breathless as I suddenly felt.

"Not can't." That butterfly-inducing grin spread across his face. "More like won't."

I did my best to act unaffected, lifting my chin and throwing in a touch of haughtiness. "Well, if you didn't already know how to dance, I would go ahead and take the lead. But since you're doing a good job, you can have it." I moved my hand from his shoulder to the back of his neck, a thrill shooting through me when he swallowed hard. "For now."

• • •

The elevator doors slid open, and Jake stepped off with me instead of riding up to his floor.

Now, I know I've gone on and on about how I don't believe two people can work out, but I am not into one-night stands, flings, or meaningless trysts either. Some girls claim they can do it, and maybe they can. One of my former coworkers claimed she could and then she'd cry when a week had gone by and the guy didn't call. So, I'm sure you're asking the same question I've asked myself: If you don't believe in relationships or flings, what *do* you believe in?

I wasn't exactly sure. What's between monogamy and promiscuity? The basic idea was to have a string of semi-long-term, low-risk relationships. Like serial monogamy. I know it sounds impossible, but I was still working on it. All I knew was unavoidable daily awkwardness was something I wanted to stay far, far away from.

Yet Jake possessed a certain je ne sais quoi. And I'd had more fun with him tonight than I'd had in a long time.

Don't even think about it, Darby. You see him every day. You eat at Blue all the time. Friends is the way to go.

I probably shouldn't have flirted with him all night, then.

Or pressed my body against his. Heat wound through my core just thinking about it. *And if he can dance like that...* My heart jolted and my pulse pounded. Man, it'd been a long time since I'd even kissed a guy.

Remember the rules. Stick to the rules.

Shaking off the memory of how his firm body felt next to mine, I dug into my purse and took out my keys. I unlocked the door, then twisted around to end the date. "I had a good—"

Jake's lips cut me off before I could go into why it was probably for the best if we didn't go out again. It was a quick, chaste kiss, over before I had a chance to latch onto it, but it still sent a spike of electricity through me. He stepped away, said good night, and then headed back toward the elevator.

No words came out as I watched him. The farther he got, the stupider it seemed to yell out a good-bye. So I walked into my condo and locked the door behind me.

Well, that was about the worst preemptive breakup speech I've ever given.

Chapter Nine

"Tell me everything," Steph said, stepping into my place. She'd brought a box of doughnuts to keep us sugared up for all the wedding-planning stuff we had to go over.

"I've got a ton of work to do and my computer keeps acting up. I'm about to throw it out the window."

"When I said everything, I meant about Jake."

I sat on my couch, closed my temperamental laptop, and set it off to the side. "I told you everything over the phone. We had a fun time, quick kiss, that's it."

"Yeah, but did he say he'd call?"

"Actually, he doesn't have my number." I opened the box she'd placed on my coffee table and selected a cinnamon-swirled pastry. "It doesn't matter, though, because I was about to tell him we couldn't be more than friends. Had he said anything about calling, I would've told him it wasn't a good idea."

Stephanie plunked her giant wedding-planner binder next to the box of doughnuts, selected a maple one out of the box, and sat back on my couch. Her red shirt matched the color of my couch so well, everything but her head and arms disappeared. "How can you just blow him off like that? You said you had a good time."

"You, of all people, know why. Now let's get started."

"Since Anthony's aunts are in a fight now, I have to redo the whole seating chart again and it's a mess." Steph sat up and flipped open her book. "Here you are. Ooh, look at my little pink friend Darby. And there's still an empty seat next to you in case you want to invite Jake."

"I'm *not* going to invite Jake. Wedding dates are the worst." Before she could argue, like I could see she was going to, I said, "Need I remind you what happened last time I took a date to a wedding?"

Steph's lip curled. "Okay, so it was bad." She scooted forward. "But that was totally different. You know Jake. Is inviting him really worse than having everyone looking at you all sad because you don't have a date to your best friend's wedding?"

Honestly, Steph's wedding was going to be a hard day for me. I was worried I would lose my best friend, and even more worried she'd eventually get her heart trampled beyond repair. Once there were joint mortgages and bank accounts and that marriage certificate involved, breaking up wasn't just a cry fest with a side of calorie binging. It was unwinding your entire life from his, one painful string at a time. But I was working on keeping from blurting out those kinds of thoughts, so I went with something else that was also true. "I'd rather be there alone, than be on a date that could go down in flames during one of your big moments."

"I remember back when Jimmy Delfino dumped me and *I* was the pessimist. You kept insisting I'd meet someone better, pushing me to date all those other guys so I could find my true love. Now I have, and you're the one who doesn't believe in it."

"That's because I hadn't broken free of the brainwashing yet. And better than Jimmy Delfino wasn't really hard to find. He was an *awful* boyfriend."

"He was pretty awful." Stephanie looked at me, and I had

the feeling she wanted me to tell her it would be different with Anthony. I'd decided to support her in her decision, but false assurances weren't my thing. For one, she'd see through it. So in the end, I turned to the wedding-planning book and acted really interested.

Stephanie moved a few figures on the seating chart around. "I'll keep you next to Drew and his plus one, Dwight and your mom, and Devin and Anne, in case you end up solo. But I still believe you'll find the right guy. And you never know. Maybe you already have." She gave me her no-nonsense glare. "Promise me you'll give Jake a chance."

I wiped my hands together, trying to get the glaze off my fingers. Apparently, I was going to have to say something. What was with everyone pushing me to open up lately? "Steph, I'm glad you found Anthony. I really am. I'm glad you've worked things out with his mom, even though she constantly pushes her way into you and Anthony's business."

"She just loves her son and is having a hard time letting go."

"See, you look for the good in everybody. I used to do that and I got knocked down over and over again. I just don't think I can pick myself up anymore. It's one thing to get over the jerks— they shook my trust, hurt me, and made me feel like crap—but I could see them for what they were afterward. It's another thing altogether to get over the good ones."

"And you're afraid Jake might be one of the good ones?"

I stared at Steph, not sure what to say to that. So far, everything about Jake was great. But seriously, it had only been a little more than a week since I'd met him. I didn't know anything about him. I *did* know that knowing stuff only got you in deeper.

"How long have we been friends?" Stephanie asked.

"Since the middle of junior year when you moved in and I discovered girls could actually be cool."

"I am the coolest," Steph said with a smile. "That's been

fourteen years now—Wow, we're getting old."

I frowned. "Hey, speak for yourself."

"Anyway, I know you better than anyone. Your family might come close, but I'd still say I have them beat. My point is, I only want the best for you. Laying out our horrible relationships was therapeutic—after that I decided to stop going for the bad boys. It's why I gave Anthony a chance." The dreamy look Stephanie got whenever she was thinking about her fiancé crossed her features. "And look what happened. I'm about to get married to a guy I'm crazy about. Instead of using your case studies as a guide, you decided to stop believing in love. Now you won't even give Jake a chance, just because he has one tiny thing in common with Evan."

"You haven't even met Jake," I said. "What makes you so insistent on me giving him a chance?"

"Because he's all you've talked about since you met him. And when it comes to you, that's saying something."

• • •

For a week, Jake had been everywhere. After our date, he was nowhere. Nowhere I was, anyway. Monday came and went. Tuesday. Wednesday. On Thursday, I was starting to think he must be going out of his way to avoid me.

I sat in front of my computer at work and played with my design software, clicking paint colors and moving digital appliances.

Kathy, our receptionist, called me on my intercom. "Stephanie's here."

I picked up my phone's receiver. "Send her on back."

A minute later, Steph walked into my office. Her eyes glistened with unshed tears and her features were pinched. Then the tears broke free.

I stood, alarm pumping through my veins. "What happened?" I asked, even though I was sure Anthony had done something horrible. I was going to kill him.

"It's stupid, I know. I can't believe I'm getting so emotional over it, but after planning and planning..." Steph flopped into the chair opposite my desk and sniffed. "They're broken. Five of them are broken, and they can't send more because everything's on back order for three months. There's no way we'd get them in time for the wedding."

The tension in my body eased. Anthony was safe. For now.

"What's broken?"

"My centerpieces."

"The pink heart vases?"

Steph fell forward, putting her head into her hands. "Yes. The florist called to tell me they got the shipment and that some of them broke during shipping. She argued with the company, I argued with them. They gave me a big discount, so I thought I could fix it. But I've been all over the city and no one even has heart vases."

"No one's going to notice the vases aren't the same," I said. "We'll find some that look nice. It'll just give your tables variety."

"Anthony and I had a big argument last night, too. I told him his mom was overstepping a little bit, changing things without talking to me, and he got upset because she's just trying to help." Stephanie wiped a few tears. "Go ahead and say it. Tell me you saw it coming."

Now that she was asking me to say it, I couldn't. Not when she already looked so crushed. I stepped around the front of my desk and sat down on the edge of it, choosing to focus on the other problem first. "We'll fix this. Let's go get something to eat and we'll figure it all out. We'll write everything down in an organized list and you'll feel better." *And my boss will probably have a fit if she finds out I'm away from my desk, even though I'm caught up, but that's just too bad, because this is an emergency bride situation.*

Stephanie got out a tissue and wiped her nose. "Okay. You want to go to Blue?"

"No way."

"Come on. We can feel him out. It'll help me get my mind off my problems."

"I already know what happened. We went out, he decided I'm not that cool, so he's avoiding me. It saves me a lot of trouble, actually. Things will be a little strange when I bump into him, but it won't be horrible. Not like if we'd done a big, full-blown relationship." I grabbed my purse. "That said, I'm not ready to face him yet. I'm in the mood for Mexican food anyway."

. . .

After eating food swimming in chili sauce and cheese, Steph and I started on the wedding problems. I wrote down all the places I could think of that might have workable vases. The heart-shaped ones she'd special ordered were pink-and-white swirled glass. Because they had to be tall enough to hold the cherry blossoms, they were an uncommon size.

With everything else that was going to be on the tables at the reception, I doubted anyone would notice if some of the vases weren't exactly the same. It would bother Stephanie, but she'd probably be distracted enough with everything else going on to get over it.

Then again, her expression said it was the end of the world, so maybe not.

Anthony called as I was finishing up my list. A few minutes into their conversation, they were saying things like, "No, I'm sorry," and "I love you so much." All the makeup stuff couples say. No matter how cynical and pessimistic I was, I really did think Stephanie and Anthony went well together. I knew they'd be back to hourly phone calls by the time Steph and I figured out what to do about her vases.

My phone rang and I answered it. Mrs. Crabtree told me how much she loved the sculpture I'd picked out for her bathroom, which gave me an idea for Steph's problem.

When Steph and I finished our respective phone calls, I tore off the list of places and shoved the paper in my purse. "I've got an idea. I'm not sure what it'll cost or if she'll do it, but we can try."

Twenty minutes later, Stephanie and I were in the gallery where Tina's artwork was on display. "Good to see you again." Tina looked from me to Stephanie. "Whoa. I can tell you guys are sisters. You look so much alike."

"We're not, actually." Stephanie draped her arm over my shoulders. "I consider her the sister I never had, though."

I quickly explained the situation to Tina, and asked her if she'd be offended at the idea of creating similar-looking vases for Steph—I knew some artists considered recreating someone else's work for money selling out. "It's six weeks away, and we need five vases."

Tina studied the picture. "Like yea big"—she held out her hands—"with a skinny hole to place the cherry blossoms?"

"Exactly."

"No worries. You front me the money to get the supplies, and I can have them done in a few weeks."

"Really?" Stephanie shrieked. "That's just the best news!" She pulled me into a hug. "You're the best! You don't even believe in marriage and you're still fixing mine."

"I'm fixing your reception," I said. "You're going to have to do all the work on the marriage."

"Don't ruin my mood, Darby. Everything's perfect and I'm happy." Steph jostled me. "Just be happy with me."

I smiled and acted excited, too. I'd learned to never argue with a bride before her wedding.

Rapunzel Case Study: Ralph/The Prince
My Age: 23
There are several princes who remain unnamed in fairy tales.

It's like all they had to do was be a prince to make the girl happy. Sometimes, though, if you get desperate enough, anyone will do. I'm sure Rapunzel felt that way. When you've been locked in a tower all your life, you take what you can get.

I hadn't been locked in a tower, but I'd landed point on my first account. I threw myself into my work to make sure I didn't screw it up. I hardly left my office; my hair was long and ratty because I was in desperate need of a trim. On top of everything else, I was trying to help Mom as she helped Devin and his fiancée, Anne, plan their wedding.

After dating Anne all through college, Devin asked her to marry him. Back when they'd first started planning the wedding, I'd been dating Charlie, so I'd sent back the RSVP card for both of us. I guess Anne and Devin never got the memo about my breakup.

When I informed Anne the Saturday before her wedding that I was going to be dateless, she exploded. Everything was planned, food had been ordered, and she wanted me to have a date. I would've taken Stephanie, but the reason she wasn't coming in the first place was she was flying to Florida to see her grandparents.

Later that night, I took Devin aside. "How am I going to find a date for next weekend? It's not like you go pick one up at a grocery store. And when did Anne get so crazy?"

Devin peeked around the corner, then leaned in. "It's the wedding stuff. It makes girls go crazy. It's enough to scare the crap out of a guy, you know."

I smiled. "So, what you're saying is she's acting like *a girl* about her wedding?"

He scowled at me. "It's not funny, Darby. Just find a date so she's happy. I've never asked you for much, but—"

"You ask me for stuff constantly. You've still got half my CD collection."

"Hon? Where are you?" Anne walked into the kitchen. She

narrowed her eyes at Devin and me huddled together. "What's going on?"

Devin looked at her, panic flashing across his face. "Um, Darby was saying she knows a guy she can bring."

My jaw dropped. He totally threw me under the bus! The crazy-bride bus.

Anne's face lit up. "Oh good. I know it seems strange that I care about stuff like that, but I've been so stressed and I just want everything to be perfect."

Devin walked over and put his arms around her. "Of course you do. You deserve the best."

They started kissing, so I left the room, wondering how I was going to scrounge up a date. Asking a guy to go to a wedding with you isn't exactly like asking him to dinner or the movies. To a guy, it's the equivalent of saying, *Hey, I want to marry you someday, so let's go see how another couple does it.*

Not wanting to risk ruining Devin and Anne's special day, my top priority became getting a date. Steph and Jimmy Delfino were hot and heavy yet again, so when I got really desperate, I asked him if he had any single friends.

That's how I ended up taking Ralph to my brother's wedding. When I showed up at Ralph's door to pick him up, the first thing he said was, "You're not ugly. I thought since you couldn't find a date, you'd be ugly."

I should've run, should've given up on the whole mandatory-date thing right then and there. You gotta wonder what Rapunzel thought after she was saved. Did she look at the prince and think, *Wow, I feel like I owe him, but he's really not who I want to be with*? If he was anything like Ralph, that's exactly what happened. I pulled him into my life, then immediately regretted it. I wished I would've let him walk on by.

All during the ceremony, I had to keep pushing Ralph's hand off my leg. He'd set it on my thigh and inch it up a little at a time.

We were in a *chapel*, and he was trying to feel me up! After the ceremony, I wanted to tell him to go, but I was his ride. I owed him for doing me this big favor.

Things at the reception only got worse. When Ralph called me a prude and took off, I was relieved. He could go eat and drink and leave me alone. It was nice to not have to be constantly pushing him off me.

I laughed and caught up with my seven giants. Drew, Devin, Gil—the whole gang was there. We laughed and even did some dancing.

I'd just gotten back to my table when one of Anne's bridesmaid's came up to me and pulled me aside. "You need to do something about your boyfriend. He's hitting on all of the bridesmaids, and he just told Anne that he liked married women, so to give him a call. She won't say anything to Devin because the last thing she wants at her wedding is for her groom to get into a fight."

I groaned, not wanting to deal with my date. This was all Anne's fault anyway, and now she wanted me to take care of it?

"Hey, baby!" Ralph said as I walked up to him. His breath reeked of alcohol. He grabbed my hand and tugged me toward the dance floor. Once we got there, he pulled me to him—like suffocatingly close—put his hands on my butt, and whispered in my ear the dirtiest thing I've ever heard. Something that I still can't bring myself to repeat, but it was wrong and suggestive and explicit.

Without thinking, I pulled back and slapped him across the face. I reached into my purse, took out several bills, and shoved them into his hand. "There. Take a cab home. I hope I never ever see you again."

People stared, mouths open, eyes wide, as I pushed Ralph toward the elevator. Anne was upset I'd caused a scene, but Drew and the rest of the guys thought it was the coolest thing they'd ever seen. At least I didn't just freeze, like I'd done so many times before.

Time Wasted: It was only one day, but the entire time was miserable, so it seemed longer. And obviously everyone remembers how charming I was at Devin and Anne's wedding. The story is legendary.

Lessons Learned:

Brides are emotional time bombs. (I bet Anne wishes she would've just let me go solo.)

Never take anyone you don't know to a wedding.

Jimmy Delfino actually looks like a gem next to his obnoxious friends.

Slapping someone across the face can feel very exhilarating.

*Sidenote (added in 2011) – Despite my ban on fairy tales, I did accidentally watch *Tangled* one day with my nephew. Yes, the Disney version added girl power, which was pretty cool. And Flynn Rider was hard not to fall for and I *might* have been cheering for him in the end. But, like Aladdin, he was a liar (real name, Eugene Fitzherbert, and he happens to be a criminal). So while charming, he's automatically disqualified. But I do consider slapping Ralph the equivalent of Rapunzel and her frying pan. Bonus points for girl power.

CHAPTER TEN

Since I'd spent a few hours with Stephanie over lunch—and had received a passive-aggressive e-mail from my boss—I'd stayed at the office late to do everything Patricia insisted was so urgent, even though I knew the client meeting wasn't until next week. The last thing I felt like doing when I got home was cooking. I was tempted to call in a take-out order to Blue, thinking I'd just slip in and out. But the risk of seeing Jake was too great. I searched my fridge and cupboards and decided to make a ham-and-cheese sandwich. Unfortunately, I only had two heels of bread left, and I only ate them if I had absolutely no other options. Like now. The entire time I choked my sandwich down, I wished it was something more appealing.

I'd barely finished putting the dish away when there was a knock at my door.

Like I said, the beauty of needing to be buzzed into the building is never being surprised. Since I hadn't buzzed anyone up, it had to be Steph or Drew. Or someone who'd gotten the wrong door. I walked over and stared out the peephole. *Jake.*

I ran a hand through my hair, swiped my tongue over my teeth to make sure they didn't have food stuck in them, then opened my door.

"Spontaneous visits," he said with a smile. "Another perk of living in the same building."

I tried to play it cool, even though my heart was doing a happy dance inside. Okay, maybe I'd missed him the tiniest bit, and the fact that he hadn't come to see me since our date had me feeling a little rejected—never fun, even if you aren't planning on something serious with a guy.

He held out a DVD—*Just Friends*. "Tell me you're up for a movie."

Seems like he's trying to tell me something with the movie title. Which is good. Telling myself that wasn't enough to keep my nerves from bouncing up and down in my stomach. Or from noticing the way his gray T-shirt showed off his toned arms and made his eyes look a little more green than blue.

And now I'm totally staring at him, probably drooling. "Come on in." I stepped aside and gestured to the couch. "Have a seat."

I was glad I hadn't changed into my pajamas yet. I had, however, worn a skirt today, and I didn't want to sit all proper through an entire movie. "I'm just going to go change into something more comfortable."

Until I said it aloud, I hadn't realized how it was going to sound—like the line the girl delivers in the movie before coming out in lingerie. "And by comfortable, I mean jeans and a T-shirt." Clarifying made me feel even stupider, but I couldn't seem to stop. "I didn't want you to think that I… I mean I'm not like… I'll be right back."

I hurried back to my room before I made it worse—although I didn't think it could get much worse. It's not like I thought I was some female Casanova or something, but usually I did okay with the guys.

I'm sure it's just because it's been a while. Relax and you'll be fine.

I threw on a black tank top and a pair of jeans. My hair looked pretty flat, so I gathered it up into a messy bun.

I walked back into the kitchen and put a bag of popcorn in the microwave. "Last week you were unavoidable and this week I haven't seen you around. Blue must be busy."

"It's been pretty hectic," Jake said. "You should come in sometime. According to everybody there, you're usually in a couple times a week."

"Oh, well, I haven't had client meetings this week, so…" I grabbed a bowl out of my cupboard. "Then today, my friend Stephanie—the one I was telling you about who's getting married—had a centerpiece tragedy. But Tina's going to whip up a few replacement vases, so crisis averted."

I dumped the popcorn into the bowl and headed to the couch. Since he'd flashed the *Just Friends* movie at me, I wasn't sure what to think. Sitting right next to him seemed desperate, sitting far away a snub. *Okay, not the very end, but not too close, either. Safe middle ground.*

Typical guy, he already had control of the remote. Drew had wired my system, and it took a specific combination to get it to work, so I was impressed Jake had already figured it out. He pressed play and the movie started up.

Jake looked at me. "Are you really going to sit all the way over there?"

Traitorous butterflies filled my tummy. *Okay, so he's still interested.*

"I can't even reach the popcorn."

Oh, right. The popcorn. That effectively killed the butterflies.

But when I scooted over, Jake put his arm over my shoulders and barely touched the popcorn. I stuck the bowl on the coffee table, tucked my legs up, and settled in next to him. The movie was funny, and the romance in it was more on the believable side, which gave me that little heart tug I hadn't felt in a while from a movie.

When the credits rolled up the screen, Jake leaned down and brushed his lips against mine. My breath caught in my throat, and before I could recover it, he kissed me. My lips automatically started moving against his, my heart beating wildly in my chest. He deepened the kiss, taking things slow yet demanding enough that tingly heat wound through my entire body. It had been a while since I'd gotten to first base, and I'd forgotten how nice it could be.

"I thought you were trying to send me a message with this movie," I said.

"I was." His lips hovered inches from mine. "I'm making sure to keep myself out of the friend zone."

He closed the gap and kissed me again. Then I was pulling him closer, getting lost in the feel of his body against mine, his lips, his tongue. Part of me was screaming, *Shut it down! This is a bad idea!*

But that part kept getting overruled by the part of me that was enjoying kissing Jake.

CHAPTER ELEVEN

Stephanie parked her car in front of her parents' house. The usually empty street was lined with a variety of cars and trucks. She'd spent most of the hour-long ride from Denver to Longmont on the phone with Anthony—there'd been some miscommunication about if and when his uncle and four kids were coming down for the wedding.

Once she got off the phone, she pressed me for more information on Jake, since I'd filled her in on our impromptu Thursday-night hangout.

A crease formed between her eyebrows. "So you had a nice time, kissed, and then you haven't seen him since?"

"You say it like it's been forever. It's only Saturday morning." I climbed out of the car and breathed in the fresh country air.

Steph came around the hood. "But he hasn't called?"

"We're not in some big relationship, Steph, and that's the way I want to keep it. He mentioned he'd be working this weekend, but that I should swing by Blue if I got the chance." I started across the grass, dodging the many lawn ornaments. There were birdbaths, fairies, and shiny spheres in every color. "Oh no, she lost her head again." I pointed at the fairy statue that was forever being glued back together.

"Stupid kids." Steph bent to pick up the head. The neighborhood kids liked to rearrange, steal, and destroy Mrs. Taylor's lawn decorations. When Zeus, the family's Rottweiler, was alive, the statues stopped being vandalized. Since Zeus had passed on—old age, but still sad—the kids were back at it again.

Fairy head under her arm, Steph walked up the steps to her house. "So you're going to go to Blue tonight to say hi, right?"

"I'm going to hang out with my family after this shindig is over, actually. I decided to spend the night at the ranch. Drew's not going to take me back into the city till tomorrow."

Stephanie shook her head but didn't give me the relationship advice I'd expected. Instead, she pulled open the screen door and we stepped inside. High-pitched greetings and congratulations erupted as soon as Stephanie walked into the living room. The entire community of women was packed into the house for the bridal shower.

Mrs. Taylor stuck a clothespin on me and explained that I couldn't say anything wedding related or I'd lose it. The person with the most clothespins was going to get a prize at the end of the game. I didn't know what the prize was, but the clothespin didn't accessorize my outfit very well.

I looked from face to face until I found the one I was searching for. Mom moved a big white gift bag off the chair next to her and patted it. *Aw, she saved me a seat.*

I left Stephanie's side as she showed off her ring to the women swarming around her.

"How're you doing, sweetheart?" Mom asked as I sat down.

There was always something about seeing my mom that made everything seem better. "Good now." I lowered my voice. "Hurry and fill me in on all the local gossip while everyone's distracted." Mom glanced around, then leaned in to give me the scoop.

It wasn't long before the shower officially got started and we were playing torturous games that would make even the most hardened terrorists crack, I was sure of it. Maybe I was just missing whatever girl gene was supposed to make this kind of thing fun.

The shrieking only got louder as the party continued. Mrs. Taylor passed around cards so everyone could write down wedding advice for the bride-to-be. Since *Don't get married* seemed inappropriate, I decided to write, *Call me when he's being a jackhole – Darby*

Mrs. Taylor and Mom were both sticklers about cussing, so Steph and I had made up that insult. We thought we were so clever.

The next game was How Well Do You Know the Bride?

"This is going to be cake," I said as I read the first few questions.

"Give it to me!" Mrs. Hildabrand said, pawing at my shirt. "You said cake!"

It took a few seconds for me to understand why she was attacking me, but when I did, I quickly relinquished my clothespin before she ripped it off me. After fixing the collar of my shirt, I turned my attention back to my sheet of paper. It had everything from favorite color to shoe size. I knew them all. When I blew the competition away, Mrs. Taylor handed me the prize—a tiny potted plant.

As I studied the little blue flowers, I thought about how Jake had teased me about my sickly plant. I smiled to myself and raised the prize. "You're going to have to be tough to live with me," I said, then tucked it under my chair.

The hostesses took a break from games and pointed toward the food. It provided the perfect opportunity for everyone I'd ever known to come over and ask me if I was dating anyone, even though I was sure they'd already asked Mom about it. After telling the first few people I didn't have a boyfriend right now, they patted my hand, that poor-you look in their eyes.

"Don't worry, dearie," Mrs. Hildabrand said. "You'll find someone."

"I guess if he is out there, he's going to have to find me, because I'm not looking." Of course the second the words left my mouth, Jake's face popped into my mind. No way in hell was I going to say anything about him, though.

I could see Mrs. Hildabrand was going to add something else, but Mom stepped in for the save. "Didn't you make the dip, Martha? It's marvelous."

Since the woman loved to be complimented on her food, the distraction worked like a charm. After a few minutes, Mrs. Taylor stood up to announce the next game. "We're going to go around the room and listen to everyone's love stories. You can tell us about where you met, your first kiss, or how he proposed."

I glanced around the room. I was the only one not married. Besides Stephanie, of course, who would tell everyone how Anthony took her to the Garden Café where they'd had their first date and proposed to her. They'd all swoon.

Mrs. Smith got up to tell her story. It started with, "I fell in love with Melvin the first night we met…"

Somebody shoot me now.

• • •

I survived the bridal shower, but only in the most literal sense of the word. I was a little dead inside from all the talk of love at first sight. I'd heard at least half of those women trashing their husbands when they got together at community events. If anything, it only reaffirmed that I'd chosen the right way to look at romance.

Being at the ranch instantly made me feel better. After changing into some jeans, a T-shirt, and my worn-in boots, I climbed the fence behind the house and whistled. It only took a moment for one of the few males in my life who'd never let me down to come running.

"Good boy, Major," I said to the sorrel horse as he approached. I held out the bucket of grain and let him take a few bites. While he munched, I ran a hand down his muscular reddish-brown neck, then scratched the white stripe on his face.

I placed the bucket outside the fence, grabbed my saddle, and heaved it onto him. "You ready to go for a run?" I asked as I fastened everything onto him.

He whinnied, which I took as a yes. Gripping the saddle horn, I put my foot in the stirrup and pulled myself onto him. "Let's go!" Major took off toward the distant trees where the pond, one of my favorite places in the whole world, was.

The Wilson Ranch spread out across three hundred acres. Before I'd come to live on the ranch, I'd been a bona-fide city girl. The sprawling fields, home decorated like a log cabin, and horses and cows hadn't impressed me. I was into fashion and decorating. And as my stepbrothers pointed out, I did everything like a girl.

Little by little, though, I found the joy in a long bike ride. Devin and Drew taught me to drive the four-wheeler and I'd take that out to the pond when I wanted to go for a swim or get away from everything for a while.

I'd lived at the Wilson ranch for about a year when Dwight came into the house and knocked on my bedroom door. "Darby, I need to show you something."

I'd opened the door and stared at him. Dwight had been nothing but nice, but our relationship was mostly common courtesy. A word or two when we passed. Drew, Devin, and I had started to do more and more together, but if I ever found myself alone with their dad, I usually headed to my bedroom.

He hooked his thumbs in the pockets of his Wranglers. "Get on some work clothes and come outside with me."

If Mom had been home, I would've asked her to tell Dwight I wasn't interested in forced bonding time. But I reluctantly changed into my jeans with holes in the knees, threw on a T-shirt, and headed outside.

Dwight was leading a young reddish-brown horse out of the

trailer. "I just bought this gelding down at the auction. And this summer, you're going to help me break him in."

I stared into the pony's big, dark eyes. "But I don't know anything about horses."

"He doesn't know much about humans, either. That's what we're going to change." Dwight patted him. "Why don't you come over here and let him get to know you."

The horse lifted his tail and pooped on the ground. *Great. A summer dodging horse crap. Just what I wanted.*

"Pick a name," Dwight said, "and nothing girlie or hippie."

"How about Major?" I asked. Major was the name of Cinderella's horse.

Dwight looked from me to the horse. "I like it."

Once I started working with Major, I fell in love. Dwight was always there, helping me, talking with me about this, that, and the other as we worked. And somewhere along the way I started loving Dwight, too.

When we'd finished breaking him in, Dwight sat me down. "Darby, I want you to know that I consider you part of my family. I know it was hard for you to get used to us boys, and they might not show it, but Drew and Devin like having you and Janet around. And I do, too."

"I like it here, too," I said.

"There're two things my kids need to have. Names that start with D—see, you already have that down—and a horse. That's why Major's yours. If you want him."

My heart swelled. "Mine?"

"You'll have to take care of him."

I nodded. "I will. Thank you so much." I'd never been a hugger, but my arms were around Dwight before I'd even realized I was going to hug him.

He patted me on the back and then told me to go feed my horse.

When I had to go back to school, I'd been pretty upset about leaving Major all day. He went through a rebellious phase, too, trying to buck off anyone else who tried to ride him. And while I knew I shouldn't be proud of that fact, I was.

"Whoa," I said now, pulling on the reins and slowing him down to a trot as we approached the pond. I slid off him and sat in the shade of the tree while he drank some water. Even now, he was picky about riders. He tolerated Dwight, Drew, and Devin, and would slowly make his way over when they called. But he only came running for me.

I laid back in the grass and saw the initials carved into the tree. That had been a romantic story at one point, just like any one of the stories I'd heard today at Steph's shower. Yet throwing your initials together with *equals true love forever* doesn't actually make it so. Even in my happy place, I had proof that relationships—even good ones—don't last.

. . .

The raised voices drifted through the front door, combined with the sound of a crying baby. I stood on the porch of the house, wondering how long they'd be at it this time.

"I took care of her all day yesterday," Anne yelled. "I think you can handle a few hours."

"I'm taking her," Devin said. "I just wanted to know if you'd be back before I needed to drive home and put the kids to bed."

"I don't know. All I know is I've got to get out of here before I go insane!" Anne swung the screen door open with such force that I had to jump out of the way. She charged down the stairs and climbed into her car. I don't even think she saw me.

I stepped into the house and saw Devin holding Ava, while Levi, my five-year-old nephew with hair so blond it was almost white, was parked in front of the television, watching cartoons.

I gave Devin a tight smile. "Hey. I'd ask how it's going, but I'm pretty sure I already know."

Devin shook his head. "Ava's teething, so she's crabby, and I've been working long hours, helping out with the cows and getting the machines ready for first cutting." He ran a hand through his hair. His eyes were bloodshot with dark circles underneath. "Needless to say, things are a little tense lately. I try to keep the mood light by joking around. Back when we were dating, Anne said she loved my sense of humor. Lately all I get when I tell a joke is a glare."

I looked down at Ava and her epically chubby cheeks. In her six months on earth, all I'd ever seen her do was cry or sleep. With her dad bouncing her around, though, she seemed pretty happy. "On the bright side, you two sure do have cute kids."

"That's about all we have," Devin said.

Ava seemed to take offense to this, even though we'd been calling her cute, and started screaming again.

"I'm going to go walk her around outside. Janet and Dad ran to the store, but they should be back in a few minutes. Until then, could you keep an eye on Levi for me?"

"Sure."

I felt bad for Devin, but I also felt bad for Anne. Everyone talked about how much she'd changed. I once heard this statement that women marry men hoping to change them, while men marry women hoping they'll never change.

So maybe it's a little true. After all, there are definitely some fixer-uppers out there that could use a good coat of-paint. Or five. And while I've never been married, I've been in long-term relationships before. I've also been around my fair share of married people. And it did seem like the men always complained about how much their girlfriends and wives had changed. But men change, too. While there used to be a little effort put into date night, he now drapes his smelly feet over his significant other and sits blank-faced, staring at the television with little conversation besides, "What we got to eat?"

He used to dress up; now he doesn't even bother getting dressed. Responsibilities and stress replace the romance. So, yes, things change. Really, guys? You didn't see that coming?

Okay, rant over.

I sat down next to my nephew. "Hey, Levi. How are you doing?"

He peeled his gaze off the TV and looked at me. "Ava cries all the time. Then Mommy does. It's lots of crying at my house."

I ran my hand over his head. "It'll get better." *I hope.*

A few minutes later, Mom walked in the door holding Ava. Mom had this gift with babies. Whereas my first instinct was to run from a screaming kid, hers was to take the child and comfort him or her.

Devin and Dwight came in, arms loaded with groceries.

"Are there any more?" I asked, motioning to the bags.

"Nah. We got 'em all," Dwight said.

I stood and followed everyone into the kitchen. Dwight set down the bags on the table, then turned and gave me a hug. "How's my girl? Still showing everyone in the city what's what?"

"I'm not sure about that," I said. "I do show them how to rearrange their homes, though. Plus spending other people's money is always fun."

Dwight pulled out a bar stool for me and then sat down on the one next to it. "You take Major out?"

"Of course. How's he doing?"

"Damn thing bit Caleb the other day."

Mom stopped her humming and shot Dwight a look. She'd been trying to get him to break his cussing habit for seventeen years, and obviously had no intention of giving up.

Dwight continued his story about Caleb, the neighbor kid who sometimes worked on the farm. "Anyway, while Caleb's trying to saddle him, Major kept biting him. So Caleb smacked him on the nose."

"Oh no," I said, already knowing it was going to be bad. Not only was Major stubborn, he also held grudges. You had to show him who was boss, but you had to be careful about it.

"Since he's such a vindictive SOB, Major lets Caleb step into the stirrup, then takes off running and kicking."

"Is Caleb okay?"

"He won't go near your horse anymore, but he's fine. Just a few bruises." Dwight shook his head. "You spoiled that horse rotten. Now he only loves you, barely tolerates me, and bites, kicks, or bucks when anyone else looks his way."

"But he loves me," I said with a shrug and a grin.

Dwight shook his head. "Damn horse," he muttered.

Ava started screaming again. Mom bounced her up and down and hummed louder.

Devin held out his arms. "Need me to take her?" His exhausted tone said it was the last thing in the world he wanted to do.

"I'll go give her a bath and see if that makes her happy," Mom said. "There's some leftover stew in the fridge if you get hungry." Mom walked out of the room with Ava, the crying getting quieter as she headed upstairs.

Devin leaned his elbows against the counter and put his head in his hands. "I'm so tired of the crying. And I'm worried about Anne. She won't listen to me, but I think she needs to talk to someone before the depression gets worse. It's like it was after Levi."

Dwight patted Devin on the back. "It'll get better, son."

Devin sighed. "I don't know how much longer I can do it." He looked at me. "Maybe you're right to keep your anti-marriage stance. I love Anne and the kids to death, but marriage is a lot harder than I thought it'd be."

"Funny, all I heard at Stephanie's bridal shower was how wonderful marriage is. I think it's one of those grass is always greener on the other side things. No matter what you've decided, you always wonder if something else would've been the better pick."

I would know. I'd been thinking about the greener grass all day.

Grownup Fairy Tales Case Study: Gil/the perfect guy from romance movies

My Age: 17

Yes, I realize this breaks the mold a bit. It's not a prince or princess story. But really, Gil broke the mold. And it happened to be around the time I'd moved on from Disney movies to romantic comedies. These were the kind of stories that could *actually happen*. Or so I'd been foolish enough to believe, anyway.

We've all seen the chick flicks with the amazing, cute guy friend. Somehow, the girl doesn't realize how amazing he is or that he's head over heels in love with her. Sometimes it's the guy who doesn't realize he's in love with his best girl friend. There are several variations, but they all end with discovering they love each other.

After the whole debacle with Sherman, I was crushed. It was hard to see him at school, especially since he and Tabitha were playing tonsil hockey in the halls all the time. He'd hurt me, and as dumb as it was, I kept thinking up scenarios where he'd realize he was a fool for losing me, and how after a long period of him making it up to me, we'd get back together.

It didn't happen. In fact, I don't think he thought twice about me—which stung even more because it meant he never cared about me at all. I hung out with my brothers and their friends a lot. We spent a lot of time at Margie's, the local diner. The guys kept me from moping around. In fact, when I tried to mope, Drew or Devin would tell me to stop being a girl and suck it up.

January of my junior year, Stephanie moved to town. We

had a class together, and we instantly hit it off. Even then, people commented on how much we looked alike. Steph was into fashion, too. Before long, I was spending most of my free time with her.

One day when I was outside brushing down Major, Gil walked up to me.

"Hey, Gil," I said. "I think Drew and Devin had to go get parts for the John Deere, but they should be back soon."

"I wanted to talk to you, actually."

Annoyed he wasn't getting all my attention anymore, Major reached his head around and bit at Gil.

I put my hands on the side of my horse's big head and looked him in the eye. "No biting, Major!" I held up the bucket of grain. "You want this?"

He whinnied, leaning for it.

I swung it back. "Then no biting."

Major hung his head like he was the most picked-on thing in the world.

"Sorry," I said, turning to Gil. "What's up?"

Gil leaned on the fence. "You haven't been around much since you met your new friend."

"It has been nice to have someone in my same class—not to mention getting a little girl time in." I set down the bucket of grain. "Stephanie and I aren't doing anything tonight, though. What's everyone doing later?"

Gil sighed. "I don't think you get it. *I* miss you."

I looked up, meeting his gaze. "Wait, are you saying...?" I wasn't sure I could finish. Not without making a fool of myself.

Instead of answering with words, Gil stepped forward and kissed me, a soft kiss that caused my pulse to skitter. "I like you, Darby," he said when his lips left mine. "I've liked you for a long time. I kept waiting to make my move, thinking I'd say something next time we were alone. But then I waited too long and you stopped hanging out with us. Anyway, think about it. If you just want to be friends, I hope things won't be awkward between us."

I finally got past being stunned and really saw Gil for the first time. With his curly, black hair and big brown eyes, he was definitely cute. Then I thought about the way he always checked on me when we were out as a group—how he'd been there to pick me up the night I watched Sherman cheat on me. I'd never thought of any of my brothers' friends as possible boyfriends, simply because we'd been close for so long. I thought that to them, I was just an annoying girl.

"Do it again," I whispered.

"What part?" Gil asked.

My heart was pounding so hard I could feel every thump. "The kissing part."

He grinned, then pulled me into his arms and kissed me again, one kiss after another, until they merged together and made the world spin.

The rest of the guys weren't sure what to think about Gil and me as a couple. It took them a little while to adjust, but before too long, they all got used to the idea. Steph and Drew started dating, too—though they only lasted a month. Things were tense between them for a couple weeks, but then they got over it. They had to. That's the curse and blessing of small-town dating.

On warmer days, Gil and I would go to the pond to relax or swim. One day he got out his pocketknife and carved our initials in the tree. He told me he loved me, and I returned the sentiment. About a month later, under the shade of that same tree, Gil and I lost our virginity together. He was thoughtful and careful and checked on me afterward. I'd been a little scared it would change everything. It did in a lot of ways, but not in the way I'd worried. Things between us couldn't have been better.

Then he graduated high school and our relationship suddenly had an expiration date—he was going to college in California, and we agreed that the long-distance thing would be too hard.

We spent the entire summer together, soaking in every spare minute we could. The night before he left for California, we went to our usual spot near the pond and said our good-byes. I did my best not to cry, but I shed a few tears. Okay, a *lot* of tears.

When the sun dipped low in the sky, all but disappearing, Gil stood and extended his hand to me. "You ready to go back?"

I shook my head. "I'm going to stay here."

"I've got to go. My parents are waiting." He bent down and kissed me. The kiss was filled with love and sorrow, an accumulation of an almost yearlong relationship and more than three years of friendship. It left me hollow and full, all at the same time. "Good-bye, Darby. I love you."

I didn't bother holding back the tears anymore. "Love you, too."

I thought it was the end of the world, and for a while, it was.

When Gil came home for Christmas break, he and I spent three blissful weeks together, everything the way it was before he'd left for college. I was sure that we were destined to be together. Waiting until summer wouldn't be easy, but when he came back for summer vacation, we'd be able to pick up where we left off.

But Gil got a job out in California. Steph and I had talked about going to school in Denver. I'd applied to the Rocky Mountain College of Art and Design and she was planning on going to Metropolitan State. I'd also applied to a school out in California in case Gil and I got serious over the summer. Without him coming home, though, things just fizzled out. It was over. I needed to move on.

So I did.

Then Devin and Anne got married and I saw Gil again. He looked great, asked me to dance, and as we spun around the floor, I felt seventeen all over again. Things with us were always so comfortable. Easy.

Then the whole thing with Ralph and me happened. Everyone

loves the story about me slapping him and telling him off; my favorite part of the night happened a couple of minutes after that.

I'd just shoved the money in Ralph's hand and watched him get into the elevator when I heard someone say, "You have really bad taste in guys."

I whipped around, ready to let whoever it was have it. Gil was smiling at me. "Yeah, I do," I said. "I can think of only one exception."

Gil pointed to himself, a hopeful look on his face.

I shook my head. "No. It was..." I grinned and gave him a playful shove. "Yes, you. Honestly, you're about the only guy I've dated who hasn't been a total jackhole. Although, for the record, that guy wasn't my choice. He was a setup. A very bad setup."

Drew walked up to me and threw his hand in the air. "That. Was. Awesome!"

I gave him his high five. That's when I noticed all the people looking at me. "Wow, everyone's still staring. It's like they've never seen a guy get slapped at a wedding before."

"Oh, there's the guy with the camcorder," Drew said, pointing to the videographer. "I'm going to go see if he got it." He took off across the floor.

I leaned closer to Gil and whispered, "Does Anne look really mad?"

Gil glanced over my shoulder. "I think Devin's talking her down."

"Great. She was already annoyed with me, and now all everyone's going to remember about this night is how I slapped my date."

"Let's give them something else to talk about, then." Gil cupped my chin and brought his mouth down on mine. I wrapped my arms around his waist, parted my lips, and kissed him back. Kissing Gil was just like I remembered it. Amazing.

Gil sighed and placed his forehead against mine. "I wanted to do that since I first got here. I was pretty sad you showed up with a date."

I gazed into his big brown eyes. "I guess getting rid of him was a good move, then."

And even though I knew it couldn't work out—we still lived in different cities—I spent the next few days glued to Gil's side. Over that time, I wanted to bring up the long-distance thing and ask him if he thought we could figure out a way to still make us work. But I didn't want to ruin it. Maybe I knew deep down that a relationship like that would be too difficult, and I also knew I'd be crushed if he said he didn't care enough to try. So I'd held back what I wanted, and simply told him good-bye when it was time for him to go back to California.

About a year later, I got his wedding invitation in the mail. He'd met a beautiful girl and fallen in love.

Part of me had always thought that Gil and I would get back together. Like we were one of those couples who kept being brought together until we got the timing right, just like in those damn romance movies.

I went to his wedding with Drew, Devin, and Anne. If I were a character in one of the movies I used to love watching, I would've stood up and announced my feelings for Gil. He would've left his modelesque bride at the altar, taken me in his arms, and kissed me. Fade out. Roll credits.

Instead, I sat there in the chapel and watched the only good boyfriend I'd ever had—my first love—marry someone else.

So thanks a lot, Julia Roberts, for making me think love always worked out, even if you made money working on street corners or ran from guys who loved you. And you, too, Molly Ringwald— maybe you had to be a redhead to land the guy you loved. Except Sandra Bullock always got her man, too. In romance movies, everything always works out, because people who are destined to be together always find a way somehow.

And the brainwashing continues…

Time Wasted: I refuse to call my relationship with Gil a waste. We dated nine months in high school, a couple weeks over Christmas break, and three days after Devin's wedding. I did, however, waste a few years thinking that we'd eventually get back together.

Lessons Learned:

There are a few guys who aren't complete jerks. But it doesn't even matter. Because Fate can be such a bitch.

Chapter Twelve

The narrator of my audiobook started right where I'd left off: female FBI agent closing in on the serial killer who preyed on young females living alone.

I stepped onto the treadmill and turned it on. Before long my heart was racing—not only because of the exercise, but also because I was scared for the protagonist. The killer was hiding under the bed, waiting for her to go to sleep.

Don't go to sleep.

The FBI agent had gotten a tip, but I wasn't sure she was going to make it in time.

The killer was sliding out, ready to make his move. Planning on killing another girl.

"Hey," Jake said, stepping in front of the treadmill.

Stumbling over my feet, I gripped the rail to keep from going down, then barely managed to get my footing back. I stopped the treadmill and paused my book. My breaths sawed in and out of my mouth.

"I just thought I'd say hi. I didn't realize it would scare you."

"It does when you do it at the same time the killer is making his move."

Confusion flashed across Jake's features.

I pointed at my earphones. "I'm listening to a book. It's at an intense part." Glancing at the digital readout, I saw I'd run two miles.

Enough for today.

I patted my face with my towel and climbed off the treadmill. "How was the weekend rush at Blue?"

"Busy. I kept hoping for someone to come in and make it more enjoyable, but she never showed. Mindy informed me I was being snubbed."

I leaned against the wall and took a swig of my water bottle. "Snubbed by this person who never showed?"

Jake stuck his hand on the wall next to my head and locked eyes with me. "According to her, if you liked me at all, you would've come in, and I should just take a hint."

"I dropped some rather big hints before, and in my experience, you're not very good at taking them." I smiled, so he'd know I was teasing him. With him leaning over me, my hyperawareness kicked in. I noticed the pulse beating at the base of his neck, a pale scar on the bottom of his chin, and how everything about him screamed strong and confident. My skin hummed from his closeness and I was tempted to reach out and run my hand down his chest.

I think he noticed my appraisal because a triumphant grin hit his lips. "I guess that's why I'm going to ask what you're doing later. I've got today off, and I think we should go out."

Regardless of how much I was enjoying being this close to him again, it was time to be honest. With him and myself. I did like being around him, and I *had* said I wanted a decent, longish-term relationship. He lived in my building, but I supposed I could deal with bumping into him as long as we didn't get too serious.

"I don't know what you're expecting the outcome of this to

be, but I want to keep this—whatever we've got going—light. I don't want to explore my past or yours, or get into all the big relationship drama."

Jake didn't skip a beat. "I'll pick you up at six."

• • •

At six on the dot, there was a knock on my door. I opened it and invited Jake in. "Just let me water my plants real quick, before I forget." I filled a cup and walked across the room to my window.

"You got another one?" Jake asked as I poured water into the dark soil of my new plant.

"I won it at a bridal shower yesterday, since I knew the bride best."

Jake came up behind me and put his arms around me. "And you didn't think you should give it to someone who doesn't kill plants?"

I elbowed him in the gut. "Hey, be nice. It tipped over and lost some dirt on the ride home, but I'm sure it'll perk up soon." I pointed at the larger plant that had been with me since I bought the place. "And look how good my one green blade is still doing."

"I think you should just put them both out of their misery." Jake kissed my neck, sending pleasant chills through my entire body.

I set my cup on the window ledge and twisted to face him, placing my hands on his arms. "Aren't you supposed to be impressing me, not making fun of my lack of gardening skills?"

Jake grinned. "Let's go, then, before you change your mind." He grabbed my hand and walked me out of the building and into the parking garage. He led me to a Chevy Camaro Z28. Classic, most likely late sixties, painted black with white racing stripes on the hood—hanging with mostly guys in high school, I'd learned a lot about cars.

Drew and Devin would die to ride in one of these. Hell,

I wanted to ride in it, too. But I couldn't help thinking of Allen and his Dodge Viper, and how I had a rule about guys who were obsessed with their cars.

"Nice car," I said, kind of wishing it wasn't, but failing to be unimpressed.

"Thanks. I like her." He opened the passenger door.

If I follow my rules, this is definitely strike three. Then again, he didn't exactly sound *obsessed*, and the classic variety gave him a couple of bonus points, at least. *So maybe, like, half a strike.*

After a moment's hesitation, I slid inside. The steering wheel was skinny, the windows were the roll-down kind, and there were gages on the middle console, along with a silver-knobbed shifter.

Jake got inside, filling the car with the scent of his familiar musky cologne. "I was thinking we might drive a bit. There's a place in Boulder that's—"

"I'd rather not go to Boulder," I blurted out, a bad sense of déjà vu hitting me.

"In case you have to bail early? Like with that counselor guy?"

"Exactly," I said, working at sounding casual about it. "Who knows when you're going to say something that sends me running?"

"Okay. I know a place that's closer to home."

I was overreacting, but I couldn't help it. Because of Allen, even the mention of Boulder for dinner struck a raw nerve. Especially combined with the fast car thing. I realized that I hadn't seen Jake's place yet and started to panic.

What's he hiding?

I reached for my seat belt. My stomach was churning, so I took a deep breath to try to calm down and think about things rationally. Jake and I lived in the same building; he'd introduced me to his friend Tina; he kept insisting I go to Blue. Oh, and Virginia Hammond wanted to set us up. All things that suggested he wasn't married.

Okay, minor freak-out over.

The engine roared to life, then quieted down to a purr. "Did you get a chance to listen to more of your book?" Jake asked, maneuvering out of the parking garage. "It seemed to have you on edge earlier."

"Even if I was listening to music, I still would've jumped when you snuck up on me. Whenever I get on the treadmill, I check out of the real world." I glanced at him. "But the book was definitely a nail-biter. The end was so intense I couldn't put it down—or whatever you say when you don't actually have the book in your hands."

"So you like to read? Or listen, anyway?"

"I've found it helps me stay on the treadmill longer. But I always like to have a paperback on hand, too. I need to swing by the bookstore for another one, actually."

"We can stop there after we eat, then." Jake reached over and took my hand, lacing his fingers with mine. There was something about the smallest gestures with him that made me feel like a teenager again. I told myself to just enjoy it.

Still, at the back of my mind, I heard that nagging voice saying, *Good things never last.*

• • •

"I told you the food was amazing," Jake said. "The good thing about knowing one of the best chefs in town is you know all the great places to eat."

I took a sip of my water. "How'd you get into the restaurant business anyway?"

"Long story."

I stabbed a tortellini with my fork. "And you're thinking of bolting soon? I haven't even told you about my creepy porcelain doll collection yet."

He shot me a quick smile. "I thought you wanted to keep things light? Talk only about superficial things." He raised his eyebrows. "Weren't those the terms?"

"Yes, but your refusal to tell the story makes me think it's a good one, and now I'm really interested."

"Well, it was between being a professional clown or starting a restaurant." Jake sighed, a tragic look on his face. "Unfortunately, I flunked out of clown school, and my parents disowned me. They kicked me out of the tiny car holding twelve other clowns and sent me on my way."

I shook my head, fighting a smile. "I can't believe you flunked out, when you're obviously so good at it."

Jake grinned. "I am a natural."

"Don't think you're getting out of telling me the real story, you clown-school dropout."

Jake pushed his plate aside and propped his forearms on the table. "My dad built the Knight Marketing & Advertising Group in New York from the ground up. He was big on learning how to work, so he told me I'd have to qualify to get a job in his company. I went to NYU and got my degree in Marketing, with a minor in Economics. As soon as I graduated, I started working for my dad, made some good money sitting behind a desk all day, and hated every minute of it.

"One day I ran into Brent—he and I had roomed together in New York while he was going to culinary school. He was back in town for a week visiting family. Anyway, we got to talking, and he told me that he'd moved to Denver and was trying to open his own restaurant. When I asked how it was going, he said he was having a hard time getting a place, but he wasn't going to give up."

The waitress came by with a pitcher of water, refilled our drinks, and asked if we needed anything else.

"Where was I?" Jake asked when she walked away.

I placed my napkin over my plate. "Brent was trying to open a place here."

"As he talked, my mind automatically started thinking about

the business side of things. I made a few suggestions and told him what I could to help him out. Then he made a joke about how we could open the place together. The joke was on him, because I flew to Denver to check it out, and the rest is history."

"Was your dad upset about you leaving the family business?"

"I think he was a little disappointed, but he's always encouraged my sister and me to do something we love. She still works for my dad, because she has a passion for it."

"I like that story," I said. "Not as scandalous as I thought it'd be, but nice."

Jake leveled his eyes on me—they were even bluer tonight, since he was wearing a navy button-down. "What about you? Why'd you choose interior design?"

"I love throwing things together and transforming a place. I know it's not saving lives, but I have fun doing it, and I'm good at it."

Jake ran his finger along the rim of his glass. "I think it's important to enjoy what you're doing. Sure, there will be crazy, crappy days where work sucks, but there's got to be some good ones, too."

"Exactly," I said. Lately, I'd been enjoying being at the office less and less, but I still loved what I did. "And who couldn't use a nice sanctuary to go home to at the end of the night? That's where I come in."

"I'm afraid you'll be disappointed with my place. It's really boring and bare."

I leaned in. "Who said anything about going to your place?"

"Well, that's where dessert's going to be." A devilish grin spread across his face. "And trust me, you want dessert."

• • •

Jake paused near the erotica shelves of the bookstore. "Isn't this your favorite section?"

Heat spread through my cheeks. "I was trying to avoid you and just happened to hide there. I didn't realize where I was until I looked at the book in my hands." I glanced up at him. "And in case you didn't notice, I'm into bondage, so I could tie you up and no one would ever find you. Don't mess with me."

"I wouldn't dare." He put his arm around me, hooking his hand on my hip. "Where to, then?"

"Mystery."

We walked toward the back of the store. I browsed the titles, waiting for something to catch my interest.

Jake picked up one and studied the back. "What are you looking for?"

I slid out a book, then pushed it back in. "Something intense. The scarier the better."

Jake ran his knuckle down my arm, my blood rushing to every place his skin had touched mine. "How scared do you have to be to call me up and tell me to come over?"

"And admit I need anyone but me, myself, and I?" I joked, shaking my head. "Never going to happen."

He gave me a quick peck on the lips. "I'm going to go browse the history section."

"How boring does your book have to be before you call me up and tell me to come over?"

"Not very. I don't mind admitting I need someone else." Jake tugged me closer and pressed his lips to mine again, lingering for long enough to make me lightheaded, then walked away.

Grinning like an idiot, I turned my attention back to the shelf. After a few minutes, I selected a Lehane novel and headed to the front to purchase it.

"Darby?"

I turned toward the voice. My heart dropped when I saw Allen. Of all the bookstores in all the world, he had to come walking into mine. He leaned in like he was going to hug me, and I stepped back.

Allen dropped his hands, hurt etched across his face. The lines in his forehead were more pronounced than they used to be, but he still looked handsome. For a no-good, cheating liar. "After all these years, you're still mad?"

"Am I still mad?" Heat wound through my veins and my breaths came quicker and quicker. "You made me the other woman without my knowing it. So yeah, I'm still mad."

"Alicia and I ended up getting divorced about a year after we had our daughter. We just couldn't work it out."

"Even if I could believe anything you're saying, it doesn't matter. I don't care about you and your wife or ex-wife, or whatever your situation is."

"Look, I'm trying to apologize here. I didn't mean to involve you in my messy marriage. I really did care about you, and I'm sorry that you got hurt." Allen took a step toward me. "I just wish that things had gone —"

"Don't even start with your wishes," I said, throwing up a hand. "You don't get any more wishes."

An arm wrapped around my waist. "Is everything okay here?" Jake asked.

"I'm ready to go." Being here suddenly felt suffocating. I set my novel down on a random display and charged out of the store, into the cool night air.

A moment later, Jake stepped next to me. "What was that all about?"

"Nothing."

He grabbed my hand. "For nothing, you sure seem upset."

"I don't want to talk about it." I pulled on his hand and headed toward his car.

Seeing Allen had put a damper on the whole night. I'd managed to avoid him for eight years. Why did he have to pop up on the one night I was starting to rethink my stance on relationships? If I would've just let Jake take me to Boulder for dinner, I wouldn't have run into Allen.

The irony wasn't lost on me.

Jake drove the couple blocks to our building, the ride passing in silence. When we got into the elevator, I was half expecting him to push my floor and drop me off. Instead, he chose the button for the twentieth floor. With no others lit, we buzzed up fast enough that my stomach lurched when we stopped.

Jake led me past several doors to the end of the hall. As we stepped inside, he flipped on the lights. He wasn't kidding about his lack of decorating. A black couch sat in the middle of the living room, and a giant flat-screen TV—on a tiny side table—was opposite it. *Typical guy. Huge TV and nothing else.*

The far wall had floor-to-ceiling windows overlooking the city.

"It's kind of plain right now," Jake said.

"Lack of decorating is better than bad decorating, in my opinion."

He walked into the kitchen and took a couple bowls out of his cupboard. "I did a little homework, and according to the people I talked to, when you order dessert, you go for chocolate." He grabbed a pan off the top of his oven. "So I made brownies."

"You made them?"

"I'm a pretty good cook, actually. When you have a chef roommate, you pick up a few things." Jake grabbed a carton of ice cream from the freezer and took some chocolate syrup out of the fridge.

I leaned against the cool granite countertop of his island, which was about twice the size of mine. "And what else did everyone at Blue say?"

"That you come in a lot—or used to before you met me, apparently. You have client meetings there, you're always friendly, a good tipper, and that you would never go out with me. They said you'd stopped dating since your last boyfriend…" Jake stopped, looking like he wanted to take back the last sentence. He scooted one of the bowls toward me and handed me the syrup.

The staff at Blue could've only been talking about one guy. "That's the problem with sticking to one place. People start to know too much about you."

"Everyone likes you. They actually told me they'd be mad if you stopped coming in because of me—or Mindy did, anyway. She's the only one bold enough to tell me something like that."

We covered our ice cream in syrup, then headed over to the couch to eat dessert.

What a night. I run into Allen, plus get a reminder of what happened the last time I let myself fall.

I knew Jake and I would have an awkward pause eventually. At least I had the brownie to keep me busy during it. Jake didn't have a coffee table, so when I finished my dessert, I glanced around for a place to set my empty bowl.

"Here," he said, taking it from me and sticking it in his. He headed to the kitchen, and I walked across the room to the giant windows. The moon peeked out between thin gray clouds. Down below, tiny headlights and taillights moved up and down the streets. I wondered where all those people were going, what their stories were.

Jake came up behind me and put his arms around me. He was warm and solid, and I was starting to like the way he always enveloped me in his arms. His breath stirred my hair. "So, what was up with that guy in the bookstore?"

I ran my fingers across Jake's forearm, over the coarse hair and the raised veins on the back of his hand. "He's a mistake from a long time ago. Also known as why I don't date liars."

Jake's lips brushed my temple. "I remember you mentioning that. After you thought I might be one."

"I'm still not sure you're not a liar. The problem with liars is, you never really know they're liars until you catch them."

"What did he lie about? Something big, I'm guessing."

"It was pretty big." I sighed. "Allen was married while we were dating. I should've seen the signs. I just…didn't."

Things were getting too deep. This was more than I wanted to tell him, and I couldn't figure out why I hadn't simply sidestepped the question. I moved away from the window, pulling free of Jake's arms. "I should get going."

"Oh, that's right," he said. "We've got to keep everything light." There was a hint of frustration in his words.

I leaned in and gave him a quick peck on the lips. "I've already broken enough rules for one night."

CHAPTER THIRTEEN

I sat down at my desk Monday morning, logged onto my computer, and opened up the Internet. Pictures flashed in one corner, advertising a diet plan; the weather report was in the other corner. One of the stories of the day was titled, "Tips on dating from NFL stars."

"Yeah, the first tip is to be an NFL star," I muttered. Since I wasn't really interested in what a bunch of jocks said about dating, I opened my e-mail. Most of the messages declared there was some amazing sale I couldn't miss—that's what happens when you indulge in online shopping.

Nadine walked into my office, cup of coffee in hand. "Hey, I'm meeting with a new prospective client at Blue today. I was hoping you'd come with me and help convince Ms. Covington to work with us. I already called in a reservation for noon."

For so long, I'd fought running into Jake, but right now, going to Blue and running into him seemed like the perfect way to break up my day. Avoiding him had made things seem more complicated, anyway. I was perfectly capable of seeing him and not making a big deal about it. Plus, I missed the food. "I'm in."

"Great." Nadine stepped out of my office, then backtracked. "Do you have the stuff on the counters we did for Virginia? I think that's the feel she's going for."

"I'll bring what I have."

Most designers had very specific ideas and hated working with other people. There were power struggles and it was a mess. I'd been part of a few teams that had so many divas I thought I was on a VH1 reality show.

Nadine and I, on the other hand, worked really well together. We bounced ideas off each other and made each other's work stronger. Together we'd made beautiful transformations, one of which was featured in *Modern Homes* magazine. That had brought in enough local clients to keep Patricia happy with our collaborating on projects. For a little while, anyway. With her, that was all you could ask for.

I glanced at my clock, mentally counting down the minutes till lunch.

Hmm. Maybe I'll tell Nadine to meet me there, so I can go early and steal a few minutes with Jake.

• • •

Blue was getting busy, and I decided coming early had been a bad idea.

Mindy spotted me and waved. "Hey, Darby." She glanced down at the list. "Are you going to be meeting with Nadine?"

"Yeah. I'm a little early." I stepped forward so we wouldn't be talking over the rest of the people in the lobby, wondering if I should ask for Jake.

"You want me to tell Jake you're here?" Mindy asked with a smile. Apparently the girl could read minds.

"I'm sure he's busy."

"I'm sure he'll make time for you." Mindy scanned her list of names. "Let me seat this couple and I'll find Jake on my way back."

A few minutes later, Jake walked up front, a big grin on his face. "Finally, she comes to see me." He pulled me into his arms and kissed me. A little deeper than I was expecting.

My rapid pulse pounded through my head, and it took me a moment to catch my breath and compose myself. "I'm actually meeting a client here in about fifteen minutes—not that I didn't come to see you, I did. I just don't think it would be very professional to be seen kissing in the lobby when she and Nadine get here."

"I guess we better go kiss in private instead, then." Jake took my hand and led me to the back of the restaurant. He opened the office door and walked into the tiny room. Stacks of paperwork lined the top of the desk. "So, how's work going?" he asked.

"Kind of hectic. Nadine and I are trying to land a new client. I'm lining up the painters for Mrs. Crabtree, and..." I looked up at him. "You don't really care."

"I care."

"Well, I don't. Not right now, anyway." I threw my arms around his neck and pressed my lips to his. I'd left too fast last night, and I'd regretted it ever since. Jake took no time responding, pulling me close and parting my lips with his. With every stroke of his tongue, the temperature rose. Thoughts got fuzzy. I couldn't catch my breath, but right now breathing seemed totally overrated.

My fingers traveled over the buttons of his shirt, and I was seriously tempted to start undoing them and get a better view of the body underneath. Only I knew that would move things faster than I wanted to go. Plus, we were in an office where someone might interrupt any second, and I had a prospective client to impress.

My chest heaving against his, I reluctantly broke the kiss and groaned at the time. "I should probably get out there," I said. "I don't want to be late."

Jake buried his face in my neck and kissed a burning trail up it and along my jaw. "Should I ride the elevator of our building up and down all night, hoping you'll show?" he asked, his voice husky. "Or should we just plan to meet?"

I ran my hand along his side, surprised at how disappointed I was that I had other plans. Usually I lived for the nights I got to go out. "I actually have a get-together with Stephanie, her fiancé, and his friends tonight. It's probably going to be a long night with a bunch of guys telling boring stories. It'll be extra-awkward because Karl the marriage counselor will be there."

"If you happen to get home early…" Jake nipped at my bottom lip, and a spike of desire shot through my core. "You know where I live."

"I think I remember," I muttered against his lips. I pressed another hard kiss on his mouth, then pulled away before I lost all reason. I straightened my shirt and skirt, making sure they were all in place, and exited the office.

Nadine and a well-dressed woman with short, highlighted hair walked into the restaurant, and I quickened my pace to go meet them. Nadine introduced me to Ms. Barbara Covington and Mindy seated us immediately.

I waited for Ms. Covington to put down her menu to start talking business. "If you don't mind catching me up a bit, what exactly do you want done?" I asked.

"I just got a fat settlement in my divorce and I want to redo *everything*." Barbara swung her hand through the air. "Kick that guy to the curb and use his money to start over again. Men always have expiration dates. I say get rid of them before things go sour."

"That's how Darby feels, too," Nadine said.

Jake chose that moment to arrive at our table. His raised eyebrows made me think he'd overheard the previous comments.

I set my glass off to the side of my plate. "I wouldn't say that. I simply think that people get too wrapped up in this unrealistic view of happy relationships that last forever."

"They don't last forever," Barbara said. "That's why you choose someone with money. *That* lasts longer."

A knot formed in my gut. I looked at Jake, pleading with my eyes for him to not take this conversation the wrong way. I'd be mortified if he thought I cared about a guy's money. Rich or poor didn't have any sway on if I thought a relationship would work out.

"Sorry to interrupt." He held up my keys. "Look familiar? They were on the floor of the office."

The keys jangled together as I took them from him. "Yeah, I probably need those."

Nadine looked at me, her eyes wide and questioning.

"You ladies let me know if you need anything." Jake smiled at me, and the heat still filling his eyes sent a swirl of warmth through me.

"Sorry about that," I said after he walked away, working to turn my thoughts back to the job at hand instead of when I could kiss Jake next. "Where were we?"

We talked color scheme and style, and by the end of the meal, Nadine and I had landed a new client.

A client who made me worry about how people saw me and my anti-relationship stance.

Chapter Fourteen

$\mathcal{I}$ got into Stephanie's car and relaxed on the cushy passenger seat. It seemed like Steph and I hardly got to talk anymore, and I was excited to spend time with her.

Stephanie turned down her radio. "Dish before my phone rings."

"Maybe you should just silence your phone," I said as she pulled out of the parking garage and onto the street. At least Steph had e-mail capability on her phone. It was turning into our main form of communication. "If we were sinking and you could save me or your phone, which would you pick?"

"If I had my phone to call for help, I could save you, my phone, *and* myself."

I shook my head. "Too bad I went under and you can't find me now. Hope you and your phone have a lovely life together."

Steph reached out and took my hand. "I'll never let you go," she said, doing her best Kate Winslet in *Titanic* impression.

I laughed. "Can you believe we watched that movie in the theater over and over?"

"What was it, like, three times?"

"I think it was four. And we cried every time." I shot her a mock-stern look. "Tell anyone that, though, and I'll have to disown you."

Steph laughed, and then her phone's ring broke through. She glanced at the display and sent it to voice mail. "I feel like I'm on the phone all day long, lately, and rarely talking to the people I want to. It'll get better after the wedding, though."

"But then you'll be a busy wife. It's okay. I've only got twenty years before I retire and move in with Drew." I injected my words with sarcasm. "I'm sure it'll fly right by."

"Stop changing the subject. Tell me about seeing Jake today."

"He took me back to his office and we kissed for a few minutes." My lips tingled at the memory of those minutes. Damn, that guy could kiss. I told Steph about my new client and how Nadine had told her she and I had the same values, then threw my hand up to my chest. "*I'm* not a gold digger. I have no desire to marry men and take their money. She even said to never marry poor, because when the relationship fails, you need to get something out of it."

"She's even more cynical than you," Steph said. "And she's found a way to make money off it."

The air vent was blowing right in my eyes, so I turned it away from me. "As my recently shitty luck would have it, Jake came to bring me my keys at the same time Nadine said I felt the same way, so that was nice and uncomfortable."

Stephanie took a sharp turn, and I gripped the handle over the door. "Sorry," she said. "I didn't realize we were so close to the turn." Her GPS spoke in the background, giving the next set of directions. "You like Jake, though, right? So far so good?"

"Yeah, I like him. I have fun when I'm with him, and he's funny, and he does have the smokin'-hot thing going for him. Plus, he's well aware of all my rules. He said something about hanging out tonight, but since I had this thing, I told him I couldn't."

"Hello? Why didn't you invite him to come along?"

I looked at her, mouth hanging open like the idiot I was. "I didn't even think of it." All I would've had to do was ask, and I could've had Jake by my side all night, making everything better… or further complicating it. "It's probably a good thing I didn't invite him. If we start hanging out all the time, someone's going to get clingy. I'm not even saying it won't be me. Then there will be the 'where are you right now' phone calls, and 'why didn't you call me.' I don't want to get into all that."

"But serial monogamy is what you say you want, right? Wasn't that your decision?"

I bit my lip. "That's the theory. It's still in the testing phase."

Steph took another right-hand turn. "You don't want to miss that puppy-love phase, though. It's one of the best parts of a relationship."

"But how do you have that all-about-you period without getting attached?"

"You don't."

I threw my head back and groaned. "I'm starting to think my plan has a few flaws."

"Girl, I've been telling you that for the past year." Stephanie parallel parked in front of a bar called Hot Shots. "Wow, this place looks kind of ghetto. Anthony said it was supposed to be the new, hip nightclub."

The run-down bar had a layer of dust on the windows, as well as neon flashing booze signs hanging half-lit around the place. There was no nightclub about it. Several people sat along the bar, drinking and watching the game. Pool tables lined the other side of the room. The people there didn't look like they cared about name-brand clothes or drinking the fanciest wine in the place— one guy even had his butt-crack hanging out for the world to see. Anthony usually made a point of hitting the newest and hottest places in the city. So where were we?

Anthony, Karl, and Finn, Anthony's other college friend and

groomsman, walked up to Steph and me, and Anthony kissed Steph on the cheek. "I got the place wrong," he said. "This place is Hot Shots. The place I meant to go is called Shots." He wrinkled his nose as he surveyed the place. "It's up north. You want to go?"

Even though he hadn't asked for my opinion, I gave it anyway. "I say we stay. If we drive up there now, we'll spend most of our night in the car." *And I'm not about to drive with Finn and Karl like you would surely suggest.* "We can get some greasy food and shoot some pool. How bad could it be?"

Steph put her arms around Anthony. "I don't really care where I am, as long as I'm with you."

Sure, I was happy for Steph and her lovey-dovey phase, but I occasionally missed the girl who used to tell boys how it was while they cowered in fear.

Anthony gestured to a table in the corner. "Let's have a seat, then." As we walked, he looked at me. "You remember Finn, of course."

I smiled. "Of course. Hey, Finn."

He gave a tiny nod. "Darby."

That was about all you'd get out of Finn. He didn't say much. According to Anthony he used to be a party animal but had mellowed over the years. I wasn't sure if Anthony was qualified to define a party animal.

Anthony pulled out a chair for Stephanie. "And you and Karl just met a week or so ago."

Karl sat across from me. "We did. She told me that I only preach communication to keep getting paid. *I* have a bachelor's degree in psychology and a master's in marriage and family counseling. I teach workshops, yet she apparently knows more about it than I do."

I gritted my teeth, trying to remain calm. "You're twisting my words. I simply expressed my opinion on communication between men and women."

"Yeah, that they shouldn't even try to communicate," Karl said.

Anthony waved his hand in the air, a nervous expression on his face. "Where is our waiter?"

Anthony's obvious discomfort didn't deter me. If Karl thought he could slam me and have the final word, he was mistaken. "What I said was everyone preaches communication like men and women have the *capability* of communicating the same way. My personal belief is that if we realize we'll *never* understand each other, we wouldn't all feel like failures. The part about counselors preaching it to get paid was thrown in for a joke. Obviously counselors don't know anything about that, either." I shot Karl a smile. "And I didn't even need a degree to figure that out."

"Let's go play some pool," Stephanie said. "I'm not that hungry."

"But I'm hungry," Anthony said.

I kept my eyes on Karl. "See right there? Stephanie was trying to subtly change the subject to keep you and me from communicating our bitter feelings toward each other. Since Anthony isn't a woman, he didn't pick up on that. He simply heard her saying she wasn't hungry."

Karl leaned forward. "I'm not that hungry, either. How about instead of passive aggressively jabbing at each other all night, we go play a game of pool. Loser buys dinner."

"You're on." The legs of my chair scraped the floor as I stood. "Would now be a good time to communicate to you that I'm rather good at pool?"

"I personally prefer to show," Karl said. "Sometimes nonverbal communication can be *rather* effective."

"Hmm. Maybe you aren't so bad at the jokes after all."

• • •

Karl and I were pretty evenly matched and had each done our

fair share of smack talking during our game of pool. As he aimed a nearly impossible shot at his last striped ball, I mentally chanted for him to scratch.

"Oh man!" a guy from the next table over yelled. "Eat that!"

The group of guys playing pool next to us had gotten louder and louder. They were now sloppy drunk, hollering and laughing at everything. I tried to ignore them, but one of them kept "accidently rubbing up against me" as he walked by, thinking he was funny and clever, I'm sure.

Karl's ball bounced next to the pocket but didn't go in.

Looking for my best shot, I leaned across the table. For the third time, the guy rubbed up against me, and this time, he'd gotten even more suggestive about it.

I whipped around and shoved him. "Look, buddy, that's enough."

The man stepped up to me, pointing a finger in my face. "Don't you dare shove me, woman!"

I threw my hands up. "What are you going to do, hit me? Will that make you feel cool in front of your friends?"

Karl stepped between the guy and me. "I think you better back off, sir."

"Oh, listen to you, mister hoity-toity. You better keep your woman in line before I have to put her in line for you."

"How about you just go back to your game of pool," Karl said, his voice calm, "and we'll go back to ours?"

The guy's friends had surrounded us, and they egged their friend on, shouting insults at Karl. "Kick his ass," one of them said.

"We're not going to fight," Karl said. "We're just going to settle this like—"

The guy swung. I tried to shout a warning, but it was too late— his fist hit Karl's face with a loud *smack*. Karl stumbled back, into the pool table. I quickly moved to steady him, a mix of disbelief and anger pumping through my veins.

"What do you think about that, hoity-toity?" the guy said.

Karl had a dazed look on his face, as though he wasn't entirely sure what had happened. "That was such a cheap shot," I said. "If I were you, I wouldn't be bragging about it."

Stephanie, Anthony, and Finn showed up at the same time a large guy—the bouncer, I presumed—made an appearance. He stepped between us and the other group and told us to break it up.

"I think we better go," Stephanie said, tugging on my arm.

"I think that would be a good idea," the bouncer said, like we'd been the ones causing all the trouble.

Not wanting things to get any worse, I fought back the urge to yell at the bouncer and all the other idiots, and let Stephanie pull me away.

As our group headed outside, the other group continued hurling insults at us.

"Well, that was fun," Karl said, flinching as he patted the red mark next to his eye.

I took his chin in my hand and tilted his head toward the streetlight so I could get a closer look. "You're going to need to ice it. How bad will it be for you to show up at the office tomorrow with a black eye?"

"It'll probably scare my clients. I suppose I could claim basketball injury or something. I hate lying, though. My office is supposed to be a place of honesty."

"Then just claim you got it playing pool." I stepped back, looking at the guy I couldn't stand at the beginning of the night. Somehow, I'd ended up getting him into a fight—because he'd stuck up for me. "Thanks for…stepping in back there. I thought I'd just humiliate him and he'd back off. Sometimes my temper gets me into trouble."

"No," Karl said, like he was shocked. Then one corner of his mouth twisted up. "I probably shouldn't say this, since I'm all about peacefully working things out, but I guess you've gotta get punched once in your life. It's kind of a rite of passage for a guy."

"I wouldn't suggest making it a habit. Girls aren't as crazy about it as you'd think."

"Darby, do you mind riding home with Karl?" Anthony asked. "I'd like to go with my lovely fiancée. And Finn lives pretty close to us."

Stephanie gave me that what-can-you-do look.

It's not like I had a choice. "Sure." I held my hand out to Karl. "Give me your keys. I think I better drive."

. . .

By the time we got to my place, Karl's eye was nice and puffy. "How far away do you live?"

"It's about another forty minutes north."

"I think you should come up and ice your eye. See if you can get the swelling down before driving home." I pulled the keys out of the ignition. "Besides, I feel like I owe you. I still think I would've won our game of pool"—I flashed him a smile to let him know I was joking around—"but you didn't get to eat, and I'm sure you're hungry."

I headed through the lobby of the building with Karl. I decided to stop at the vending machine and grab a couple of sodas. I needed some caffeine. "What do you want?"

"I'll take a Pepsi," Karl said.

I bought a Pepsi for him and a Mountain Dew for myself, then we got on the elevator. I held my cold can of Mountain Dew on Karl's eye. "Here, this should help." Metal and cold worked wonders on swelling.

The doors of the elevator opened back up and Jake stepped inside. Of course.

"Don't worry," I said as the elevator lifted. "I didn't punch him that hard."

Karl laughed. "After everything you put me through tonight,

at least let me keep my dignity."

"But if you don't have any dignity, how can I let you keep it?"

"I thought we were at peace now."

"Sorry. It might take me a few days to switch gears to being nice to you." The elevator stopped, opening up on my floor. "This is me."

Karl walked into the hall. I stuck my hand over the elevator door so it wouldn't shut, then twisted back to Jake. "Long story. The short version is it's not as bad as it looks."

"You have my number," Jake said. "And you know where I live."

I smiled at him. "I *think* I remember." I let go of the door and blew Jake a kiss good-bye as my view of him narrowed.

As soon as Karl and I got to my apartment, I pointed him to the couch. "Have a seat and I'll get you some ice. The can probably isn't cold enough anymore." I headed to the fridge and dug out a bag of frozen peas, then walked over to the couch and handed it to him. "Peas do a good job because they conform."

"You have lots of experience in this kind of thing?"

"Too much. Combination of breaking in a horse and having a boyfriend who liked to get into fights."

Karl sat there, holding the bag of peas on his face. "Who could've seen this coming after our disastrous date? You're actually pretty nice when you want to be."

"Don't tell anyone. I've got to keep up my reputation."

Karl smiled, then winced. "I know it wouldn't have solved anything, but I kind of wish I would've at least taken a swing at the guy."

"Then you'd just have cut-up knuckles to go with your busted eye." I leaned back on my couch. "I would've really liked to see that guy go down, though. Freakin' jackhole."

Twenty minutes later, the swelling had lessened, the ibuprofen had kicked in, and we'd filled up on grilled-cheese sandwiches.

Karl decided he was good to drive home, so we said our good-byes and I sent him on his way.

What a night.

I picked up the bag of soggy peas. *Now this brings back some memories...*

Beauty and the Beast Case Study: Boone/The Beast
My Age: 19

I started college with the feeling that no matter who I met, he'd never be as good as Gil. In a lot of ways, this was true. Still, there comes a point when you've got to try to move on.

Boone was in one of my study groups sophomore year. The first time I met him, I wouldn't have used the words *cute, hot,* or any other flattering word to describe him. He had a big nose and out-of-control, dark hair that stuck in all directions. But there was something about him—the whole tortured-artist thing—that drew me in.

We started flirting and he seemed better-looking every time I saw him. He took me to his place and showed me his paintings. His artwork had this deep, disturbing quality. The nightmare images displayed pain, anger, and suffering. Simply looking at them made me feel a mix of emotions, and I thought that was powerful.

After dropping a few hints that I was into him, I still couldn't tell how he felt about me. So one night when we were studying, I finally got the courage to say something. "Boone, if I told you I was interested in being more than friends, how would you take that?"

He stared at me like I'd asked him to travel to the moon with me.

My cheeks blazed. "Forget it." I started gathering my books, desperate to get away from the humiliation.

Boone put his hand on my wrist. "Why would *you* like *me*? You're really pretty. And smart. And I'm just...not those things."

"You don't give yourself enough credit. I think you're funny, I like hanging out with you, and your artwork is amazing."

He slowly leaned in and we shared an awkward, all-open-mouth first kiss. It got better over time. Before long, we went everywhere together. But the more time I spent with him, the more I saw him lose his temper. When his painting wasn't going well, he'd throw paintbrushes and yell; he had several arguments with his roommates; his road rage was bad enough I started driving everywhere we went. Then he'd always calm down and go back to the guy I knew.

He began calling all the time to "check in." Being somewhere he didn't think I should be started an argument. If I ever talked to another guy at a party, on campus, or in class, he'd go off about it. He started throwing punches at other guys on a regular basis. Eventually, the fight would be broken up. Afterward, we'd go back to his or my place and I'd ice his bruises, soak his cuts, and he'd tell me that he couldn't stand the thought of losing me. I felt like if I just stuck by his side, he'd see that I cared about him, and he'd stop fighting everyone else.

Instead of getting better, it got worse.

"Did you drink all of the juice?" Boone asked one day while we were at his apartment.

I looked up from my book. "No. I haven't touched the juice. Didn't you finish it off yesterday?"

"I think I would've remembered that. You think I'm stupid?"

I stood and hugged my book to my chest. "I'm not going to sit here and let you yell at me. I don't deserve to be treated like that."

"There you go, overreacting like you always do. I swear, you make every little thing into a big deal."

"I think you yelling at me over juice *is* a big deal." Every time I said anything, he acted like I was completely crazy. Like I was some psycho chick who was irrational. The guy who yelled at me over juice insisted *I* was irrational. "I'm going home. Call me when you decide to stop being a jerk."

I opened the door, but he slammed it closed from behind me and put his foot in the way, so I couldn't pull it open again. I twisted to face him. "Come on, Boone. Move so I can go."

"You leave, you leave for good."

I stared at him, my heart racing. "I guess this is good-bye forever, then."

He punched the door and I flinched, thinking I was next. He let out a stream of profanities, then stormed back to his room.

The next weekend I was at a party with Stephanie, talking to Carlos, who lived in our same building. I saw Boone walk in and immediately panicked. He met my gaze from across the room and started toward us. My pulse sped up with each step that brought him closer.

"Who's this?" he asked, glaring at Carlos.

"He's just a friend," I said.

Boone stepped closer to Carlos, getting in his face. "Why are you all over my girlfriend?"

"Calm down, dude," Carlos said. "Darby and I are just talking."

"That's the problem. You need to stop."

I tried to sound as firm as I could. "*You* need to stop, Boone. I'm not your girlfriend anymore, and if you're going to be like this, you need to leave."

Boone took a few steps away from us and I let out a shaky breath.

Carlos put his hand on my shoulder. "You okay?"

Boone glanced back, saw the contact, and went crazy. He charged Carlos, throwing wild fists through the air. Unfortunately for Boone, he finally picked on someone too big. Carlos's main hobby was working out—at a boxing gym—and Boone was no match. It took several people to break up the fight, and by the time they did, Boone's nose was gushing blood, and I suspected he'd have a black eye, if not two.

I stared at him, thinking that he'd gotten uglier and uglier over the past few months. And yeah, that does kind of happen in *Beauty and the Beast*, too. All that time spent waiting for the prince, and then he turns human and you think, man, he was cuter as an animal. Who knew you'd be asking for bestiality in the end?

My grandma always hated the story, claiming it was ridiculous that a pretty girl would fall for a beast. It used to be one of my favorites, though—one of those true-love-will-fix-anything stories. Belle was so patient and overlooked his temper, even ignoring the fact that he almost killed her dad and imprisoned her. I'm not sure it's a good idea to make girls think they can heal a guy with love and patience, though. Because most guys don't ever change. At least in the movie, the beast really does learn to love, and his mean streak is broken. I don't know if Boone ever had his mean streak broken, but I knew I couldn't stick around to find out.

Time Wasted: Three and a half months

Lessons Learned:

Getting mad once in a while is normal. Flying off the handle over every little thing is a sign to run.

No aggressive or overly jealous guys.

No letting a guy walk all over you.

You can't fix people. They have to learn to fix themselves.

CHAPTER FIFTEEN

Unable to concentrate on work, I sat at my desk, drumming my fingers along the top of it. I imagined Jake was starting to wonder what he'd gotten himself into with me. I probably shouldn't have made that joke about punching Karl. Especially since he'd heard the story about me slapping Ralph. But he got that I was kidding, right? I'd even blown him a kiss to show him he was still the guy for me. I mean, if I were choosing guys. Which I…wasn't? No. Jake and I were free agents, keeping everything light. Still, I wanted to give him a full explanation. If the tables were reversed, I know I'd want one.

I waited until I was sure Jake would be awake and called his cell. The call rolled to voice mail, so I cleared my throat, readying myself to leave a message. "Hey, it's me." I hated it when people said that. Most of the time I didn't know who it was until halfway through the message. "I guess that's pretty arrogant, assuming you'll recognize my voice. Or maybe I'm already programmed into your phone. Not that I'm saying…" I wanted to start over. Be calm and collected. "Anyway, it's Darby. Who else would leave you a rambling message without ever getting to the point? The point is give me a call. If you want to. Last night was crazy, and I just wanted to tell you that—"

A loud beep cut me off.

Awesome. I left a drunken message without the benefit of actually being drunk.

Calling back to finish seemed extra desperate. Especially if he'd been screening me on purpose.

I tossed my phone on my desk and ran my hands over my face. "Urgh. This is why I don't do relationships."

My phone chirped and I picked it back up. A text from an unfamiliar number. When I opened it, I saw a picture of Karl. Underneath his eye was a line of purple and red. At least it wasn't swollen shut.

THOUGHT YOU'D ENJOY THIS. EVERYONE AT THE OFFICE SURE IS. THEY'RE ALL SO CONFUSED WHEN I SAY I GOT IT PLAYING POOL. THEY SEEM TO LIKE "GOT INTO A BAR BRAWL BECAUSE OF A GIRL" MUCH BETTER.

My fingers flew over my keypad.

I THINK IT'S ONLY CONSIDERED A BRAWL IF TWO PEOPLE ARE INVOLVED. YOU WERE MORE LIKE A PUNCHING BAG FOR A DRUNK GUY BECAUSE OF A GIRL.

I hit send, then set down my phone and opened up my files for Mrs. Crabtree. Another chirp caught my attention. Karl had sent a message back.

YEAH, I LIKE MY VERSION BETTER. I GUESS YOU AND I JUST COMMUNICATE DIFFERENTLY.

I laughed and then sent another message:

I SWEAR I HEARD THIS REALLY SMART PERSON SAY THAT MEN AND WOMEN COULDN'T COMMUNICATE VERY WELL… I BETTER GET TO WORK. I'M SURE I'LL BE SEEING YOU AROUND.

I was surprised how much I'd ended up liking Karl by the end of last night. While I knew Stephanie had initially set us up hoping for a romance, that kind of spark wasn't there. But I thought we might get to be friends eventually. It'd be nice to have him to talk to at all of Anthony and Stephanie's upcoming wedding events. And even though I still wasn't totally sold on the marriage counseling thing, he did see a lot of different types of couples, and it gave me hope that he thought Anthony and Stephanie would make it. Regardless of my jaded stance on forever love, I really wanted them to be one of those couples who defied the odds.

And if they can make it... I thought of Jake, the way I seemed to be doing more often than not lately. I could feel a glimmer of hope trying to wedge its way into my heart, whispering that maybe this time, it could actually be different.

Don't do it. Hope only leads to depression.

But it was already giving me that warm, light feeling. Steph was right. I didn't want to miss the puppy-love phase.

I wanted to dive in and enjoy it.

Patricia charged into my office, dousing all the happy vibes with her stern expression. "Did you and Nadine land that account yesterday?"

"Yes."

"Then where's the contract? I don't have it yet."

I was pretty sure Nadine had it, but not 100 percent sure, so this was one of those lose-lose moments, where no matter what I said, it made me look like I didn't know what was going on. "I'll get right on it."

She stared at me for long enough that it became uncomfortable, then sighed in that I-work-with-idiots way. I had a feeling that this was going to be a long day.

• • •

I shifted my bag of groceries to the other hand and dug through my purse to get my ringing phone. I glanced at the display. *Jake.*

"You just wanted to tell me what?" Jake said when I answered.

"Huh?" I asked.

"Your message. It cut out."

I readjusted my groceries and my cell phone slipped from my shoulder and clattered to the floor. Instead of dropping everything, I set my groceries in front of my door and picked my phone back up, relieved to see my case and screen were still intact. "Jake?"

"Yeah."

"Sorry, I dropped my phone. Anyway, I guess I owe you a story. What are you doing tonight?" Work was extra crappy today, and I wanted nothing more than to kick back with Jake and forget about everything else for a while.

"Things are crazy here at Blue, so I'll be working even later than usual."

I wasn't sure if he was brushing me off. "Okay. Well, good luck with that."

A loud banging noise came across the line, accompanied by yelling. Someone next to Jake wasn't happy with whatever was going on. "Another problem just came up. I've gotta go."

"Okay, I'll talk to you later, then." I hung up and frowned at my groceries. It seemed like I'd made a big deal about a relationship that wasn't even happening. My heart sank. Had I read him wrong? He did sound busy, and maybe that was all it was. I was just taking it harder because of the stress at work—that had to be it.

Stupid hope. I knew it'd bite me in the butt if I let it slip in.

I unlocked my door and picked up my bag. I wouldn't let myself start analyzing or stare at the phone, waiting for him to call. I'd invited him to hang out, and he'd declined.

Ball's in his court now.

• • •

First thing Wednesday morning, Nadine and I headed to Barbara Covington's house to start our new project. Nadine pulled her car up in front of the wrought-iron gate and glanced at the house. "Whoa."

"Whoa is right," I said. "So that's what fifteen thousand square feet looks like. I think living all by yourself in a house that big would just accentuate the lonely."

"No kidding." Nadine rolled down her window and announced that we were here to see Ms. Covington. A moment later, the gate swung open and Nadine drove through. "I've been chatting with a nice guy online, and I think we might meet up this weekend. I'm telling you, the Help From Cupid site is really good. You'd be surprised by how many good-looking eligible men you find."

She'd wanted me to join this online dating site with her a few months ago. The last guy she had met had been close to a perfect match, but after a couple of months things fizzled, so she was trying again. Which always led to her wanting me to try again, too. "Come on," she said, pulling her car up to the house. "When's the last time you went on a date that wasn't awful?"

"Sunday, actually."

Nadine whipped her head toward me. "You're dating someone? Dish."

"I'm not really dating him. It's Jake."

"I knew it! I knew there was something going on between you two."

I leaned back in my seat and sighed. "I'm not sure if anything's going on between us anymore. I'm...I'm not sure what we're doing." He hadn't called, and I was starting to think our whatever was already over. Which sucked, not only because I now felt the need to avoid Blue, but also because I really had enjoyed spending time with him.

Moving on. "Let's go see what we've got to work with."

Ms. Covington ushered Nadine and me inside. The place looked like no one lived there, the walls and floors completely bare. Still, the bare bones were beautiful: vaulted ceilings, a staircase that twisted up to the top floor, and giant windows facing the mountains.

"I just told them to get rid of all of it," Barbara said as she gave us the tour. "Let him deal with that stuffy old furniture. I know this little place we should go for lunch, and then I'll swing you by my friend's house and show you some of the things she's done that I love."

We followed Barbara to her three-car garage and got into her BMW 7-series. The entire drive, Barbara talked. About redecorating; about starting over; about how her husband was already looking for a new, younger model. "You see, in my first marriage, I was a fool for the man. He had no money, but I thought our love would be enough. When our daughter was two, I found out he'd been unfaithful. After that, I knew I needed a way to support myself and my daughter…"

And on she went about her other husbands all through lunch, and all while we toured her friend's place. She hadn't loved husband number two, but he was wealthy; three she'd had lukewarm feelings for—he was even wealthier; and number four was a fairy-tale beginning, including being flown to other countries.

By the time I'd heard all about her many men, I felt like I never wanted to deal with one again. If I was pessimistic, Barbara was the eternal pessimist. Yet she managed to find optimism in her pessimism. Her philosophy seemed to be: "If life hands you husbands who don't work out, make millionaire-ade."

At the end of the day, as Nadine and I drove away from Barbara's, I said, "Take it back."

Nadine furrowed her brow. "Take what back?"

"That I'm anything like Barbara. That's not my philosophy on love. It's so depressing."

"Your philosophy is pretty depressing, too. At least she makes money off it."

"You're jumping on the gold-digger idea now?"

Nadine laughed. "No. I don't really think she's as happy and chipper as she claims. She just talks like that to make it seem like she's in control. No one wants to feel like they don't have power." She pulled onto the freeway. "It's like those people who claim they're anti-marriage because they really want to get married, but no one's asked them."

I groaned. "This is getting worse and worse."

"I'm not talking about you," Nadine said. "You had your chance to get married and you turned it down. Twice."

"Not twice."

"I bet he would've asked if you would've—"

"I don't want to talk about it." I let out a long breath. "All those stories Barbara told, that's why I don't want to get married. I'm wondering if she had them all fooled. They all thought she loved them, but she just loved their money."

"Now we get to love their money, too. This project's going to be hard, but we'll be getting fat commissions."

My phone rang. I dug it out and looked at the display. It was Jake.

I'd wanted to talk to him so badly for three days, but after spending the afternoon with Barbara, I was grouchy and back to feeling like relationships were all crap. *If I talk to him right now, there's a good chance I'll screw up everything.*

Not willing to risk it, I sent the call to voice mail. Nadine's comment about my missed chances at marriage dug at me, my heart squeezing as I thought about how I'd let hope seep in, only to be crushed again.

No hope was sad, but having it was dangerous. I suppose the real question was would I be better or worse off in the end?

Chapter Sixteen

As I drove back to Barbara's house on Thursday morning, I stuck in my earpiece and called Jake. All he'd said in his message last night was, "Give me a call," so I decided to follow his instructions and see what happened.

"What time should I pick you up for dinner?"

I glanced at my phone to make sure I'd called Jake—yep. "I think you're confused. This is Darby."

"I know who it is. So what time works for you?"

"You just sounded like you'd already made plans, and I thought you must not realize it was me."

"I did already make plans," Jake said. "All you have to do is say yes."

I found myself smiling, the stirrings of butterflies low in my stomach. "I'm free anytime after six."

"Six thirty it is."

Several hours later, I was thinking I'd never survive the day, much less make it to six thirty. *Of all the days I could've chosen to break in my new gray heels, why'd it have to be today?*

We were already on our sixth furniture store, and Nadine and

I could hardly keep up with Barbara. The woman could win a gold medal in shopping. When she'd temporarily run out of things to say about her husbands, she'd asked Nadine and me about our love lives. When neither of us had much to say on the subject, she pursed her lips and studied us. "Hmm. Two pretty, smart girls who have never been married? I was on my second marriage by your age. I'll tell you what's wrong—you're too intimidating to men. Do you rent or own?"

"Own," Nadine said.

"I own, too," I said.

Barbara frowned. For some reason it felt like we were getting scolded for being independent and good at our jobs. "Guys want a girl they can take care of. I read this book about it between numbers two and three…" Barbara went on to talk about what guys wanted in a domestic partner. Apparently, just because I wore a dress and heels sometimes didn't make me feminine enough. I needed to act more desperate. To show a guy how much I needed him.

If I had to act needy and helpless to keep a guy, then I'd rather not have one. Nadine, on the other hand, was soaking it all in. In fact, while Barbara asked the salesman a question, Nadine got out her phone and made notes on all the books Barbara had suggested.

I peeked over her shoulder as she put the information into her phone. "You're not seriously going to read those, are you?"

Nadine shrugged. "What's the harm in seeing what they say? I don't want to settle for anyone, and I'm not into marrying only for money, but I would like to get married. I've only got so long before my opportune time for having babies runs out. I've always wanted kids."

After seeing what having kids could do to a relationship, I didn't know why anyone had more than one.

"Did you two see this sofa?" Barbara said. "It's simply hideous!"

My aching feet protested at the thought of walking around

again. Money does talk, though—louder than feet—so I forced myself to shake it off and go see the hideous couch.

And it *was* hideous. The diamond-and-square, brown-and-orange print made me feel like I was having a seizure.

"Suddenly antique is taking on a horrible meaning." Barbara looped her elbow through mine. "I know a place just up the street. Let's go check it out."

Some clients looked at a few samples and told you to do whatever; others wanted to be involved. Barbara wanted to oversee *everything*. Already, she was getting involved not only with the decorating, but also our personal lives.

"I'm having this function next weekend and you two must come," Barbara said as we charged up the sidewalk. "You might have to settle for an older gentleman, but they have money and they will spoil you rotten. Of course if you want younger, some of my exes have handsome sons…"

As she rattled on and on, I felt myself growing more and more cynical.

• • •

Jake hadn't specified a location, so I'd thrown on a black-sequined top and a pair of dark dressy jeans. Four- to five-inch heels were what I wore most days and I'd never had a problem before. But after all day shopping with Barbara, the thought of having to walk again—in heels of any kind—exhausted me. So I went with my black ballet flats.

I dropped onto my couch and watched TV until there was a knock on the door.

After checking it was Jake, I opened the door and leaned against the frame. "Hey, you're not planning on going dancing or anything crazy like that, are you?"

"I'm open," Jake said. "Why? Where do you want to go?"

"Somewhere we won't have to walk much. I wore new shoes

today and my client could outshop anyone. I'm exhausted."

"I just got groceries. I'll whip us up something to eat and we'll stay in."

"I don't want you to have to go to all that trouble," I said. "It's not like I can't walk. I just don't want to be on my feet all night."

"It's no trouble. In fact, it'll be nice. I've been going all day." Jake extended his hand. "You ready?"

Jake and I made the short journey up to his place. Admittedly, his living in my same building was a perk tonight.

He opened the fridge and stared inside. "How does lemon-pepper chicken sound?"

"Sounds amazing." I leaned back against the island counter as he pulled out the ingredients. "What do you need me to do?"

"Just keep me company." Within a few minutes, the lemony scent of the grilling chicken filled the air, making my mouth water. Jake washed his hands then turned to me. "So, about the guy in the elevator the other night…?"

"I practically forgot about that." I wondered how Karl's eye was shaping up. Probably more yellow than purple. "It seems like ages ago."

"I was worried that's why you were avoiding me."

"I wasn't avoiding you, I swear. Everything's been crazy lately." I put more of my weight on the counter and crossed my ankles. I told him about ending up in the wrong bar, and as I gave the recap of the pool game gone wrong, the muscles along Jake's jaw tensed.

"What happened to the other guy?" he asked. "At least tell me they threw him out."

"I think they were regulars, because the bouncer picked them over us."

Jake shook his head. "I would've taken his head off for something like that." The protective way he said it made my heart skip a couple of beats.

"Believe me, I wanted to. Anyway, Karl's eye was swelling

pretty badly, and since he lives in north Boulder, I had him come up to ice his eye. The guy can actually be pretty funny when he wants to be."

Jake braced his hands on the island on either side of me. "Sounds like I have some competition. I better step up my game."

I placed my hand on his bicep and brushed my thumb across the curve of it. "I'm your only competition."

He cocked his head, confusion creasing his features. "You're my competition to win you over?"

"Yep. Me and all my issues. And the exes who gave me issues. Oh, and Ms. Barbara Covington."

Jake's eyebrows shot up. "This is getting more interesting by the second."

"She's my new client—the one I was with at Blue on Monday. She's had four husbands and all she talks about is how horrible the marriages were."

"So let me guess, she's telling you that you should never get married."

"Actually, she told me I should find a wealthy man and marry him so that when it ends, I can console myself with the finer things in life. I told her that in my experience, men like that are either workaholics who ignore you or rich, lazy pricks." I ran my hand up his arm and placed it on the side of his neck. "She suggested I go for the workaholic so I can take a lover."

"Nice," he said, and I could feel his deep voice vibrate through my palm.

"She also has this strange philosophy about how a woman should reel in a man." I shook my head. "I don't really want to get into it, because just thinking about it makes me angry." I looked into his blue eyes—they were pale tonight, no hint of the green I saw the other day.

Then it hit me. Maybe Barbara was right. "Do you think I'm some damsel in distress who needs a big strong man to save me?

Is that the appeal of this…?" I motioned between us.

Jake laughed. "Are you serious?"

"Every time I'm around you, I'm a complete mess. It's the only explanation for why you keep asking me out. You think I need rescuing."

Jake closed the gap between us, pinning me against the counter. His eyes locked onto mine. "I like you, Darby. *That's* why I keep asking you out. You act tough—and I'm not saying you're not—but you've also got a kind heart. You're funny. And instead of playing games, you tell me what you're thinking."

He leaned down and lightly pressed his lips against mine. "And you're really sexy." He ran his tongue along my bottom lip, his weight holding me in place. My knees went weak and a whole lot of fire, fire, fire wound through every inch of my body.

"I like you, too," I said, my voice coming out breathy. "But I always choose the wrong guys. *Always.* Trust me, I've studied all my relationships in and out, and no matter how much I learn, I still choose wrong."

Jake put his hand on my hip, like he had done so many times before, and slid his thumb between my shirt and pants, brushing the skin underneath. "I guess it's a good thing I chose you, then."

The way he was looking at me made it hard to breathe. Thinking clearly wasn't really possible with his lips so close to mine either. So instead of trying to come up with something to say, I closed the gap and kissed him. I didn't hold back, putting all the overwhelming emotions swirling through me into the kiss.

He made a low sound in the back of his throat, and it seemed to take him great effort to pull away. He exhaled, then turned to the stove and flipped the chicken.

I walked up behind him, put my arms around him, and leaned my head on his strong back. "Sweet talk *and* a guy who knows how to cook? A girl could get used to this."

CHAPTER SEVENTEEN

Stephanie had shown up at my office on Friday and announced we were going to Blue for our weekly wedding planning session so she could meet "this Jake guy." When I couldn't talk her out of it, I'd reminded her that he and I were keeping things light, no matter what she thought of him. The fact that she'd rolled her eyes and said, *Yeah, I've heard the speech. Numerous times*, didn't give me a whole lot of confidence in how this lunch was about to go down.

After Mindy seated us, Stephanie shook her head, her disappointed expression aimed at me. "I can't believe you didn't ask for him."

I placed my napkin on my lap. "I'm not going to march in unannounced and demand to see him. Mindy will tell him I'm here, and he'll come over if he gets a chance."

Stephanie picked up her phone when it rang. To my surprise, she sent the call to voice mail. I watched her turn it off and toss it in her purse. "Whatever it is, it can wait."

"If reaching over the table and checking your temperature wouldn't knock over our water glasses, I'd do it."

"I feel like I never see you anymore. Our short e-mails and

texts just aren't enough." Stephanie placed her purse in the seat next to her. "By the way, Karl called and got your number. I hope that was okay."

"Yeah, it's cool. He sent me a picture of his black eye and we made jokes back and forth. He's actually pretty funny."

Stephanie leaned in. "You two aren't...starting something?"

"No. Nothing like that. But we don't hate each other anymore."

"I never know with your philosophy on relationships..."

Jake neared the table. He smiled at me and I smiled back, my heart skipping a couple beats.

"...maybe you're juggling half the guys in the city and you just forgot to tell me," Stephanie finished.

My smile faded. I wasn't sure what to say. Every damn time he came around, someone said something about me that I wished they hadn't.

"I guess I should just feel lucky I'm one of them," Jake said from behind Steph, causing her to jump.

That made my smile reappear. "Stephanie, I'd like you to meet Jake. Jake, my best friend, Stephanie."

Stephanie twisted toward him. "That part about her juggling lots of guys was a joke. She's really not."

Jake sat next to me and draped his arm over my shoulders. "I know you have a no-kissing policy in front of clients. What're the rules about kissing in front of your friends?"

I leaned in and pressed my lips against his. "I don't have rules about *everything*."

Jake shot me a skeptical glance, then turned his attention to Stephanie. "I hear you're getting married soon."

"In five weeks and one day." That faraway, dreamy gleam entered her eye. "I can't wait." She sighed, then snapped out of it and pointed a finger at me. "I don't want to hear it."

I held my hands up. "I wasn't going to say anything about your very specific countdown."

Sarah walked over, pen and pad out.

"I guess that's my cue." Jake kissed my cheek. He dragged his nose across my skin, and when he spoke, his lips brushed my ear. "If you get a chance, come back to my office and say goodbye. Otherwise, I suppose I'll just have to wait until you're done juggling all your other guys."

My skin was now covered in goose bumps. "I'll try to squeeze you in. It was Jack, right?"

He flashed me a mischievous smile. "You can call me whatever you like, as long as you call me."

If anyone but Stephanie was with me, I might've tried to play it cool. Instead I watched him walk away, grinning like an idiot.

After Sarah took our order, Stephanie leaned in. "Wow, Darby. He's really hot."

"I told you he was."

"Yeah, but, dang. And he's nice, and so all about you. How are you not in love with him already?"

Just the mention of the word *love* set off alarms, making my entire body tense up. I wasn't in love with Jake, but I was starting to tip toward falling, and while it terrified me, there was a thrill hidden underneath the fear as well. If I said that, though, I'd never hear the end of it, so I shrugged and played it off. "I guess I know better. The only thing I've ever gotten from falling fast and hard is hurt."

"I don't want you to ruin things with him because of all your rules."

I ran my fingers along the edge of the table. Keeping things from Stephanie never worked. We'd been friends too long and I needed to talk to her if I was really letting go—even if it was only a little bit. "I'm starting to rethink my rules. It's not like they've worked out for me so well."

A huge grin lit up Stephanie's face. "Are you saying that—"

"No," I said, holding up a stop-right-there hand. "I'm not

disregarding them all. I did that for Porter, remember? I'm saying *some* of my rules I'm breaking—like letting it slide that Jake lives in my building and has a classic car and works at my favorite restaurant. I'm going to let myself enjoy the beginning, exciting part of our relationship. But some things, like the not getting too serious, are still firmly in place."

Stephanie stuck out her lips, shifting them one way then the other. "I guess it's better than nothing." She tapped her fingers on the table, then glanced at her purse, and her fingers started moving faster.

"You can check it if you want to."

Stephanie looked back up at me. "I wasn't… I just worry that Anthony might be trying to get ahold of me."

"It's okay. Unlike you, I've accepted you the way you are. I'm done trying to change you."

Steph reached for her purse. Halfway there, she dropped her hand. "No. You know what? If it's important, it'll be there in an hour." She looked at me, a smug expression on her face. "See, people change. One small victory at a time."

Jake walked into my line of sight. He said something to Chad, then glanced over at me. My instincts told me to look away and play it cool. Jake smiled at me, though, and I smiled back.

Maybe Stephanie was right. I wasn't going to change my entire philosophy, but I was going to learn to be open to the possibility of a good relationship, even knowing it wasn't going to last forever. Like she said, one small victory at a time.

Chapter Eighteen

It's pretty impressive what you can get done when you have a Friday night to yourself. I ran three miles, mopped my floors, put the finishing touches on a couple of proposals, and took a trip to the bookstore. Luckily, I didn't run into an old boyfriend or have to hide in the erotica section.

What's devastating about getting so much done on a Friday night, is it makes you feel like a loser. The rest of the world was out there celebrating the start of the weekend, while I sat by myself on my couch, wondering what I should do next.

Admittedly, I started to feel the tiniest bit sorry for myself. I know, it's not very Independent Woman thinking of me. It's not like I *needed* a guy. But someone to hang out with would be nice.

Nadine was with her Help From Cupid matchup, Steph and Anthony were having dinner with Steph's parents, and Jake was working.

I guess I should've gone to the ranch for the night.

It's too late now. Mom will be getting ready for bed by the time I show up.

I'm not much of a phone-talker, but when I get bored enough,

I start calling everyone I know to say hi. Half the time I regret it around minute three and then spend the rest of the time trying to figure out how to nicely end the call.

If I was going to shoot the breeze with someone, though, Drew was my first choice. I picked up my phone and dialed his number. After four rings, it rolled over to his voice mail. Mom didn't answer, either. I scrolled up and down through my contacts—mostly work associates. Then I saw Jake's name. Calling for no reason was such a relationship-y thing.

Don't do it.

I set my phone down on my coffee table and sat back on my couch. Looking for something to keep me busy, I picked up the remote and searched through the onscreen guide. Three times.

I had a staring contest with my phone for about a minute— that thing didn't blink once. I picked it off the coffee table, scrolled down to Jake's number, and pushed the call button.

What am I going to say if he picks up?

Back in high school, this was the point I would've realized my mistake and hung up; nowadays, technology didn't let you chicken out. Already, my number was going to be on his phone, showing the exact time I called.

What am I going to say if it goes to voice mail?

"Hey, gorgeous," Jake said.

My heart went all fluttery on me. "Hey. Are you busy right now?"

I smacked my forehead with the palm of my hand. *Of course he's busy, stupid. He's at work.*

"For you, I'm sure I can find a few minutes."

The pressure to come up with something to say sent me into panic mode. Work was boring, I hadn't done anything today worth mentioning, and my mind scrambled for something—anything— to say to him.

"Guess who came into Blue tonight for dinner," Jake said.

"If I missed Christian Bale, I'm going to be so upset."

He laughed. "Close. The Crabtrees. Mrs. Crabtree asked about you, so I told her you'd finally broken down and gone out with me. She hugged me, then lectured me on being a gentleman and treating you right. She's surprisingly scary for an older lady."

Picturing Mrs. Crabtree and Jake having that conversation made me smile. "It's nice to know she's got my back."

"Yeah, with those bar fights you get into, you need all the extra help you can get."

And just like that, we eased into an effortless conversation that surpassed my normal three-minute mark.

• • •

When my phone rang Saturday morning, I fumbled around for a few minutes before finding it. *Drew.*

I hit the accept button and put the phone up to my ear. "You better be dying."

"Good morning to you, too," Drew said, his voice way too chipper. "I'm coming down. Now, get out of bed. You're sleeping the day away."

I squinted at my alarm clock until the red digits sharpened enough I could read them. "Eight o' clock is not sleeping the day away."

"I've been up for two hours. I've checked on the horses, made sure the newborn calves have sucked, and doctored a few cows. What've you done?"

"I've been coming up with a plan to power the world using smiles and laughter," I said. "Beat that."

"One of the calves crapped on me when I picked him up and took him to the barn, and I thought that was a good bullshit story. But I think yours is even more full of crap."

I laughed. "I'm too tired to come up with a response to that. I'm sure I'll think of a good one by the time you get here."

"Okay. It'll probably be about ten."

"See you in a while, then." I hung up and put a pillow over my head, hoping to catch a few more minutes of sleep before having to start my day.

By the time Drew made it down, I was not only ready, but also feeling ahead of the game thanks to all the work I'd done last night. As he and I settled onto the couch, I asked, "Isn't this the second Saturday in a row you've spent with the redhead?"

"Her name is Lisa, and yes it is." He kicked off his shoes and stuck his feet on my coffee table. I'd given up on asking him not to. "We actually met in Broomfield on Wednesday, too. And we've been talking on the phone."

"You hate talking on the phone."

Drew shrugged. "I usually do." A slow smile spread across his face. "But I've been talking to Lisa for at least an hour every night."

"Does Michelle know she's already been replaced?"

"Michelle went a little crazy. She kept coming to the house and yelling at me. She told me I was a loser who still lived at home and went on and on about how stupid I was. So then I was like, 'If I'm a loser, why do you want me?' Then she cried and begged me to take her back." Drew shook his head. "Finally I just had to tell her, making sure I jabbed hard enough for her to get the point, that we were over and there was no chance of ever getting back together. Then she went all *Fatal Attraction* on me."

"She boiled your bunny?"

"She keyed my truck."

I shook my head. "You sure know how to pick them."

"Lisa's different, though."

"Until you dump her and you learn how crazy she really is." If there was a mentally unstable girl, Drew was drawn to her. For about two to three months.

"She won't. In fact, she'll probably dump *me*, and I'll be the one who calls her at all hours of the day, begging for a second chance." Drew leaned forward, propping his forearms on his knees. "So what's going on with you?"

"I'm kind of dating this guy. Keeping it light, that kind of thing. Oh, and I got one of Anthony's friends punched in the face while we were at a bar."

"And you say I'm trouble." Drew nudged me with his elbow. "Tell me about the fight. You get any hits in?"

"I wish." I told Drew the story, then grabbed my phone off the table and showed him the picture of Karl's black eye. "His job is about peacefully resolving things, and he had to walk in looking like this."

"But this isn't the guy you're dating?"

I shook my head. "No, this guy's just a… I guess he's a friend now."

"So when do I get to meet your boyfriend? I've got to see if he's good enough. That's a brother's job, you know."

I set my phone down. "One, he's not my boyfriend. And two, you and Devin seem to think it's your job to torture my boyfriends."

"That's 'cause you always date city boys who can't take a joke. I don't think you've had a decent boyfriend yet. Except Gil, and that was forever ago."

"Thanks for rubbing it in, jerkface." I scooted to the edge of the couch. "Let's go get something to eat, I'm starving."

Drew took his feet off my coffee table and slipped on his shoes. "After, let's go to the mall and you can help me pick out a shirt. Just nothing too prissy. I want to impress Lisa, not have her question my sexuality."

I stared at Drew, thinking I must have misheard him. "You're going to let me pick out a shirt for you? Hmm. Maybe there really is something different about this girl."

"Damn straight."

My phone rang. "I bet that's the devil, calling to tell me he's freezing his ass off."

It wasn't actually Lucifer. Just a charming guy with devilish good looks, calling to ask me what I was doing tomorrow night.

Chapter Nineteen

$\mathcal{W}$hen I heard knocking, I glanced at the clock.

He must be excited to get going, because he's a few minutes early. Jake wanted me to help him pick out furniture for his place. First order of business was going to be finding a coffee table. He'd been eating at the restaurant or off his lap since he'd moved in.

I stuck in my hoop earrings and hurried to my door. Swinging it open, I said, "Hey, I—"

Instead of Jake, Stephanie stood there, tears streaming down her face.

"What's wrong?"

"Anthony and I got into this huge fight," Stephanie said. "I should've warned you I was coming. But I'm so mad and sad and argh! I just punched in the code and hurried up, hoping you were home. I decided that even if you weren't, I'd hide out here for a while."

"Come on in. You know you can always stay here, even if I'm gone."

We walked across the room and sat down on the couch.

Stephanie rubbed her temples. "We never used to fight. But

lately…everything's just such a struggle. It's like we don't even speak the same language. He was such a jackhole tonight, then he tells me *I'm* overreacting."

I put my hand on her back. "What happened?"

She shook her head and took a deep breath. "I didn't know he was a chauvinistic pig. He expects me to be sitting at home like a fifties housewife, with the house all cleaned and dinner cooked and ready the instant he steps in the door. I work, too!"

"You do. I don't know how you get so much done."

"I know I'm not working as many hours right now, but that's because I'm doing all the planning for the wedding. Any time I ask his opinion, he says he doesn't care, but his mom cares about *everything*. And then there's this typo I'm dealing with, and all he can say when he gets home is, 'What's for dinner?' Like I'm his maid or cook." Stephanie's voice got higher and higher with each sentence. "Is this how it's going to be the rest of my life? I should've never moved in with him. I wish I was still living with you."

A loud knock sounded on my door.

"I'll be right back." I crossed the room and answered the door.

Jake leaned in and gave me a peck on the lips, his hand going to that spot on my hip that drove me crazy. "Ready, gorgeous?"

"Um…" I glanced back at Stephanie. "I've got a situation."

"I'm sorry," Stephanie said, wiping tears off her face. "I didn't realize you were busy. You two go out. I'll just hang here if that's okay."

"I'm not going to leave you like this," I said.

Jake stepped into the room, looking from Steph to me, then back to Steph. "Is everything okay?"

Stephanie sniffed. "I'm sorry. I'm a big fan of you and the changes I've seen in Darby since you two have been dating—or whatever she's allowing it to be called. Now here I am, ruining it all by coming and telling her how horrible men are. Even the ones you think are good." A couple more tears escaped and ran down her cheeks. "It turns out she was right all along," she said, her voice so high I could barely make out the words. She jerked her thumb toward the bathroom. "I'm going to go get a tissue."

I turned to Jake and kept my voice low. "She and Anthony got into a fight. I'm not sure exactly what happened yet. You see, something happens to a girl when she gets engaged that makes everything seem like a bigger deal. I've learned that brides-to-be tend to get a little…dramatic."

Jake nodded like he understood, although I doubted he did.

"Anyway. I'm thinking our furniture shopping is going to need to be postponed."

Stephanie reentered the room, a wadded-up tissue in her hand, and flopped back down on the couch. "Hey, you're a guy," she said, looking up at Jake. "Maybe you can tell me why guys think it's a woman's job to take care of everything."

I put a hand on Jake's chest. "You might want to run while you can," I whispered. "You don't have to stay."

Jake grabbed my hand and led me to the couch. He sat on the far end but angled his body to face Stephanie. "Tell me what happened, and I'll try to clue you in on the guy perspective."

Stephanie kicked off her shoes and tucked her legs under her. "All day long I'd been excited to see him. Then he finally comes home, and the first thing he does is ask me what's for dinner."

Both Jake and I stared, waiting for the rest.

"Like I'm supposed to serve him or something," Stephanie said. "Why's it my job to make dinner?"

"Guys just don't think sometimes," Jake said. "We say whatever pops into our heads. All he was probably thinking was that he was hungry. I bet if you would've said something like, 'I don't know. Where are you taking me?' he would've been happy to go out."

"But…" Stephanie's eyebrows scrunched together.

"Do you take turns cooking dinner or do you usually cook or

do you go out most nights?"

"Most nights I cook. I actually like cooking most of the time." Stephanie leaned back into the cushions. "Great, now I feel like an idiot. This wedding stuff's making me crazy. Just today, I got the thank-you cards in the mail and they spelled my name wrong, so thinking of what to do about that on top of what to make for dinner, it all seemed like too much." She frowned. "And the more I explain it, the stupider I feel. I better call Anthony." She grabbed her phone and disappeared down the hall.

I twisted to face Jake, still processing how easily that had gone. "You fixed that in record time. I probably would've just complained about guys all night with her until she calmed down. You come in, say a few words, and now she's already calling Anthony to explain." I narrowed my eyes. "You're not secretly trained in counseling or something, are you?"

Jake put his arm over the back of the couch. His fingers grazed my shoulder, then he twisted them in the ends of my hair, sending a tingly sensation along my scalp "Nope. Just had some experience with stuff like this before."

"You think you've got women all figured out, then, do you?"

Jake shook his head. "No way. Every time you think you do, they change the rules on you. Like they could love the way you were yesterday and hate it the next day."

"Every now and then, we change our minds. It's our prerogative. The big secret is"—I leaned in conspiratorially—"sometimes, even *we* don't know why. There are times after we pick a fight where we're as confused as you are. But there's no way we're admitting it." I shrugged a shoulder. "That's why we have boobs."

Jake's eyebrows shot up.

"See, after we've acted crazy, and the guy's wondering what he's doing with us, we use them to mesmerize him, so he forgets that we're crazy." I shot Jake my most seductive smile and leaned the assets in question against his arm. "And by the way, if you look at my cleavage right now, even though I'm the one talking about it, I'll accuse you of not caring about what I say and of just treating me like an object."

Jake swallowed hard, keeping eye contact with me, though I could tell he was fighting his impulse to look down. A mischievous glint flickered through his eyes. "And treating you like an object would be bad?"

"It depends on how big a deal you make about how smart, funny, talented, etcetera, etcetera I am first."

Jake slid his hand behind my neck and swept his thumb along my jaw. "Have I told you how smart, funny, talented, and etcetera I think you are?"

"You think I'm going to fall for that when I just fed you the lines?" Before he could answer, I kissed him. Using his hand on my neck, he pulled me closer, forcing my lips open with his tongue. His other hand slid up my thigh, and even through jeans, my skin burned from his touch.

Stephanie's voice got a little louder. I pulled away from Jake, my breaths coming out shaky. I'd momentarily forgotten my best friend was even here. I only heard snippets of the conversation, but whatever she was saying, it sounded tense.

"Maybe I didn't do such a great job of fixing things after all," Jake said. "I'm assuming her fiancé isn't a complete jerk."

"He's very nice, actually. They have small fights here and there, like all couples do." I listened for a second and caught the word *mother*. "Sounds like they're onto fighting about his mom now. Every relationship's got a sore subject; theirs is his mother. It's the kind of problem girls get together to complain about, but after a little venting it doesn't seem like such a big deal. It's the big stuff—like lying and cheating—that's unforgivable." I pulled my attention off Steph's conversation and looked back at Jake. "You claim guys say whatever they're thinking, like they're honest all the time. I've been around too many liars to believe that."

"The things we think will get us into trouble, we keep in," Jake said. "That's why when we say something we think is totally innocent, we're so shocked and confused when you get mad. Then we use the classic, 'You're overreacting.'"

"Which, by the way, women really hate. If you want me to overreact or be grouchy, just tell me that I am."

"Just like that?"

"Just like that."

"Let's try this out," Jake said.

I raised an eyebrow, silently warning him he better be careful.

"You're completely crazy...about me." He leaned in, his lips near mine. "Did it work?"

I shook my head, but couldn't help smiling. "See, this is the problem. You know how to spin everything to your advantage. In my experience, it's the charming guys who are the most dangerous. They make you think they care, but they've got ulterior motives. In fact, you just told me that you'd keep in the things that would get you into trouble. So how am I supposed to trust you?"

He put his hand on my knee and ran his thumb across the top of it. "I guess my insisting that you can won't change your mind if you don't trust me in the first place."

"Exactly."

"I guess I'll just have to prove it, then." His eyes locked onto mine. "However long it takes."

CHAPTER TWENTY

Stephanie rinsed off her plate and stuck it in my dishwasher. "Last night was just what I needed. It felt good to relax and laugh and forget about everything else for a while." She wiped her hands on the dishtowel hanging from my oven handle and spun to face me. "I still feel bad for messing up your date with Jake, though."

I drained my glass of orange juice. "You didn't mess it up. Jake's lived without a coffee table for weeks. Another day's not going to make a difference to him."

"You know, back when I dated bad boys, I was always yelling and fighting with them—"

"Then making up with them and breaking up the next day."

"Only to make up again." She shook her head. "What a mess. But Anthony and I never fight. We occasionally disagree, sure, but not the yelling fight like we got into last night." She leaned against the counter. "I thought that getting together with Anthony had made me mellow. Turns out, I can still get fired up."

"Nothing wrong with that." I stuck my glass in the dishwasher and closed it. "It'll keep him on his toes."

"I read this article that said the reason you fight more when you get engaged is because you're more committed to the relationship. Since you're working to stay together, the little things seem more important."

The way Stephanie looked at me, I knew I was supposed to step in and make her feel better. "You know that your married friends would be better for this 'everything's going to be great' pep talk."

"I want to hear it from you," she said. I could see the vulnerability in her eyes and hear it in her voice.

I thought of the things Karl had said about her and Anthony, how I could recite his opinion but knew it would come out insincere. I wanted to tell her that it was going to be difficult, but they could give it a fighting chance, and not to take it too hard if it didn't work out. That wasn't what she needed either, though. So I dug down deep, focused on the hope I was working on letting in, and said, "Anthony loves you, you love him, and your minor problems are ones that you can easily work through and live with. You two are going to make it." I shot her a smile. "If only to prove me wrong."

She pulled me into a hug. "Thanks. I needed to hear that." She glanced at her watch and sighed. "I better get going. Thanks for the loaner outfit. Slumber parties are awesome. We should've never stopped having them."

"I'm game anytime."

"I should probably call first. You and Jake might want to have a few slumber parties of your own."

"Okay, let's not get carried away. I've barely been semi-dating him for a few weeks, and as you know, I have a strict rule about that."

"Ah, yes," Stephanie said. "The No-love, no-making-love rule. Now that's one I agree with."

"Yes and it's a rule that no one, regardless of how hot or amazing he is, will convince me to break."

A crease formed between Stephanie's eyebrows. "I'm confused. If you follow all your rules, and make sure to not fall in love again, that means you're planning on being celibate for the rest of your life."

"*Falling* is the key word. You can care about someone, enough to have feelings of love, without being in love."

"That doesn't make sense."

"What I mean is there's a more realistic love than the love that you think is going to last forever." I shook my head. "Look, I've already admitted I'm a little shaky on the details. You know, you don't always have to point out the flaws with my plan."

"Why not?" Stephanie asked. "You point out how flawed marriage is all the time."

I wanted to argue, but she had me there. It couldn't be easy to work so hard planning a wedding with me by her side, and she'd still stuck with me, the way she had since the day we met. "You're right. And the truth is, I'm not sure what I'm going to do about the sex part of the relationship yet. I need to at least know the guy for a while, enough to care about him, but just realize that the love has an expiration date. Or something like that." I blew out my breath, confused at my own logic, wishing it made more sense. "Until I figure out how to deal with the feelings that come along with sex, I'm not going to be crossing that line.

"Besides, this week I'll be spending a lot of time with Barbara." I grabbed my purse off the counter. "I doubt I'll believe in anything resembling love after she's done with me."

• • •

On my shopping excursion with Barbara, I'd discovered a new furniture store on the west end of town. After we had wrapped up our day, I'd called Jake and asked him if he wanted to meet me at Odds and Ends Furniture Store.

I'd barely had enough time to eat a sandwich and get back

to the store before Jake showed up. I led him toward the middle, where mini-living rooms surrounded us on all sides. Most of the rooms were monochromatic—not really how I liked to go—but they had several unique pieces.

"You said you wanted simple and modern. How do you feel about this set up?" I pointed to the black coffee table with chrome.

Jake stared at it, brow furrowed. "Why's it so short?"

I tapped my finger to my lip as I studied it. "Hmm. It is a little short. There's the three-tiered coffee table over there." I motioned to the faux room to the right. "It'd be handy for hiding all your remotes. You can also twist it however you want, so think of the hours of entertainment. Or, if you like the futuristic, there's a glossy white one…"

I searched around, trying to remember where I'd seen it. "Um, there. In that living room set up that looks like the North Pole. We wouldn't go all white, but a little would work if we kept the other things more black than white."

"How are you guys doing today?" a female voice asked.

I turned in search of the voice and saw a saleswoman with a red-lipped smile. Except for the black jacket—the jacket over her boob-squeezing corset top—she looked more like a stripper than a furniture saleswoman.

"We're good," I said. "We're just looking around for living room furniture, seeing what hits us."

She looked from me to Jake. "Oh, are you guys redecorating and working with what you have? Or are you moving into a new place?"

"Neither. We're not living together. I'm his…" I wasn't sure what to say. "I'm an interior designer. He's got an empty bachelor pad, and I'm helping him decorate it. Our main focus is a coffee table so his dates don't have to eat off their laps."

The saleswoman ran a hand through her dark hair. "We can't have that." She put her hand on Jake's elbow. "Come with me," she purred. "I think I have just what you need."

Rude! She's totally flirting with him right in front of me.

I started to follow the two of them, but got distracted when I saw a lamp in the corner that would go great in my bedroom.

After a quick detour to get a closer look, I walked toward the back where I could see Jake and the saleswoman. Standing really close together.

"If you go with something like this, it's more like a work of art than an ordinary table." She leaned in, pressing up against him. "Girls like that."

The coffee table was made up of clear cubes that flipped out every which way. "I think it looks pretentious," I said. "Besides, it wouldn't hide anything."

Her eyes flicked to me, back to the coffee table, then landed on Jake. "I think it's really hip. Some people can't pull it off." Those red lips of her curved into a flirtatious grin as she stared up at Jake. "But I think you could."

I put my hand in the crook of Jake's elbow—the one the salesgirl wasn't plastered against. "I want to show you something." I shot Miss Perky a tight smile. "Thanks for your help, but I think we'll just wander around a bit. If we have any questions, we'll let you know."

"No problem." She pulled a card out of her pocket and handed it to Jake. "Take this. That way if you have any questions later, you'll know how to reach me."

Just because Jake and I didn't have a label on our relationship didn't mean I wanted to watch a girl throw herself at him. I tightened my grip on his arm and led him toward a mock living room with a rug you could lose a zebra in. "Wow, that girl was all over you. Does that happen everywhere you go?"

The corners of his mouth turned up. "Why? Are you jealous?"

"Of course not. I just don't think it was very professional. Unless her real profession is an escort. She is kind of dressed for it."

"You're the one who said you were my interior designer." Jake hugged me into him, a smug expression on his face. "How much do I owe you, by the way?"

"You couldn't afford me." I glanced around, looking for where to go next. When I saw Miss Perky watching us, I grabbed Jake's shirt and pulled him in for a kiss—the kind of kiss I don't normally do in a public place.

Jake moved his lips to my ear and whispered, "I'm going to have to bring you here more often."

While he was obviously amused by my jealousy, panic was winding through me, mixing in and making my stomach clench. This level of jealousy scared me because it burned more than it should.

Because it was the way I usually felt *after* I'd already fallen for a guy.

CHAPTER TWENTY-ONE

"They delivered the furniture and everything else," Jake said when I answered my phone. "So whenever you're free, I need you to get up here and tell me where to put it all. I don't want to do it wrong."

For a couple of days I'd kept busy, keeping my contact with Jake to a text here and there. I was better now. A little jealousy could totally happen pre-fall. Besides, I was his interior designer; I had to do my job, right? And if the thought of seeing him to do my job sent excitement zipping through me, that was an added bonus. "I'll be right there."

I moved to my closet, scanning it for my sneakers—not what I'd normally wear to see Jake, but they were the best option when it came to moving furniture.

"I didn't mean you have to come now. Don't get me wrong, I'd love to see you, but I know you go to work earlier than I do. It doesn't have to be tonight."

I tugged on one sneaker, then switched the phone to my other ear and put on the other one. "It's not that much stuff, so it won't take us very long. Besides, this is my favorite part."

"I'll see you in a few minutes, then," he said.

I hung up and tossed the phone onto my bed, already planning the layout of Jake's living room. He'd bought a coffee table and matching entertainment center. Unable to help myself, I'd pointed out a few other things that would pull his room together. I'd convinced them to knock 20 percent off Jake's purchase, got my lamp for next to nothing, *and* got them to throw in free delivery. Jake said he was impressed by my mad bargaining skills.

A short elevator ride later, I arrived at Jake's, toolbox in hand.

"I have tools," he said.

"Well, you never know." I set the box down on the floor. "First the rug, then we'll get everything set up around it."

Over the next forty-five minutes, we positioned and rearranged the room. Once I got started, I liked to go until I was happy with it.

I stepped back and looked at the finished project. "What d'ya think? Personally, I really like the black-and-white landscape picture there, but if you don't agree, let me know. You can be honest if you hate it. Any of it."

"I like it. It's homey." Jake grabbed my hand. "We better try out the couch."

"The couch is the same."

"But it might feel different now."

"It's late, and I've got to be up early for a meeting."

Ignoring my protest, he tugged me toward the couch. He sat, pulling me with him, reclining back against the arm. He wrapped his arms around me and pressed a kiss to my temple. "It definitely feels better."

I kicked off my shoes, tucked my feet up, and leaned my head against his chest. "It is pretty comfortable."

"So, is this about what you do with most of your clients?" Jake asked.

"Cuddle afterward?"

He laughed. "Yes. That's exactly what I meant."

"Usually people who hire me want big remodeling done. We build shelves or knock down walls—I hire people to do it, anyway. New paint, flooring, lots of decorations and knickknacks. Some people prefer textures and patterns. I tend to keep things simpler with clean lines and comfort in mind."

"At least now I have a place to rest my food and feet."

"Yeah, those together don't really sound like a good idea." I lifted my hand and ran it along his jaw. Strange how dark prickly hair could look so hot on a guy. "You give up shaving?"

"Lazy one day, slept in the next. I swore I was going to shave it today, but Lindsay—my sister—called. I hadn't talked to her in forever, so I left the house again without shaving."

"You and your sister are close, then?"

"I'd say we're pretty close," he agreed. "We used to fight some growing up, but as we got older, we got closer. My niece, Addie, is going through the terrible-two thing. Lindsay's always calling to tell me something funny Addie did, or to tell me about the huge messes she makes."

"And you said your sister still works with your dad, right?"

He nodded. "She loves it. Her husband's an illustrator, so he works from home and takes care of Addie. She draws next to him while he works, and then he works a couple more hours when Lindsay comes home."

Jake ran his fingers up and down my back, his touch relaxing me so much I had to fight to keep my eyes open. "I was surprised when I first met Cameron," he said. "He was the opposite of who I pictured Lindsay with. But they work well together. My parents are really good at that, too. I think first you've got to find the right person, then you have to work hard to keep the relationship going strong."

If I wasn't feeling so drowsy, I might've lifted my head and told him I wasn't sure I agreed. Instead, I decided to change the subject. "You think you'll ever go back to New York and open a restaurant there?"

"The restaurant market in New York is much tougher. Vegas is really competitive, too, but we set up in one of the newer hotels and it's been doing really well."

I'd been dumped for the city of New York once before, so I wanted to know how likely it was that Jake would be going back. Even if it involved a little bit of breaking my rules and talking about the future. "Do you ever think about going back there and doing something else? Maybe someday you'll want to be back behind the desk."

"I'd never say never, but right now, I'm very happy where I am."

I wasn't sure whether he meant with the restaurant or this moment. I was going to make a joke about it, but talking seemed like too much effort. Suddenly, I found it hard to form words or even keep my eyes open.

• • •

Nothing seemed right when I woke up. My neck and back ached, and after a confusing moment wondering where I was and what was going on, I realized that instead of being in my bed, I was sleeping against Jake. He groaned as I untangled myself from him.

I searched the room for a clock but couldn't find one. *Note to self: get Jake a clock.*

My phone wasn't in my pocket. I tried to remember when I'd had it last. *I think I left it in my bedroom.*

Stifling a yawn, I stood and stretched. The sunlight coming through the windows seemed brighter than normal, but I figured it was because the windows in his place were so big. I stepped toward the kitchen and looked at the oven clock.

"Is this right?" I asked, panic filling me. "Tell me that isn't set to the right time."

Jake sat up and squinted against the light. He pulled his phone out of his pocket. "It's eight thirty."

"No, no, no. This can't be happening. Not today. Any day but today. I've got to meet my boss at nine. If I didn't live two minutes away, I'd be screwed." I stepped into my shoes, not bothering to tie them. "Even then, I don't know if I'll make it. She's huge on punctuality, and I really, really hate being late. Today, it's just not an option."

Jake stood and ran his hand down my arm. "You've got some time."

"I'm not a guy. It takes me a while to put myself together."

"You look fine the way you are right now."

I waved him off. "Don't start with the sweet talk. I've got to go." I grabbed my keys off the coffee table and rushed out the door.

The elevator chose this morning to run slow, and I couldn't cross the short distance to my place fast enough. I hurried inside, took the quickest shower of my life, and threw my hair in a wet bun. I ran a coat of mascara over my eyelashes and rushed out the door, praying I'd make it in time.

Of course traffic was thick and the stoplights all red. I was muttering swear words under my breath as I half ran, half speed-walked to my office. I scooped up my trusty binder and slid into the conference room at 9:01.

My boss shot me a look that meant she noticed, and the meeting went downhill from there. Twenty minutes in I was scrambling through the contents of my binder, looking completely unprepared for the day, much less the meeting.

Patricia frowned at me. "Do you have it or not?"

"I know it's in here somewhere." Not only could I not find what I needed, I was blanking on everything. The one day I really needed to be on top of my game, and I was totally off.

Nadine handed a sheet of paper to Patricia. "Here it is. I know they'll work with us if we do a large order like we did on the condos. Darby's the one who got them to agree to it last time."

Patricia arched an overly filled-in eyebrow at me. "Do you think you can manage to do that again?"

"Tell me what you need and I'll get on it." Normally, I got to pick and choose my clients. Occasionally, though, we got a company-wide account—like we did with the building I lived in. Patricia was working on a presentation for a new hotel renovation, which meant she'd tell everyone else what to do for it.

"I hope you haven't been getting lazy. This deal with The Lion Inn is big for us. You've got to be a team player sometimes." Patricia clicked a button on her laptop, changing the slide being projected onto the front of the room.

After going over the rest of the layout of the Red Lion Inn, Patricia dismissed us.

I hurried out of the conference room, toward my office. A person could work her butt off impressing Patricia and never get more than the tiniest acknowledgment. Screw up once, and she remembered it forever.

"Everything okay with you?" Nadine asked, stepping next to me.

"I didn't get up early enough to organize all my notes, and my mind just wasn't working as fast as normal," I said. "Thanks for stepping in back there."

"Of course. The only reason I had the information was because you'd given it to me." Nadine stopped in front of her office door. "Barbara wants to know if she should put you down for one or two tomorrow night."

One or two? It took me a moment to figure out what Nadine was talking about. "Right. Barbara's party. In all the excitement last night, I forgot to ask Jake." I wasn't sure if I even should ask him to go with me. "Fridays are usually busy nights for him."

"You know that she's going to be setting you up all night if you don't have a date." Nadine shrugged. "Maybe there will be some interesting guys there."

"Yeah, interesting like they have money and one to three ex-wives." I sighed. "Let me call him and I'll get back to you."

I walked the rest of the way to my office and tossed my binder on the desk. It slid off the edge and fell to the floor. When I bent down to retrieve it, I noticed it had opened to the page I couldn't find earlier. "Figures."

After how bitchy I'd been this morning, I wouldn't be surprised if Jake avoided me for a few days. I definitely I owed him an apology. And I'd much rather have him at the party with me than deal with the men Barbara would try to set me up with. I grabbed my phone and called him.

"Hey, how was your meeting?" he asked.

"Awful. I was disorganized and my boss called me out on it. Basically, it was my worst meeting ever." I sat in my chair and scooted it closer to my desk. I'd never been great at apologies and my nerves were twisting around in my gut. "Look, I'm sorry about this morning. I was stressed and late. I really hate being late. But I shouldn't have talked to you like that."

"Meet me at Blue and we'll have lunch. End on a better note."

"I'd love to, but I can't. I've got to fast track my current jobs and draw up a proposal so my boss doesn't think I'm incompetent. I do have a question for you, though…" I picked up my pen and started doodling on my notepad. "There's this party tomorrow night. The client with all the ex-husbands is throwing it, and I've got to go. I know it's last minute, and that Fridays are really busy for you. I'm also sure it's going to be boring. Anyway, if you can't go, I completely understand. But if you don't come with me, I'll be forced to meet rich, eligible bachelors who may or may not have all their original teeth and hair."

I bit my nail as I waited for his answer, trying to prepare myself for the possibility he couldn't go.

"You're not really giving me much of a choice," Jake said. "Not when I know you've got a weakness for bald men with dentures."

I grinned, getting that tingling-tummy sensation that flirting with Jake always brought. "The money eases those minor flaws. I'm really shallow like that."

Patricia walked past my office window, slowing in the way that meant she was coming in. She always saved the meanest comments for when she sat down for a one-on-one meeting.

Apprehension replaced my momentary happiness. I had a feeling my day was about to go down in flames.

• • •

Only a few people remained in Blue, finishing up their meals. In five minutes, the place was closing for the night. After working late, going for a run, and pacing my apartment, I couldn't get over my horrible day at work. I wanted to talk to someone about it but kept getting halfway through a number and hanging up. Steph was stressed enough with all her wedding stuff, and Mom would just tell me to do whatever I felt was right. So I decided to go for a walk around downtown.

After wandering in and out of a couple stores in the area, I'd ended up near Blue. I walked past once. Then doubled back. Then decided to go in.

Sitting across from Jake, picking at the chocolate-lava cake, I was getting more and more fired up. "Patricia's made good money off jobs Nadine and I do all the work on. And I'm the one with the good rapport with all the vendors. Whenever they call, they request me. I'll admit I wasn't the most prepared for the meeting this morning, thanks to certain events…"

"That's why I brought the chocolate." Jake took a bite of the rich cake, then slid the plate back toward me.

I swirled the fork through the thick syrup. "I don't even like doing the commercial jobs. They're so plain and impersonal. Then to get yelled at about it, when I'm the one who has all the contacts in the first place, was really infuriating."

"Have you ever looked at going into business on your own? Or with Nadine?"

"I considered it about a year ago," I said. "But that was more of a relocation thing."

"Where were you going to move?"

"I toyed around with New York for a while before coming to my senses." I didn't want to get into that, so I kept talking before he could ask why. "The thing is, I got my start at Metamorphosis. I've worked there for eight years. All my clients signed contracts with me through the company, so they'd be considered Metamorphosis's clients, not mine. I only keep them if I stay with the company."

"But how many of them are going to need their places redone again? If they refer someone else, I'm guessing they refer them to you, not the company." Jake set down his fork. "I could crunch some numbers and set up a business plan if you want me to. It's kind of my specialty, you know."

I took another bite of the cake and pushed the plate back to Jake. "The only time I really have to deal with Patricia is when I do the commercial jobs. I can power through it, like I did last time. I just wish they didn't take so long."

"Lots of people get comfortable with where they're at and are too afraid to change, so they settle with what they've got."

"Sounds like my stance on relationships."

"Well, in any relationship," Jake said, meeting my gaze, "including your business ones, you have to decide if you're going to put in the effort to make it work."

I slumped back in my chair. "Great. Not even a job I love has a happy ending."

"You decide the ending. If you don't like something, all you have to do is find a way to change it."

"It sounds like a good idea and all, but I know better." That awful sense that my life was about to get more complicated burned away at my gut. "Things never end the way you want them to."

I knew that better than anyone.

Chapter Twenty-two

Barbara's party had a good chance of being boring, but at least it gave me an excuse to wear my new silver-and-black print dress. I twisted my hair into a loose bun at the base of my neck, then pulled out a few face-framing strands. After looking over my collection of shoes, I decided to add some color with my plum heels. Dangly purple earrings completed the look.

There was a knock on my door, and I went to answer it. Jake stood in the hall wearing a black suit and looking like a million bucks. He leaned in and gave me a kiss. "Hey, gorgeous."

Just like that, the stress filling me melted away. I put my arms around him, soaking in the way he looked, smelled, and felt. Then I tipped onto my toes and kissed his freshly shaven cheek. "You look nice."

My cell phone rang and I groaned. Since Patricia had been calling nonstop, I'd programmed a special ring for her. "I've got to get that."

"Where's my report?" Patricia asked the second I answered.

"In your inbox. I stuck it there before I left."

"I'm not going to the office tonight. E-mail it to me."

Working to control my voice, I took a deep breath. I'd wanted to e-mail it in the first place; she was the one who'd insisted she wanted the large printout. "I can't. I'm on my way to Barbara's party and the files are on my work computer."

"I thought you were going to be a team player. Now you can't do it because of a party?"

"A party for one of our high-paying clients. It's a great chance for me to network. I'll e-mail you the information first thing tomorrow morning."

Silence hung in the air for a few seconds before she snapped, "Fine. You know this is a big account. We can't afford to screw it up."

"I've got all the groundwork laid already. You just need to make the final decisions, then we'll present it."

"I expect it to be in my e-mail first thing tomorrow morning."

"It'll be there." I let out a breath, frustration burning through me. Getting to choose my clients over the past year had spoiled me. Already this hotel thing was becoming a big headache.

When I ended the call, Jake was standing at my window, pouring a glass of water into my mostly dead plant. "I thought you said watering it was a waste of time," I said.

"At first I thought you should put it out of its misery, but it won't give up and I admire that." Jake glanced around. "Where's the other one?"

"It gave up." His I-knew-it expression caused me to add, "I swear it wasn't my fault. It was already on its way out when I got it here." I tossed my keys and cell into my beaded clutch and hooked my hand in his elbow. "Now let's go party."

• • •

Waiters circled the large room, handing out champagne and appetizers. Nadine walked through the crowd, up to Jake and me. "I'm glad you guys are finally here."

"That bad, huh?" I asked.

"I've been introduced to two different men who are about the same age as my grandfather."

"And how's Barbara tonight?"

"In top form. I think she's got her eye on a new man. She'll probably have husband number five before I've even had one."

"That's because you and Barbara have different criteria when it comes to husbands." I glanced up. "Here she comes."

Barbara greeted me with a couple of air kisses. "Good evening, darling." She raised her eyebrows as her appraising gaze ran over my date. "And who's this handsome gentleman?"

"This is Jake Knight," I said. "Jake, Barbara Covington."

Jake extended his hand. "Nice to meet you, Ms. Covington."

"Call me Barbara." She placed a hand on his forearm. "Darby, I'm going to steal your man and introduce him around the room." She indicated a table in the corner. "My friends over there want to meet my fabulous decorators. After I showed them what you ladies are planning to do for me, several of them are thinking of remodeling, too. You should go introduce yourselves."

Jake released my hand and followed Barbara, leaving Nadine and me standing alone.

"What now?" I asked.

"I guess we go try to land a few clients," Nadine said. "Even though we won't have time to do another job for months. I hate these commercial projects. Most of the year, you and I bring in our own clients and make Patricia a ton of money. The minute she gets the commercial jobs, she treats us like idiots."

"I suppose we'll just have to take turns working on our current projects and power through. Then we'll get back to the fun ones."

We put on our game faces and approached Barbara's group of friends. Twenty minutes of talking about the many options and styles of decorating later, I started to worry about Jake. I glanced around the room and spotted him in the corner, several men and a few women around him. Barbara stood off to his left, talking to an impeccably dressed older man with a shiny bald head.

"I'm going to go reclaim my date," I whispered to Nadine.

Nadine leaned closer. "If you see any guys under the age of forty-five, fifty, send them my way, will you?"

I think she was only half kidding. Setting my sights on Jake, I crossed the room. His back was to me as he spoke to the people around him. I squeezed my way into the group and put my hand on his elbow.

He glanced down and put his arm around me. "It was nice meeting you all."

A couple of the men shook his hand before letting us go.

"What was that all about?" I asked, keeping a tight grip on him as we wove through the crowd. Finally we got to a fairly open space where we could stand without people bumping into us.

"When Barbara tried to feel out my financial stability, I told her I ran a taco shack," Jake said.

I laughed. "You did not."

"I teased her for a bit before telling her about Blue. Apparently it wasn't impressive enough. She wanted to introduce me to a few people who might be able to help me find a better job. She said that if I wanted to be with a girl like you, I needed to get serious about providing you with all the luxuries you deserved."

"I think she means well. I just don't know why she insists you need to be in a relationship to be happy."

Jake gripped the sides of my waist and drew me to him. "Well, there is something great about being with someone who knows how to cheer you up."

I ran my fingers up his arms and hooked them behind his neck. "Or someone who will go to a boring party with you when you need him to?"

That irresistible smile of his spread across his face. "See, you're finally getting it. Relationships aren't all bad." His hands moved to my back, pressing me against him. "Some of them work."

I swallowed past my suddenly dry throat. I was having a hard time not focusing on his lips and thinking about what I wanted them to do to me. "I never said they were all bad." My heart picked up speed, hammering against my rib cage. His gaze ran down me, burning everywhere it touched. Passion lit his eyes, leaving little question what he was thinking. It wasn't just passion, though; there was tenderness there, too.

I could feel the threads forming, from my heart to his. Threads that would become strings, until I was all wrapped up in him and couldn't separate myself from him without feeling like half a person.

Oh, shit, I'm in over my head. Panic squeezed my lungs, stealing my breath. I'd been here before too many times, and the last couple of relationships had nearly crushed me. They'd messed with my job, my sense of self—everything. *I have to do something before it's too late. I can't do this to myself again. I* won't *do this again.* I took a step back, and the space between us felt wrong and torturous—another sure sign that this was getting too serious.

Jake's eyebrows drew together, the confusion on his features clear.

I rubbed the back of my neck. "I like spending time with you, Jake. You've been really great, and I'm afraid I'm starting to give you the wrong impression. I'm not going to change my mind about doing the relationship thing." Looking at him was painful, so I dropped my gaze, focusing on the refracted light bouncing off the wall. "I think we should stop spending so much time together before someone ends up getting hurt."

I jumped when a hand came down on my shoulder.

"How are you two doing?" It was Barbara. After all the hours I'd spent listening to her talk, her voice was ingrained in my head. "Several of my friends are talking about working with you and Nadine." Barbara glanced at Jake, her lips curving up. "And I've heard nothing but good things about you, young man. I'm sure there will be several business opportunities coming your way soon."

"That's good to hear," Jake said. I could tell he had to work at a smile. Knowing there was pain buried in it—and that it was my fault—sent a pang through my chest. "But honestly, I'm very happy with my job. And Darby's made it clear she doesn't need or want anyone to take care of her."

The ache in my chest deepened, and tears pricked my eyes. I quickly blinked them away. *Don't cry, don't cry, don't cry.*

Barbara dismissed the idea with a wave of her hand. "That's what women always say. Secretly they love a man to come in and sweep them off their feet."

"I prefer to have my feet on the ground, actually," I said. "That way you always remember how to walk on your own."

"Darling, you'll miss out if you don't allow yourself to be swept away now and then." Barbara patted Jake's arm. "I can tell this guy cares about you. He held up very well under my scrutiny." She glanced around. "I better go attend to some of my other guests, but you two have a wonderful evening."

Not wanting to deal with the weirdness I was sure Jake and I were about to have, I watched her walk away. Finally, I looked at him. "I can get Nadine to give me a ride home."

Jake ran a hand through his hair. "A few minutes ago we were fine, and suddenly you can't even stand me for the rest of the night?"

"I'm just saying if you want to leave, you can. I'd understand."

"Do you want me to go?"

I shook my head. "Like I said, I have fun with you. I'm only trying to be honest." *Only trying to keep my heart in one piece so it won't get ripped apart again.*

Over the next hour, Jake stuck by my side, almost as if nothing happened, but the smiles and casual touches were gone. We heard stories about grandkids, all about what companies to invest in, and heated discussions on the state the country was in.

When we got back to our building, I punched the elevator button for my floor. The ride took an eternity, and it felt like the walls were closing in on me. Everything was awkward and strained, the ease of the past few weeks with Jake effectively destroyed.

The doors opened and Jake started to step off the elevator with me.

"You don't have to walk me to my door," I said.

Jake put his hand on my back, guiding me down the hall anyway. Part of me wondered if he'd heard me at all tonight. Did he get that everything needed to change? That if I didn't draw a line, we'd both regret it later?

The walk down the hall took three times as long as it usually did. Finally, miracle of all miracles, we reached my door. Knowing looking at Jake was dangerous, I focused on my hands, twisting the bracelet on my wrist. "Thanks again for coming with me tonight. I'm sure I'll see you around."

Jake exhaled, and I could hear the frustration in it. "Is that your way of telling me not to call you?"

I continued spinning the bracelet, round and round. "No. But I'm going to be busy with this job, and I should be helping Steph with the wedding planning more."

Jake put his hand on my wrist, making it impossible to keep spinning my bracelet. "So if I asked you to hang out with me on Sunday morning?"

Slipping would be so easy, and I couldn't let myself do it. I kept my eyes glued to his long fingers wrapped around my wrist. "I'd say it's not a good idea."

Jake put his other hand under my chin, gently tipping it up until I had no choice but to look at him. He pressed a gentle kiss to my lips. "I'll see you around, Darby."

I watched him walk away. Waiting around until I found his

fatal flaw was taking too long, and I just couldn't afford to get more attached. Already, I'd been relying on him too much. I couldn't deal with everything going down at work *and* a relationship that was getting too serious. When the relationship failed, I'd still need my job. It's what got me through every time my heart had been broken, and I couldn't screw it up.

I felt each one of the threads that had started to form between us snap, a dozen pricks of pain in my heart. They stung, but at least I knew I could survive them.

Good-bye, Jake.

Next time I decided to have a semi-long-term relationship, I was going to go for someone who wasn't so hard to resist.

Chapter Twenty-three

There were two relationships I tried not to think about—unless it was to remind myself of the pain love could bring. So whenever I started thinking I was an idiot for letting Jake go, I opened up those memories and let the residual heartache wash over me. I even went so far as to break out my case studies.

I stared at Robert's name until the letters bled together. Before I'd met him, I'd decided all guys were immature idiots. But he was different. I remember thinking it was a miracle that I'd met a mature, amazing, and funny guy.

I thought he might just be the one.

Robin Hood Case Study: Robert/Robin Hood
My Age: 25

I was at The Bullpen Bar with Steph, Nadine, and a few other friends. After giving up on a waiter to come by, I'd left my friends at the table to go get a drink. I was waiting by the packed bar when someone tapped me on the shoulder.

"Hey, you," a male voice said. "Come look at this."

Not bothering to glance at him, I said, "I'm sorry, I don't respond to, 'hey you.' Get someone else to look at it."

"What's your name?"

I turned back to tell the guy to get lost. But his green eyes, strong jaw, and wavy, blond hair made me rethink blowing him off. It took a few seconds to figure out why he was looking at me, eyebrows raised, like he was waiting for something. *Oh, right. He asked me a question.*

"Darby. My name's Darby."

"Hi, Darby. I'm Robert. Now, will you come look at this for me? It's pretty important, and my friend and I need an objective eye." He glanced at the money in my hand. "Afterward, I'll buy you a drink."

I eyed him for a moment. *What's the worst that could happen?*

"Okay," I said, backing away from the bar. "Show me what's so important."

Robert grabbed my hand and led me across the room. "Don't you dare touch it, Joe," he said as we approached a pudgy guy. "I swear if you cheated—"

"I don't need to cheat," Joe said. "Because I already won."

"Darby's going to judge it." Robert stopped in front of the dartboard hanging on the wall.

I pointed at it. "This? This is what's so important?"

"Look, we've got fifty bucks on this. Joe thinks—"

"Hey, no biasing her," Joe said.

"Okay, add up the points of the red darts and the blue darts. I won't even tell you whose is whose. Then tell us the score."

The board was older, beat-up. Unlike some of the ones I'd seen, it didn't have metallic dividers. A few darts had hit right on the line, making it hard to decide what score to go with. Specifically, there was one blue dart between the six-point white and ten-point black. I leaned in and studied it.

Looks more six than ten to me.

"Red's the winner," I said.

"No way!" Joe yelled.

Robert shouted, "Suck it!" while pumping his fists in the air. (I know I said mature, and this isn't exactly a mature moment, but I'll get to that part later.) He put his arm around me. "Come on, Darby. Let's get you that drink."

When I got back to my table a few minutes later, Steph leaned in and whispered, "Who was that guy?"

"His name's Robert. He needed me to judge a game of darts."

"Did he get your number?"

I shook my head. "It's not like he handpicked me. I just happened to be the first person he could find."

Stephanie looked over my head at Robert and Joe. "He's cute. You should go get his number."

"Don't stare." I raised my voice to talk to the rest of the girls. "What did I miss?"

The girls caught me up on their conversation, which had mostly been about Nadine's recently exed-boyfriend.

Stephanie nudged me. "He's coming over here."

Robert walked up to our table, his eyes on me. One corner of his mouth lifted. "Hey, you. Up for a game of darts?"

"You forgot my name already?" I asked.

The other side of his mouth got in on the smile. "No. But since you made it clear how much you like to be called, 'hey you,' I decided to go with that." He put his hand on the back of my chair. "Come on. Joe's lost three in a row, so I'll send him over to talk to your friends."

"Make sure you show our girl a good time." Steph pushed me, hard enough I almost fell out of my chair.

I shot her a dirty look, then followed Robert back to the dartboard. He handed me the three red darts. "You can go first."

I'd never played darts before, but I figured it couldn't be that difficult. I aimed and tossed one. It barely landed in the bottom of the board, giving me all of three points. "Wow, it's harder than it looks."

"Here, I'll show you how to throw it." Robert stepped behind me.

"You're not going to do that whole put-your-arms-around-me-because-you-think-I'm-too-stupid-to-get-it-from-a-simple-explanation thing, are you?"

Robert dropped his arms. "Not anymore."

I aimed higher, tossed my second dart, and watched it land to the right of the bull's-eye, giving me thirteen points. "I think I got it."

After several games—all of which I'd lost, even with the pity points he gave me—Robert held up his last dart. "Okay, how about if I hit the bull's-eye, you go out with me this weekend."

I hadn't flirted in a while, but the guy was cute, and I figured I didn't really have much to lose. "Are you that sure you can hit it? Or are your feelings for me so mediocre you'd risk it all on a game of darts?"

A cocky smile spread across his face. "I figure if I actually hit the bull's-eye you'll go out with me. But if I don't, you'll be so flattered that I've worked so hard to win you over, you'll at least give me your number."

"That's twisting the game so that no matter what happens, you still win." I leaned toward him, close enough our bodies were almost touching. "It's cheating."

"I happen to be a lawyer, so I know how to bend the rules to my advantage."

"*Ooh*, a professional liar. Now I can't go out with you, even if you do hit the bull's-eye. You see, I don't date liars. It's a good way to get burned."

Robert put his arm around me and locked his hand on my hip. He looked at the board and lined up his shot. With a quick toss, the dart flew through the air and hit the red center.

"I guess I'll just have to take my prize now." Before I could ask what he meant, he used the arm he had around me to pull me closer and planted a kiss on my lips. My knees went weak and I found myself parting my lips and kissing him deeper, while the rest of the world spun out of focus.

Two days later, we had our first official date.

Robert was a public defender. He was the "if you cannot afford an attorney, one will be appointed to you" kind of lawyer. Which meant he was overworked, underpaid, and took cases home with him.

He was confident and smart, and I loved how passionate he was about his job. Sometimes that meant he got swamped and we couldn't do much. But he still made an effort to meet up for quick lunches or dinners. If we couldn't swing getting together, we'd talk over the phone, often into the early hours of the morning.

Even with our hectic schedules, we managed to make things work. He told me how smart and beautiful he thought I was, he remembered the things I liked and didn't like, and when I surprised him at work when he couldn't get away, he thanked me for being so understanding and showed me off to his associates.

For five months, everything was great.

Then we had our first fight.

Robert had come over to my place for dinner. We'd both had stressful weeks, but we tried to at least spend one night together, no matter how exhausted we were.

As we ate, he filled me in on how his case had gone. "So we were able to get him off since the police officer didn't follow procedure," he finished.

"But he was guilty?" I asked. Earlier in the conversation, Robert had implied as much.

"Oh, for sure."

"It doesn't seem right. I admire you for keeping innocent

people out of jail. But the guilty people should be *in* jail, not released for stupid reasons."

"Honey, this is how the law works. If the police don't follow procedure, innocent people would be convicted. So if they screw up, sometimes guilty people get off, too. Don't worry, though, it was just minor stuff. A little larceny."

"And he'll probably do it again. Don't you feel a bit responsible?"

"I feel responsible for making sure the law is enforced," Robert said, his words clipped. "If the police have hard evidence, we plea and the guy does time. If not, he gets off."

I frowned. "I'm not sure I could do it. I'd want to make sure he got what he deserved."

"Then I guess it's a good thing I'm the lawyer, and you're a decorator."

The condescending way he'd said *decorator* irritated me. "You make my job sound so unimportant. I'm not saying I'm saving lives, but turning someone's home into a place he or she loves makes a difference."

"I doubt many of them even realize how lucky they are to have nice things to put in their big houses. Several of my clients don't have anything but a bare bed in a tiny room."

"I get that, but think of how sad it would be if there was no color in the world. No beauty. No art."

Robert took a sip of his water. "It'd be depressing, but it's not like you need it to survive or anything."

Anger bubbled up in me. "You know what else doesn't help survival? Criminals being on the loose because their lawyers put them back on the streets!"

Robert threw up his hands and scooted away from the table. "All right, I guess I'll go back to my drab apartment and figure out a way to keep more criminals on the street. You have fun in your fancy, well-decorated place."

I didn't even try to stop him from going.

Over the next few days, I missed Robert like crazy. I missed talking to him. Missed the way he always made me laugh. I thought over and over again, *who am I to judge who goes free and why.*

I realized I was in love with him.

I decided that after work I was going to drive to his office and tell him so, but before I could, he showed up at my work, told me he was miserable without me, and apologized for everything he'd said. I apologized, and told him I loved him. He said he loved me, too. Things went back to perfect.

Three months later, we started discussing our future. We talked about buying a place; the M-word was mentioned. We were at my kitchen table, looking at flyers for homes when the topic of having kids came up.

"We'll start in a home like this," Robert said, picking up one of the flyers. "But we'll need to move to a bigger place once we start having kids."

"I'm a little shaky on the kids issue." I swallowed the bite of cookie I had in my mouth. "If we do decide to have one or two kids, though, three bedrooms should be enough." I popped the rest of my cookie in my mouth and wiped the crumbs from my hands.

"I'm thinking more like five or six kids."

I almost choked. "What? I'm not having five or six kids. After my parents got divorced, I went through this phase where I didn't think I wanted kids at all. Drew and Devin pretty much solidified my stance on it. I'm barely getting used to the idea of having kids at all."

"Since I've met Drew and Devin," Robert said, "I completely understand."

"Hey, those are my brothers you're talking about. I can slam them, but no one else can. Besides, they're not so bad now."

"Yeah, I loved it when they dragged me along to show me" — he made air quotes — "real men's work." And how they called me a city boy when I fell off a horse. Or when they didn't tell me that a giant bull was in the pen, so I climbed over the fence after them and came face-to-face with the beast."

"Tiny's the most gentle creature on the farm," I said, picturing the enormous black bull Dwight treated like a puppy.

"He rammed me with his head."

"He nudged you because he wanted his head scratched. You're just lucky you weren't holding a stick. Tiny loves to get scratched with a big rough stick. He'll come running at you if you've got one of those in your hand."

Robert exhaled, managing to convey with the sound how frustrated he was. "Anyway, all I'm saying is that I grew up with seven kids, and I've always wanted to have a big family. It's crazy, but it's fun. And we'll have them all close together so they always have someone to play with."

"You've got cases piled up all the time. How are you going to have time to take care of six kids?" I put a hand on my chest. "I'm not raising six kids by myself. I'm not even going to raise one kid by myself. Not to mention we can't afford to have that many kids."

"You can work from home. We'll buy a fixer-upper. With how great you are at your job, you'll find a way to make it nice."

As nice as that vote of confidence was, frustration welled up in me. Cleary, he didn't get what I did. "I can't paint over bad plumbing or holes in the wall. And there's no way I could work from home while taking care of kids. Don't you remember what it was like last week at my parents' house? Devin *and* Anne were about to go crazy taking care of Levi. He just cried and cried and nothing made him happy."

I shook my head. "I can't do that. I'm not even sure if I can do more than one baby. Then there's the whole issue that most of the time my job involves working in the home I'm renovating."

Robert tossed the flyer back down on the table. "We don't have to figure everything out right now."

I didn't want to talk about it anymore, either. But in the back of my mind, I knew this was a problem we couldn't ignore forever. I told myself it was okay, though. This was what people meant when they said relationships were about compromise. We just had to find the right balance.

A couple more months went by. I was working on a condo project that was hectic and stressful, and Robert had more and more cases piling up. We looked at homes whenever we could squeeze time into our crazy schedules. I kept telling myself we'd figure everything out. We did love each other, after all.

Flash forward to my twenty-sixth birthday. I sat by myself at Little Italy for thirty minutes, waiting for Robert to show up. He'd said he wanted to do something just the two of us, so Steph and I were going to celebrate the next day.

As I was waiting, I kept thinking about the conversation Robert and I'd had a few days before. The conversation where he'd gone on and on about how great it was that his mom had stayed at home to take care of him and his brothers and sisters. He'd followed it up with, "Maybe we should look for places in Longmont once we have kids, so you could be close to your mom. Then it won't be so hard when I'm not home."

"That would mean we'd both have at least an hour commute each way," I'd said.

"But if you stayed home, then I'd be the only one doing the commute." It ended the same way it always did. With Robert saying, "It's not something we have to decide now, but I think you'll find you want to stay home once we have kids."

And maybe he was right. But there was also a chance he was wrong.

When Robert finally walked up to the table, I felt like crying. Everything suddenly felt wrong and I didn't know what to do about it.

"Sorry I'm so late," he said. "I know you hate waiting, but you know how it is. One thing leads to another..." He leaned down and gave me a quick peck before sitting across from me.

My breaths came out shallow, and my nerves were all jittery. "I was starting to think I'd be celebrating my birthday by myself."

"Well, I'm here now. And I don't want to wait any longer to give you your present. I've been excited about it all day."

"What if I don't want to stay home with our kids?" I blurted out. "What if I only want a small family, and I don't want to move out to the suburbs? Lately, your hours have been crazy. This is the first time I've seen you all week, and I have a feeling it's only going to get worse."

"I don't want to be some housewife with kids hanging off me, wishing I would've said something before it was too late. These are some big issues, and I'm not sure we're ever going to agree on them."

Robert blinked, obviously taken aback by my words. "We can figure that out later." He recovered and placed his hand over mine. "Now, just wait until you see your present." He reached into his coat pocket.

"Robert, I don't know if I—"

"Darby Quinn, will you marry me?" He pulled out a black velvet box and popped open the lid.

I stared at the ring. A simple silver band with a solitaire diamond winking in the middle.

If he'd asked me the day before, I would've said yes. I wanted to say yes now. I knew he was passionate about his job. So was I. Sure, I wasn't keeping innocent people out of jail—of course, he wasn't all the time, either, which still bothered me a little bit—but I loved my job. It made me happy. But he thought what I did was a frivolous waste.

As I sat there, my dream bubble bursting, I realized Robert and I didn't want the same things out of life, either. Not just with the kid issue, but where we wanted to live, how we wanted to raise our kids (six if he had his way), the lifestyle we'd lead. I'd tried to be understanding about it, but the fact that he was always late drove me crazy.

There was also a struggle over visiting our families. He rarely had time to go with me to see mine, yet we managed to make it to his twice a month. And when we did visit his family, he'd disappear to hang out with his brothers, leaving me with his sisters and mom, who I had nothing in common with.

If only one of these things had been an issue, maybe we could work them out. All of them together were too many.

Tears filled my eyes, and the pain in my chest made it hard to breathe.

I can't believe this is happening.

Robert moved the box closer to me. "Darby, say yes already. I'm starting to get worried."

"I can't do it. I love you, I really do, but we don't want the same things. I tried to tell myself it'd all be okay, but…" My words came in a high-pitched squeak. "It's not going to work."

People around us were staring. A few people started clapping. They thought we were getting engaged; they didn't realize we were in the middle of breaking up.

That was the day I realized I'd been lied to. Even though I'd found an amazing, mature guy who I loved, who loved me back, it still wasn't enough. I was crushed. And pissed. And totally heartbroken.

Time Wasted: I refuse to say any of our ten months together were a waste. I learned a lot about myself. I got to experience the most intense love I'd ever had up till then. I also had to get over it, which wasn't easy. I became bitter and went through a zombie/ horror film phase. My favorite part was when everyone died. If someone actually found love in the movie, I booed and threw popcorn at the screen.

Lessons Learned:

My family is really, really important to me.

I want someone with enough free time to spend some with me (a.k.a. no workaholics).

Never date someone who wants six kids.

The hardest lesson: Sometimes love's just not enough.

• • •

Stephanie, Anthony, Karl, and I sat down at a table near the bar. I'd called Stephanie, desperate to get out after spending all day working, and we'd met at Shots, the place Anthony had originally meant for us to go. Saturday nights were apparently popular, because it was hard to move. When a group got up to leave, we snatched the table.

"So what happened?" Steph asked.

I knew what she was talking about, but I didn't want to get into it. The whole point of getting out was to stop thinking about *him*.

She scooted her chair closer to mine. "You know I'm not going to leave you alone until you tell me what happened with Jake."

I sighed, nice and dramatic so that she got how much I didn't want to talk about it. "He kept trying to convince me that some relationships are good."

Steph tilted her head and stared at me. "Oh, Darby. Surely there's more than that."

"I called him for no reason but to chat, even though he was in the middle of work. When I had a bad day, I complained about it to him. I had him go to a boring party with me. I was relying on him too much. I could just feel it starting to get messy."

Karl leaned in, yelling over the music. "What's going on?"

"Darby dropped a guy because he liked her and she was starting to like him back," Steph said.

I scowled at her. "Thanks for making it sound as horrible as possible."

"I guess I should consider myself lucky that you were appalled by me," Karl said with a smile.

"You better watch it. Getting someone in this place to punch you might be harder than at Hot Shots, but I like a challenge." Usually I would've delivered that line much better, but it came out kind of sad, thanks to the fact that his statement was a little too true. Maybe my exes had a list of what not to look for in a girlfriend with all my qualities listed.

Anthony held his hand out to Stephanie. "You want to dance?"

Stephanie glanced at me.

"I'm fine," I said, pushing her toward her fiancé. "Go dance."

Anthony hated to dance, but Steph loved it. I knew Anthony suffered through it because of how happy it made Stephanie.

As soon as they were gone, Karl asked, "You want to talk about your relationship? I know you don't believe in what I do, but I might just impress you with what I know."

"I don't need a therapist to tell me that my views on relationships are screwed up." I glanced at him. "I hope this doesn't come across as offensive, because I don't mean it that way, but don't you have a hard time convincing your clients you know what you're talking about when you're not married?"

Karl's lips thinned. He took a swig of his drink. "I was married. For six years. My wife had cystic fibrosis. They wanted to do a lung transplant, but they couldn't find a donor in time. So she passed away. A little more than two years ago."

"That's… I'm so sorry. I can't believe Stephanie didn't tell me."

"I asked her not to. I don't want it to be the first thing people know about me. I'd rather tell them in my own time." He sat back. "Everyone keeps saying I should get back out there. But it's impossible not to compare them all to Monica."

"At least you had training on how to make those six years good."

"You'd think. She used to get mad whenever I'd ask her

counseling-type questions. I had to word them differently so she didn't know what I was doing, and even then, she caught on pretty quick." He stared at the table, a faraway look on his face. One corner of his mouth twisted up. "She taught me the real-world experience I needed."

"So after going through that, don't you hesitate to do it all again?" I asked.

Karl nodded. "Sure. It's why I'm sitting here with you right now instead of going over to the blonde at the end of the bar and asking her out."

Trying to be subtle, I checked out the girl he was talking about. She was pretty, dressed in clothes that were sexy but not completely revealing, and had these cute black glasses.

"You should go," I said. "The worst she could say is no."

Karl shot me a sidelong glance. "I'm not sure I should be taking relationship advice from someone who dumped a perfectly good guy."

"Just because I'm a big failure at relationships doesn't mean I'm not right about the blonde. She keeps looking back here, and she's going to think you and I are together." I nudged Karl with the tip of my shoe. "Go."

He reluctantly stood up and headed over to the bar.

Another song started and Stephanie and Anthony didn't come back. When I'd thought about getting out, sitting in a nightclub by myself wasn't what I had in mind.

Is that my phone? I could barely hear it over the noise. I dug my cell out of my purse and stared at the display. *Jake.*

Finger over the accept button, I went back and forth on whether I should answer.

"You look sad sitting here all by yourself," a guy said as he approached, interrupting my dilemma. He extended his hand. "Come dance with me."

I was going to say I should save the table, but Anthony and

Stephanie were making their way back.

What the hell? I might as well try to have a good time while I'm here.

I took his outstretched hand and let him lead me to the dance floor. It had been a while since I'd danced in a nightclub. Not much had changed: girls in Barbie-size clothes danced like they were auditioning to be America's next top stripper; one look-at-me girl was dancing on the platform; people grinded against one another.

The guy who'd led me to the floor threw his arms around me and started swaying to the beat. Within seconds, he leaned in for a kiss.

I jerked away. "Whoa, buddy. Aren't you supposed to buy a girl a drink first?"

"I've got some wine at my apartment." He pulled me closer. "It's only a few blocks away."

"How nice for you." I stepped back. "I'm all danced out."

I huffed off the floor and went back to sit with Stephanie and Anthony.

"That was quick," Steph said.

"Yeah. He thought I'd be interested in the fact that he has an apartment a few blocks away. I wasn't."

Stephanie leaned her head on Anthony's shoulder. "I'm so glad I don't have to deal with that anymore." She shot a pointed look at me. "You wouldn't have to deal with it either if you weren't so stubborn."

"The point was to forget about everything, not have it rubbed in my face."

"But part of a best friend's duty is pointing out things you might not want to hear."

Karl sat down in the chair next to me. "How'd it go with the blonde?" I asked.

"Had a nice conversation. Got her number. So, we'll see."

The four of us sat there, listening to the music as the lights bounced around the room. Watching all the other people mingle wasn't making me feel better. I'd wanted to get out so badly, but now that I was out, I kept thinking it really wasn't all that great.

Chapter Twenty-four

Since I had a basic idea of Jake's schedule, it wasn't too hard to keep from running into him. I headed to the office early and made sure to avoid coming or going into the building around the time Blue closed.

The Lion Inn job was becoming an even bigger mess by the day. Now the owners were talking about adding a few extended-stay suites. They wanted a whole different look for the rooms, and I just didn't have the same passion that I had for my residential jobs.

At least I get to see Mrs. Crabtree today, I thought as I pulled into her neighborhood. She'd asked if I wanted to do lunch at Blue first—her treat—but I told her I couldn't get away from the office that early. Which was true. But mostly I couldn't see Jake. It was only Wednesday and I was going through withdrawals.

Mrs. Crabtree greeted me in typical grandmother form, offering cookies and asking about my day. She led me to the bathroom and I studied the pink-striped wall. The painters had done a great job on it. I bent down and studied the new baseboards. "I think it looks great. Do you like it?"

Mrs. Crabtree nodded enthusiastically. "I really do. Clyde told me he thought I was crazy for wanting a pink bathroom. When I showed it to him, he put his arm around me and said if I'm happy, he's happy. I think once we get everything else into place it's going to be perfect."

"I better get to work, then."

I kicked off my ruffled, red suede pumps and worked on getting the bathroom together. I hung shadow boxes, filled them with knickknacks—one of them being the sculpture I'd bought from Tina. Looking at the glass-blown flower made me think about how Jake had carried it home for me. If only I'd said no that night, I wouldn't be thinking about him now.

I shook that thought from my head and got to work on the last touches: hanging pink daisy towels and placing the rugs around the room. I'd had it all planned out in my mind, but it turned out even better than expected.

Mrs. Crabtree beamed when she saw the finished room. "I've got to go get Clyde and show him. I bet he's reading the paper in his den."

I put my shoes back on, gathered my leveler and hammer, stuck them back into my toolbox, and set it by my purse.

Then I heard an awful noise. A noise I couldn't quite place, but immediately told me something was wrong. I hurried through the house, searching for where it was coming from. Through the open door of the den, I saw Mrs. Crabtree leaning over her husband.

"Something's wrong with him," she cried.

The antique desk in the corner had a phone on top. I picked it up and punched in 911.

• • •

I pulled my car into the parking garage and made my way to the elevator. I'd been trying to hold it together, but I could feel myself cracking. My eyes burned, a giant lump had permanently lodged in my throat, and a steady rhythm of pain pounded through my head.

I climbed on the elevator, leaned against the wall, and ran a hand through my hair. The elevator stopped on the first floor and Jake got on. I didn't say anything for fear I'd start crying.

Jake's eyebrows drew together. He reached out and put his hand on my arm, his eyes searching mine. "Darby? What's wrong?"

If he wouldn't have asked, I might've made it. "Mrs. Crabtree's husband had a stroke. I went to the hospital with her and it was awful." I felt a tear slide down my cheek. "All while we waited for the rest of her family to get there, Mrs. Crabtree told me stories of their sixty years together. I kept praying Clyde would be okay, but…" I forced the last few words out. "He didn't make it."

Jake pulled me to him and I buried my head in his chest. I'd wanted to get home before losing it. Now that he had his arms around me, though, I couldn't keep it in any longer. The tears broke free and the raw achy sensation in my chest spread until I thought I might crumble to the ground. Mrs. Crabtree was one of my favorite clients, and I'd had to sit there and watch her world get turned upside down.

Jake kept me tucked against him as we stepped off the elevator and walked down the hall to my door. Once inside, he led me to the couch and sat down next to me.

"I hardly even knew him, but it was so sad." I leaned my head on Jake's shoulder. He put his arm around me and ran his hand up and down my arm. My phone rang again. I didn't bother moving.

"You need to get that?" he asked softly.

"It's my boss. She's called me about ten times, but I was too drained to answer. I'm sure she's upset about something." His shirt smelled like cologne and faintly like Blue. The thought of food made my stomach growl. I put my arm over it, trying to quiet it.

"Have you eaten dinner yet?"

"I'm fine. I'll grab some cereal in a minute."

Jake patted my knee. "You sit here. I'll whip something up."

"You don't have to. I'm fine. Really." The fact he was being so nice—especially after everything that happened between us—made me feel like a huge jerk.

"I know I don't have to." Jake walked over to my kitchen. He opened cupboards and studied the things I had—a whole lot of nothing. "How do you feel about pancakes?"

"Sounds perfect."

After I collected myself, I listened to the messages from Patricia. I didn't have the energy to explain everything that had happened, and I didn't want to talk to her anyway, so I sent her a lengthy text with the important details.

Jake set a giant stack of pancakes in front of me, along with a bottle of syrup. "I've got to get back to work. Do you need anything else before I go?"

I shook my head. "Thank you, Jake. I don't deserve it."

He cupped my cheek and wiped a tear away with his thumb. "Call me if you need anything."

I barely restrained myself from begging him not to go.

• • •

Mrs. Crabtree and her stories about her husband stuck with me. I went to bed thinking about her, and immediately thought of her again the next morning. As soon as I got into the office, I sent flowers, wishing I could do something more helpful.

Jake was also on my mind. He'd come in and made me dinner, even after I'd basically dumped and avoided him. Digging into the Lion Inn account seemed like an impossible task, but I didn't have a choice. With all the catching up I had to do, I worked through lunch.

At five, I couldn't take it anymore.

The walk to Blue was nice. It gave me the chance to prepare a speech thanking Jake for his help last night and telling him how much I appreciated his friendship, then reaffirming that he deserved a girl who had the same stance as he did on relationships.

When I got to Blue, Mindy informed me Jake wasn't in.

I walked back to the office, got my car, and headed home. My speech got lengthier on the drive. The more I thought about it, the more I knew it was the right thing to do. Tell him I cared, but insist he'd be better off without me. Surely he'd understand that he meant a lot to me even though we couldn't be together.

Worried I might lose the courage to give my speech if I went to my place first, I got into the elevator and punched the button for the twentieth floor.

My heart raced as I stepped out of the elevator. My stomach churned as I walked down the hall. By the time I knocked on the door, I was a nervous, sweaty wreck.

Jake opened the door and all the words I planned on saying flew out of my head. I threw my arms around his neck, and smashed my mouth to his, kissing him the way I'd been thinking about kissing him for days.

Jake pulled me into his place, closed the door, and pinned me against it. With each caress of his tongue, heat built up in my body, until every inch of me was burning. I was seconds from getting carried away and ripping off his shirt when he broke the kiss.

His chest rose and fell against mine. He ran his nose across the top of my cheek and kissed the sensitive spot under my ear, sending a delicious chill down my spine. "Hey."

I bit my lip, barely managing to suppress a moan. "I came to thank you for last night."

His warm breath tickled my neck. "Much better than a card."

This was the moment to follow up with the rest of it.

"I'm on my way to meet some friends for dinner," Jake said. "You wanna come with me?"

"I wouldn't want to intrude on your plans. I just wanted to let you know how much I appreciate what you did last night. Even though I didn't deserve it."

Jake put a hand on my hip, the way he had the first night we met. And like the first night we met, it sent my pulse skyrocketing. "You wouldn't be intruding. We're just meeting at Buffalo Wild Wings to watch the game. Tina and her boyfriend will be there, and a couple of guys I play in a basketball league with."

Meeting his friends. More entanglement. Opposite of what I was supposed to be doing...

He slipped his hand behind me and pulled me tighter against him, making my thoughts go fuzzy. "Come on. It'll be fun."

The grin he flashed did me in. Especially as I took in his T-shirt, jeans, and baseball cap. Casual and sporty looked good on him. I, on the other hand, was wearing a cream-colored silk shirt that didn't seem like a good idea when it came to eating bright orange wings. "Do I have time to change?"

. . .

Jake and I walked into Buffalo Wild Wings. Flat-screen televisions hung on every wall, so no matter where you were, you could see some kind of sporting event playing out. He grabbed my hand and led me to a table in the back with a great view of a giant screen.

"Hey, everyone," Jake said. "This is Darby."

A sea of greetings came at me.

"You know Tina." She was next to an attractive guy with a shaved head and the biggest arms I'd ever seen. "That's Vinnie."

"Adam..." Jake pointed at the scrawny guy with the goatee, then the athletic-looking guy with the dirty-blond hair. "And that's Pete."

"Nice to meet you all." I scooted in next to Tina and Jake sat on the other side of me.

"I'm almost done with your friend's vases," Tina said. "They're turning out really well, if I do say so myself."

"You totally saved the day."

"I owe you, too. I've had several people come in and tell me you referred them."

Jake put his arm around me. "So which wings do you want? They have just about every kind you can think of. We usually get a big thing and mix and match."

My phone rang and I groaned. "Sorry. It's my boss again. Just get whatever; I'm not picky."

With the music and the talking, I couldn't hear myself think, much less what Patricia was saying. I nudged Jake. He moved, and I tried to get away from the noise.

I stepped into the quietest corner I could find, pressed my phone to my ear, and used my free hand to plug the other ear. "What was that?"

"Where's Nadine?" Patricia asked, annoyance filling her voice.

"I have no idea. Did you call her cell?"

"Of course I did. I need a number from her, but she's not picking up. I was hoping you had it."

"Didn't Nadine give you the entire vendor list?"

Patricia exhaled loudly enough I could hear it through the phone. "I'm out to dinner. I don't have it *with* me."

Sure, she *gets to go out to dinner.*

As luck would have it, I had the number she was looking for stored in my phone. I rattled it off, hung up, and headed back to the table.

"So she's just going to come in and out whenever she feels like it?" Tina asked.

Jake shrugged. "It's not like —"

"Hey, Darby," Adam said, nice and loud, leading me to believe that Jake and Tina were talking about me.

"Sorry about that," I said. "I've got this big project at work that my boss won't leave me alone about."

Jake stepped aside so I could get to my seat, then sat back down beside me. The guys were all focused on the Rockies game going on the wall opposite us. A guy from the Yankees caught the ball that the batter popped into the air.

Everyone groaned except Jake. His lips curved into a megawatt grin. "You guys are so going down tonight."

Adam reached for a fried mozzarella stick. "No way. We can still win."

Glancing at the score, I saw the Rockies were down by seven. "So you're a Yankees fan," I said to Jake, though it was pretty obvious, what with the cheering and the Yankees cap he was sporting.

"Born and raised. Every year these guys claim the Rockies are going to win one, but they always lose." He put his hand on my thigh. "You care about baseball?"

"Uh, no. The only more boring sport on TV is golf. Or bowling. I can handle a football game now and then, but I don't care enough to go out of my way to watch one."

Adam's mouth dropped. "I don't know if we can let you hang out with us if you don't care about sports. It's what we're all about."

"I'll let you in on a secret. Most girls don't care about sports. They just say they do to impress you. Once you're hooked, they'll start complaining about how much you watch. Only a select few actually like to sit around yelling at the TV, acting like they can influence the outcome of the game."

"She's right," Pete said. "I've had girlfriends who say they're huge sports fans, then a few months in, they want to go out when the game's on. And if you come to a place like this, they accuse you of ignoring them."

"Tina likes sports," Vinnie said.

Tina nodded. "I do. I grew up in a house with four brothers and played every sport I could in high school. I don't yell at the TV, though."

"Oh!" Jake hollered. "Look at that hit! Go three, go three." The batter rounded the bases, making it to third seconds before the baseman caught the ball. Jake inclined his head to me, though his gaze remained on the TV screen. "See, if the Rockies win, I have to buy. If the Yankees win, they have to pay." He raised his voice, glancing around the table. "What are we up to now? Like, three in a row?"

The other guys complained and grumbled. I sat there, listening to them discuss the best teams, thinking about my no-sports-fanatics rule.

How do I know if Jake's just your average fan or the guy who can't miss a game? And how much does it matter, since I can't stop breaking my rules with him anyway?

A few minutes later, a heated debate about pitchers broke out. None of them could agree who was the best, and they all had strong opinions about it.

Jake nudged me. "Care to weigh in?"

"My favorite pitcher is glass," I said. "I got it at Pottery Barn. It's handblown—kind of like what Tina does, but not as colorful. I especially like it when it's full of something to drink."

Jake shook his head, but he was smiling. "Pretty funny. Since you don't really care, just say Mariano Rivera. The guy's won five World Series with the Yankees and is one of the best closers of all time. Isn't that impressive?"

I put my hand on his neck and ran my fingers through the ends of his hair. "Next time I can't fall asleep, I'm going to call you and have you tell me baseball stats. I'm sure I'll be asleep in no time."

Adam jumped up, rocking the table. "Look at that! He's out." He pointed at Jake. "So much for your big hitter."

The trash talk started up again, barely settling down when the waitress brought a giant platter of wings, fries, and onion rings.

I sat back and ate, watching everyone else get really into the game. Every now and then Jake would smile at me, squeeze my thigh, give me a quick kiss, or ask how I was doing. The bustle of the place, the way the guys got so into the game—I was actually enjoying watching it all unfold.

"That's game," Jake said as both teams came onto the field. "Sorry, suckers. Maybe next year."

Pete, Vinnie, and Adam frowned and hung their heads like they'd had something to do with the loss.

Adam tossed a napkin onto his plate. "I'm so sick of losing. Maybe I'll just jump on the bandwagon and switch teams."

As they argued the strategy needed for the Rockies to start winning, Jake took the black binder holding the check, put several bills into it, and held it out low for the waitress as she walked by. He gave me a quick peck on the lips. "Hope that wasn't too boring."

"I had a good time," I said. "It's been a while since I've been around crazy sports enthusiasts. And I forgot how good an entire meal of fried stuff could be."

He laced his fingers with mine. "Ready to go?"

He'd paid the bill even though his team had won, and now he was going to sneak away before his friends found out. Steph was right. I was an idiot for not holding on to him.

Jake helped me to my feet and wrapped his arm around me. "See you guys later. Ball on Saturday morning, right?"

I waved. "It was nice meeting you all."

Earlier I'd been prepared to give my speech about not getting too involved; walking out of the restaurant with Jake's arm around me, I was sure it was way too late.

CHAPTER TWENTY-FIVE

 $\mathcal{Y}$ ou can tell a lot about people by the way they act when they don't think anyone's looking. I lingered near the bar of the restaurant, watching Drew and Lisa laughing and talking. I couldn't believe I'd let him convince me to go to dinner with them—I was the third wheel way too often. But Drew was right. There *was* something different about Lisa. For one, I didn't immediately dislike her. Most of the girls he dated got on my nerves within the first thirty minutes. But Lisa was actually easy to talk to and totally down to earth.

"Can I get you something?" the bartender asked, drawing my attention away from my brother and his girlfriend.

"No thanks." I walked across the room and sat opposite Drew and Lisa.

She leaned her elbows on the table. "Drew talks to me about all the stuff he has to do on the ranch, and it sounds like a lot of long, hard days. How'd you like growing up there?"

"I hated it at first," I said. "Moving there at thirteen wasn't exactly easy."

Her brows knit together as she turned to Drew. "I thought you said you lived there your whole life?"

"I did. Darby and Janet didn't move in until Janet and my dad got married. I was fourteen."

"Oh. I knew Janet was your stepmom. I guess I didn't realize Darby was your stepsister. You two are so close."

"It wasn't always that way. I thought Drew and Devin hated me. I didn't realize that's just how brothers are." I picked up a fry, swiped it through the puddle of ketchup, and tossed it in my mouth. "I never would've survived high school without them, though."

"Darby learned to be tough by the end of her time on the ranch," Drew said. "She actually turned into a pretty good cowgirl."

"Aw, thanks." I took a sip of my drink and turned my attention back on Lisa. "Drew tells me you're a veterinarian."

She tucked her red hair behind an ear. "I specialize in dogs and cats. I haven't seen horses or cows since vet school."

Most of the girls Drew dated couldn't handle the farm. It never made any sense to me. They didn't want to be there but freaked out when he dumped them, even though being with him would mean being on the farm. Sitting here, I started to wonder if Drew was actually going to break his pattern.

Great. If Drew falls in love and does the wedding thing, I'm going to have no one to hang out with. Or live with.

Lisa kissed Drew's cheek. "Excuse me, honey. I've got to go to the bathroom."

Drew moved out of her way, then watched her walk away, a goofy grin on his face.

"Traitor," I said.

He grinned at me. "I told you she was great."

• • •

Monday after he got off work, Jake came over, even though he'd spent most of yesterday evening at my place as well. I'm pretty anti-let-me-cook-and-serve-you when it comes to men, but Jake had cooked for me twice—three times if you count the brownies. So I'd made him Sunday dinner, going so far as to set my table with candles and buy a good bottle of wine. It felt like a big step, and for me, it was. I was preparing meals and making plans that revolved around his schedule. We talked about my job, and options for my career if things at work continued going badly. And instead of pushing him away because of that, I just went with it. Mostly because I was so damn happy around him I couldn't help myself.

We ate the leftovers and settled onto the couch to watch a movie. I scrolled through the selection on my TV, enjoying being tucked next to him. "How about this one?"

His eyebrows lowered. "It looks…awful. The guy in it bugs me."

"He's funny."

"Go down two more. I remember thinking that one sounded good."

I clicked down to the movie he wanted and hit the info button. I started reading about the true-life events of two brave men in World War I. And then my mind shut down. "I can't even read what it's about without getting bored. After my day today, I need something funny. And this one," I said, scrolling back up to my original choice, "will be funny." I stuck out my lower lip. "Are you telling me that you won't watch it with me?"

"Don't," Jake said, the corners of his mouth twitching from fighting a smile. "That's not fair."

I worked at looking even sadder. "All I want is to sit back with a funny movie, and even after I watched baseball with you, you're going to make me see it all alone?" I leaned in and kissed his neck. "Come on. You know you want to watch it with me."

Jake laughed. "You think you can just pout and get your way?"

"Uh-huh."

"Fine. We'll watch your stupid movie."

I grinned at him. "Oh, okay. If you insist." I bought the

comedy and settled in next to Jake, happy to have a simple night at home to relax and watch a movie with my really cute… whatever he was.

Shortly after the movie got going, my eyelids felt heavy—I'd stayed up too late with Jake last night and it was catching up with me. I blinked a couple times, and with each blink it took a little longer to keep my eyes open. I rested my head on Jake's shoulder, thinking I'd just close my eyes for a minute.

When I awoke, the credits were rolling up my TV screen, accompanied by an obnoxious wannabe rap song. Apparently, my minute had turned into two hours.

"You know how you pouted to get your way?" Jake asked.

"Nope," I said with a smile. "I don't remember that at all."

"Then you fell asleep, leaving me to watch this stupid movie by myself. I kept eyeing the remote on the coffee table, wanting to turn it off and watch something else, but I didn't want to wake you up."

I stifled a yawn. "The twenty or so minutes I saw of it weren't that bad."

Jake kissed my forehead, leaving his lips there as he spoke. "Next time, I'm going to rent the war drama."

The clock on the cable box read 1:34. In a little over five hours, my alarm would go off. "I don't think I can do this anymore."

Jake sighed. "Not this again."

It took me a second to put it together. "I mean staying up this late night after night Dragging myself out of bed in the morning is going to be killer, and I'm already having enough stress at work without adding lack of sleep."

"I guess I should go then."

"I guess so," I said, but I didn't move. "It's just that you're really comfortable. And you're warm and you smell nice…"

He ran his fingers down my back, and I had to fight hard to keep my eyes open. I pushed myself up. "Okay, I've got to get to bed before I fall asleep again and then you have to deal with me being grouchy in the morning."

Just before we reached the door, Jake turned and wrapped his arms around my waist. "You know, you forced me to watch a horrible movie—which you slept through—and I still had a good time. You know what that means, right?"

I tipped onto my toes and kissed his perfect lips, one kiss to hold onto tonight. Another to get me through the hours until I could see him again. "That pouting works better than I thought?"

Jake smiled, then his expression turned serious. The way his eyes were boring into mine somehow sent both heat and nerves through my stomach. "I want to tell you something, but I'm afraid it'll freak you out."

I swallowed, the gesture taking a lot more effort than usual. I suspected it might include the L-word, and he was right about it freaking me out. Things were finally easy between us again, and I didn't want to step into the dangerous, serious zone. "Then you better not say it."

He pulled me closer, our hips bumping together, and covered my mouth with his. As tired as I was a few seconds ago, every part of me was suddenly very alert. He slid a hand under my shirt, his fingertips stroking my bare back. I bit lightly at his bottom lip. He groaned and crushed me to him. Then he thrust his tongue in to meet mine, kissing me so deeply the room spun.

I clung onto him, losing myself in the moment, wanting to drag him to my bedroom but knowing I couldn't yet. For some reason…I was having trouble remembering it right now. I broke the kiss and worked on getting air back into my lungs.

Jake blew out his breath. He raked a hand through his hair, making it messy. He looked so hot I had to work at holding back my surging hormones. "Good night," he said, his voice husky. Then he shot me a roguish smile that sent desire burning through my veins. "Sweet dreams."

Oh, I was pretty sure my dreams would be featuring him tonight. And they'd probably be more dirty than sweet.

Chapter Twenty-six

Stephanie paused outside of the gallery, her hand on the door. Instead of pulling it open like I thought she was going to, she spun around to face me. "I just realized something. Charlie wasn't Prince Charming. Jake is."

As we'd walked down the sidewalk, I'd been gushing about Jake, telling her all about how great he was and how much fun I'd been having with him lately. I should've known better.

"Don't do that," I said. "I don't want to think about my stupid case studies right now." I simply wanted to enjoy being with a guy who made me happy and not worry about the future or how he tied in to all my past exes.

"But think about it. You lost your shoe at the restaurant and you went dancing together. He cares about your job. He's not deterred when you try to push him away. He's totally Prince Charming."

"The whole point of putting those case studies together was to prove that there is no Prince Charming. Fairy tales and real life are nothing alike."

"Yeah, real life's harder, blah, blah, blah." Steph crossed her arms and raised a challenging eyebrow. "You're just too scared to see if you're wrong. Because it means putting yourself out there again."

I thought about last night, how Jake had said he wanted to tell me something. I went back and forth on whether I should've let him tell me. If I could handle it. It was getting harder and harder to live life halfway with him, and I wasn't sure I wanted to hold back anymore. I was too stubborn to admit she was the tiniest bit right, though, so I changed the subject. "Time crunch, remember? Patricia's been commenting on how long my lunches are."

"You normally love your work," Stephanie said. "Maybe Jake's right about you branching off on your own."

"Maybe. But right now, I've got to focus on this job. After we get your vases. Because nothing's as important as your wedding."

Smiling, Steph nodded. "That's right."

Mission accomplished. When desperate for a distraction, the wedding's always a winner. She pulled the door open and we headed back to Tina's display room. Tina was talking to a woman in the corner, explaining the inspiration behind one of her larger pieces.

A red-and-blue heart sculpture that looked partway melted caught my eye. "I think I need this to remind myself that heartbreak—or heart melt—is inevitable."

"*Phfft.* Like you need a reminder to be Debbie Downer," Steph said.

Tina invited the woman to look around, then walked up to Stephanie and me. "Come on back and I'll show you the vases before we pack them up."

"I can't thank you enough for doing this last minute," I said.

Stephanie and I followed Tina through a small door. The walk-in closet had that stuffy smell that comes from lack of fresh air. Various glass pieces dotted the shelves and the heart vases sat on a desk.

Steph picked one up and studied it. "They're even prettier than the vases I special ordered." The three of us started bubble wrapping and placing them into little square cardboard places in the box. "Do you have your maid of honor speech prepared yet?"

I ripped off a sheet of bubble wrap. "Not yet."

"You're not going to say anything anti-marriage or anti-love, right?"

"Do you really have to ask?"

Steph raised her eyebrows, answering by not answering.

I scowled at her. "I'm not *that* bad. You know I want everything to go right for you on your big day. I'm sure I'll find something great to say about love and the institution of marriage."

Tina tucked the last vase inside the box, then straightened and stared at me. "I keep going back and forth on whether I should say something, but I can't help myself. I've always been a loudmouth."

I leaned against the table, waiting for whatever she was going to say.

"Jake could have his pick of nice girls, but for some reason, he always chooses girls who don't appreciate him," Tina said. "You know I like you. I think you're funny, and you've been really great for my business. I just don't think you're good for Jake."

Stunned would be an understatement. Stephanie stood there next to me, mouth hanging open, eyes wide, and I was sure my expression matched—if not surpassed—hers.

Tina lifted her chin, her jaw set. "Jake and I have been friends for a long time. He's a great guy, and I feel like you're messing with him. And he'll let you because he likes you."

I took a deep breath to steady my voice. "I'm not trying to mess with him. I told him from the beginning that I don't do the big relationship thing. Maybe that doesn't make sense to you or to him or to anyone. But this is who I am, and he says he's okay with it."

"He says that, but he's lying. Lying to himself. I'm not going to give the whole 'if you hurt him' speech. All I'm saying is that if you really don't think there's something there, you shouldn't waste any more of his time."

Needless to say, things were a little weird after Tina's speech. It was a relief when Steph and I finally made it back to my car. Steph stuck the box filled with her vases in the backseat, eased the door closed, and put a hand on my shoulder. "I totally get it. I've watched you get hurt over and over again." Her eyes met mine. "But what if this time really is different? I don't think you should dump him because of what Tina said. You're not wasting his time."

I bit my lip. "Despite my best efforts, I'm afraid I'm already too attached. I even tried to pull away, but it didn't work. If I don't have a good reason, I'll just get sucked back in." I leaned against my car, trying to figure out what I was going to do. "I need to find that thing that'll eventually break us apart before I end up repeating all my past mistakes."

"Just take him to meet Drew and Devin," Stephanie said with a smile. "Those boys always cause fights between you and your boyfriends."

I stared at her for a moment. Hadn't I just rehashed how much conflict Robert and my clashing over our families had caused? "You're right. I've got to put him through the real test before letting my guard down."

Stephanie put her hands on my shoulders. "Darby, I was kidding. Don't you have a rule about not taking a guy home until you absolutely have to?"

"I've already been breaking all the rules." I shrugged. "What's one more?"

• • •

Jake invited me to "come on in."

His giant flat-screen TV was tuned to the Yankees game. One of the players spit, and with the hugeness and the high-defness, I saw—way too clearly—a leftover bubble of saliva on his lip.

"You've really got to be committed to be a baseball fan," I said, sitting next to him on the couch. "There's a game on, like, every night."

"This one's pretty much over." Jake picked up the remote, hovered his finger over the power button, and watched the next play.

"Go ahead and watch it. You just owe me dessert afterward."

Jake set his hand on my thigh and squeezed. "You're awesome, you know that?"

I smiled at him. "I know."

All through the game, I chewed on my fingernail, going back and forth on my plan to take Jake home with me. Earlier today I'd been so sure; now I was wondering if I was ready for this casual, easy fun to end.

But Tina thinks I'm wasting his time. And maybe I am. I took in his profile, the stubble on his chin, how his eyes had a hint of green, since he was wearing black today. *Who am I kidding? We already passed the casual stage. It's time for the make-or-break one.*

When the game was over, I picked up the remote—just to see how much I could get away with. Jake didn't rip it out of my hands; he didn't even say anything about it. *Divine Design* was on the HGTV channel, so I stopped there, waiting for the protests.

Jake didn't protest. He started kissing my neck, then trailed kisses along my jaw. After that, I didn't care what was on television anyway. Within a few minutes we ended up horizontal on the couch. The weight of his body made me feel secure and dizzy, all at the same time. Still, he didn't seem close enough. I hooked my leg over his, bringing our bodies together. Delicious heat wound through me. His tongue rolled over mine.

I arched into him and shockwaves shot through my core. He moaned and slid his hands up my shirt. His fingers brushed the bottom of my bra. One more inch and this was happening—I'd never be able to stop.

Shit, shit, shit!

I pressed my hand to his chest, pushing him back. "I think…I think we better slow down." Closing my eyes, I blew out my breath. My rules about sex had been in place long before I typed up my case studies. I only crossed that line when I was sure I was ready for the next step, and I didn't plan on breaking that for anyone.

I opened my eyes, bracing for the anger or for him telling me I was a tease or worse—I'd gotten it before. When it came to sex, women were called a prude, a tease, or a slut. No in between and nothing flattering. No good job, you've waited the perfect amount of time and had the exact right number of partners.

Jake leaned his forehead on my shoulder and I could feel his breath coming in and out against my skin.

"Sorry," I said. "I shouldn't have let it get that far."

"I just…need a minute." He took a couple more deep breaths, lifted his head, and gave me a quick kiss on the lips, then slowly sat back up, pulling me with him.

I straightened my shirt, unable to look at him.

He cupped my chin and gently turned my face toward his. "I'll wait."

For the life of me, I couldn't figure out why he would. No doubt he'd be able to find another woman willing to go all the way. I'd be lying if I said I wasn't tempted to just say screw it, do my best to not think about what would happen afterward, and finish what we started. But I couldn't. It wasn't me, and I still wasn't willing to put my heart out there that much quite yet. "I just can't… Not until…"

"I'll wait," he repeated.

Tina's words ran though my head again: *If you really don't think there's something there, you shouldn't waste any more of his time.*

There's definitely something, I thought. *But I'm not sure if it's enough. Or if I can really do this to myself again.* I leaned into his chest and inhaled his familiar musky and woodsy-smelling cologne. *Time to put him to the real test.*

"I was wondering..." I almost chickened out. But then I thought about how close I'd been to ignoring my rules a moment ago and charged on with it. "My stepdad's birthday is on Sunday, so I'm going to Longmont." I glanced up, looking into his eyes. "I was wondering if you wanted to come with me."

A smile spread across his face, sending a pang of guilt through my gut. "Really? *You* want *me* to meet your family."

Is it too late to take it back?

"You don't have to. The ranch is kind of in the middle of nowhere. I've just got to drive over and—"

"I'll go."

The guilt running through me deepened as I stared at him.

He doesn't stand a chance.

Chapter Twenty-seven

As the city fell away to a whole lot of nothing, I glanced at Jake. He'd asked several questions about my family during the drive, and I'd filled him in on the basics. After all the effort he'd put into learning the names and history of my family, I decided I should let him know what he was in for.

"My brothers usually give my…" *Boyfriend* still wouldn't roll off my tongue. "They like to give everyone who comes home with me a bad time. You don't have to try to impress them. They might call you a city boy or whatever, but that's just the way they are. They have a strange sense of humor. If they ask you to do anything you're not comfortable with, just say no."

Jake grinned. "That's so sweet. Darby Quinn's worried about me meeting her family. It almost seems like you care about me."

My phone rang, saving me from coming up with something to say to that. When I saw it was my mom, I answered.

"Hey, sweetheart," Mom said. "I wanted to make garlic toast to go with dinner, but I forgot the French bread. I'm in the middle of frosting the cake and I was hoping you could swing into Johnson's Market and pick it up for me."

"No problem. One loaf or two?"

"Two. And could you get some more Mountain Dew? I think we're low. Oh, and another gallon of vanilla ice cream, because I thought we had some, but I think the guys got into it earlier this week."

I hit my blinker and turned into the grocery store parking lot. "I'm at Johnson's now, so we'll get the stuff and be there soon." I hung up and glanced at Jake. "My mom needs a few things from the store. Looks like you get the whole small-town treatment."

We got out of the car and walked across the parking lot. I dislodged a cart from the others and pushed it toward the bakery section. The grocery store near my condo was always rearranging everything, making it impossible to find something you knew had been there last time. Johnson's Market—which had been operating since basically the dawn of time—always had everything in the same place. I grabbed two loaves of bread, then headed over to the soda aisle.

Jake lifted a case of Mountain Dew.

"Better get two. Actually, make it three. They go through a lot." I left the cart by him and stepped around a display to find the oatmeal-chocolate-chip cookies Dwight loved.

"Darby Wilson!" a voice shrieked at an octave so high, I expected dogs to come running. "Is that you?"

Tabitha Newton, the witch who made my high school experience hell, stood in the aisle. I fought the urge to turn and run. She'd stuck with "The Rachel" haircut, so she looked about the same as she did in high school. A little outdated, but still pretty.

I forced the corners of my mouth into a smile. "Hi, Tabitha. How are you?"

She stepped forward and hugged me like we were the best of friends instead of torturer and torturee. "I'm just so good. I've got this little angel." She gestured to the chubby toddler sitting in her cart. A sucker stick poked out of his mouth, a stream of red drool coated his chin. "Sherman and I also have a little girl in first grade now, can you believe it? I mean, where does the time go? We've been married for ten years and it's been such a wonderful adventure."

"That's... Wow." I turned back, ready to introduce Jake, but didn't get the words out before Sherman came around the aisle and tossed two boxes of cereal into the cart.

"Look who it is," Tabitha said, pointing at me.

Sherman's eyebrows drew together. He stared at me for what seemed like forever, then recognition flashed across his features. "Darby. Hey. I thought you and Gil lived in California."

"Darby didn't marry Gil." Tabitha rolled her eyes. "He never remembers anything."

Including who his wife is, if the rumors about him cheating are true.

Tabitha placed a hand on his shoulder and spoke slowly. "Gil married some other girl. Darby's not married yet." She turned to me, a big grin on her face. "I'm sure there's someone out there for you, don't you worry."

Desperate to get her to shut up, I clamped onto Jake's arm and pulled him forward. "This is Jake. Jake, this is Tabitha and Sherman. We went to high school together." *It was awful.*

Jake draped his arm over my shoulders and gave Tabitha and Sherman a polite smile. "Nice to meet you."

The toddler started making this whine/moan noise while pawing at Tabitha. I know as a woman I'm supposed to have this innate love of babies, but the truth is, they kind of remind me of zombies. They stumble around, arms out, moaning. And if they get ahold of you, they suck the energy out of you.

I wrapped my arm around Jake's waist, keeping my fake smile plastered on my face. "We better get going. It's Dwight's birthday, so they're expecting us at the ranch."

The kid's moaning grew louder. Sherman turned away from it

and studied the cookies, while Tabitha took her son out of the car and stuck him on her hip. "Well, tell your family I say hello. It's so nice to see you."

There's that saying about if you can't say anything nice, don't say anything at all. I had to say something, though, so I went with, "I will. You guys have a good day."

• • •

"I thought your last name was Quinn," Jake said as we put the groceries into the trunk of my car.

"Since I lived with the Wilsons, people forget my real last name. Or maybe they don't even remember I'm not one. Who knows?" I slammed my trunk down and we got into the car.

"For friends, you didn't seem that happy to see them," Jake said.

"You caught that?" I started the car and turned down the radio.

"I'm not sure if that dude even knew where he was."

"Yeah, that's my ex-boyfriend. Real gem of a guy. Our relationship ended when I caught him with his tongue down Tabitha's throat. They did end up getting married, so I guess you could say it was meant to be. But from what I hear, he's not exactly faithful to her, either. I suppose she did me a favor, really."

I put my car into drive and pulled onto the road. "I think she wanted to show me how happy she was to save face. I actually feel a little bad for her, even though she went out of her way to be awful to me in high school. Seriously, if it weren't for my brothers and their friends, I never would've survived. Luckily, before the guys graduated and left me, Steph showed up. Which is why I owe her. Enough to help her plan her dream wedding." I glanced at Jake. "Sorry. Guess that just drudged up some old drama."

He put his hand on my thigh. "No worries. I got you now, babe."

Warmth filled me, that peace and security I got around Jake—especially when he said things like that—and then I was rethinking this plan all over again.

Better to find out now than when I truly can't pull away, right? Before there's talk of the future and houses and kids and things that made my blood pressure rise, even when they were only hypothetical.

Five miles later, we pulled off the main road. The change in my ashtray clanged together as we drove down the bumpy dirt road leading to the ranch. I slowed to a stop in front of the house and waited for the cloud of dirt around us to settle before getting out.

"So, here we are." I exited the car and took a deep breath of dust-and-manure-tinged air.

Ah. Smells like home.

On the way to the trunk to grab the groceries, a *mew* caught my attention. "Hi, Swampthing." I squatted down and ran my hand down the cat's back. She had long multicolored hair that was matted in places, sticking straight up in others. Even her purr sounded rattley. Which was why Drew had named her Swampthing.

Mom and Dwight came out of the house to greet us. "Hello," Mom said to Jake, positively beaming at him. I'd been blunt about my relationship stance, but I could tell by the way she looked at Jake that she hoped I'd changed my mind.

I introduced everyone, and Dwight gave Jake a firm handshake.

Mom was a hugger, so she went for one. "It's so nice to meet you." She turned and threw her arms around me. I was several inches taller, even without my heels, so I had to hunch over.

"We'd better get the ice cream in." I used my keychain to pop the trunk and everyone pitched in to take the groceries into the house.

Drew and Devin walked into the kitchen as we were putting the last of the food away.

"Hey," Drew said to me, then turned to Jake, hand extended. "I'm… Have we met? You look kind of familiar."

Jake shook Drew's hand. "I live in Darby's building. I ran into you two in the elevator one night."

Drew furrowed his brow. "I guess Darby forgot to introduce us. She thinks I'm embarrassing."

"You were telling the story about how I slapped Ralph at Devin and Anne's wedding. You *are* embarrassing." I pointed to Drew. "This is Drew, and that's Devin. Guys, this is Jake."

Jake looked from Devin to Drew. "It might take me a little while to get names straight." I never thought they looked that much alike. Not like most twins I'd seen.

Drew gave Jake a firm pat on the back. "Let us show you around, Jake. We'll leave Darby here to do girl stuff."

I shot Drew a dirty look. "If you don't watch it, I'm going to pop you one, then we'll see who's crying like a girl."

"Which reminds me," Drew said as he and Devin led Jake out of the room, "we do have the footage of Darby slapping that guy if you want to see it later."

They insisted on doing the tour—the tour they gave to all "city boys"—alone. The few times my brothers and I had fought about it, my boyfriend at the time always insisted he'd be fine without me there. So I'd stopped fighting. I probably should've done a better job warning Jake what he was in for, but then again, I might as well see if he could handle it now. Then I wouldn't have a big what-if hanging over me.

Mom pulled vegetables out of the fridge and placed them on the counter. I sat on a stool opposite her. "Need help?"

Mom slid the cutting board, carrots, tomatoes, and lettuce toward me. "You can make the salad."

Noticing how quiet the house was, I asked, "Where are Anne and the kids?"

"They'll be up in a few. Ava was napping and Anne didn't want to wake her. Devin was excited to come down and show Jake around, though." Mom glanced out the window. "I hope they're nice to him. He seems like a good guy."

"Don't they all in the beginning." I headed to the sink to wash my hands.

"I worry about you, sweetheart. You used to be all about love and romance. Somewhere along the way you got so down on it, and I don't want you to live like that. Finding someone you love is really great."

I dried my hands on a dishtowel. "I'm glad you have Dwight. But didn't you feel that way at first about Dad, too?"

Mom sighed. "Your father and I, we were young, and I didn't realize how much work marriage takes. I can look back now and see all the mistakes I made, but hindsight is always twenty-twenty."

I grabbed the lettuce and knife and sat back down.

"With Dwight, I got married knowing it wasn't going to be easy," Mom said. "Sometimes I'm so mad at him I can't even talk to him. And sometimes, I know that no one else in the world will understand me like he does. It's a nice thing to have." Mom sprinkled seasoning over the steaks and put them in the fridge. "Now if you ask me, you've got a perfectly nice man who's crazy about you." She raised her eyebrows. "Trust me. Moms can sense that thing. I think you should give him a chance."

I ran the knife through the lettuce. "I *am* giving him a chance. That's why I brought him here. Since fairy tales aren't realistic, I've decided to revert back to gladiator times. If he survives the arena—a.k.a. Drew and Devin's tour of the ranch—then I'll know he's worth taking a risk on." Using the knife, I scraped the lettuce into the salad bowl. "I have a feeling, though, that things will go downhill after this."

Mom shook her head. "That's not really giving him a chance."

"It is when you don't believe in chances."

• • •

The boys' signature tour usually lasted about forty-five minutes to an hour, depending on how upset my boyfriends got after the first few challenges. Drew and Devin took the guys into the bull pen with Tiny, rode around the ranch on horseback, and tested their lassoing skills.

At the hour and a half mark, I started to get anxious. My foot took on a life of its own, tapping and shaking. When I couldn't sit still any longer, I paced the floor.

It didn't help that Ava had been crying since Anne had arrived with her and Levi. The screaming seemed to make time stand still. Finally, when the crying reached the I'm-so-mad-I'm-not-breathing-anymore, Mom brought Ava outside.

"What's taking them so long?" Anne asked, glancing out front again.

I realized, sitting here trying to think of something to say to Anne, that I didn't really know her all that well. She'd been in the family for years, but we'd rarely been left one-on-one. I sat on the loveseat across from her. "I know. If they don't get back soon, I'm going to hunt them down."

Anne's lips thinned and the crease in her forehead deepened. "Devin always leaves me here with the kids while he gets to go out and have fun. If it wasn't for Janet's help, I think I would've lost my mind already. Sometimes it seems like I have three kids to take care of."

I always wanted to stick up for Devin when she complained about him. But I could tell she was stressed and knew she only wanted to vent, so I didn't say anything. From what I'd seen, raising two kids wasn't easy.

I'd sometimes wondered if I could've made it work with Robert—if I hadn't been too brash in calling things off. Seeing the stress having kids put on Devin and Anne, though, I knew I'd chosen right. Robert and I would've never been strong enough to make it. Not on top of the other issues we had.

I wonder if he ever found someone to have all his kids.

I heard guys' voices and shot out of my chair. Devin, Drew, and Jake walked in, all dirtier than when they left.

"You'll never guess what happened," Devin said, his eyes lit up with excitement.

"Jake rode Major," Drew said before anyone had the chance to guess.

"What?" I looked from Drew to Devin. "You let him ride Major?"

Devin shrugged. "We didn't think he'd get the saddle on. It was supposed to be funny. The joke was on us because he not only got the saddle on, but he rode him. Without getting bucked off."

I scowled at my brothers. "You guys could've hurt him."

Jake put his hand on my back, then leaned down and kissed my cheek. "It was fun. I haven't been on a horse in a long time."

Dwight and Mom, who was still holding Ava, came in from the backyard. Steam and the scent of cooked meat rose off the platter Dwight was holding. "Steaks are done. Let's eat."

A few minutes later, everyone was sitting around the table, their plates filled with food. Ava didn't want to be put down, so Devin had her on his lap.

Dwight stabbed his steak and sawed at a corner with his knife. "Dang, my arm's still sore. I swear, that heifer was already late as it is, then the second she starts giving birth, she's running around, calf halfway out, acting like a chicken with her head cut off."

Drew swallowed the bite of food in his mouth. "We had to lasso her and tie her to a post to pull her calf. It was one of the biggest I've ever seen."

"That's why I had to stick my hand up there and help her get him out," Dwight continued. "And my arm was so numb I could hardly stand it. It's still killing me."

"Yeah, poor you," I muttered. "The cow's only having a huge baby, but your poor arm."

I'd gotten used to talk like this. Pretty much every guy I ever dated, though, including Evan, the carefree, whatever-goes guy, hated when I spoke of anything remotely bloody while we were eating. Once over dinner I'd started to tell him about watching a surgery on TLC. He'd dropped his fork and said, "Jeez, Darb, not while we're eating."

I glanced at Jake to gauge his reaction.

"I remember the first time I pulled a calf," he said. "I could tell the cow was in trouble, so I had to help her out. My arm was sore for days."

Wait. What?

Jake wiped his mouth with a napkin. "The limousine bull my granddad used that year gave us lots of trouble. The calves were just too big."

I stared at Jake, wondering what he'd reveal next. *Who is this guy?*

Dwight talked about a limousine bull he used to have, then the conversation drifted to the other bulls he'd used over the years, and Jake chimed in with his opinion on the different breeds.

The entire time he talked, I kept thinking I'd only scratched the surface of who Jake was. And as much as I tried to tell myself that I was perfectly good with what I already knew—that knowing more meant getting in deeper—I wanted to know more.

I wanted to know everything.

Chapter Twenty-eight

Because the weather was so nice, we'd eaten cake and ice cream in the backyard. I'd left Jake out there with Dwight, Mom, Anne, and the kids, and headed inside to grab a Mountain Dew. And also because I was freaking out a little bit. After everything Jake had revealed at dinner, I wanted to get him alone, yet I was terrified of the idea at the same time.

Devin and Drew looked up at me as I walked into the kitchen. "You finally brought home someone cool," Drew said. "Looks like you're going to settle down after all."

"Let's not get carried away. I'm considering a steady relationship, not settling down. I see what happens to people when they get married and have kids."

Devin crossed his arms. "Oh really? What happens?"

"You know what I mean. I can't believe you're not with me on this. You and Anne don't even get along anymore."

"That's marriage. Sometimes we get along, sometimes we struggle. But I know we'll work it out because we love each other." Devin locked eyes with me. "Having kids, the ups and downs. You won't have those—won't know the joy that comes along with it—

because of your stupid theory on relationships. Not letting that into your life doesn't make you smarter than me, it just makes you a chicken." He picked up his can of Mountain Dew and headed outside, slamming the door behind him.

"Ouch," I said.

Drew leaned against the counter next to me. "It's okay. I'm a chicken, too. Of course, I'm starting to rethink things a bit."

"Already? You and Lisa just barely met."

"She's smart and funny and she calls me on my crap. I think about her all the time. I think I'm falling for her, Darby. Strike that. I'm totally whipped and I don't even mind admitting it. And if you don't give Jake a chance, you might miss out on something great."

I glanced outside, where I could just make out Jake's profile. I was cracking, I knew—my heart even gave a hopeful flutter as I took him in. But that didn't mean I wasn't going to fight it, despite the overwhelming desire to jump in. "Or I might just get hurt and be forced to start all over again."

"I guess you're going to have to decide right now if you want to be a chicken."

Right now my relationship with Jake felt safe. I liked safe. But what if what was beyond safe was…better? Not that I was going to admit that to Drew. I shrugged. "I'm okay with being a chicken."

Drew pushed me toward the back door. "Wrong answer."

• • •

I pulled back on the reins, bringing Major to a halt near the pond. I swung my foot over and dismounted. Jake brought Sonny up next to me and climbed off.

I draped the reins around the saddle horn and turned to Jake. "You never told me you worked on a farm before."

"You never asked."

I crossed my arms and tilted my head.

"Don't give me that look," Jake said. "I never know what's on the approved list of topics. I do recall something about you not wanting to get into my past."

"I didn't mean you couldn't tell me that kind of stuff. I just meant…" It was hard to clarify when I wasn't sure what I meant anymore. I decided to change the subject instead of try to explain. "So, you know how to ride a horse and you've pulled a calf before. How did you fair in the roping contest?"

"Not as good as your brothers, but I did okay. My dad wanted me to learn to work like he had as a kid, so I spent a few summers on my granddad's farm." He jerked his chin toward Major. "You never told me you had a horse as stubborn as you. Drew and Devin made it sound like I had a smooth ride on him. I was able to get on, but he fought me the entire time."

I ran my hand down my horse's neck. "Major and I have a special bond. He doesn't trust just anyone."

"And neither do you." Jake grabbed my hand and drew me to him. "I know this was a big deal for you, bringing me home. But I'm glad that you did. I like seeing this other side of you."

A knot formed in my chest. "Great. Now you're making me feel guilty." I bit my lip. "I have a confession. I invited you because Tina told me to stop wasting your time if I wasn't going to get serious."

Jake's posture stiffened. "What else did she say?"

"That's about it. So I decided to invite you along to put a strain on things. Normally, my brothers drive guys away. My exes and I have gotten into huge fights about it."

"So you brought me here to dump me?"

"No, I brought you here to have a reason to." I looked up to find him looking down at me. "You messed it all up, though. Now I just like you more." I grabbed a fistful of his T-shirt, pulled him to me, and kissed him.

We'd shared a lot of kisses before, but this one felt different. I let myself melt into it and get carried away in every detail, from his soft lips to the brush of his stubble on my chin. The way his fingers dug into my sides, how he took his time exploring every inch of my mouth. I thought of how he seemed to get me, how he'd been patient, even when I freaked out or pushed him away.

Major nudged me with his nose, whinnying his dislike for not being the center of my attention.

Jake never took his eyes off me, the desire in them clear. I wasn't ready to go all the way, but a little less clothing…I thought it was definitely time for that.

I glanced at the pond, watching the sunlight glimmering on its surface. "Wanna go for a swim?"

"Now?"

I took a deep breath and then peeled off my shirt, glad I'd worn my sexy black lace underwear today. I watched Jake's Adam's apple bob up and down as he ran his gaze over me. I shot him a smile. "Unless you're scared of a little pond scum."

• • •

After our swim, Jake and I laid out on the grass to dry off. I knew that shirtless Jake would be hot, but once I saw the real thing—pecs, abs, and a whole lot of skin that just begged to be touched—I seriously reconsidered my decision to wait.

I rolled onto my stomach and watched his well-toned chest rise and fall with each breath.

He pointed to the initials on the tree. "Looks like you bring all the guys here."

"That's from high school when I was dating one of my brothers' friends." I sat up, pulling my hair to the side and twisting all the water I could get out of it. "Actually, this is one of my favorite places. I've never brought anyone but Gil here because I knew they wouldn't appreciate it. Not to mention after Drew and Devin got ahold of the others, they refused to get on a horse again." I put my hand on Jake's firm chest and smiled. "Since you're apparently part farm boy, I figured you could handle the horse ride it takes to get here."

Jake sat up and kissed my shoulder. "It's nice. Peaceful."

"This is where I used to come to get away from everything and everyone. Moving to the ranch was a rough transition for me." I told Jake about how things were at first, my brothers coming to my rescue at school, and Dwight getting me involved by training Major. "We're not your conventional family, but they took me in, taught me a lot about what family really means, and I love them."

"What about your dad? You don't talk about him much."

I looked out over the water. I'd only talked about my relationship with my dad with one other guy. "Before he and my mom got divorced, they fought *all* the time. Still, they were my parents. I didn't want our family split. When I saw how happy they were apart, though, I finally got it. My mom found Dwight and my dad got remarried and moved to Florida with his wife. For a lot of years, he and I didn't have a very good relationship, but we finally worked past our issues, and now we talk on the phone and visit back and forth when we can."

Jake took my hand and laced his fingers through mine. "I'm sure that was hard. I get how something like that might make you question love."

I shook my head. "Even after my parents divorced, I still believed in love. It was all the relationships I had after it that beat it out of me. That taught me better." My chest squeezed. I wanted to try, I did, but my heart remembered this painful path way too well, and it was shouting a warning at me I couldn't ignore.

I can't do it. I'd rather be a chicken than open myself up to getting hurt again. "We should probably get back."

When I tried to stand, Jake tugged my arm, keeping me next to him. "Anything worth having takes hard work and a little risk." He slipped his hand behind my neck and gently pressed his lips to mine. He kept it short and sweet, but there was enough tenderness behind the kiss that when he pulled away and looked in my eyes, I knew he was trying to tell me that he wasn't giving up on me.

Hope rose up, taking the edge off the fear lodged in my chest. I wasn't sure how I'd gotten lucky enough to meet this guy, and I didn't know if we could have a real relationship, but I knew I didn't want to let him go.

We put on our clothes, climbed on the horses, and rode back across the ranch. After getting oats for the horses, I walked over to Jake and hugged him. It felt like we were under an enchanted spell and I was afraid leaving would break it.

I knew it was time to say good-bye to my family, but knowing it didn't make it any easier. When we got inside the house, Jake and Drew started talking, and I went in search of Devin. I found him in the backyard, pushing Ava and Levi on the swings. Anne was standing next to him, her arm wrapped around his waist. I hadn't seen them like that in a long time.

Devin glanced back just as I was about to retreat instead of interrupt.

"Can I talk to you real fast?" I asked. He gave Levi a big push, then crossed the yard to me.

I kicked at the dandelion sticking up in the grass, sending the yellow flower bobbing. "About what I said earlier, I was out of line." I lifted my eyes to Devin's. "I'm sorry."

Devin shrugged. "No big deal. Guess I was a little harsh, too."

"You know I love you and Anne. And the kids."

Devin glanced at his wife, who was now a dark outline against the setting sun. "I know you've seen us at our worst, but it's not always like that. Anne has a hard time with the baby stage. We fight more. Then we work it out because that's what you do. Every day I wake up and see my beautiful family, I think I'm one of the luckiest people in the world."

Devin didn't do the big talks or show his emotions often. Not with me, anyway. I could tell he meant what he'd said. My heart dropped when I thought about all the times I'd made derogatory comments about his marriage.

"Daddy, I need another push," Levi said.

"I'm sure you'll figure out what'll make you happy," Devin said. "Just don't be scared to go for it when you do." He mussed my hair like he used to when we were growing up, then strode over to Levi and got him swinging high through the air again.

Sometimes, you just need a little push.

Chapter Twenty-nine

The new layout of the extended-stay suites lit up my computer screen. My eyes were trained on it, but my mind was elsewhere. On the drive home from Longmont, Jake had finally convinced me to let him run the numbers on branching off on my own. I'd sent him all the information I had first thing this morning like I promised I would. But it wasn't just the future of my career crowding my thoughts. It was Jake. Taking him home had been a chance. One I thought he'd fail. Instead, he'd gone above and beyond my expectations, winning my whole family over. Including me.

He gave me hope when I thought there was none. He'd stuck with me regardless of all the times I'd tried to push him away. I wanted to call him, even if I didn't have anything in particular to talk about. I wanted to take him to Stephanie's wedding. To tell people he was my boyfriend.

I wanted him to be mine.

Of course, there was only one way to make that happen...
Time to take a chance.

I knew he'd worked the early shift today, which meant he'd probably be home. The thought of having a serious talk of any kind made me nauseous, but I was going to do it anyway.

The entire drive home, my stomach churned. Knowing I'd chicken out if I didn't go straight to his place, I rode the elevator to the top floor. My rapid pulse hammered in my ears as I raised my fist to knock.

When Jake opened the door, his hair was disheveled, the top few buttons of his shirt undone. A volatile mix of desire and anxiety shot through me. I wasn't sure if I was going to jump him or throw up on him. Hopefully not both, because this conversation was going to be hard enough as it was.

"Um, am I interrupting something?" I asked.

"I'm just going through some reports for Blue, trying to figure out a few things. Would you like to come in?"

I stood there for a few seconds, trying to kick my pink, glittery pumps into motion—they seemed to be glued to the floor. "Sure," I said, wishing this wasn't so damn hard. I'd never been one to wish I was normal, but in this moment, I wanted to be at least functional. Not shaking like a leaf because I wanted to ask a guy to be my boyfriend.

Jake seemed slightly distracted and also looked like he'd had a long day—still hot, of course, but in a crumpled, tired way. "I was about to grab a drink. You want one?"

"I'll just take water." *What am I saying? I need something to calm my nerves.* "Or whatever you're having. Anything's fine."

I sat down on the couch while he went to the kitchen, and I took a deep breath. Even when I was in relationships, I rarely did the big-talk thing. I usually waited until things were out of control before saying anything, and by then, it was too late anyway.

I can do this, I can do this.

"I'll warn you that I might not be the best company tonight," Jake said as he walked toward the couch, two glasses in his hands. "Rough day at work, and now I'm trying to figure out this new business deal. I've got a guy who's supposed to call. You'll probably be bored."

"If I get too bored, I'll just find a baseball game on TV and take a nap," I teased.

At least that got a smile out of him. He handed me a glass—I took a large sip, disappointed when it was only water. Another sign that I was going crazy. I basically asked for water, he gave it to me, and here I was disappointed. When I went to set the glass on the coffee table, I noticed the papers spread across it. "What's all this?"

"I'm trying to figure out if we should open a restaurant in Salt Lake. Vegas has been doing really well, and there's this great space in downtown Salt Lake that has good potential."

My heart dropped as I realized another deal meant he'd be gone again. "How long did the Vegas location take?"

"It was built from the ground up, so longer than normal. Supposed to take six months, but ended up taking eight to get it running well enough I could trust it to the management there."

I did my best to sound calm and collected about this new information. "How long would the one in Salt Lake take?"

"The renovation wouldn't be much. After that, there's hiring the staff and all that. Hopefully four months. Maybe five."

Five months? A tight band formed around my chest, and each breath I took strained against it. Now what was I supposed to do? There was no point in pouring my heart out if he was going to be leaving.

Jake stacked the papers. "Brent and I just have to decide if it's worth it. With me gone, he has to do more management and less cooking, which he doesn't really like. I also need to keep tabs on Vegas. But will another opportunity like this come up? I don't know." He tucked the papers into a file. "Sorry, I'm sure this is all really boring to you."

All I could concentrate on was how he was going to leave. Just like the last guy. Throbbing pain radiated out from my heart, old and new. "It's kind of eye-opening, actually."

"What do you mean?" His phone rang and he glanced at the display. "That's my call." He gave me a quick peck on the cheek and then answered.

Just when I'd accepted the fact I was in a relationship that might actually be going somewhere, he decided to go somewhere. By himself.

• • •

Having a breakdown in front of Jake wasn't an option. That was why last night, while he was still on the phone, I'd gone back to my place and had a pity party involving brownies, Mountain Dew, and an overly violent action flick.

Jake had called me on his way into work this morning and insisted I let him make last night up to me. I told him there was no need—that I'd been the one who showed up unannounced. Not to mention I wasn't sure how to deal with him anymore, knowing he was probably leaving for several months.

"Just let me take you out already," he'd said. So I'd agreed—I did want to see him, even though things were turning out differently than I'd wanted them to. In theory, I could still keep things light, and that was the smartest move right now, with his plans up in the air.

Since he had to run documents to FedEx and I was going to be up north with Barbara, we'd decided to meet at Sparrow, this trendy, upscale restaurant Anthony and Stephanie had recommended.

I'd been sitting in the restaurant for thirty minutes by myself, getting more annoyed by the minute. The battery in my cell had died, so I couldn't even call Jake and ask where he was. Or if he was still coming.

"It's about time," I said when I felt a hand on my shoulder. I looked up and saw not Jake, but my ex-boyfriend, Porter.

Not just my ex. But THE ex.

Also known as my relapse. All I could do for a moment was blink, blink, blink, sure he was a mirage.

"I thought that was you." Porter grabbed my hand and glided me into a hug.

His signature Acqua Di Gio cologne surrounded me, his hand pressed into the small of my back, and I knew it wasn't a mirage. I took a shaky breath, trying to recover from the shock of seeing him. "In town for a visit?"

"Actually, I just moved back. New York wasn't for me." He looked me up and down and then his pale green eyes lit up as he flashed me a smile. "You look amazing."

It was impossible not to relive a dozen memories of back when we were together and he'd give me that exact same look, completely undoing me with such little effort. I swiped a piece of hair behind my ear. "Thanks. You look good, too." As usual, his clothing was impeccable. Tonight he wore a fitted, striped button-down that probably cost more than I spent on groceries in a month.

"There you are," Jake said, coming around the table. "Did you get my message?"

I lowered my eyebrows. "Message?"

"I called to tell you I was running late."

"My phone's dead."

Jake's eyes flicked from me, to Porter, to Porter's hand on my waist. Porter dropped it, and there were a couple of awkward seconds before I realized it was my job to make introductions. "Oh. Um. This is Porter. Porter, Jake. Jake owns Blue."

"The little place on Fifteenth you like to take all your clients to?" Porter asked.

"That's the one."

"It's a great place," he said to Jake, polite as ever. "I suppose I better get back to my party." He gave me another quick hug. "It was good to see you again, Darby."

"Don't tell me that was another one of your ex-boyfriends,"

Jake said as he pulled my chair out for me.

I was still a little irritated at him for being late, so I said, "Okay, I won't tell you."

Jake sat across from me. "Man, they seem to be everywhere."

I looked at Jake, wondering how long it'd take before I was referring to him as an ex. Or if I even could refer to him as that, since we'd never used the boyfriend-girlfriend label. "You're telling me."

Sleeping Beauty Case Study: Porter/Prince Phillip
My Age: 28

Prince Phillip, in my always right opinion, was the best prince. Sure, I'd be a little weirded out if a guy started singing about waiting to find his special someone in the woods, but that's Disney for you. And at least he had good dance moves and a nice voice. Unlike several of the other princes, he had more than that as well. He was determined to marry a peasant girl instead of a princess, regardless of what his dad said, and the guy fought a dragon to get back to the girl he loved.

You've got to admire a guy willing to fight for what he wants.

After my almost engagement to Robert, I vowed never to fall again. I bought one of the condos that Robert had said would be too small to start a family in and dropped a large sum of money on a comfortable mattress. I came home exhausted, hit the soft bed, and slept until morning. On the weekends, I didn't roll out of bed until noon. There was no point in getting up anyway. Steph and Anthony were in that can't-stand-to-be-apart phase, leaving me to hang out with me, myself, and I.

At least I had my job to keep me busy.

Searching for the perfect pieces to go in Virginia Hammond's newly remodeled living room, I popped into a furniture store in Greenwood Village. Opera music floated through the room, giving off an air of sophistication.

I stared at a mock living room with aspen tree wallpaper for a good five minutes, trying to decide if it was the fake trees or the tree-trunk side tables I hated more.

Why am I staring at this stuff? I need to find a couch to match Virginia's room, not a woodland area.

As I turned to see what else the store had, I brushed against someone. "Sorry," I said, looking up at the guy I'd run into. He had short, sandy-colored hair and a dimpled chin. His style was impeccable—dark suit that fit perfectly, black silk tie. His whole look screamed business and money, and he made it look good.

"What do you think about that couch?" he asked, pointing at a shiny black leather sectional.

"Looks slippery and will forever have a dead cowhide smell. If you want that whole bachelor pad look, then that's the way to go. Why guys all love black leather, I'll never quite know."

"Not a fan of black leather, huh?" His deep, rich voice held a touch of humor.

"Not especially. I like a couch that I can cuddle up on without having to unstick myself every time the room gets above seventy degrees. There's a couch over there…" I pointed to the next "room" over. "Black, still very masculine, and much more comfortable."

He cocked his head and studied me. "You know, you look really familiar. Do I know you from somewhere?"

If you think that line's going to work on me, you're dreaming. Even if you are very attractive. "I don't think so."

"Are you sure we haven't met before?" His eyebrows lowered as he stared at me. "Where do you work?"

He sounded genuine enough that I started to think it wasn't a line, but I would've remembered meeting a guy who looked like he did. "I work as an interior designer for Metamorphosis Interior Designs."

"So you pick out furniture for other people?" One corner of

his mouth twisted up. "Even if what they want smells like dead cow?"

"If that's what they want. Then I just silently judge them while I decorate."

He laughed, and his smile lit up his pale green eyes. "Well, I'm sick of trying to decorate my place. Maybe I should hire you."

"Maybe you should." I'd thrown it out there, but I hadn't expected him to actually consider it. Something about the guy unsettled me in a hard-to-place way. It wasn't a scary feeling, but a kind of magnetic pull that made me feel like I should run and move closer at the same time. I pulled a card out of my purse and handed it to him, more to have something to do than anything else. The way he was looking at me had my heart beating faster and faster and I couldn't have that. I'd sworn off men.

"I better get back to work." I shot him a quick smile, then continued my search through the store.

Two days later, Porter Montgomery called and hired me to redecorate his place.

"I figured out where I saw you," Porter said when I showed up at his house to see what the job was going to entail. "The Building Hope dinner. At the time, you were with someone else." He leaned against the door frame, his eyes locked on mine. "Are you still with him?"

I'd attended that dinner with Robert. The old scars from that relationship rose up, making my chest constrict. "I'm not with anyone right now."

"So, how about you and me—"

"Let's have a look around and get started on your place," I said, stepping past him and into the expansive entry.

Over the course of the next few months, I redid every room in his giant four-bedroom house. He constantly flirted with me; I remained professional. After all, I didn't believe in love or relationships anymore.

But occasionally I slipped with Porter, getting drawn into conversations with him that felt like only minutes but lasted an hour. Once it was about classic cars. Then an interesting art piece he'd gotten in Italy. He'd visited countries I'd always dreamed of going to, and he had all these pictures and stories—the way he told them made me feel like I was there. He always asked questions about my hobbies and opinions, and he really listened when I talked.

There was this crazy chemistry between us, like the air was charged every time we were in the same room. But whenever he brought up doing anything together outside of decorating, I brushed him off and got back to work.

Then he sent me flowers, with a note insisting I let him take me to dinner. I told him I didn't date clients. He let it go after that, and I volleyed between relief and disappointment.

The job ended, we settled the account, and I went on my way.

A week later, he called and told me I had no excuse to not go out with him anymore. I caved—I couldn't help it. I tried to keep things light, but Porter didn't believe in light. He threw himself into whatever he did, whether it was his work, sports—he liked lacrosse—or being with me. We attended functions, dined at nice restaurants, and spent time strolling around downtown. We had a blast when we went out, and our time in was even better. If he was going to have late meetings, he'd join me for lunch at Blue so we wouldn't have to go days without seeing each other.

Porter had money and liked to have fun like Charlie, only he had ambition and talked respectfully about women. He was everything Robert was, in that he was kind and driven, only he got how much I loved my job and talked about it like it was important. Basically, he had all the best qualities of every guy I'd ever dated, without any flaws. On top of all that, he got me in a way no one else ever had.

After two months of dating, he told me he loved me. It took

me another month to be able to say it back.

When the dragon tried to step in and ruin things, he slayed her.

Okay, I suppose calling his mother a dragon is a little unfair. The woman actually blew smoke out of her nostrils, though. Instead of smoking "poor people" cigarettes, she smoked Fantasia Lights. They had gold filter tips and came in a rainbow of colors.

At one of the Montgomery parties, while Eleanor Montgomery was puffing away on a cigarette, Porter escorted me over to say hi to her—despite my objections. I already knew she didn't like me, even though Porter claimed it wasn't true.

Eleanor turned to me, and if her face hadn't been filled with so much Botox, I'm sure she would've scowled. She looked from me to Porter. "Darling, I thought you were bringing Catherine tonight."

Porter put his arm around me. "Why would I bring her, when I have a lovely girlfriend to come with me?"

"As we discussed over the phone, I'd hate for Darby to be uncomfortable…"

The way you're discussing me as if I'm not here is making me uncomfortable.

Eleanor took another drag on her cigarette. "It's just that most people here went to Ivy League colleges. I'm not sure that art school's prepared Darby for the topics discussed at this party." She glanced at me. "Nothing personal, dear, but we've got to keep good relations with all of our friends. We tend to stick together in a tight-knit group and they might not accept you like…Porter has." Smoke filled the air around us. "I'd hate for anyone to insinuate you're with him because of his financial status."

"That's enough," Porter said, stepping closer to his mother, his voice low. "You can either be nice to Darby, or we'll leave."

Her hand shot to her chest. "I'm being nice, I just—"

Porter grabbed my hand. "Good-bye, Mother. Give everyone my regards." With that, he and I left the stuffy party.

Porter's standing up to his mother, especially since it was in my defense, impressed me. I was so impressed, I decided it was time to take him to the ranch to meet my family. Porter owned a business empire. He came from old money. I worried that he, Drew, and Devin wouldn't mesh very well. I warned Porter about my brothers, warned my brothers about the way Porter was, and threatened them to all be nice to each other.

Porter didn't do very well with the whole tour-the-ranch thing, but he was a better sport about it than Robert. He didn't have anything in common with my family besides me, but he tried. He invited them to the city and took them to dinner. He informed his mother she could accept me or deal with not seeing him as much, so she and I learned to tolerate each other. It wasn't perfect, but we worked at it.

One night when we were talking about our childhoods, Porter asked about my father. Dad was one of those subjects that made an achy, raw feeling form over my heart, and I didn't like talking about him. But when Porter wrapped his arms around me, I finally did it—I dropped all my walls. I told him how it hurt that my dad didn't try to spend more time with me when I was younger or even now, and how I missed him all the same.

After talking it through with Porter, he convinced me to reach out to my dad, telling me that he'd be there for me if it went badly. Because of him giving me that nudge, I started talking to my dad more and more. For Thanksgiving that year, Porter surprised me by flying Dad and his wife in so we could be together. I think I spent most of the day crying.

Week after week passed and things just kept getting better. While I hadn't moved into his place, I stayed there most nights and had a whole closet set aside just for me. He worked crazy hours sometimes, but he'd bring his laptop to bed and occasionally reach out and squeeze my hand or kiss my cheek, just to show me he was glad I was there.

Life was perfect, and I felt my abandonment issues melting away and my faith in love returning. Something whispered to me, *This is it. He's the one.*

Then Porter hit me with his "great news."

"My company's merging with another," he said one night over a candlelit dinner. "It's a great opportunity, and I think it's going to be great for business. There's just one thing...I've got to move to New York to oversee it."

Who knows, maybe after Sleeping Beauty and Prince Phillip got together, he informed her that he needed to go settle another kingdom. Maybe that's the part of the story they decided was best not to show.

All I could do was stare across the table at Porter, feeling betrayed that he'd leave me after everything we'd been through. My heart started to crack; my perfect world crumbled around me.

"I was thinking, though..." Porter scooted forward and put his hand over mine. "You could go with me. We can try out living together. See what happens."

Try it out? See what happens? Thoughts swam through my head, too many to focus on at once and not a single solid one to grab hold of. Finally they started separating, the more logical pushing past the oh-holy-crap ones.

"What about my job?" I asked. "My family? My place that I just bought. They're all here."

"Baby, I know it's not ideal, but I *have* to go." He brushed his thumb over my knuckles. "The past six months with you have been amazing. I'll take care of everything until you find a job—I know you love what you do, and I'm sure you can find something similar there. Just think about it."

I continued to stare, still trying to put it all together. After being hesitant for most of our relationship, I'd finally gone all in— or at least I thought I had. But this was big. Bigger than big. And I was tempted to say, *Let's do it!* But I couldn't stop thinking of all the things that could go wrong. What would I do if I got to New York and he changed his mind? Panic wound up, suffocating me one slow inch at a time. What if he was busy all the time and I was alone without my family and friends?

I took a few days to think about it, unable to sleep or eat much, all my old insecurities flaring up until I was a nervous wreck. I kept thinking that maybe if we'd been together a little longer, I'd be sure. If we'd already tried living together and knew we could make it work. But all the huge changes at once felt like too much.

So in the end, I told him I couldn't go, trying to hide that my heart was breaking, one tiny shard at a time, until I was sure nothing was left.

Aurora, renamed Briar Rose, stumbled across her true love in the woods. If I tried that method, I'd probably run into a bear and become his lunch. But no, she made me think it was as simple as a lucky encounter, a duet with words you and the guy just *knew*, and a nice long nap that ended with a magical kiss.

Sleeping Beauty obviously had some poor decision-making skills. I mean, some lady in horns shows up and you go ahead and do whatever she says? Only I can't really talk now, can I? I knew I was going to get hurt, yet I'd still stretched out my hand and was surprised when I ended up on the floor with a broken heart.

After Porter left, I renewed my vow to NEVER let myself fall in love again.

Time Wasted: Six months with him. A few months wondering if I should've moved to New York and tried to make it work. Several nights re-reviewing all my case files.

Lessons Learned:

The good guys always move away and leave me behind.

If something seems too good to be true, it is.

Love never lasts. ☹ STOP TRYING ALREADY!!!!!!!!!!

CHAPTER THIRTY

"Are you mad?" Jake asked when we got to my door.

After eating dinner at Sparrow, we'd driven back in our separate cars. I'd wanted to just go home and be done with today, but he'd insisted on walking me to my door.

I turned to face him. "You like that I'm honest, right?"

Jake's shoulders sagged. "That means yes."

"I told you that you didn't need to make anything up to me, but you insisted we go out. Then you were late. And after you finally showed up, you spent the entire time on the phone. If I wanted to eat dinner by myself, I would've stayed home where I'd at least have the TV to keep me company."

I reached into my purse and ran my hand along the bottom, searching for my keys. "I understand that you need to work sometimes, but don't call and insist we go out if you need to take care of something else." Finally, I found my keys and unlocked the door.

Jake followed me in. "I wouldn't have taken the calls if they weren't important. It's like when you have to take calls from your boss. You don't want to answer, but sometimes you have to anyway."

"But my calls rarely last more than five minutes." I kicked off my shoes and sighed. "Whatever. I don't want to have a big thing about it. I'm just tired and done with today." I ran a hand through my hair. "This is the crappy relationship stuff that I hate."

"I guess it's good thing we're not in a relationship, then," he said sarcastically.

"I guess so."

The muscles along his jaw tensed as he stared at me. He took a deep breath and blew it out. "I've got a lot going on right now. I shouldn't have gone out tonight, but I was worried you'd be upset about last night, and then I ended up making you more upset, which is the complete opposite of what I was going for."

My eyes burned as I tried to keep the tears from coming. *I can't have a breakdown now. Not in front of him.* "I'm going to bed. I'll see you later."

Jake ran his hand down my arm and slipped his fingers between mine. "Darby, come on. We're going to have disagreements from time to time." His phone rang and he swore. He glanced at the display. "It's the restaurant. I've got to take it."

"I understand. I really do. You've got to take that and I've got to get to bed early so I can deal with tomorrow." I opened the door and motioned for him to go.

He kissed me on the cheek as he brushed past. "I'll call you tomorrow."

I closed the door behind him and double-checked my locks.

What a shitty night. Why'd I have to run into Porter the same day Jake and I have our first fight?

Rest was what I needed. I was sure that everything would look better tomorrow morning. I washed my face, brushed my teeth, changed into my pajamas, and crawled into bed.

But I couldn't fall asleep.

. . .

I finished typing up the options for the flooring and e-mailed the information to Patricia. *I give her ten minutes to call me and ask me about this, even though I already sent it to her.*

The phone on my desk rang. I saw it was from the front desk and hit the speaker button. "What's up?"

"You have a Mr. Porter Montgomery here to see you," Kathy said.

My throat went dry. Seeing Porter last night had stirred up issues I thought I was over. All night long I'd replayed my relationship with him, then my sort-of relationship with Jake. Everything was a big, confusing mess. And it looked like it was about to get messier.

"Go ahead and send him back."

I sat back, trying to act casual even though it felt like a swarm of bees had taken up residence in my stomach.

Porter walked through my open doorway and flashed his million-dollar smile. It brought out the cleft in his chin and lit up his eyes.

"Come on in," I said, annoyed at the way my voice wavered.

Porter closed the door behind him. He strode up to my desk, his eyes never leaving mine. "You know, when I first got to New York I missed you like crazy. In fact, I was crushed you decided not to move there with me. Before long, though, I was busy, met other people, and stopped thinking about you."

I thought of the months I'd missed him. Of how I'd reviewed my case studies and entered him in with the rest of my exes, every keystroke breaking my heart a little more. "Wow. I'm so glad you stopped by to tell me that."

Porter placed his palms on my desk and leaned toward me. "But ever since I saw you last night, you're all I can think about. The guy you were with, the guy who ignored you all night, tell me he's not your boyfriend."

I didn't know what to say about Jake. Especially after our

discussion last night. He'd made it clear we weren't in a relationship. "We're sort of...undefined."

"Let me take you out, then. Surely he can handle a little competition." Porter's expression—cocky grin, one eyebrow higher than the other—said he didn't think he'd have a problem taking out the competition.

Most of Jake's calls last night had been about opening another Blue in Salt Lake. With him leaving for months, and our whatever-it-was starting to crack, I wasn't sure what his and my future held. Or if we even had a future. My chest tightened and a lump rose in my throat. I worked to shove those emotions down and looked at Porter, trying to think objectively about the current mess I'd gotten myself into. After all, there'd been a point in my life when I'd thought Porter was "the one."

The phone on my desk rang, scattering my thoughts. "I'm really busy right now. Patricia's got me working on this project, and things are crazy."

Porter came around my desk, grabbed a Post-it and a pen, and wrote down his name and number. "Call me later." He stuck the Post-it on my computer monitor, bent down and kissed my cheek, then walked out of my office.

I answered the phone—it was Patricia, demanding I go to the contractors to look over the new plans. After I hung up, I stared at Porter's number, my heart catching at the familiar writing. Then I thought about Jake and our time together, beginning to end, and the pain in my chest deepened.

If Jake weren't leaving for months, the answer would be easy.

I shut down my computer and stood. Last minute, I turned back and ripped the Post-it off my computer screen.

• • •

As soon as I got out of the meeting with the contractors, I picked up my phone and called an emergency get-together with Stephanie.

Full-on wedding mode or not, I needed my best friend. By the time I arrived at her place, my emotions were coiled so tightly I thought I might explode. Stephanie waved me inside the home she and Anthony shared. "Come on back. I'm just packing a few things for the honeymoon."

I followed her to her bedroom and watched her consult her bullet-pointed list.

"So what's up?" she said.

"I ran into Porter last night," I said.

Steph whipped toward me, eyes wide.

"Then Jake and I had our first fight."

Steph set her pile of clothes on the bed. "Okay, this is a sit-down conversation. Let's go get something to drink and talk it out."

We went back out to the living room. I sat on the couch; Steph disappeared into the kitchen and came back with two cans of Sprite. "Sorry. This is all I've got."

I took a can from her. "That's okay. I don't mind starting with the hard stuff."

She popped the top of her soda and sat on the couch facing me. "Start with the fight."

"Jake was thirty minutes late to dinner last night, then he spent the entire time on his phone. I sat there having dinner with myself, so I was annoyed, and when he walked me home we had this big stupid thing over it."

"You wouldn't be fighting if you didn't care. I just read this article about how if you never fight, one of you isn't speaking up. It compared a good fight to getting an oil change for your car. You have to clear the gunk out to keep the ride going smoothly."

Steph and all her articles that had the answers to everything. If only they really did. I blew out my breath. "So how do you know the difference between an oil change and something that will ruin your car forever?"

"I don't know, but I don't think one bad dinner's enough." She took a swig of her soda. "Get to the part with Porter, and we'll come back to Jake."

When I told her about Porter's visit to my office, Stephanie slammed her soda can on the coffee table with a *clink* and shook her head. "That's so Porter. To just show up, make a grand gesture, and think he can get his way." When I didn't say anything, her eyes widened. "You're not seriously thinking of… Darby, no." She put her hand on my knee. "I know you loved Porter, and that since you two only broke up because he moved, you never really got closure. But he didn't offer to visit back and forth. He never even called after he moved. He blew his chance. I think you should work things out with Jake."

I slumped back against her couch. "Honestly, after I took Jake to the ranch, I decided I wanted to do the relationship thing with him. Then I found out he's thinking about opening a restaurant in Salt Lake. He'll be gone for months." Saying it aloud sent a sharp pang through my chest.

"Maybe he won't go if you tell him how much you care about him."

"I'm not going to ask him to choose me over his job," I said, shaking my head. "That's what he was on the phone about all last night and I could tell it's a big deal to him. I swear, it's like Porter all over again." I rubbed my forehead, my eyes burning from trying to hold back tears. "Gil, too. All the good ones always move away." I cracked open my soda and took a big gulp, enjoying the way the fizzy bubbles burned on the way down. "I don't know what to do about anything anymore."

Stephanie's eyes lit up and I could practically see the lightbulb blinking on over her head. "I've got just the thing." She walked over to the entertainment center and dug through her CDs. "The breakup mix we made after Gil left for school and I broke up with Paul."

Music I hadn't heard in years blasted through the room. It didn't take long for Steph and me to belt out the lyrics to "Don't Speak" along with No Doubt.

"'Good Riddance' by Green Day is coming up next," Steph said over the music.

"And how exactly is listening to this old music supposed to help?"

Steph shrugged. "We sit back and wait for inspiration to hit."

Each song produced a sea of memories—some good, some bad. Old relationships, days in the apartment with Steph, hours spent cramming for school. I leaned against Stephanie's shoulder. "Sometimes I wish we could go back to those college years when you and I lived in that tiny apartment with so few responsibilities. Then I remember Allen, Boone, Evan—you and your string of bad boyfriends. The studying, eating nothing but ramen, and our crappy, run-down apartment, and I think where I'm at isn't so bad."

"We've done pretty well for ourselves," Steph said. "And I'm getting married to an amazing man in a little more than a week."

"You're going to be the best, most beautiful bride. I'm happy for you, Steph. I know I don't say it enough."

A huge smile spread across her face. "Thanks. That means a lot to me." She leaned her head onto mine. We sat there like that, listening as The Verve's "Bitter Sweet Symphony" replaced Christina Aguilera.

When the last track on the CD ended, Stephanie sat up and twisted to face me. "Promise me you'll at least talk to Jake. He deserves a face-to-face conversation."

"And what am I supposed to say to him?"

"Hello's always a good place to start."

Chapter Thirty-one

$\mathcal{I}$ should've gone back to the office—I had more than enough work to do—but I couldn't take it anymore. I had to know where Jake and I stood. I'd gotten in the habit of spouting off reasons to not be together, and now I needed to switch gears and have a real discussion about staying together and whether that was even an option.

The fading rays of sunlight peeked between the buildings, striping the sidewalk in front of me. Even with the sun setting, the heat of the day remained. Walking only made me hotter. And sweatier, which wasn't exactly the look I'd been hoping for.

Blue's navy awning came into view, sending a panicky feeling through my chest. *I wish I could just fast forward to later when this part is over and I already know how it went.*

Still, underneath those nerves was a glimmer of hope. After our swim, Jake had talked about good things taking work and a little risk, and it'd never felt truer than now. The fact that he might leave for several months scared me, but there had to be a way to make it work. That was as optimistic as I got, and it felt scary and awesome at the same time.

My heart picked up speed as I pulled open the door to Blue. Several people stood in the lobby, waiting to be seated. Looking down the walkway gave me a good view of the main dining area. The place was busy but not packed. Butterflies filled my stomach when I saw Jake at a table near the back—even after our fight last night, all I wanted was to be in his arms again.

I can do this, I thought, taking long strides toward him, ready to spill my heart out and ask him to take me despite my issues.

Then I noticed he wasn't alone.

The woman seated across from him had strawberry-blond hair, and they seemed to be having an intense conversation. *Okay, don't jump to any conclusions. Maybe it's his sister. In the movies, it's* always *the sister.*

Then I remembered his sister had dark hair.

Maybe she dyed her hair. Or it's a cousin.

Or just someone who comes into the restaurant all the time. It's okay for him to have female friends.

But then he looked up at me and this guilty expression crossed his face.

He held up a finger to the woman and then stood, placing himself between her and me. "Hey. I thought you had to work late."

I answered on autopilot, a creeping sense of foreboding rising in me. "I needed to take care of a few other things, so I took off early. So...what're you doing?" I gave a pointed look to the blonde sitting there, poorly concealing the fact that she was staring at us.

"Darby...it's not... I meant to tell you—"

I turned, throwing a hand up. This couldn't be happening.

He caught my arm, and I whipped around. "Who is she?" My breaths were coming too fast, my pulse pounded through my head, and the room started to spin. The past few days had been a roller coaster. I always puke after roller coasters, and I felt like puking now. How could he be one of the bad ones?

"She's my ex…fiancée."

The words stabbed me in the chest, every syllable radiating pain. I tried to jerk away, but he kept hold of my arm. "Look, I can explain. Just come to my office so we don't have to do this in front of everyone in the entire restaurant."

Tears formed in my eyes, threatening to break free. "It's my fault. I played with fire and I got burned." I jabbed a finger in his chest. "I thought you were different, so I let you swoop in and change my mind, just like I swore I'd never do again."

"I'll be right back," Jake said over his shoulder, and then he nudged me toward his office. I wanted to fight him, to head in the other direction, but I was so numb that I just let him blindly lead me inside the room that had caused us to meet. That we'd later made out in.

"Look, I swear I was going to tell you about Shannon, but it never seemed like a good time. I was finally starting to get through to you and I knew you'd freak out. You'd use it to prove your theory about relationships."

"I love it when liars make it sound like it's all your fault instead of theirs. I don't know whether to be more mad about the fact you lied or about how you preached on and on about commitment and making things work."

"Hey, you were the one with the rules about no talking about the past. No mentioning anything that would freak you out. Those were *your* rules and now you're getting mad that I didn't break them?"

"You're right, okay? My rules make no sense, and it's all *my* fault that you're still meeting with your ex." Crying was something I hated doing in front of people. Usually, I could stop the tears, but I felt one roll down my cheek. "Good-bye, Jake. You were always destined to be another case study anyway. I ran out of princes, so I'll just have to smoosh you into the Cinderella case with the other Prince Charming."

I sniffed and started for the door.

Jake was faster.

He blocked the exit. "I'm not letting you leave until you allow me to explain a few things."

"I'm sure your explanation will be charming and full of crap. So no thanks."

Jake crossed his arms, not moving from his spot in the doorway. "Shannon and I had only been engaged a few months when I decided to leave my dad's company and open the restaurant. She moved to Denver with me, but she missed New York, her friends, and her family. We started fighting about everything. From how to load the dishwasher, to coasters under glasses, to how loud I was in the morning. I couldn't do anything right."

Jake ran a hand through his hair. "Don't get me wrong, I'm not saying it was all her fault. I was putting everything into opening the restaurant, gone all the time, and she and I grew apart. The little bit of time we spent together, we hardly talked. I always had to guess what she was thinking, because she wouldn't just tell me, and when I couldn't figure it out, she'd get even angrier."

He reached out and squeezed my shoulder. "That's why I like that you tell me how you feel. When we fought about my being on the phone last night, I was frustrated, but you were right. Sometimes I get so focused on work, I neglect everything else in my life. I don't want to do it again." He ran his hand down my arm. "Not with you."

"So you're telling me that it doesn't matter that you called off your engagement because it just wasn't right?"

"It *wasn't* right. It's lucky we realized that before we committed to spending the rest of our lives together."

A mirthless laugh escaped my lips. "That's the thing. People think everything will magically work out with someone else. But it's the same, no matter who you're with. Passion fades, problems arise, the world gets in the way, or you meet someone else new and exciting. Then everyone justifies that they tried, making it okay to cheat or to walk away."

"Don't you think it's a little hypocritical to lecture me on commitment when you have a problem with it, too? How many failed relationships have you had?"

"None that ever went as far as engagement," I shot back.

"And with all the walls you throw up, you never will."

I stared at him, jaw clenched, for several seconds before I found words to respond to that. "I've always said that relationships aren't meant to last. *You're* the one who insisted that as long as there's love and commitment and all that other bullshit, you could make it work." I couldn't look at him anymore. I paced the tiny place, mad at him for doing this to me, mad at myself for building him up so much in my mind that I thought he'd be different.

"I was willing to try to fix my relationship with Shannon," Jake said. "Even though things were bad between us, our families were old friends, she and I had a long history, and she'd moved to Denver with me." The muscles along Jake's jaw tightened. "But she'd already met someone else. According to her, she never cheated on me—physically, at least—but she fell in love with him. So we broke up and I moved out."

His eyes locked onto mine. I stared back, not knowing what to say. "You're not the only one who's been hurt before," he said. "It sucks, I get it. But the giving up on everybody option sucks, too."

Yes, it did. But it was the safest option as well. "She's out there in the restaurant right now, Jake. That doesn't say you're over her."

"Because of her credit, she had trouble getting a loan. Our old place was in my name, so I rented it to her. She and Andrew— who's her fiancé now—just bought the house from me. We're heading over to the realtor's office to take care of all the closing stuff as soon as he gets here." Jake stepped forward and put his hands on my hips. "I swear I was going to tell you, but I knew admitting I had been engaged before would scare you. I wanted to wait until you knew you could trust me."

Tears blurred my vision; my throat tightened. "This just proves I can't trust you."

"No, you're looking for a way to prove your theory instead of really listening to me. You never gave this a chance because you wanted to find a reason." He held my gaze for a few beats and then dropped his hands.

"I tried." I wrapped my arms around myself, wishing I could curl up in a ball until none of me was left. "I just need some space right now."

Jake hung his head and pinched the bridge of his nose. "It's never going to change, is it? I thought..." He shook his head, and then he looked at me as if he was waiting for something. He let out a rough exhale. "I'll make it easy and give you plenty of space. Good-bye, Darby. I hope you find what you're looking for someday."

A heaviness entered my chest, and no matter how many times I swallowed, the tears lodged in my throat wouldn't go away.

Jake hesitated in the doorway, and without looking back said, "Maybe if you'd have looked for a reason to be with me instead of dump me, you would've found one."

CHAPTER THIRTY-TWO

The days after my talk with Jake had gone horribly wrong weren't pretty. I moped, watched hours of the most skuzzy, awful reality TV, and cursed all happy couples—real and fictional. Panicked I'd bump into him, I rushed in and out of my building like a paranoid lunatic. Having to go through that stress every day was why I had a rule about getting involved with people I couldn't avoid. I'd outdone myself with Jake. I could avoid Blue, but I couldn't really avoid where I lived.

Relief filled me at the end of the day when I was tucked into my condo with nowhere else to go. I'd poke at whatever I managed to make for dinner—usually a frozen microwave meal with more frost than food—and feel sorry for myself. It was ridiculous, considering Jake and I had only known each other a couple of months.

On Friday, I dug the Post-it with Porter's number out of my purse and stuck it on my fridge. Every time I saw it I'd stare at it for a few seconds. Then I'd walk on.

Saturday afternoon—after a tube of uncooked cookie dough and a Lifetime movie—I broke down and called Porter.

"It's about time," he said when he answered. "So when are we going out?"

• • •

I'd tried to organize Stephanie's bachelorette party, but she kind of took over, and it ended up being more structured than I'd planned on making it: drinks at Tryst, no cutesy bridal stuff, and no males anywhere close to her.

Laura, a girl from Steph's work, tried to slip on a tiara-veil-thing as we followed the hostess to our table. "It'll be so cute, and then everyone will know that you're getting married."

Steph shot me a look, and I knew I was supposed to take care of it. I took the veil and put it in my purse. "I'll just set it aside so Stephanie can have it as a keepsake."

The seven women in our party settled into a large booth in the back. Out of the seven, two weren't married—Stephanie, the bride-to-be, and me. That, paired with the fact we were in an isolated area of Tryst, made this night more of a girls' night out than a party.

I thought back to some of the crazy bachelorette parties I'd attended in my twenties. Compared to those, Stephanie's was pathetic. Women told stories about their husbands; I heard stories about their kids. One about potty training was especially detailed and painful to sit through. All the women gushed about Anthony and what an amazing couple he and Stephanie made, while I started tossing back drinks. When the waiter came by, I asked for a sex on the beach and told him to keep them coming. The party got more interesting from there.

Once everyone worked up a buzz, they got chatty. And loud. I told stories about the horrible guys Steph used to date, and then she'd tell one about me. I heard about Stephanie's first days at work, about the change they saw when she met Anthony, and how before something was missing, but now she glowed.

Like you need a guy to swoop in to not have something missing. And what are we? Fireflies? Seriously, who wants to glow?

I was completely happy for Steph, but seeing these women—the married-with-children crowd—only reiterated how much things were about to change. In a pinch, I could still count on my best friend. But there'd be commitments to Anthony, his family, the family they planned on starting right away. Sitting there, surrounded by six other women, a feeling of intense loneliness settled over me. Even Drew—the guy who was supposed to be as calloused as I was about love—was going to abandon me for it.

Just another reason love stinks.

My next drink showed up just in time to toast that sentiment.

Guys started swinging by on a regular basis, hoping to score with the drunk chicks. Laura was nice enough to point a finger at me when a tall guy clad in a leather jacket stopped by. "She's the only one who's single."

I looked up at the guy.

The disappointment on his face was clear, which didn't do much for my already fragile ego. He stood there, looking uncomfortable for a moment.

"It's okay," I said. "I'm not interested either."

He couldn't get away fast enough.

A few minutes later, a guy tapped Steph on the shoulder. She rolled her head in his direction, then looked to me.

"She's getting married," I said. Words seemed thick and hard to get out. "This is her bachelorette party."

"How about a last fling before you settle down?" he asked, grinning at her.

"Sorry, buddy. It's a girl's night, and she's not interested in cheating on her fiancé." I gave him the scoot signal, sweeping my hand through the air. "So get lost."

He muttered something less than flattering under his breath before walking away.

I flung my arm around Stephanie's shoulder. "I wonder what Jake's doing. I mean, it's Saturday night, so I'm sure he's working, but I wonder..."

"Wonder what?" Steph slurred.

"If he misses me? Isn't it stupid to miss him so much already? I feel all needy. This is why I don't drink. I get sloppy and emotional and it's hard to comp—to compartlize—" Words weren't coming out right. I tried again. "To keep my feelings in check. Then I start making big mistakes. Like that night I met Allen."

"Jake wasn't a mistake, though."

"I screwed it all up. I can't even blame Cinderella this time." I shook my head. "It doesn't matter anymore. I pushed him too far, he's leaving, it's done." Even with the alcohol dulling my senses, I still felt the sharp pain in my heart.

The bartender brought another round of drinks and I considered them for a moment before waving them off. "I'm going to stop before I do something stupid."

Steph waved them away as well. "I had fun, celebrated my last single weekend, and now all I want to do is go home to my guy." She looked at me, a sloppy grin on her face. "Can you get me home to my guy?"

Of course getting her home was easier said than done. Stephanie had this weird fear of taxi drivers. If someone she knew was with her, she was fine. Leave her alone with the driver, and she went into panic mode. I'd ridden past my place just so she wouldn't have to be alone. As we turned down her street, I called Anthony to come get her.

When she saw him outside her door, she erupted in uncontrollable laughter.

He pulled her out of the taxi and put his arm around her.

She poked at his cheek. "You're amazing. I love you so much."

"I love you, too." He leaned over to see me, keeping Steph next to him. "You okay getting home alone?"

I knew he was being nice, so I bit back my thanks-for-rubbing-it-in comment. "I'm good."

"And you can make it into your building? You're not too—"

"*Shh!*" Steph glanced at the driver. "He'll take advantage of her." She got louder. "Keep your stun gun ready in case of trouble."

I laughed. She was more wasted than I'd realized. My head still felt fuzzy, but functioning wasn't a problem. "I'll be fine. Thanks, Anthony. See you, Steph."

She giggled and waved. Anthony turned and helped her into their house.

I gave the driver my address and sat back in the seat. *Note to self: No more bachelorette parties. They're just not as fun as they used to be.*

A few minutes later, the cab pulled up to my building. Walking in a straight line took some effort, but I was able to make it inside my building and to the elevator. The doors opened with a *bing* and I stepped inside. My hand hovered over the five button, and then I moved it up and pushed the number twenty. All night I'd felt alone, and I was sick of it. There's a reason why alcohol's sometimes referred to as *liquid courage.*

"Whoa," I said as the elevator lurched to a stop. I steadied myself, then stepped off the elevator into the empty hall. I got past the first door—only three more to go—then froze.

Oh my gosh, what am I doing? I'm going to show up drunk and desperate just so I don't feel lonely tonight? That's seriously pathetic.

I hurried back the way I'd come, the wall getting closer with each step. Stumbling, I made it back to the elevator. Pushing the button over and over, I prayed Jake wouldn't be coming up or leaving or anything that would force me to see him. *Liquid courage* was the wrong word. It gave you courage to do what you usually had common sense not to.

The doors opened and I lunged inside. For the first time

tonight, I felt lucky to be alone. I punched my floor and almost tipped over when the elevator started its descent.

Tomorrow, I'd go out with Porter. Then my life could finally get back to normal. Or what constituted as normal for an anti-love, I-don't-need-anyone-but-myself person like me.

CHAPTER THIRTY-THREE

The black wrap dress caught my eye as I scanned my closet for what to wear on my date. Going out with Porter seemed like a much better idea than starting over with someone completely new. He already knew about my stance on love, I cared about him, and he'd stuck up for me before. With him back in town, I figured he'd be someone I could spend time with when Steph was busy. In fact, I was starting to think his coming into town at the same time everything else started going wrong with Jake was a fortuitous coincidence.

My phone rang. I picked it off my nightstand and glanced at the display. *Drew.*

I bet he and Lisa broke up and he wants to come trolling for women. Maybe I won't have to live alone forever.

"What's up?" I said.

"I was thinking that tomorrow morning you and Jake might want to come get a late breakfast with Lisa and me."

"Yeah, about that… You see, Jake and I… We're not—"

"Don't tell me you broke up with the only decent guy you've dated in years," Drew said.

"Let's just say, I hope you're making enough money to find us a nice place to retire in."

"Oh sure. I'm rolling in the dough." Drew sighed. "So, what did you find wrong this time? Not stuck up enough? He got along with us?"

"Well, that did concern me," I said, attempting a joke.

Silence.

I clenched my jaw, the ache I was trying to pretend didn't exist squeezing at my heart. "Nothing, okay. He's going to start up a restaurant in another city and be gone all the time, and I ran into Porter and—"

"I swear if you go out with that prick again, I'm disowning you. Then when it doesn't work out—because we both know it's not gonna—you're going to live alone, because I'm not moving in with someone who doesn't have any common sense."

"You know what, Drew? I don't need anyone to tell me that I'm not good at relationships. Especially not someone like *you*." Fuming, I hit the disconnect button and threw my phone on my bed. "Argh!"

Who does he think he is, telling me who I can and can't date?

I took a few deep breaths to try to calm myself. *Just forget about him. He doesn't know what he's talking about.*

"I'm not moving in with you if you don't have any common sense," I said, mimicking Drew's words. "Yeah, well, I don't want to live with you, either. In fact, living alone forever suddenly doesn't seem like such a bad idea."

• • •

Porter took me to Palace Arms at the Brown Palace Hotel, the same placed he'd taken me on our first date. The first time he'd brought me there, I didn't even know what some of the things on the menu were. No matter how many times he insisted the foie gras was amazing, I didn't even like liver, much less duck liver.

While we ate, he told me all about his time in New York, how much his company had grown while he was there, and how he'd sold his shares so he could pursue other interests. I just sat there, soaking it all in. Feeling a strange sense of déjà vu.

After he'd finished his meal, he dropped his fork and looked at me. "I'm sorry. I'm so excited to see you that I've been going on and on, and you've hardly said a word. How's work going?"

"I'm busy doing this commercial job for Patricia."

"I know you get frustrated with those," Porter said.

It was nice to skip all the stupid getting-to-know-you crap. "I'm totally frustrated. I'm passing up jobs I'd love to do because of it. Jake thinks…" My stomach dropped, and it took me a moment to recover. "Uh, I've been toying with the idea of going into business for myself."

Porter steepled his hands and brought them under his chin. "It's a bit of a risky economy right now, and Metamorphosis carries a big name."

"I know. It's just that Nadine and I pull in most of the clients and I hate working on jobs I dislike while Patricia treats me like I'm an idiot."

"You're very good at your job, and Patricia gets that. Starting a new business is hard work, but I know you'll do whatever you put your mind to. If you need help with anything, all you have to do is let me know."

The offer to help—and the vote of confidence—was nice, but a good way for things to get messy, since I still wasn't sure jumping right into a relationship with him was a good idea. The fact of the matter was, I was trying to force myself to move on from Jake. I missed his voice. His cologne. Missed his sense of humor.

And I should really stop thinking about him.

I took a sip of my water. "I don't think I'm going to do it. It'd be nice, though."

Porter leaned forward and placed his hand on my knee. "Being here with you reminds me of all the good times we had together. I'm glad you called."

"I bet your mother will be horrified to know you're spending time with me again."

"Not like your family is any better."

Since I'd argued about it with Drew earlier, I could hardly insist he was wrong. "I just don't know… I don't know if this is a good idea."

He gave a couple slow nods. "So we're back to the place where you don't trust me."

"It's not that I don't trust you. I know you, and that helps. But we've been apart for a while. Things have changed since then."

"But not your opinion that relationships don't last."

"Not really." I twisted the stem of my glass in my fingers. "You only helped prove it when you left. Not that I don't understand. You did what you had to do for your career."

Porter put his hand over the glass, stopping its motion and causing me to look up at him. "But I asked you to come with me."

"You asked me to uproot my whole life—to leave my job, family, and friends—to try and make it work in an unfamiliar city, when I knew you'd be busy with your job all the time. And the way you laid it out made it seem like you didn't really care either way."

"If I didn't care, I wouldn't have asked you to move halfway across the country with me. I knew if I pushed too hard, you'd shut down. That's what you always did when I tried to get serious about us." His eyes bored into mine, and a flicker of hurt went through them. "I thought I'd finally broken through to you enough that you'd consider moving to New York with me."

"I did consider it. Then reality set in." I almost didn't say anything else, but I couldn't let it go. "What's to keep you from going back to New York? Or to another city?"

"I hope I'm looking at her."

My stomach climbed into my throat. As usual, Porter was so

certain, already throwing himself all in, when I was feeling like I was betraying Jake by being here, even after he'd dumped me.

Maybe if I'd gone after him, though…

I should've gone after him.

Porter scooted so close our knees bumped. "New York wasn't for me. Too crowded, too busy. Too many people but not the right one. I didn't realize exactly what it was until I got back. Then I saw you again, and all the pieces clicked into place. I never stopped loving you, Darby. And I'll do whatever it takes to prove it to you."

CHAPTER THIRTY-FOUR

Monday morning, Kathy walked into my office with a huge bouquet of white tulips. "Looks like someone had a good weekend."

"It was interesting, anyway," I said. Going out with Porter was supposed to put everything in perspective, but all I'd really gotten out of it was more confused.

She set the bouquet on my desk. "I'm guessing these are—" She held up a finger and pushed the button on her headset. "Metamorphosis Designs, how can I help you?" Pause. "Sure. Let me get you the number." She waved at me, then walked out of my office.

The flowers filled the air with their sweet, floral scent. I stood and plucked the card off its plastic stand. The metallic gold writing across it was so swirly, I could barely read it.

Had a great time. Hope we can do it again soon.
—Porter

Porter got extra points for remembering that tulips were my favorite. The bouquet obstructed the view of the window that looked into the hall. Since I needed all the Patricia's-coming warning I could get, I moved it to the right corner of my desk.

That was really nice of him to send flowers. He's always been sweet like that.

I sat back down in my cushy chair and twisted to my computer monitor. Thinking I should e-mail Steph about this turn of events, I pulled up my inbox. At the top was a new message from Jake. My pulse quickened, thumping through my head as I moved my cursor over his name and clicked the message.

I RAN A COUPLE OF SCENARIOS FOR YOU AND ATTACHED THE WORKSHEET. ONE WITH NADINE AND ONE WITHOUT HER. YOU MIGHT WANT TO TAKE THE INFORMATION TO YOUR BOSS AND USE IT AS LEVERAGE. SEEING THE KIND OF BUSINESS YOU AND NADINE PULL IN, I THINK PATRICIA WOULD BE A FOOL NOT TO AGREE TO THE TERMS YOU WANT. JUST REMEMBER THAT BEING HAPPY IS WORTH THE RISK.

GOOD LUCK WITH EVERYTHING,

JAKE

After rereading the message, I opened the attachment. I stared at how he'd pulled together all the information I'd given him.

Is this right?

I could hardly believe it.

Not only were the figures staggering, I found it hard to believe Jake would work this hard putting the information together for me, despite our breakup. Tears were rising, burning my throat and my eyes. I blinked like crazy, trying to get ahold of my emotions before I was the girl crying in her office.

Nadine stuck her head in the doorway. "Ready to go?" She stepped farther into my office. "Nice flowers. From Jake, I'm assuming."

Nope. Jake sent me something better. I swallowed hard, my throat still way too tight. "Porter, actually."

Her forehead puckered. "What happened to Jake? And Porter? Is he visiting or is he —"

"I'll explain everything on the way to Barbara's. Just give me a second." I printed the worksheet Jake had e-mailed me. When my printer stopped whirring, I reached over and retrieved the paper. Holding the key to my and Nadine's freedom made me want to jump up and down like a little kid. *Time to go after what I want.*

• • •

Nadine lifted her binder from my coffee table and shoved it into her laptop bag. "So we're really going to do this?"

"If Patricia doesn't agree to let us choose our own jobs and give us a ten percent bump on every project, we're walking. If she doesn't agree," I said, gesturing around my condo, "this might be our new office. Are you cool with that?"

Nadine took a deep breath. "Let's do it."

I said good-bye to Nadine, then tried to breathe out all the stress of the day. The vase of tulips perched on my kitchen counter reminded me that Porter had called earlier. Nadine and I had been going over our game plan, so I hadn't answered. I lifted my phone off the coffee table. I just had one missed call, meaning Porter hadn't left a message. I sat there, contemplating what I was going to say when I called him back. Knowing him, he'd already planned out our week together.

Last night he'd said all the right words. He'd sent me flowers. But it was all wrong. I'd gone out with Porter, hoping to prove to myself that Jake was just another guy. But all it had done was show me that he wasn't. Things were different with Jake. I had fun whether we were chilling at his place, laughing over dinner, or even watching baseball. And I really, really hated baseball. Or used to. Things were getting fuzzy. Plus, Jake took an interest in my life—all parts of my life. And then there was the way his face lit up when he saw me. How he called me gorgeous. The way I felt when he had his arms around me.

I missed him so badly that the ache in my chest overtook my heart, my lungs. I'd worked so hard to keep myself from falling, but I'd completely failed. I was totally in love with Jake.

And instead of just facing my feelings, I'd pushed him away. For what? A guy I wasn't in love with anymore? Because he'd had a relationship that failed? Because I was an idiot?

Yeah, that last one was probably the right answer.

Deciding a pity-fest was in order, I clicked on the TV. Five minutes of channel surfing didn't produce anything worth watching, so I got off the couch and walked around my apartment. My plant—the plant that refused to live or die—sat in the window, looking drier than ever.

I picked it up and walked over to my kitchen, planning on watering it. It looked so dead, so gone.

Instead of heading for the sink like I'd planned on doing, I stopped at the trash can. Stepping on the lever that lifted the lid, I hovered my plant over the open mouth, ready to toss it in with the rest of my trash. But there it was—the one green blade that kept on living. I heard Jake's voice in my head, saying he admired it for not giving up.

I hated signs. Didn't believe in them. People interpreted them to mean whatever they wanted. But right now, that blade was telling me to go fix things with the guy who'd fought so hard, despite everything I'd put him through.

Question after question ran through my head: What if he'd finally had enough? What if he told me to get lost? What if he'd already moved on?

What if he didn't love me back?

Just the thought made me want to crumple to the floor. But I was starting to think not knowing was worse than screwing up my one shot at happiness. My head pounded as I considered going upstairs and laying it all on the line.

I glanced at the clock. *He probably just got home.* I shoved the plant onto the counter, determination pumping through my veins. When I got inside the elevator, I punched number twenty, trying not to think about the painful way my heart was hammering against my rib cage.

The ride up didn't give me near enough time to prepare. Head spinning, I exited the elevator. With every step I took down the hall, my throat got drier, my stomach clenched tighter.

I stared at Jake's door for several minutes before gaining the courage to knock.

As I waited, I ran a hand through my hair, fluffing it just so. Then I ran a hand down it, to smooth it back into place. I took the lip gloss out of my pocket and swiped it across my lips.

And then it was clear he wasn't answering the door.

I retreated a couple of steps, then heard the door open. Slowly, I turned around. "Spontaneous visits. Just one of the advantages of living in the same building." My voice came out as shaky as I felt.

"I thought there weren't any advantages," Jake said, stepping farther into the hall. His hair was wet and his clothes clung to his damp body. Obviously he'd just gotten out of the shower. Despite the nerves churning through my gut, desire burned within me. I wanted my hands in his hair. On his damp skin. Even more, I wanted him to assure me everything would be okay.

I guessed the only way for that to be a possibility was if I got on with the apologizing. "Jake, I freaked out. I didn't handle that situation at the restaurant very well."

A no-shit expression crossed his face.

"Or at all, really," I said. "I guess I just got caught up in everything that could and would inevitably go wrong, that I forgot things might go right. The fact is, there's nothing really wrong with you."

Jake crossed his arms, and I couldn't help but notice the way it made the muscles in his arms stand out. "But?"

I licked my lips, tasting the cherry lip gloss I'd just put on. "There's no but. What I'm trying to say is that I don't want to date anyone else, and I don't want you to, either. I want to say we're in a relationship and do everything that people in relationships do, from the light and fun to the serious, to everything in between. Unless I've already scared you away and you want to run in the other direction." At intense moments like these, I tended to try to joke things away. "Although, since we live in the same building and we constantly bump into each other, that's going to be awkward for you."

"You're wrong."

My heart stopped, I swear it did. "Oh. I'll just go, then."

"I've got plenty wrong with me," Jake said. "For instance, I'm in love with a woman who doesn't believe in love."

Breathing became impossible. "It's not that I don't believe in it—" I threw a hand to my chest. "We're talking about me, right?"

The corners of his mouth twitched. "Do you see anyone else?"

I let out a relieved breath and looked into his blue eyes. "I only doubted that it could last."

"Maybe you just haven't met the right guy yet."

I closed the gap between us and put my hands on the sides of his waist. "Maybe I have, and I just didn't realize it."

Jake's eyebrows shot up as he pointed to his chest. "Me?"

"Do you see anyone else?" I tipped onto my toes, his arms encircled me, and my lips parted as they landed on his. We stumbled backward, through the open door and into his place. He kicked the door closed, then pinned me against it, sending fire through every inch of my body as he pressed into me.

I drank in his kiss, his taste, as we clung to each other, making up for the days we'd been apart. I ran my hand through his damp hair as I gently bit his lower lip. He groaned and then his lips left mine, traveling down my neck and across my collarbone, sending delicious chills down my spine.

"I have to tell you something," I whispered.

His lips left my neck, but he kept me pinned against the door with his body, the warmth from him soaking into my skin.

"I-I don't want you to go to Salt Lake. I understand that you need to and all, but I'll miss you." I peered into his blue, blue eyes and had to work to continue breathing. "I was about to tell you that I was ready for a real relationship, but when you talked about being gone for months, I… Getting attached right before you left seemed like a really bad idea."

"Even if the deal goes through, I'll be flying back and forth. I wasn't planning on putting us on hold for months." He put his hand on my neck and ran his thumb along my jaw. "If we're going to do this, you've got to tell me what's going on. Otherwise it's never going to work."

I nodded. "I guess I should confess something else, then."

Jake's posture stiffened.

My heart was pounding so hard it actually hurt. "I've never tried so hard to not fall for someone. And I've never fallen faster." The words were on the tip of my tongue, I simply had to force them out. "I love you, Jake."

He grinned and pulled me into his arms. I locked my hands behind his neck as he covered my mouth with his. His hands moved to my butt, lifting me off my feet, and I wrapped my legs around his waist.

"Couch or bed?" he whispered.

I brushed my lips over his. "Well, I haven't seen your bedroom yet."

• • •

I rested my head on Jake's shoulder, loving the feel of my skin against his and basking in the afterglow of being with someone I loved. I felt light-headed and happy and tired and tingly and *mmm*, did I mention happy?

Jake wound his fingers through my hair. "So, do I actually get a title now when you introduce me?"

"You want me to introduce you as my lover?" I said with a smile. "Seems a little personal, but okay."

"Hey, as long as other guys know to keep their hands off, I'll take it."

I ran my fingers down his stomach. "You still want to be my boyfriend after what I put you through?"

"What you put me through tonight was good."

I shook my head but couldn't help smiling. I propped my chin on his chest so I could see his face. "I'm all in. So if there's anything important I should know, now's the time to tell me."

"I used to have an obsession with turtles as a kid."

I tilted my head and gave him the best evil eye I could manage under the current no-clothing, just-had-amazing-sex circumstances.

"It was a problem, I'm telling you. Do you have any idea how smelly a couple of turtle aquariums can be?" He placed his hand on my back. "Okay, the serious stuff. You know about my last relationship…" He paused almost as if he was checking to see if we needed to talk about it more before he continued. "You know about my family and my work—which I love, by the way. There's nothing better than taking a run-down place and turning it into a spot where people love to eat. I'm damn good at it, too. On top of the restaurants, I also work with Virginia, taking care of the business side of her Hammond's Children's Hospital Charity.

"Let's see…what else?" He ran his fingers down my back, tickling me enough that I pressed into him. He smiled and did it again. "I'm so crazy about you that if you asked me to give up watching sports for the rest of my life, I would." Another brush of his fingers and another grin. "Except maybe the World Series, 'cause that's more religion than sport." His fingers stilled and his eyes locked onto mine. "And in case I didn't make it clear enough yet, I'm in love with you, Darby Quinn."

I scooted up to place a kiss on his lips, so much happiness bubbling up in me that I suddenly understood why someone might burst into song. For all I knew, cartoon birds were circling my head. I sighed as I sunk into his kiss, his embrace.

Then I caught sight of the alarm clock and groaned. "It's already tomorrow. I'd better go."

Jake put his arm around me, keeping me against him. "Stay."

Leaving was the last thing I wanted to do, but life— unfortunately—didn't stop simply because I was in love. "Thanks to your being a genius with numbers, Nadine and I have a meeting with Patricia tomorrow, and I've got to be in early to prepare."

Still keeping me tight against him with one arm, Jake grabbed his alarm clock with his other. "Just tell me what time you need to get up and I'll make sure you're on time."

Staying the night in Jake's arms or going to my own lonely bed?

As if there was really any choice.

CHAPTER THIRTY-FIVE

Normally, I consider myself organized; this morning as I rushed around my bedroom, I felt anything but. "Have you seen my other shoe? I swear it was right here."

Jake squinted against the morning light and sat up in bed. His hair was sticking up on one side. "If I told you I was wearing them last night, would you think it was cute or creepy?"

I laughed as I smacked his arm. "This isn't funny. Steph will kill me if I'm late."

Jake grabbed my hand, pulling me down so he could kiss my neck. His deep voice rumbled in my ear. "Well, if you're going to be late anyway…"

"Don't tempt me," I said. I gave him a quick kiss, then dropped to the floor to search for my other shoe. I'd put all my bridesmaid stuff together, but somehow, between last night and this morning, one of my dyed-pink-to-match shoes was missing.

A shoe was thrust in front of my face. "Is this what you're looking for?"

I took the other shoe from Jake, tossed it in the bag next to its mate, and kissed his cheek. "You're a lifesaver."

Jake and I had spent the last week getting to know each other better. We'd celebrated the fact that Nadine and my meeting with Patricia had gone so well that we were going to be able to take on only clients of our choice as soon as we wrapped up the Red Lion account. I dropped into Blue almost every day after work so we could have dinner together. We talked late into the night—or more like early into the next morning. He told stories about growing up, his family, and I did the same. We talked about interests, goals, everything and nothing. About the only thing we hadn't done much of was sleep.

There'd been a slightly uncomfortable phone call with Porter, where I thanked him for the flowers and for helping me with my relationship with my dad, told him he was a great guy (I know, it sorta killed me to pull out that cliché line even if it were true) but informed him my situation had changed. That I was taken.

Drew had called, too, apparently to apologize, but ended up gloating more than anything that he was right about Jake. A few last-minute bumps had come up with Stephanie's wedding, but she and I had taken care of them and made it through the rehearsal. And now it was the big day she'd been counting down for months.

Jake followed me into the living room. I draped my plastic-encased dress over my arm, then peeked in my bag one more time to check on my shoes and makeup. I'd taken the rest of it down to the car already.

"I'm pretty sure that's everything." I turned back to Jake, soaking in the image of him standing in my living room in only his boxers, and wishing that I had an extra hour to kill. I wrapped my free arm around his waist and leaned in for another kiss, taking a moment to linger and run my hand down the strong line of his back. "See you soon."

"I'll be there."

As I reached for the doorknob, I realized I'd forgotten to warn him about the people he was going to encounter at Steph's wedding. Worried I might not get another chance, I figured I better say something. "Just so you know, the people in my town are a little crazy. Since it's small and everyone knows everyone, they all think they should be involved in my life. So don't believe everything you hear, and don't freak out if they ask you when you and I are going to tie the knot."

"I'll just send them to you for the answer to that question," he said with a smile.

I rolled my eyes but couldn't help smile back. I waved good-bye and headed for the elevator, feeling surprisingly cheerful about attending a wedding.

• • •

"I'm hyperventilating," Stephanie said, fanning her face with her hand. "Why is it, like, two hundred degrees in here?"

I grabbed a magazine off a table and used it to create a breeze. "Everything's fine. You're just nervous."

"You would say it's cold feet." Steph put her hand over her heart. "I'm excited to marry Anthony. I *want* to marry him."

I could tell by her shaky voice that she was trying to convince herself as hard as she was trying to convince me. "Steph, I know you want to marry him, and I know this is the day you've been dreaming about. Still, it's perfectly fine to be nervous, even if you're excited. It's a big deal, and I'm sure it's nerve-racking thinking about all those people staring at you."

"Oh, shit. I forgot about all the staring people. What if I trip?"

"Your dad won't let you. Neither will Anthony." I put my hands on her shoulders and locked eyes with her. "But if anything goes wrong, I got your back. I'll do something crazy…like flash everyone." I looked down at my dress. "As soon as I can figure out how to."

Stephanie laughed. "You do need to do something big to outlive the slapping story."

"Yes, well, it's my goal to do something crazy at everyone I love's wedding."

Steph took a deep breath. "Okay. Freak-out over. I'm getting married, I can't wait, and everything's going to go smoothly." She flung her arms around me and I nearly toppled over. Once I was sure I was steady, I hugged my best friend back, thinking about all the good memories we'd had over the years and how my life would've totally sucked without her.

I grabbed my bouquet and handed Steph hers. "Let's do this."

Fifteen minutes later, Karl and I were marching down the aisle together, just like we'd practiced the night before. Already, several people were crying and dabbing their eyes with tissues. A couple weeks ago, I might've made a joke that they were crying because they knew that Steph's and Anthony's lives were over. But I was feeling like a glass-half-full girl today.

The audience members stood as the wedding march filled the air. Stephanie and her dad walked down the aisle. My best friend, the girl I considered my sister, looked beautiful. The beading on her bodice caught the light, her blond hair was curled and pinned up, and her smile lit the room.

Before I could prevent it—even sense its coming—a traitorous tear rolled down my cheek. *Pull it together. You can't join the rest of the hopeless romantics crying at a wedding. You're better than this.*

Another tear ran down and Laura slipped a tissue into my hand.

How embarrassing. If anyone asks, I'm crying because I'm losing my best friend. I swore I could feel Jake somewhere in the audience looking at me, too. I didn't dare try to see if I was right.

Stephanie reached Anthony and they came the rest of the way together. As she spun to face her groom, I bent down and rearranged her train.

The priest looked at the two of them, a smile on his face. "We are here to celebrate the union of Stephanie and Anthony. These two people are here to commit to spending the rest of their lives together…"

I was working on reforming my opinion of forever relationships and all, but those words still made my stomach clench. But then I happened to glance out at the audience. My eyes went to Jake as if they knew he was there before I did. He smiled at me and I turned into a bit of a mushy twitterpated mess despite myself.

• • •

Searching the reception hall for Jake, I ran into Karl. "Hey, have you seen Jake?" I asked. Karl had officially met him last night at the rehearsal dinner.

"No, but I've been busy talking to Erin," Karl said, a love-struck smile curving his lips.

I followed his gaze to the blonde, the same girl he'd met at Shots. "It seems like that's going well."

His smile widened. "She's never told me that my profession was a farce or gotten me into a bar brawl, so yeah, it's going pretty well."

"Man, you're so picky about that stuff."

He laughed, and I smiled, enjoying that we could joke like this. Then I spotted Jake. Talking to Mrs. Hildabrand.

Oh no. Anyone but her.

"Good luck with Erin. I'll catch you later," I said, already moving toward Jake and Mrs. Hildabrand.

Mrs. Hildabrand smiled at me as I approached. "Darby, I just met your beau. He's very nice and *very* handsome." She grabbed my hand and patted it. "And you wanted to give up. I told you he was out there." She twisted to face Jake. "Can you believe she tried to tell everyone she was happy on her own?"

Jake shook his head in mock disbelief. "I can't. I guess it's lucky I got to her."

"Oh, such a gentleman. You don't let her get away." She smiled at me again, and I knew whatever she was about to say was going to be bad. "You know, after you two get married, you're going to have to start your family right away. After a certain age, it gets a lot harder."

I grabbed Jake's hand. "Excuse us, Mrs. Hildabrand. I've got to go introduce Jake to some other people." I led him away from the woman as fast as I could.

Before I could say a word to Jake about what had just happened, Mrs. Taylor came up to me. "We're going to do the toasts after people have had some time to eat. Just go on up after Karl."

She eyed Jake.

"Mrs. Taylor, this is my boyfriend, Jake. Jake, this is Stephanie's mom."

Jake extended his hand to her. "Nice to meet you."

Mrs. Taylor shook his hand. "You two aren't going to get in a fight, are you?"

"Not planning on it," I said.

Mrs. Taylor shot me a look. I'd been at her house enough she didn't mind putting me in my place.

"Sorry, Mrs. Taylor. No fighting. I promise."

Jeez. You make a scene at one wedding and you're marked for life.

I led Jake over to the table where my family was seated. It really was nice to not have to worry they didn't like each other or have to take control of the conversation, but simply sit back and enjoy being around so many people I loved.

As dinner was wrapping up, I noticed Mrs. Taylor walk over to Karl and tap him on the shoulder. His toast was first, which meant I'd be going next. My stomach churned as I thought of standing up in front of everyone and giving my toast. When I first started putting my speech together, I'd searched online for help. Total waste of time. How was I supposed to read something aloud that made me gag?

There was one quote that said, "Love is when you look into someone's eyes, and see everything you need." Seems like a lot of pressure to put on someone. And everything? Really? Like, do you have a cheeseburger in there, because at some point, someone's going to get hungry.

The best one I'd read, the one I'd been thinking about, said, "A great marriage is not when the 'perfect couple' comes together. It's when an imperfect couple learns to enjoy their differences." I'd use it, but Steph might interpret it as me saying she and Anthony weren't the perfect couple.

Karl took the microphone out of its stand and cleared his throat. "Hello, everyone. I'm Karl, the best man, and it's my privilege to toast this happy couple. Earlier today, I witnessed one of my best friends marry the woman he loves. I've known Anthony for several years now, and he's always been a kind, generous person. In Stephanie, he's found someone who has those traits and complements him perfectly.

"As a marriage counselor, I've seen lots of couples in every stage of their relationships, and I can tell you that Stephanie and Anthony are a great couple. They communicate well, which everyone knows is a key to having a good relationship." Karl glanced at me and smiled. "Someone recently informed me, though, that communication isn't the key to a good relationship. It's realizing that we all communicate differently. She might've been onto something. I guess it's about figuring out how to communicate with someone different from you. So, may you learn to understand each other, even when you don't."

He raised his glass. "To the happy couple. I wish you a lifetime of happiness together."

Drew nudged me. "Go knock 'em dead." He leaned closer and whispered, "And if you see anyone who needs put in his place, you know what to do." He made a slapping motion.

CINDERELLA SCREWED ME OVER

I shot him a dirty look before making my way up front to give my toast.

"Hope I didn't steal your speech," Karl whispered as he handed me the mic.

"I just want credit when all your counseling sessions go better," I said with a smile. But the second I raised the microphone and looked out at all the people, my knees started shaking and I felt light-headed and queasy.

"For those of you who don't know me, I'm Darby, and the beautiful bride is my very best friend. She and I have gone through a lot of ups and downs together, and I'm so honored to be with her on one of the happiest days of her life." My throat went completely dry. I eyed the glasses on the table, wishing I'd brought mine with me. I cleared my throat and licked my lips. "Those of you who *do* know me know I've been skeptical about the whole happily-ever-after thing."

I could see the fear in Steph's eyes, so I charged on with the rest of it before she passed out. "But because I've known Stephanie for so long, I can see when she's truly happy. Being with Anthony has made her happier than I've ever seen her. I've watched their relationship from the beginning. Watched the way they've changed each other's lives. And I can say, without any hesitation, that these two have what it takes to make it. So today, I feel not like I'm losing a friend, but like I'm gaining one…" I twisted to Anthony. "That's right, Anthony, you should've read the fine print. You're stuck with me, too."

Laughter sounded through the crowd.

"I guess what I'm saying is that they're a great example of what love is and how amazing it can be when you find the right person." I raised my glass, happy to have the hard part out of the way. "To Anthony and Stephanie. May their union be filled with love and laughter."

Stephanie put her hand over her heart and mouthed, "Love you."

"You, too," I mouthed back.

• • •

Stephanie's dress crinkled as she threw her arms around me, and her veil pressed against my cheek. Moments ago, she and Anthony had taken their first spin around the dance floor as husband and wife. "I'm married, and your curse is broken. I knew we'd find the right guys someday."

"Hey!" I said. "I wasn't cursed."

"Yeah, you kinda were. And it's my wedding, so that means you have to listen to everything I say." She pulled back and pinned me with a serious glare. "Now that you've found him, let go of all that old crap, okay? Just let yourself be happy."

"I am really happy," I said, unable to keep a silly grin off my face—no doubt I looked like she did whenever she talked about Anthony.

"Speaking of your awesome boyfriend…"

Jake stepped up next to me and put his hand on my back. "Congratulations," he said to Stephanie.

"Thanks." Steph motioned to the dance floor. "You two should go dance. I'll say good-bye before we leave." She glanced behind me. "Mrs. Hildabrand's coming. You better go before she gives you the talk about children and being too old, like she gave me earlier."

"Yeah, we already heard it." I took Jake's hand. "But I don't really want to hear it again."

He and I stepped onto the dance floor. He put his arms around my waist and pulled me in close. I locked my hands behind his neck.

"You sounded like you really meant that toast," Jake said. "That you actually think two people can make it."

I smiled up at him. "I guess that maybe—just maybe—if you do find the right person and you're both willing to work at it, the odds get a little better."

He hugged me to him. "It's okay to say I was right, you know. I'll only hang it over your head for a month or two. A year at most."

I shook my head, moving with him as he glided us across the floor. All around us, people were dancing, laughing, and talking. Mom and Dwight were sitting at our table, big smiles on their faces; Drew and Lisa were dancing to the left of me and Jake, laughing as they spun around the floor; Devin and Anne were dancing, too, obviously enjoying their childless evening together. Stephanie and Anthony stepped onto the floor, huge grins on their faces as they gazed into each other's eyes.

I was surrounded by happy, in-love couples, and surprise, surprise, I was one of them.

The thing is, I thought I'd been in love before. I'd been sure of it. And while I did love those guys, this was something different. Just when you think you've kicked a bad habit is usually when it sneaks back up on you. I hadn't just fallen off the men sobriety bandwagon this time; I'd tumbled off and couldn't even see the wagon anymore.

Over the past several days, I'd learned a lot about Jake. He blasted awful eighties metal first thing in the morning. He was beyond crazy about knowing the score of every baseball game, no matter what teams were playing, and often went to "just check the score" and ended up watching the rest of the game. He didn't rinse his whiskers down the sink after shaving, so they crusted onto the porcelain and were almost impossible to get off. He also snored, which made it hard to fall asleep.

Eventually, I might find those idiosyncrasies a little annoying. But I was willing to overlook them because I loved the way I felt whenever I was with him. I loved the way he kissed me. Loved that he would come over and help cook dinner. Loved cuddling up next to him and falling asleep. I loved that he somehow looked past all of my issues and loved me anyway.

But mostly, because I just loved him.

Like any relationship, we'd have ups and downs. But there would also be the part where we'd share our hopes, dreams, and disappointments. In each other, we'd find the support and understanding we needed to make it through another day.

The truth is, fairy-tale beginnings are easy. It's what comes after that's hard. Life doesn't have a clean-cut ending. My relationship with Jake was better than a fairy tale, though, because it was real. Real life love requires forgiving another person's flaws and loving him or her anyway. And even though tacking the words "happily ever after" onto the end would be easier, there's something pretty amazing about loving someone else, flaws and all.

When the song came to a close, Jake lowered his lips to mine. As I kissed him back, I felt myself falling deeper. Found myself believing that the forever kind of love did exist.

That's when it hit me. I had to go through a lot of bad relationships first, but I'd finally found him. My very own Prince Charming. Turns out they do exist.

Touché, Cinderella. Touché.

Acknowledgments

This book all started with a conversation I had with Christy Walters, one of my very best girlfriends about the unrealistic ideas we had about how relationships would be. I uttered the phrase, "Yeah, Cinderella really screwed us over," and right then, I knew I needed to write a book about all the things fairy tales forgot to teach us, while somehow pulling off a romance. Thanks to my Aunt Malinda, who was one of the first people to read it and told me how much she loved it. She was also one of my very first writing cheerleaders, and I've always been grateful for that—it totally kept me going. Ariane Love, thanks for reading an early draft as well. I could go all mushy, mushy about missing you and Christy, but I'll refrain and just say thanks for being awesome girlfriends. Also to my friend, Amanda Price (I almost typed Crowther. Lol), whose character traits tend to show up in all of the girlfriends I write in my books. Thanks for saying all the right things as I was going through the editing process—I'm glad to have found another girl so much like me.

I wouldn't be where I was today if Stacy Abrams hadn't taken a chance on me. Thanks to her and Alycia Tornetta's mad editing skills, my books come out all shiny, too. Thanks for all the behind the scenes work you two do for me as well. Hugs! Entangled Publishing has been so supportive, from the authors to editors to publicists and everyone in between. I'd especially like to thank publicist ninja Heather Riccio, along with Anjana and Danielle for all of their work. Thanks to my writer friends Rachel Harris, Lisa Burstein, Brandy Vallance, and Anne Eliot for always being there and constantly making me laugh.

To my own Prince Charming—hehe, had to put that in there, babe—thanks for helping me come up with more fairy-tale tie-ins as I wrote, answering one hundred billion questions, and for reading the first draft what seems like forever ago, when I still wasn't sure I'd ever have a book published. Thanks for supporting me through my entire writing career, even before it was actually a career. Oh, and for indulging me in my shoe-collecting habit. To my daughters and son, you guys make me laugh, keep me going, and I'm amazed every day that I have such awesome kids. A lot of the farm/small-town stuff was inspired by the town I grew up in and not-so-normal conversations around the dinner table. I'll always be a farm girl at heart, even when I'm walking around in my stilettos. Mom and Dad, thanks for everything, from the way you raised me, to checking how the book stuff's going, to letting me get away with inappropriate jokes (See, it's in print, so it's permanent now). I could say a hundred nice things about my brothers and sisters, but I'll just say I love you all, and thanks for the support. Shout-out to my brother, Greg, who let me steal his phrases and stories for Drew.

Since this is getting long and I'm always scared of forgetting someone, I'll just say thanks to all the wonderful blogger and cool bookish people I've met the past few years (some, only virtually). You make writing more fun, and have been a huge help getting the word out about my books. To my girls in the TZWNDU book club, thanks for helping me out when I need feedback, and for just being awesome.

And lastly, thanks to my readers! You're the best! May you all find the perfect pair of glass slippers, or whatever shoes happen to be your preferred footwear.

About the Author

Cindi Madsen sits at her computer every chance she gets, plotting, revising, and falling in love with her characters. Sometimes it makes her a crazy person. Without it, she'd be even crazier. She has way too many shoes, but can always find a reason to buy a new pretty pair, especially if they're sparkly, colorful, or super-tall. She loves music, dancing, and wishes summer lasted all year long. She lives in Colorado (where summer is most definitely NOT all year long) with her husband and three children. She is the author of YA books *All the Broken Pieces, Cipher,* and *Demons of the Sun* and adult romances *Falling for Her Fiancé, Act Like You Love Me,* and *Cinderella Screwed Me Over.*

You can visit Cindi at: www.cindimadsen.com

Follow her on twitter @cindimadsen

Additional Entangled Select releases…

WAKING UP DEAD

by Emma Shortt

When her best friend, Tye, disappears hunting for food, kick-ass Jackson Hart's 'head south to safety' plan looks like it's dead before it's even begun. But then she meets ex-mechanic Luke Granger, who offers her protection against the zombie hordes—not that she needs it.

Luke and Jackson team up to find other humans and discover that even if flesh eating zombies are knocking down their door, there's always time for sex and even love.

Deep in Crimson

by Sarah Gilman

Kidnapped by humans and raised in a research facility, Jett was taught to believe his own race of demons insidious and violent. Jett wants to bring his captor to justice, so he join forces with the demon Guardians, and the demon child's older sister, Lexine.

Irresistible attraction grows between Jett and Lexine, but if Jett goes through the all-consuming process of becoming a Guardian, he may forfeit any chance they have of being together.

MALICIOUS MISCHIEF

by Marianne Harden

Career chameleon, Rylie Keyes, must keep her current job. If not, the tax assessor will evict her ailing grandfather and auction off their ancestral home. When a senior she shuttles for a Bellevue, Washington retirement home winds up dead in her minibus, her goal to keep her job hits a road bump.

Forced to dust off the PI training, Rylie must align with a circus-bike-wheeling Samoan to solve the murder, while juggling the attentions of two very hot police officers.